All the Places that were Hurt

Mish Cromer

LEAF BY LEAF

Published by Leaf by Leaf
an imprint of Cinnamon Press,
Office 49019, PO Box 92, Cardiff, CF11 1NB
www.cinnamonpress.com

The right of Mish Cromer to be identified as author of this work has been
asserted by her in accordance with the Copyright, Designs and Patent
Act, 1988. © 2021..
Print Edition ISBN 978-1-78864-930-8

British Library Cataloguing in Publication Data. A CIP record for this
book can be obtained from the British Library.

Designed and typeset in Adobe Jenson by Cinnamon Press.
Cover design by Adam Craig © Adam Craig.
Cinnamon Press is represented by Inpress.

Acknowledgements

My heartfelt thanks go to Adam Craig, Jan Fortune, and Rowan Fortune at Cinnamon Press who once again, in the teeth of a pandemic, turned my manuscript into a book.

To Alison Chandler and Shanti Fricker who see everything I write before anyone else and give me purpose and structure and the kind of feedback that matters. Alison, every time I find myself flagging or in the grip of self-doubt, you find ways to make things feel new again and help me to locate my courage. Thank you.

Tracy Harvey, Lindsay Latimore Masters, Jenny Olivier, Susan Olivier, Kathy Colby Scott, Harriet Wheeler, Marianna Wiener, all of you read early drafts of this and encouraged me with corrections and suggestions and general cheerleading. You cannot know how much this kept me going, thank you.

To Paul Crosfield for helping me with the Spanish, to Juana Espasa for checking the copy (any errors are mine.)

To The Muppets of Alpha Theta: thank you for giving me a home when I needed it, for encouraging me to think differently about myself and for inspiring this story; I wouldn't be the person I am without you all, and that's a good thing.

Molly, Casey and Ruby—always my inspiration, this one is for you who were there from the first storm and taught me the truth and beauty of unconditional love.

And for the late Diane Wales a dynamic and encouraging neighbour and friend who, on learning that I was secretly writing a novel, said that she believed I could do it, and that I should meet Alison. She was right about both.

All the Places that were Hurt

There is something beautiful about all scars of whatever nature. A scar means the hurt is over the wound is closed and healed, done with.

Harry Crews

For Tom—my love, healer of all the places.

PART ONE

1

In the thin and colourless light of the early morning, drifting between sleep and consciousness, she heard him say her name... once... twice, the sound riding on a sigh, a huff of breath, held out, offered, taken back. And as she emerged into the tired flatness of another day, she tried to stay soft, slip back into sleep, remain oblivious of where she was. If she could just hear it again...

May's head pounded, her mouth hard-scrabble dry. She lay listening to the rushing sound, as a fast rain fell hard and steady in the area outside her window. She peered through the open curtains at the wet, grey, concrete stairs winding from her basement flat, the damp terracotta pots climbing up the first couple, then giving up. She could just make out the black glossed iron railings at street level, edges softened by the shrouding orange cast from the street lamp.

Her eyes hurt. They hurt when she opened them and hurt when she closed them, as though her lids were a fine grade sandpaper. She lay very still for a moment, breathing, almost sucking in a deep lungful of air before letting it out long and slow and pressing the heels of her hands over her closed lids. She let go and stared up at the ceiling, motionless except for her eyes, which traced the watermark around the light fixture. She'd painted over it but still it worked its silent, persistent way through.

'Do you want some tea?'

'Hmm?' May glanced up as her older sister, Lallie, leaned through the serving hatch from the kitchen. She'd been scrabbling about, boxing up the things neither of them was keeping.

'Tea,' she said again. 'Do you want some?'

'Okay...' May murmured, looking back down. 'Thanks.'

It had been a slow and mizzling day, damp and grey, the earlier promise of a storm petering out and disappointing. She sat on the living room floor of the Shepherd's Bush house she'd grown up in, the soles of her feet together, knees splayed, going through a box of letters and photographs. There was an aching chill in the still air and she reached for her wool knit hat, pulling it on and settling it low on her brow.

'How can it be colder inside than out?' she wondered, beginning again to sort through the tissue-fine airmail paper, looking at the stamps and trying to discern dates.

'Bugger. There's no milk,' Lallie said.

May reached for her scarf. 'Doesn't matter.' She wound its length around her neck and yanked her long, dark hair out of the coils.

'Listen to this Lal, it's brilliant.' She gave a short laugh. 'Did you know that Sarah and Dad ever went to Tunisia? Where were we do you think?'

'When?'

'While they were in Tunisia?'

'What are you talking about?'

May sighed and tried again. 'There's a postcard from them to us from Tunisia, I can't see the date, but…' She gave another quick laugh. 'Listen, listen… *Girl and Small Girl, We are being spat at by camels and I have sold Sarah to a very handsome Bedouin who liked her skills with the needle. Have decided to send for you and join them in the desert. I think this would solve the unbearable problem of school and Small Girl threatening to run away if I don't Sort It Out At Once.*'

Lallie, laughing, reached through the serving hatch for the postcard. 'Let me have that… I'd forgotten you thought school was child abuse! "*Look after Granny,*" she read aloud, "*and don't let her out too often, it goes to her head. All love, Dad and Sarah x*". Oh my god that's hilarious!' Lallie handed the card back to May. 'Honeymoon maybe? Shame the date is faded.'

'I don't remember them being gone.'

'Well,' Lallie said. 'We spent so much time just you and me, maybe you didn't notice!' She wrinkled her nose at May and turned back to the kettle.

May thought about this. Before their father had met Sarah, it had been a quiet, sometimes melancholy home. Their mother had left almost before May could talk, and she'd always told anyone who asked that she'd never missed her as she'd never had her. But maybe it was me that was melancholy, she thought.

As she looked around the room, her eyes grazing and glancing off familiar objects and paintings, she realised she rarely *saw* them; the Dufy print of some high-spirited little boats, in a sun-drenched harbour, the vibrantly quilt-draped armchair Sarah's cat Orpheus had always hogged, the small collection of antique chandelier crystals that hung on a fishing line at the now dust-filmed living room window. These had been gathered and pieced together by Sarah. They'd become part of the house, bringing colour and light, structure even. To remove them now... It might fall apart. Blimey, it's true what they say, she thought with a wry grimace. Grief really can make you a bit bonkers.

She picked up a photo of Sarah and William sitting in the back of an open estate car, looking sun-browned and windswept and conspiratorially happy. A wave of loneliness, of almost unbearable longing, pulled through her.

'Come on May,' Lallie was saying. 'We need to get on. I want some time with Sam, he's going away for work tomorrow. Oh love...

What is it?'

May found she was crying, an unchecked flow of silent tears. It was the way they spilled from her, undammed, that scared her. Lallie was quickly beside her, stroking a gentle hand across her back.

'It's shit, isn't it?' she said quietly.

'Yeah.' May stood, knowing it wasn't just about Sarah, but unable yet to make sense of it she couldn't say any more to her sister and that hurt too. She padded to the armchair and reached a chilly hand to stroke the soft velvet nap on one of the quilted patches. *Crazy.* Sarah had always preferred that irregular, random form of quilting to any other. Not for her the neat precision and repetition of log cabin or birds in flight.

But it's not slapdash, she'd assert, stitching one of her exuberant pieces. *It all fits like a puzzle.* May had loved them because the colours and shapes always seemed to her to sing, or hum and dance a little as she looked at them.

'There's always something else to see if you keep looking,' she said, stroking her fingertip along some feather-stitching. 'I feel as though I've looked at every square inch, but I don't remember this. Do you think she just secretly kept adding bits whenever the fancy took her?'

Lallie came across the room laughing softly and they sat together, touching random patches, playing again the game they'd shared so often.

'Yours or mine?' she asked, tapping a light finger on a patch of deep rose satin.

'Mine,' May answered without hesitation.

Sarah had rarely sent any worn or outgrown clothes to the charity shop, preferring to use them in her textiles. *There's always a story or a memory in a piece of cloth*, she would tell them, *why get rid of it?* Lallie laughed as May jealously stroked the smooth cloth.

As a six-year-old, she had loved that dress; the way it felt, heavy and substantial, shushing her softly as she moved. She'd like to be somewhere that sounded like that, she'd think, and imagined the rolling grassland and soaring skies of the prairie books her granny had sent.

'Do you remember how furious you were when she cut that dress up? You insisted that you could still wear it—but you couldn't even button the back up!'

'I wore a cardi with it to hide the gaping at the back.'

'No you didn't. You didn't care *who* saw.'

'Really...' May hesitated, unsure now of her own recollection. She watched her sister's face, so calm and assured.

'Yours or mine?' she said in a rush, moving on to an emerald patch of baby-cord.

Lallie cocked her head for a moment, frowned squintingly, then burst out, 'Ha! Trick question!' She grinned at May before saying 'both' in triumph.

They'd fought tooth and claw over that cloak. 'Typical,' their father William had muttered, clenching his jaw and leaving them to it.

May moved to the sofa, with her cup clutched hot in her hands and sat, leaning her head back, closing her eyes.

'Sis,' Lallie said. 'Is there anything else up? Apart from having to deal with all this I mean?'

May shook her head vaguely. 'It's been a long year,' she said and felt strangely disloyal; they had always shared, but she had no idea where to begin, she barely understood herself what she was going through.

After they'd decided they'd done enough for a night, May let herself into her flat, and stood motionless in the hall. Tired, she thought. Just so tired. She sat in the deep sofa, drawing one of Sarah's soft velvet quilts around herself without bothering to turn on the lamp.

Lallie had dropped her off on her way back to Sam and the kids, shouting through the open window of her car for May to come and have supper with them in the week, before bibbing her horn lightly and driving off into the oily-dark night.

The growing silence swelled through the room, pressing against her as she sat in the dark, listening to the rain drumming like so many fingers on the roof of the conservatory. She closed her eyes with a sigh; she could never hear a hard rain now, without remembering; remembering how there'd been no rain for weeks, how the parched ground had been so cracked, that the front yard had looked as if it was crazy paving, and how everything had opened up and come alive for her after that one summer storm in Vermont, ten years before.

May flopped onto the covered porch, gasping for air and through the shimmering heat haze far down the road, saw her roommates emerge; Stella and Danielle were heading towards her. They were walking so slowly it seemed they were getting no closer, as though the heat was too thick to push through. Danielle had a sarong tied and twisted around her head and looked like a serene African princess, slowly undulating along the road. Stella, wearing only a swimsuit and someone else's boxer shorts, kept pace, her usually sleek hair pushed back from her face, damp and sticky.

As they got closer, May could hear Stella muttering, 'God damn! It's so hot the road's melting.'

They made it to the porch and collapsed onto the floor, letting out great whooshes of air as they lay sprawled, panting rhythmically like dogs.

'Man, I hope it rains soon, it feels like something's going to explode if it doesn't.'

The light was so white it hurt to look out without sunglasses and May stayed in the shade of the porch as her friends discussed the class they'd just had.

'Are you done for the day?' she asked.

'Yup. No more classes now til Monday. Party time!'

Stella raised a single eyebrow at Danielle. 'How can you even think of partying? It's too hot to do anything. I'm still hungover from last night, anyway.'

'Lightweight,' Danielle said, poking Stella with a bare foot. 'Hey! Would you look at that! Where the hell did those come from?'

Danielle jerked her head towards a bank of trees along whose edges thick, low clouds were beginning to ooze and jostle for room.

The rest of the sky soared incandescent blue, dropping a hot shimmer onto the yard.

May pushed her hair up off her forehead and let the sweat catch the air. She sighed. The minutes crawled by, heavy air sucked at her bones. Slowly, slowly the clouds built up, overflowing the confines of the horizon and occupying more and more space, bullying, cajoling. May moved herself to a half sitting position and peered out at the swollen sky.

A long, low rumble tumbled towards them from beyond the river. Her skin prickled and she sat a little straighter. Another came, grumbling and complaining, rising reluctantly.

And then a drop of rain fell. No one spoke. May held her breath, waiting for another drop. It came. Then another, fat and heavy drops that plopped into the dust. There came more fast and fat drops, steaming as they landed on the heaving ground, quicker and quicker.

May was on her feet, poised, breathless, watching it come down in sheeting torrents. The ground sighed its gratitude and in seconds she was down the sagging wooden steps and out in the bubbling, pounding rain.

Oblivious to the splitting, shattering thunder, she shook her head back and let the warm water pour hard as a massage shower onto her face. She was soaked in seconds, her skin tingled and her heart was pounding as all that energy that had been sucked up and stored in those clouds poured onto her, into her. She felt a great whooping shout of joy burst from her lungs and the others who had been stupefied, petrified, came to life and clattered down the steps into the rain as it went on, on, on.

'Who wants a swim?' May called out and ran barefoot and laughing down the middle of the deserted road, towards the Connecticut River.

As she came to the steep sweep of road that wound past woodland and down to the river, she slowed her pace and they jogged steadily, three abreast until the road met the river and a series of floating jetties.

It was deserted and the rain continued to drum onto them, thunder and lightning crashing and cracking.

Without pausing, May flung herself in, plunging under the water into a deep, full silence. She surfaced moments later to see the other two girls, one arching into a dive the other bombing with a great shout of joy into the water.

Oh! What it is to be alive, she thought as the river swelled warm and held her body, and the rain continued its tingling strum across her scalp, its swift, prickling sweep across the surface of the river sending a constant rippling quiver over to the far shore.

Stella struck out for the opposite bank and slowly the rain subsided, becoming thinner until gradually it stopped. From their shelter beneath the bridge, unseen until now, two canoes slipped, silent.

'I didn't know there were mermaids in the Connecticut River!' one of the occupants called out with a long wave as they sculled slowly over to where the girls were treading water. May hung an arm over the edge to steady herself and opened her mouth as she was offered grapes and a morsel of soft, ripe brie. Stella joined them and someone else offered them a drink over the side.

'With ice and lemon, no less,' quipped Stella. 'Classy!'

May swam off to duck Danielle. The canoes and their occupants slowly drifted away and the three girls swam to the shore. The air was still very warm, but had lost its aggressive edge and they slowly walked up the hill towards Main Street. Soaking leaves dripped from darkened branches and the sound of water rushing through the drains and gutters at the edge of the road was almost enough to drown out the first chirruping announcements of the birds, as they emerged from their shelter.

'Oh my God—I can't believe we did that,' burbled Stella, 'Tanqueray and Tonic in the Connecticut river in a thunder storm. It didn't even occur to me how dangerous that might be. Lightening, alcohol, water. May, you're crazy.'

She shrugged. 'You loved it.'

She lay, sleepless and exhausted, her mind grabbing at vanishing details that felt crucial to recall until she did. Eventually she got up and wrapping herself in her quilt, padded on chilly feet into the kitchen to make herself some chamomile tea. Standing on one foot, rubbing the other for warmth on the back of her calf, she stared at the pin board above the counter, layered with postcards, receipts, photos, tickets, eyes drifting, unseeing, the sound of the kettle, rolling loud, louder than it ever seemed to in the daylight.

Something caught at her eye, whisper light but persistent. She reached out and pulled at the corner of a photo behind a postcard of *The New Yorker*. She laughed, then her eyes filled with tears. You're a bloody wreck, May.

Someone had taken it during her first year in Vermont, on one of the many days she'd spent by the river with Stella, Danielle, Courtney… It looked as though it was towards the end of a fine summer day. The angled sun slanted golden bright through slender, fir-fringed branches that reached towards the water's edge, making this shallow, rocky part of the river look as though it had been embellished with silver leaf.

In the lower left-hand corner of the photo, May crouched, bare-armed, bare-legged, hair caught up in a loose knot on top of her bowed head, as she looked down into the water. A box or basket of some kind sat just behind her along with a jumble of… what, clothes? It was hard to make out any detail because of the angle of the sun. It was the overall impression that felt important to May; it was why she'd kept this photo where she could see it, before it had slowly disappeared behind a steady build-up of the receipts and reminders of a life lived full of distracting activity.

As she continued to stare into the photo, she felt a hard knot in her chest, twisting and holding fast. The tenderness of the warm air, the sun filtering through the trees and warming that body—her body, her skin—was unreachable now. She looked at that girl and felt again that she'd left herself behind. How careless. Almost without thinking, she picked up the phone and dialled Stella's number in Vermont, mentally counting backward five hours to reassure herself she wouldn't be waking anyone.

'Mayflower! Yay!' Her friend's voice came tumbling over the line, so warm and full of laughter she had to squeeze her eyes and draw a deep breath to stop herself from crying. 'What time is it there?' Stella sounded breathy, rushed.

'Oh, late. One... something. Don't know. I just wanted to see how you were.'

Stella laughed with her but May could hear the concern in her voice. 'Are you okay?'

'Yeah, yes. I'm fine. I miss you. And we've been going through all Sarah's stuff...'

'We miss you too!' Stella broke off and May heard her muffled voice say something before she became clear again and said, 'Honey, I'm real sorry but I can't talk right now. I have a faculty meeting and Pete says he can give me a ride if we split now. How about I call you tomorrow, what time's good for you?'

'Oh don't worry,' May wished she had not made the call. 'You're busy, I'm busy. It was just on the off chance.'

'Hey! Don't be doing that! This is *me* you're talking to, not some any-ol-body. I'll call you tomorrow.' Stella was emphatic. 'I was going to call you anyways to see how you and Lallie were doing, but when I have time, it's the wrong time for you—I can never get my head round the time difference. Go *nowhere* tomorrow. Call in to work "stupid" and sit by the phone until I call!'

May laughed and the tinny echo of the long-distance line threw her laugh back at her, making it sound forced and self-conscious. The voice in the background was more persistent and Stella said in a low urgent tone, 'Quit, Pete, it's May.'

Pete's voice called loudly for May to 'come visit'.

'Honey, I'm so sorry, I really have to go, Pete can't wait and it's snow up to here and I don't want to walk...'

'It's fine, Stella. Don't worry, I'm fine.'

May put down the phone and felt lonelier than ever.

2

'Alex told me I have to reapply for a job at the magazine.' May was making soup in her sister's kitchen a few nights later. 'They're "restructuring". They've already fired half the PR department and want it to get sucked up by production.'

She could hear Tillie, and her little brother, Max, shrieking and splashing upstairs. Their father, Sam, was admonishing them to 'pipe down.' She knocked a lump of pale butter into a pan and watched it slide about and melt.

'Oh no!' Lallie stopped fighting with the booster seat she was trying to attach to the edge of the table and scrunched her face in sympathy. 'That's awful. You love that job.'

'No, not really. Not for a long time and Alex knows it. She says I've lost my spark and she's right.'

Lallie looked furious. 'Of course you've lost your spark!' she exploded and May flinched. 'You were nursing your dying stepmother and trying to produce a glossy-bloody-fashion mag for *her*. Alex did know, right? You did tell her, didn't you?'

'Yes, Lallie,' she said wearily. 'Of course I told her and she was brilliant about it. But she's not stupid. She knows my heart's not in it any more. I was feeling like this long before Sarah got ill.'

Lallie was at a loss, and hurt. 'Why didn't you say anything? To me I mean?' Then, changing gear abruptly to a brisk upbeat tone. 'Anyway, you'll be fine. I'm sure it's a formality on their part. You'll walk it.'

May turned to put a pan of potatoes on the hob, listening for the click, click, click, voomph of the gas as it caught light. She left it to boil and sliced leeks with long, clean strokes, scooping the fragments in two hands and dropping them into the foaming butter.

'I'm not going to apply, Lal. I loathe PR. I'm going to take redundancy.'

'Not going to… what? It's your job! You need to keep some structure in your life; the last thing you need is too much time on your hands.'

May had an urge to bite something. 'I spoke to Stella the other night.' She hoped a change of subject might ease the tension.

Her sister paused. 'Oh yea? How is she?'

'Good, I think. Settling into her new job. She sends her love.' She felt a ratcheting, tightening sensation in her belly. Why am I nervous? 'Lallie…'

'What?' she'd given up on the booster and was piling books on a chair. 'Max'll have to sit on these until Sam can fix this bloody thing.'

'I might take a bit of time and go out there.' She hadn't planned to say this, hadn't even consciously decided to visit, but now the words were out, she felt it was the only thing she knew for certain.

'Really?' Lallie sounded wary. 'When were you thinking of going?'

'Soon I suppose. Couple of weeks? I haven't made plans.'

'Hang on a minute.' May thought she heard something combative crouching in her sister's words. 'Stella's new teaching job. It's at her old university, isn't it?'

'Yes!' May tried to sound bright, casual. 'Well remembered. It's funny that she should end up teaching back at Hartland.'

'Hmm.' The sound came out as a kind of grunt. 'But not so funny if *you* end up back there.'

May tensed. 'What do you mean? It's a lovely town. I had a great time there.'

'Yeah. Until you didn't.'

May flushed, but before she could say anything Sam ambled in chatting, Max in his arms rosy and damp haired and cosy looking. Tillie scampered along beside him talking and clutching a picture book.

'Oh!' she yelped, then looked accusingly up at her father. 'You didn't tell me Aunt May's here. He didn't say, did he Maxie? Aunt May, he didn't say!'

Max shrugged sleepily and snuggled closer against his father. May stroked Max's hair and scooped Tillie up.

'Hello, my darling, I should've shouted up, I'm sorry. Come on.' She settled her more comfortably on her hip. 'Help me with the supper.'

They peered into the pot at the glistening leeks, pale and limp against the black of the pan and together turned and stirred, turned and stirred, scraping the bottom with the wooden spoon.

'There's nothing worse than a burnt leek,' May said, adding the cooked potatoes to the softened mass before filling up the pot with pale, golden stock. 'Unless it's garlic.' She pulled a face. 'Ugh! Burnt garlic is the *worst*.'

Tillie giggled and slid down as May loosened her hold. She lifted a spoonful of the soup to her lips, slurping in air so as not to burn her mouth.

'It's ready, sit everyone.'

Lallie gave her a smile as she settled the children and reached for the bread Sam was buttering, but May, strangely ashamed by her sister's earlier reaction, found it hard to smile back and focused on the children.

'What's that book you've been carting around with you, Tillie?'

'It's Katie, and she can climb into the pictures in the gal-er-ee, and be there with all the people in the pictures, and the animals, and she has all adventures and… Can you read it? Can she Mama? Can she read my story?'

Lallie raised her eyebrows questioningly at May and she nodded vigorously.

'Love to, darling. After supper, yes?'

After the children settled in bed and Sam had left them to talk, Lallie pressed the heels of her hands into her closed eyes and sighed. May waited, reluctant to open it up herself.

'May, is this really the right time to be visiting Stella?'

'Why wouldn't it be?'

Lallie shuffled. 'It feels impulsive. A bit...' she trailed momentarily, while May thought to herself, that ten years spent thinking about whether to go back was hardly impulsive. She said nothing and her sister went on. 'A bit Running Away.'

'Can we not make a big deal out of it? It rather neatly coincides with me being out of a job, don't you think?'

'Well, you're not officially out of a job. Not yet. But if you're not careful you will be.' May tried to respond, but Lallie raised her voice. 'But it's not so much that, that's bothering me. I get you need a break; I knew it was getting too much. I should have helped you more when Sarah was ill, but I...'

'You had the kids and Sam,' May managed to break in. 'You couldn't have done more and I keep trying to tell you, it's not just about Sarah.' She flushed hot all over. 'Lallie, I'm not in a good way, I'm ill all the time, I'm too thin, my skin's crap. Don't say you haven't noticed.' She could see from Lallie's face that she couldn't deny it. 'I've got—nothing. Nothing, Lallie. Look at you—all this. Home, kids, Sam. A job you love.' She hated how this sounded; childish, jealous. 'I'm nearly thirty years old and I feel like an old woman.'

'And that's *exactly* why going to Hartland right now would be an absolute bloody disaster! When you lived there before, it wasn't real life, it was a gap-year, you were just bumming around with a bunch of students.' Lallie grasped May's forearm. 'It won't be the same.'

May withdrew inside. Just let her get on with it, she thought. No point arguing. She stared at the floor as her sister pressed on.

'And clearly you don't remember the state you were in when you came home. Sarah and I were so worried.'

But she *did* remember. It wasn't the kind of thing you forgot; that kind of desolation. It had haunted her.

'Lallie, this has got nothing to do with that. I want to be with Stella, that's where she is and—and if you must know, Hartland is the one place I have ever felt really at home.'

She had a vivid image of the river, the sun leaping about, of tumbling clouds and most particularly, feeling alive.

'I think I'd go back, Stella or no Stella. I still miss it. I loved it there.'

And never, not once did I stop missing it, she thought. Why has it taken me this long? She was crying, and felt stupid and vulnerable for showing how unravelled she was. Lallie would never take her plans seriously, now.

'Oh, May,' Lallie said, sounding almost relieved, as though she now knew that this would blow over because May was just overwrought. 'Don't you know it won't be the same? It will have changed and that happiness—it was because you were in love. Don't you see?'

But May knew that it was her sister who didn't see, who couldn't know that she had loved the place, long before she had loved Harley.

At the top of the hill, she stopped walking and looked along the road towards the house, then back towards the centre of town and hesitated.

'Who's hungry?' Stella asked and without waiting for an answer headed off. May broke into a jog and she and Danielle caught up with their friend as she stopped in front of Everybody's and peered in to the steamed-up windows.

'Uh huh!' she said in a low but triumphant voice and May smiled as she saw Stella's new boyfriend Pete, sitting with a crowd of their friends.

'Didn't know you meant that kind of hungry...' she murmured,

just loud enough for Stella to hear. Pushing open the plate glass door, she flung a bare, brown arm around her friend and, dripping rainwater all over the greasy, tan, carpet tiles of the campus pizza joint, headed towards Pete's crowded table.

'Hey-hey!' he called out with a great friendly grin. 'Why are you so wet?'

Stella rolled her eyes, but May glanced down at herself and laughed. They really were very wet.

'It's been absolutely pissing with rain,' she said in her clipped English. 'And we've been jumping in puddles.'

She wasn't sure why, but something made her look over at the next booth and a dark-haired boy, whose long legs were jutting out into the aisle, caught her eye. He was staring intensely at her. May felt aware of herself; of her mouth moving clumsily over her teeth as she spoke, of her wet boxer shorts and t-shirt, her hair sticking to her back. She smiled at him and he looked abruptly away, as though she'd severed something.

'Scoot over guys, c'mon,' Stella ordered and perched on the edge of the highly-glazed bench of the packed booth.

'Aww, quit it Stella, you're peeing rainwater all over me,' said Pete, but he squeezed closer to her rather than further away.

'Yeah well, it's a fuckin monsoon out there you wuss, where've you been hiding?' Pete ducked as she aimed a swipe at his head and he grabbed her round the waist, butting at her middle with his head like a young steer.

'You'll never win!' May raised her voice above the row. 'You do know you're messing with the new captain of the women's soccer team?'

There was a clash of raised voices as Pete leapt up, sending a tray of red plastic cups filled with iced water crashing over the table. Delight wreathed his messy features as he failed to notice his companions' frenzied moppings and groaning, complaints that he always did that.

'No way! When did this happen?' he asked and without waiting for an answer, enveloped Stella in a huge hug. 'That is awesome.'

Then, 'Man, you're wet.'

'That, my friend, is cause and effect. What's the matter with you? I thought you were a science major. You're just a big fraud!' Pete went for her again.

'Back off man—it's all gonna change now. You can look at the merchandise but no touching. I'm out of your league now.'

Everyone laughed and from across the aisle, as the noise level decreased, the dark boy tilted his head back fractionally and looked out from under his hair.

'Way to go, Stella,' he said, his voice low and ever so slightly gravely around the edges. May thought she noticed a familiar Southern warmth about it, but couldn't be certain.

'Thanks!' Stella's smile was a dazzler, 'I'm really psyched.'

May stood at the edge of the table feeling the air conditioning vent blasting her wet legs and looking curiously at the boy, trying and failing to place him, when a waiter came scuttling, brandishing a huge pile of paper towels and looking embarrassed.

'I'm sorry, we have a no shoes policy,' he said, as he started mopping up the spills.

May lifted one of her bare feet and smiled, 'What a coincidence, so do I.'

The waiter looked crestfallen and began stumblingly to explain, but May cut him off. 'Oh I'm only teasing, don't worry, we'll just order a takeaway quickly and wait outside.'

The young waiter glanced furtively around. 'Uh, it's okay, I guess. You can sit with your friends while you wait. Shall I take your order?'

May thanked him as she and Stella, who kept chuckling and shaking her head, somehow found space to sit.

'That accent sure is strong currency,' she teased. 'You don't have to develop a personality at all, you still get all the perks! Like overly pretty girls. No impetus to develop a personality.'

'So how come you got one, hmm?' Pete said and everyone groaned, laughing.

The talk turned from raucous banter to which campus party to go to that night.

'We have to go to Dougie's,' someone shouted above the voices. 'It's his birthday and he's bought a keg of decent beer.'

'What? Not your usual gnat's piss?' May asked mockingly.

'Yay! Then we can get May drunk and she'll forget she's too cool for school and dance with us!' Stella added.

'What are you talking about? I always dance,' protested May, but stopped when she saw the look in Stella's eye. 'Oh, okay,' she backtracked hurriedly. 'You mean that Dance.' She mimicked Stella's deep Missouri accent artfully, earning herself another swipe at the head. 'You're right, I'd have to be pretty wasted to do that with you.'

There was general jeering and Stella said, 'See, too cool for school. I rest my case.'

The dark boy remained quiet, his eyes tracking back and forth to whoever was speaking, smiling when they laughed, body relaxed and slightly slumped against the bench. He was just removed from the group, May thought, his face occasionally betraying a flicker of something difficult to read; an ironic dismissal, but not quite. He looked unbelievably chilled and yet the fingers of one hand seemed to be drumming out a continual phrase on a table top piano.

Their order arrived and as the two girls got up to leave, he addressed May directly for the first time. His hand closed briefly around her forearm as she moved past.

'Well?' he asked, voice low, 'Are y'all going to be drinking Dougie's beer tonight?'

May shivered. The air conditioning vent on her legs? The warmth of his grasp? She looked over at Stella, eyebrows raised in question.

'Yeah. Maybe. Whatever.'

May chuckled. 'I just love that decisive quality of yours, Stel.' She turned back to the boy. 'Look out for us,' she said, 'it sounds as though we might, maybe, whatever be there.'

There was a flash of what was perhaps a smile and May thought he said 'cool' but couldn't be sure.

As she and Stella walked up Main Street, through the now fine, misting rain, trying to keep her voice light and casual, May asked,

'Who was that boy?'

Stella lowered her head and kicked a puddle at May, her laughter bouncing off the walls of the library as they passed. '"That boy", oh Best Beloved, is Harley Daniels. And no, you are not the first new girl in town to ask.' She laughed as May shot her a filthy look.

'How do you know him?'

'Oh, we met my Freshman year at some party. He was a Senior then.'

'Oh. So he's not a student?'

'Grad student. I'm not sure if he's done yet, but he works at Hartland Strings... the music shop? Up the far end of Main Street.'

'Where's he from?' May asked, wanting to flatter herself that she'd clocked his accent correctly.

'His Mom is from one of the North Dakota tribes, South Dakota. I don't know. Somewhere out in the Mid-West I think. Oh who cares, May?' she finished with a laugh, kicking at a puddle in May's direction again.

The night before her flight to Boston, May stayed at her sister's.

'Do you remember, Lal, how Sarah used to tell us stories of our life?'

'Of course,' said Lallie. A smile softened her face. 'She always said that no matter what, no one could change what we already had.'

'Ours' for keeps.' May thought about Sarah's passionate belief that life was about experiences, shared and otherwise.

Anyone can take stuff from you, she used to say. You lose things and they rot and decay, but memories of the things you've done... people you've loved... good food you've eaten... they'll sustain you always.

At bedtimes, even the night of their father William's funeral, she sat by their bunks. Holding their hands, one arm reaching up to Lallie on top, the other holding May's. She said as she had for as long as May could remember, 'Best thing about today?' and then, 'Worst thing?'

'Do you think that's a bit weird now?' asked May as though Lallie could read her mind.

'What?'

'That even the day of Dad's funeral, she asked the bedtime questions?'

'Yeah, maybe. But that was so Sarah, wasn't it?'

'I didn't think anything at the time...' but May didn't want to tell her sister that she wished just sometimes she'd been allowed to wallow. 'Can you remember what she said was *her* best thing?' she asked instead.

'That the robin came into the kitchen for something to eat.'

'I couldn't remember. I thought it was something about the birdfeeder. I remember now, she was just so genuinely touched that Dad's robin had come. And I do remember I couldn't think of a single best thing that had happened,' said May. 'Dad dying was all there was.'

May remembered also the confusion of defiance and guilt she'd felt when she'd said it. Not playing the game, letting Sarah down. Letting the side down.

'Sarah said that there would be days like that and that was when you use your memories.'

And that's what I've been doing for the past ten years, thought May.

'I don't want to spend my life being sustained by the past, Lallie. I want...'

'May,' her sister broke in, 'I can see you need to do this and get it out of your system. My hope is that in a month or so, with a bit of distance and perspective, you'll see that what you've got going for you here is pretty good. And just remember that wherever you go...'

'Yeah, yeah...' May said and they finished together, *'there you are.'*

3

An exhilarating shock of biting wind came from the direction of the ocean hitting her full in the cheeks and she threw back her shoulders and looked up, almost laughing. The icy blue sky spread with soaring clarity above her.

After a moment, she looked for signs to the bus stop and picked her way across the salt and grit of the walkways. Stella had tried to insist on meeting her at the airport, but May had been firm. She wanted, once again, to see the country unfold quietly from the picture window of the bus, just as she had ten years before.

'No,' she'd said emphatically. 'I'm feeling nostalgic.'

Everything around her dazzled and shone; great expanses of glass in the terminal building reflected the sharp winter sun; chrome, steel and the shining white curves of aircraft flashed and winked with shafts of light. She felt about in her bag for her sunglasses and, impatient to see the countryside she'd come for, waited restlessly.

The afternoon rush hour traffic seemed to stand still and yet the bus managed slowly to edge forward onto I-93 and begin its journey north. The tangle of flyovers and freeways, gleaming office blocks and construction works gave way to frost-fringed trees and snowy fields whose swooping dips and thickly drifted hills picked up the cool pinks and purples of the now setting sun.

She was tired and ready to be there as the bus slowly pulled up at the stop opposite the Hartland Inn. May's eyes felt sandy and hot behind her lids and the skin on her face, tight and grimy. Her knees creaked and clicked as she stood; three hours on a bus, on top of the transatlantic flight, had left her cramped and stiff.

The driver hauled himself out of his seat and thump-thumped down the steps onto the slushy roadside. May peered round his dark, polyester bulk into the belly of the bus, indicating which bags were hers and helped him drag them out.

'Thanks very much,' she said.

'No problem ma'am, enjoy your visit.'

She smiled at this unfamiliar nicety and stood where she was for a minute watching the bus pull out and head off down the road towards the river, leaving her in the quiet darkness of a glittering cold.

On the far side of the snow covered green, the illuminated clock tower showed 7.20; it was after midnight at home, no wonder she was tired. It took her a moment to recognise that what she was also feeling, was excitement. It's been a long time, she thought. She stood there in the dark, looking around at the shadowy shapes of faculty buildings and the dim warmth of the shops and businesses lit behind her along Main Street. She snuggled her scarf around her neck more securely.

She was really beginning to feel the cold after the drowsy, drying heat of the bus, when a large, murky jeep pulled alongside and a familiar voice drawled through the open passenger window. 'Hey lady! You wanna date?'

'Stella!' cried May as a bundle of quilted jacket, jeans and Timberland boots fell out of the door into her arms. Her throat tightened sharply as they stood hugging and rocking from side to side, snuggling into one another's necks, babbling you're here and I'm here and I can't believe it and nothing that really mattered.

It was Stella who loosened her hold first. 'Well, let me look at you!'

May drew back and, wiping her eyes, saw the swiftly concealed shock in Stella's face.

'Honey, you got so thin,' she said.

'Don't be daft.' May laughed it off and noticed Pete for the first time, hovering just behind Stella, big and rangy and muffled in a trapper hat and down coat.

'Hello,' he said, drawing the word out long and friendly; his warm smile touched May in such a tender and vulnerable place she felt almost scared at how raw she was.

'I'm getting in back with you,' Stella said, putting a possessive hand through the crook of May's arm. 'Drive on, my man!' she called out to Pete, in what May always used to call her Lady Penelope voice.

It was a short drive to Stella and Pete's house, made shorter by the buzzing whirl of chatter and silly jokes. May felt at once overwhelmed and delighted that they did seem to pick up where they had left off.

It had always been this way. Each summer after Stella's family had relocated back to America, they had returned to England to visit and May had looked forward to these long summers and the annual fusing of their two families, unflaggingly. Stella's quick, covetable wit coupled with her unselfconscious, sincere warmth had been the icebreaker every time. Stella loved her friends, and nothing ever seemed to interfere with that.

'Stella,' May said with a shudder. 'That is the most disgustingly enormous pizza I have ever seen. Are you expecting company?' She was sitting on the floor in front of a cast-iron wood burner an hour later and Stella was opening a huge flat box that had just been delivered.

'Lady, you have been gone waaay too long. This is a *regular* pizza. Regular.' She handed her a bottle of Rolling Rock and they settled back on the floor, the pizza between them.

'Pete? Play May's song,' she said as he returned from the kitchen with a bottle opener and some paper napkins. He looked briefly puzzled, then his face cleared and with a huge smile he went over to the stereo and flipped it on. Van Morrison sang *Brown Eyed Girl*.

'Oh my god, Stella! Not this,' May said with a groan, but she couldn't help grinning.

'You *love* this,' Stella giggled and sang along into her beer bottle, then hugged May. '*You're our—da-da-da—Brown Eyed Girl!*'

The room was almost too warm from the fire and it wasn't long before May wilted.

'Come on, honey,' Stella hoiked herself off the floor. 'Let me show you your home from home.'

May woke the next morning with the sun in her eyes, unsure where she was. She felt disorientated about where she lay in relation to the door. Surely the door should be over there, in the direction her feet pointed. As she became fully awake, she remembered with a melting pleasure.

There was a quiet stillness, dotted with birdsong, and as she lay on her back, her thoughts meandering lazily, she could hear the town waking. The steady, unhurried crunch of feet on the pavement beyond the front garden; the slow spattered crinkling of tyres on the road; a screen door slamming and a faraway dog answering one closer by.

She turned onto her side and propped herself on one elbow. Reaching for a glass of water, she drank thirstily and looked out of the window. The sky was a bright, soft blue with puffs of white speeding across, high, in billowy gusts. The road beyond the wide, short garden lawn was dark with the wet of melted slush and mud as each solitary car, usually a jeep-type thing, crept by, the wheels spattered mud and gritty slush all over the sidewalk and the deep piles of shovelled snow. The little house was very quiet and still.

In the kitchen, a note was propped against a jug of pale tulips, so open and relaxed they looked as though they had taken their corsets off and were lolling around with the girls. May smiled as she read:

Mayflower,
  Didn't want to wake you, there's coffee on the counter. I'll be back

around 5. My extension # is 6531 if anything comes up.
  Love Stellaxxxx

She pottered around the little kitchen, finding a mug and some milk and spreading peanut butter onto toast. She had forgotten how sweet everything tasted and glanced down the list of ingredients on the jar, curling her lip. How could there be so many in a thing as simple as ground up peanuts? She sat and drank her coffee, idly sifting through newspaper clippings and correspondence and last Sunday's *New York Times*, looking in a vague purposeless way for something to read. It was not as late as she had thought, Stella and Pete must have had an early start. The day stretched ahead, unplanned.

She spent the morning unpacking, making the little bedroom hers. All the forgotten aspects of American life came back, familiar again the instant they happened; the soft foaminess of the tap water; the way the phone rang—long, bubbling, trilling; the brightness of everything; the Now! Hey! Wow-ness of packet labels and adverts and magazine covers; the insistent, endless advertisements on the radio, with the voice-over rushing the words out, then inhumanly speeding to spit out the disclaimer at the end and wash their hands of it all.

The house was warm and May stepped out onto the deck to feel the air. It was much colder than the clear blue sky and sharp white sunlight promised and she scurried inside to pull on another layer. Looking at herself in the mirror on the back of her bedroom door, she quickly twisted her hair into a long plait, not bothering to comb out the infernal tangle of knots and, unsure whether she would need a hat, tucked one into her pocket.

4

Pete and Stella's house was on a side street less than half a mile from the town's main street and the college buildings they worked at, although you wouldn't know, reflected May wryly, as she noticed both cars were missing from the driveway. It was typical of many houses in the area; detached, single-storey, white clap-boarded buildings, with green painted shutters and a fenceless lawn that ran in a short slope down to the pavement and the road beyond. The only thing that showed the boundaries to each property were the mailboxes, standing like wading birds on a long thin leg, and the placement of dustbins and driveways.

As she made her way along the smooth tarmac pavement, flanked by lawns on one side and a narrow verge on the other, peppered by fire hydrants and cavernous gutters, she was reminded again of the American fondness for flags and whimsy. She passed dog walkers, commuting cars and huddles of kids walking to school; she wanted to call out, 'Hey! Look! I'm back!'

She took a left at the end of the street and headed uphill along a wide, curving road banked by high, snowy inclines and woodland, then turned and stood, in the middle of the steep sweep of road, watching as it disappeared around a knot of trees heading for the river. How often had she and her friends walked this way, killing time, making each other laugh? I wonder where they all are now, she thought. Danielle... Courtney? Scattered across the states, like a handful of chicken feed. And what of Harley? He would have left Hartland long ago, she knew, camera on his shoulder, focussing on something or someone else.

The road came out at the green in the town centre, marking the beginning of Main Street. May hesitated. Main Street could be covered in ten minutes if you strolled. She decided to walk around the green and then up toward the old co-ed house she had shared with Stella and her college friends nearly ten years before, and then do Main Street, maybe stop at Lou's for a coffee, if it was still there.

She was unprepared for the swell of love and sadness when she saw the old house. It looked tired and in need of sunshine. The pine trees that shielded it from the road had grown surprisingly tall and been badly neglected. Someone had attempted to cut back some of the branches that would make access through the front door a little tricky; it seemed as though they had not had the right tools, their cuts were ragged and torn. She wondered if the trees knocked on that upper bedroom window on windy nights, as she stepped tentatively up towards the front door and tried the handle. It never used to be locked and she remembered that the brass handle was always loose and wobbly. You could always hear when someone was trying to sneak in, by the familiar rattle, just so long as the music wasn't too loud. She turned the stiff knob and nothing happened. Locked. Things change.

Stepping back, she looked up at the second storey sun porch. The only way to access it was either by climbing the iron fire escape, or through the window that looked out onto it. That had been May's old bedroom. Well, not hers exactly. It was Stella's and her roommate Danielle's, while they were undergrads. She'd come to visit Stella for a couple of weeks in what was meant to be a gap-year of travel, and stayed put. It occurred, surely not for the first time, that they had been unbelievably relaxed and generous. How many people would tolerate a person crashing in their room like that? For a week or so maybe, but months? How had she been so lucky? She looked up at the window as though she might see an old friend appear.

She turned onto Main Street, thoughts still far away in that old house, remembering hot summers and breathless nights, getting bitten to pieces by mosquitoes, drinking weak beer, smoking far too much and singing, and she was just crossing the road at the edge of the green when a swift prickle of pins and needles netted across her scalp. She stopped walking, paralysed and conspicuous.

A man was leaning into the open bonnet of a black pickup, parked by the kerbside, stretching and muttering something to the engine, the mannerisms so familiar to her that she knew just before he did it that he would rub an open palm thoughtfully over his mouth and shake his hair out of his eyes as soon as he straightened. Wiping his hands on a rag and slamming the bonnet, he turned towards her and for a moment went utterly still.

There was no mistaking him. Same faded jeans and heavy boots and his thick, dark hair, although shorter than she remembered, still long enough over his brow for her to recognise the characteristic way he slightly cocked and tilted his head back to look out from under it. It gave him a slightly arrogant, appraising air she knew was deceptive.

His breath held stillness was somehow contagious. She stood motionless until she heard him say, 'Piper, get up,' in a low imperative voice and point through the open door at the inside of the truck. A sleek, black dog leapt then scrambled up into the passenger seat, and the man's face broke into a beautiful, flashing smile as he praised her. He jerked his head from May, jumped into his truck and drove off, music pounding out of the open window.

A rush of tears, which she managed to hold back fiercely, almost overwhelmed her and she stood there until the pounding in her ears had subsided. Seeing him like that frightened her. And yet to see him there, amongst all that was familiar and beloved felt right; it fit. He was as much part of this place as the trees and the river and she'd been a fool to think he wouldn't have been, even if he had been gone.

She waited in the lush chill until her pumping veins had stilled a little and headed, subdued, towards Lou's.

In the pounding smoke and roaring darkness of the house party, May leaned against a basement wall and watched Stella and Danielle shooting a game of pool with another of their housemates, Courtney.

'I see you found your shoes.'

She turned to see the dark boy standing beside her. Breathe, she told herself, pulse banging. He was not as tall as he had looked, all stretched out in the pizza place earlier, but she still had to look up and his eyes, oh… they were so dark it was hard to tell where the iris ended and pupil began. Mesmerising, she thought.

'Well, what about that?' May said, smiling at him. 'So I did. I was just thinking about you. Did you just get here?'

'Nah…' He pulled out a packet of Marlboro Lights, and raised his eyebrow in a question.

'Sure.' She nodded, congratulating herself on how cool she was managing to be.

'I've been stuck over there with the guys.' He indicated with a nod to the other side of the crowded basement and she wondered how she'd missed him.

'I managed to make my excuses when they started in on a game of beer-pong.' She gave him a quizzical look. 'You don't want a know.'

He lit a cigarette, took a drag and passed it to her. She was surprised by the gesture, hesitated, then took it, saying with a suppressed smile, 'That's very Now Voyager! Are you a film studies major?'

His eyes were lowered as he lit another for himself, but she could see the crinkles of a smile and when he looked at her again she realised with something like shock, that his smile made him completely visible. It was in the way his eyes flashed, unguarded. She wanted to make him smile like that again. He looked at her steadily.

'No,' he said and the corner of his mouth tipped up a little. 'And anyway, it was two. He always lit two at a time.' May laughed and was about to ask what he did study, when he continued. 'You look different from today.'

She wondered if that was good or bad; his tone was so neutral. 'Really?' she said, knowing that she must do. 'How so?'

'Well…' he drew the word out, considering. 'Your hair. It's got a curl to it. It was so wet this afternoon, it looked straight.' He put out a hand and she felt its warmth briefly on her neck as he picked up a lock, straightening it slowly until the end touched her elbow. 'And… you're wearing clothes.'

She held her breath. He darted a smile at her and May felt a warmth course through her, then slowly, slowly, subside. He looked at her sideways, head tilted slightly back and started off in another direction.

'So, how come I've never seen you around if you're a friend of Stella's? Are you a student?'

'No. Stella and I kind of grew up together and she invited me for a visit about two months ago now she's at college. I haven't been able to leave. I'm vicariously living through her. You know, all the perks of college life but none of the hard work?'

'How'd y'all grow up together, English girl?'

This always confused people and May laughed. 'Our parents were friends. My dad was born in the same town as hers in South Carolina, but moved to London for work and they visited every year. Stella's mum's English.'

'Cool.'

'Yes. It was. How about you? Where did you grow up?'

Harley seemed for a fraction of a second to stop breathing. 'Oh all over really,' he said, tone even.

'Like where? Come on, name names!' she pressed, laughing.

She'd been right about his accent although he seemed to slip in and out of the dialect at will, but the idea that he might be connected to the red clay her father's family came from appealed to her. He gave her a quizzical look, tempered with something like reluctance she read simply as teasing.

'Oh, you know… Midwest, then Alabama, Mississippi, Georgia, some.'

May heard these names and they touched her deep-rooted romantic sense of the country. To her it sounded wonderfully free; an unshackled itinerant life. She longed to go, to feel the space and sky *and freedom, but before she could share this with him he almost blurted, 'So, how do you like Hartland?'*

'Enough to get myself a job. I'm waitressing at Molly's Balloon. I'm crap, but it's fun.'

He raised his eyebrows. 'You like it that much? Okay.'

'Well, and I ran out of money.' They laughed, but then she added because it seemed to matter that he understood, 'I really do like it, though. It's been quite an eye opener. Very different from what I'm used to. It's hard to explain, but I like the way the people here are so open, so frank; I like the way that other things matter here, or the things I'm used to, don't matter. How you look, who you know, what music you like…' She looked at him, weighing whether it was worth saying what was truly an eye opener, and swiftly realised that the couple of beers she'd had were enough; she had what her stepmother Sarah always called The Fuck-Its. 'I've felt more myself here, than at any other time in my life.'

'Oh!' he gave a kind of half laugh emphasising the husky edge to his voice. 'And you an old lady of… what? Nineteen? Twenty?' He shifted slightly.

'Nineteen,' she confirmed with dignity, and drew back a little. Harley smiled lazily and, touching the top of his beer bottle briefly to his lip, offered it to her. It was an oddly intimate gesture and May hesitated, struck by how she couldn't get the measure of him. She took the bottle and a swig, eyes on his mouth.

'Well how old are you then, Ol Man River?' she asked, feeling childish but curiosity getting the better of her. He smiled, looking out over the crowded room.

'Twenty-four,' he said, then somewhat ambiguously added, 'Not too old I hope?'

May looked at him, hoping his face might give something away, but found he was looking at her with such intensity she had to look away. She tried to make out Stella and the girls through the smoke and was just thinking of a way to ask him what he did on campus that would not sound like an interrogation, when he said, 'Film making.' He smiled, emphasising the second word. 'Not studies. With social anthropology.'

'Aah…' They both laughed and settled closer together against the wall. Their heads were turned towards one another, eyes roaming over each other's faces, connecting, smiling, saying nothing until a rolling crescendo of music and voices swelled through the packed basement room and Harley said, 'Do you want to go outside? It might be a little easier to talk.'

May looked about briefly for Stella who was still shooting pool and signalled to her that she was going outside. Stella responded with a cartoonish raising of her eyebrows and went on with her game. Harley took her hand lightly and led her up the narrow basement stairs letting go as soon as they reached the top. They passed by shouting, drinking, laughing students. Someone was hollering a loud call for anyone to line up for a chugging competition. They continued through the darkened house to a back door that gave onto a wooden porch with some scattered outdoor furniture and a swing sofa. A small huddle of kids was crouched around a bong made from an empty tequila bottle, trying to get it to light and arguing over why it wasn't working.

The throb of music and roar of voices became a backdrop to the thick, dark night, as they leaned side by side against the back wall. May could feel heat coming through Harley's faded shirt, as his upper arm rested against her shoulder. She was acutely aware of his eyes flicking towards a sound, darting over towards any slight movement even though he kept physically still, his head quiet and bent towards her as they spoke. She felt as though she was doing all the talking, opening up, unable to stop herself.

'So,' Harley gave her a long, slow smile, his eyes half closed. 'What're y'all reading right now?'

'You really want to know what I'm reading?' she said, wondering if she should fib and think of something erudite. He jerked his head in an upward nod, eyes flicking towards the sudden sound of breaking glass. His shoulders relaxed, as shouts of laughter followed.

'Yeah,' he said. 'Right now, don't dress it up. No lyin.'

May laughed and flushed. 'I wouldn't lie!'

He raised his eyebrows. 'Yeah? Wouldn't? Everybody lies,

sweetheart. But just so you know, I don't.'

'That's quite a statement,' May said, feeling out of her depth. 'Never? Not even to save someone's feelings?'

'Especially not to save someone's feelings.' His eyes tracked her face slowly and May's blood rose, languorous and hot.

'Isn't that a bit cruel?'

Harley was quiet for a while, pondering. 'Mmm… maybe. I guess, but discovering the truth later, isn't that worse?'

'Yes,' May said emphatically then looked away. Harley nudged himself abruptly from the wall and faced her.

'You know,' he said, whispering the tips of his fingers on the underside of her wrists, 'we've been talking all this time and I don't even know your name.'

With the lightest touch, his fingertips traced the inside of her warm, bare arm, stopping at the crook of her elbows. She felt it everywhere, stillness gripped her.

Harley dipped his face towards her and his breath, barely there, was warm on her cheek and then her neck. His nose just tipped a nudge at her earlobe and he drew back a little.

She realised she was staring at him, breathless, when he said, 'Well? You have a name?'

'I do. My name is May.'

'Hello, May,' he said and kissed her on her mouth, long and slow, drawing her hips close against his. 'I've been thinking about doing that all day,' he said, keeping his hands cupped around her hips as he swayed a little, a gentle dance, slowly, slowly, looking down at her. 'Is that okay?'

She was so affected by the sincerity in his voice that she couldn't answer, so she just touched his mouth and he nipped gently at her finger with his lips. Curling her other arm closely around his waist she felt his back through the heavy, supple cotton of his shirt, firm and intensely warm.

'Of course.' The tension in her belly began to melt. She'd been wanting to touch him since his first honest smile.

'Well that's good,' he said, then picked up her hand and put his warm lips on her wrist. 'You want to come home with me?' he asked.

The swift kick of euphoria and lust surprised her. She looked at his profile as he leaned back loose limbed and relaxed against the wall and lit another cigarette.

'Is that a euphemism?' Her pulse was racing. Harley gave a low laugh, dropping his head in a sideways glance. He took a couple of drags and handed his cigarette to her.

'Yes,' he said, his voice full of smiles, 'that is a euphemism.'

'Well, that's a relief.'

They walked slowly through the dark streets, music receding and fading as they came to the edge of town where other sounds and silence took over. Their boots made a light crunching on the gravely sidewalk. They talked as they walked and Harley kept his arm slung loosely around her neck, twisting his fingers through her hair every now and then. She could smell the clean, potent heat of him, feel the warm skin of his forearm brushing at her cheek and neck and tried to concentrate on what he was saying about Native American voters rights, but all she could think was, any minute now, I'll feel all his skin on my body. He stopped and looked at her.

'What?'

He gave her a sweet half smile. 'I can't think about politics when I think I'm about to shag you. I'm feeling very distracted.' She smiled, wondering when she'd ever been this honest with a boy. It was the first time she heard him laugh and it was so free and uninhibited he seemed younger. She couldn't take her eyes off him.

'Shag? That's a state dance in the South. I'm guessing that might translate somewhat differently where you're from?'

It was May's turn to laugh. 'Yep.'

'Well, you sure are shallow, English girl! Here I am trying to educate you about corruption and the disenfranchisement of an indigenous people and all you're doing is thinking about fucking!' He flashed his teeth at her wolfishly.

'I know. I am shallow, but you started it!'

He turned serious again and looked at her unwaveringly as he took her in his arms and pulled her against him, one arm around her waist, the other holding the back of her head, fingers restlessly moving, always moving.

'No,' he said. 'You started it. When you came dancin into Everybody's all rain slicked and—were you singing? Laughing? I don't know, but you, girl, you started it.' His eyes were full of dark heat and May was swept up in him. They swayed in the moonlight hip to hip, kissing, until Harley broke off. 'I live right here.'

He took her around to the side gate of a large detached house set back from the road. She couldn't make out much in the dark shadows, but Harley led her through the long, rustling grass to a small cabin tucked among trees. Just like a little Wendy House, she thought.

Inside, the air was hot and still and he lit candles stuck in bottles that gave off a soft, warm glow and switched on a fan, which provided some relief. The ringing, rhythmic sounds of the Vermont summer night intensified.

'So...' Harley took May in his arms and kissed her, his hands roaming, pushing at bits of her clothing impatiently. 'You want a dance?'

'I saw Harley Daniels today.' May dropped it casually, but felt a flush creep up over her and burn, burn at her ears. She felt slightly sick.

'I knew there was something I forgot to tell you!' Stella slapped herself on the forehead. 'He knocked me flying a while ago, just after I spoke to you that night you were having a meltdown...'

'I was not melting down,' shot May.

'You were.' Stella grinned. 'Anyway, I was on my way somewhere going down Main Street and he was just running backwards.'

'Backwards?

'Running backwards, yelling to someone.'

'Yelling?'

'Oh, "later buddy," something like that, and he swung

right round into me—wham, boom!—and we said, "Hi, hi" you know, that sort of thing, but,' she slowed down a little, 'he was so *weird* when I said I'd spoken to you.'

There was a rather awkward silence while May pondered. 'You told him?'

'Mmm hmm.' Stella sounded momentarily distracted and then continued in a puzzled tone, 'I don't remember if I even managed to tell him that you were coming back. Maybe just that you'd called.' Stella screwed up her face in a quick grimace. 'And I kept wondering why he acted so weird when I mentioned your name, didn't I Pete?'

With a grunt, Pete picked up the TV guide and flicked through, his boisterous limbs jostling for space on the sofa. His face was so mobile and expressive, May only needed to watch it to see what he was reading. Garbage... garbage... *interesting*, What? Nothing, nothing. Aha! She almost laughed.

'He probably couldn't remember who she was, honey,' Pete said absently, reading on. Then he darted a swift look at the two women and said, 'What? Harley Daniels dated every girl that stepped off the bus, why would he remember her? No offence, May, the guy's nuts.'

'*I* didn't date him!' Stella exclaimed, laughing indignantly.

'Yeah well, you're about the only one who didn't, but you probably wanted to!' He ducked as his wife made a swipe at his head.

'Come on, Pete. You know Harley was crazy about May.' Then to May she said, 'I always thought you two would, I don't know...' she trailed off thoughtfully and then went on, 'He hasn't changed that much you know, still *very* mmm hmmm.' She smirked. 'If you like that sort of thing.'

Pete snorted and May snapped, 'Yeah, well we didn't,' then tried to soften her reaction with a smile. Stella gave her a pondering look and May blushed again.

'He says he's working as a sound tech at the Roth,' Stella

said. The vast, modern cultural centre dominated the small college town and May knew that the basketball courts where Pete coached the college team were in there somewhere. 'Hey! How come you haven't bumped into him yet?'

'It wasn't deliberate, Stella,' Pete teased. May giggled. 'But I saw Ethan—you remember him, May? Owned the music store Harley worked in?'

She smiled a nod. 'He had the most almighty crush on Danielle and never did anything about it.'

'Oh didn't he?' intoned Stella with a lewd smirk.

'Really? Wow, I so missed that!'

'You had your mind on other things, my dear,' Stella said.

'Anyhow,' Pete went on. 'Ethan mentioned something about Harley having a workshop just behind his lot, so I figured he must be around. Seems he has a nice little side line in carpentry. Regular renaissance guy,' he finished dryly.

Stella was piqued. 'Why didn't you tell me?'

'What?'

'That he was back in town?'

Pete, unmoved, shrugged. 'I don't know. Didn't seem important.' He carried on trawling through the TV guide.

Stella sat bolt upright, indignation crackling off her.

'Well quite beside the fact he and May were an item, he became a good friend of ours. How could that not seem important?'

'Stella? What? I failed to mention, that someone mentioned an old pal. What's the big deal? I'm sure one of us will run into him again soon, it's a small town, remember?' He pulled a face at her.

'Anyway,' May said. 'You're right, Pete. He didn't remember me. Or recognise me.' She felt sad saying this. 'I suppose I've changed a lot?' She looked first at Stella, then Pete.

'I'm sure that's it,' Stella reassured, while her husband looked uncertain. 'Pete,' she said briskly, 'haven't you got a ball game to watch or something?'

Pete stood and hugged his wife's head against his belly. 'As a matter of fact, I've got a ball game to *play*.' He grinned at them and sloped off into the hall, calling as he put on his jacket, 'Want to swing by Molly's for a beer later? I know the guys would love to meet you, May.'

Stella raised her eyebrows at her. 'Want to?' May nodded, smiling. 'Sure, hon,' Stella called out. 'We'll see you about 9.30.'

The purplish light of evening crept out of the woods and down over the roofs and gardens, softly shrouding everything.

'So, you've been having a pretty shitty time,' Stella said with her usual inflection of laughter behind sober words. May nodded.

'Looking after dying people sucks,' she said, trying to match Stella's tone. 'Especially when you love them and you're trying to ignore the fact that they're dying.'

'Mmm hmm…'

May looked at her friend and her gentle, affectionate expression was too much. 'I miss her.' She didn't even try to stop the tears and it felt so good just to let them come.

The pressure from Stella's warm hand felt good on her back, with its slow and rhythmic strokes, but it undid something too. May hunched over the table, forehead on her hands and felt herself come apart. 'She was my mum,' she sobbed. 'Never had one and then she came along and now she's gone.'

'Oh May, I know.'

'And too young. She would have been fifty-six this year.' May scrubbed at her eyes. 'Would it be too much of a cliché to say—I mean, what if *I've* only got twenty-five years left?' Stella tried to break in but May pressed on. 'You never know, do you? Sarah was never ill and then boom, cancer, dead within eighteen months. My own mother killed by a car after she left us. You just never know.'

'May! Don't.' Stella looked dismayed and May leaned over to hold her arm.

'And Dad. He didn't even make it to fifty.'

'Jeez, May, when you lay it out like that it's…'

'I don't mean to be morbid,' May broke in. 'That's not what I mean. I just mean… I don't want to wake up in the mornings wondering what's the point of it all. And I'm glad I'm here.'

Stella smiled. 'Existential here, or Hartland, Vermont here?'

That made May laugh. 'Both?' she said and reached for a tissue. 'Oh my god, I'm disgusting!'

Her nose was swollen and stuffed up from crying and her skin felt hot and stretched across her face.

'No, darlin,' drawled Stella. 'I've always said you're at your most beautiful when you cry.'

May stuck out her tongue. 'You can't tell anyway; it's got awfully dark in here.'

'I've got infra-red eyes, Ms Smarty-Pants!'

Stella looked at her watch and stood to switch some lights on. Everything in the kitchen sprung and pulsed as the light threw itself over the curves and planes.

'Still feel up to a beer with the guys? Or even a Long Island ice tea, for old time's sake?'

'Blimey, I'd forgotten those. I don't know if I still have the constitution I did, but I suppose there's only one way to find out. What time did Pete say to meet them?'

'Oh it's easy; they'll be there from about eight-thirty.'

May stood and stretched, yawning theatrically. 'I think I'll just go and stick a brush through this mop, if I can. I didn't realise it had got so late.'

'I love that you've kept it long,' said Stella, lifting a handful of May's hair and letting it fall through her fingers. 'I really regret cutting mine, now I'm too impatient to grow it back.'

'And I'm just too cheap to go to a hairdresser.' May laughed.

The sky was frosted with stars and May's breath furred out in front of her as she and Stella walked, footsteps ringing out rhythmically. People walked about ducking into restaurants and bars, calling out across the street and talking by the light of the shop fronts, making eye contact and saying 'Hi' as they passed.

Halfway down Main Street, the familiar green and white striped awning of Molly's Balloon came into view and May felt a spark of anticipation. She'd waitressed there years before and her memories of it were good.

'I wonder if I'll still know anyone,' she said, slipping her arm through Stella's.

'Oh definitely you will, things turnover slowly around here if you're not a student, including the menu!'

May laughed. 'Still one thousand different types of "gourmet" burgers and "our famous Mexican menu"?'

'Mmmhmm… but *man* they do it well,' Stella said with a grin.

May gave Stella a sceptical look. 'How many Mexican chefs cover everything with Monterey Jack cheese?'

'Stop, with that! It's good.'

They slammed through the door into a little storm shelter, then into the restaurant and were greeted by a young girl with a thorough smile, showing teeth that put her trainers to shame. 'Hi!' she exclaimed. 'My name is Kelly?' she made it sound like a question, 'How many are you this evening?'

Stella began to speak, but Pete was already calling, 'Hey, Stella!' across the restaurant. May wondered if she was the only one to think of Marlon Brando when he hollered. She smiled apologetically at Kelly and they made their way to the rowdy table at the window overlooking Main Street. Pete stood as they got closer, calling, 'Come on guys, scoot over! Grab another chair, Doug! Hey! Everyone! This is our good friend May-From-London! Kelly, honey, bring us another pitcher!'

May didn't know anyone besides Stella and Pete, but allowed herself to be drawn in, warming to the easy, relaxed atmosphere. Most of the talk was of the basketball game the men had just played and involved a lot of humour that challenged each other's masculinity.

She was sitting between Stella and a sandy coloured, crop-haired fellow with pale eyes and a loud voice. Doug rocked when he laughed, shaking and bowing his head. He was so long limbed, he kept knocking things as he moved.

'Man, your accent is awesome!' he bellowed above the bar room noise. 'My mom had a cousin who visited London once. My dream is to go to a real London pub, you have awesome pubs in London. Did you know that all those names of pubs have a meaning?' May nodded and he lolloped on. 'You know, like The King's Head? It's named after the real king who… they cut his head off and as a kind of warning they named the pub after it.' May tried not to look at Stella, who had dropped her jaw exaggeratedly, but it wasn't easy and she was afraid she might laugh.

'But it's not just that,' Doug continued. 'Every single pub is named after real people or events.'

'Yeah… like the Slug and Lettuce,' muttered Stella and May giggled and took a swift swig of her drink.

She leaned forward to pour herself another from the jug in the centre of the table and caught a look passing between Pete and Stella. Following the direction of Stella's briefly darting glance, her breath rose and slammed to an abrupt halt in her throat. Oh god, she thought for the second time that day, it's Harley.

Self-contained, watchful, while everyone around jostled

and roared; she would know him anywhere. It was in the tilt of his head, the way the tips of his fingers tap-tapped on his mouth, before he rubbed them lightly across, then back, while he listened to the man wedged against the bar to his left. And while she was clocking this, May realised with a lurch of panic that any moment, he would look over in their direction, because that's what he always did; checked out the room. Always looking for the emergency exit, she used to think.

She couldn't stop staring, in case... what, she never saw him again? She smiled ruefully to herself just as he caught her eye and looked away, turning abruptly back to a man at the bar who she now recognised as his old friend Rob Something. What *was* his last name? They'd been knock about drinking buddies when May lived there and as she watched them, laidback and familiar, something touched her. I'm glad you've got an old friend, she thought.

She was so acutely aware of him being on the other side of the room that she could barely hear what Doug was saying. She forced herself to listen to the words, if not the meaning, and pulled her attention back to the people she was with, realising with a start, that Doug was expecting a response.

'I'm sorry, Doug. Jet lag. Go on.' He had what he needed and galloped on.

May's mood had flattened and she struggled, trying to find a conversational thread. It had become a succession of shouted observations and retorts, followed by explosions of laughter that made her jump inside. She was wondering if it would be too soon to tell Stella she was ready to bail, when a familiar, humorous voice broke into her thoughts and she looked up into the bristly smile of her old restaurant boss.

'May! It *is* you!'

'Turtle!' She jumped up, delighted, and hugged him tight.

He was a small wiry man and although May was only a few inches above average height, she felt she was enveloping him. She stood back and looked at him.

'Oh, Turtle! How lovely!' She couldn't help but give him another hug and they laughed. 'I thought you opened your own restaurant, you're still here?'

Turtle grimaced. 'Well, we did, but it didn't pan out. Tell you about it another time. But this is great! How long are you here for? Just passing through or staying a while?'

'Staying awhile, I think, things haven't quite panned out for me either.'

May mirrored Turtle's cartoonish expression of sympathy back at him, making him laugh.

'Well come in sometime when it's quiet and we can catch up, have a coffee. Hey,' he said, 'did you and Harley keep up after you left?' He turned, raising his arm and before May could say anything, called out, 'Yo, Harley! Look who's just blown in! Get over here!'

Harley, who was still propping up the bar holding a bottle of Bass, turned and smiled at Turtle and saying something first to Rob, picked his way through the packed bar. May felt an urge to get away and looked helplessly at Stella, who just smiled as though she didn't quite understand. She swallowed and made herself breathe as she watched Harley appear and disappear around and behind people, then materialise beside Turtle. He towered over him, giving the impression he was a man of extreme height and now he was up close, May could see that he had changed. Of course he had, he was nearly ten years older and his features had a strength and definition about them that had only been hinted at before. Why this should make her feel so sad, she had no idea. Where a boy once stood, she thought, then smiled and greeted him brightly.

'Hello, May,' he said, as though this happened every day. 'Stella.' His brief smile warmed and opened a little as he looked at her.

'The last thing you were expecting, huh?' Turtle

exclaimed.

'I guess it might have been,' Harley said, looking back at May, 'but we ran into each other earlier.'

Until that moment, May believed he hadn't known her; she'd even toyed with the idea he hadn't seen her properly. It happened, she'd told herself; out of context, out of time it was easy to miss someone who shouldn't really be there. Now her cheeks burned with humiliation; he seemed to be making it clear he had not only seen her, but known her. She felt stupid, but more than anything, hurt.

'So you blanked me, then?' May smiled, trying for humorous bravado and not feeling it. 'I thought you hadn't recognised me. I mean, it has been a long time.'

Harley's answering smile was brief as he shrugged. 'Not so long.'

May clammed up, exposed, uncertain.

'So, what do you think of the old place?' Turtle was saying. 'Any surprises, or is it just the same?'

'I only just got here,' May said, 'so I wouldn't want to be too hasty, but I have seen quite a few familiar faces, which is lovely.'

She glanced quickly at Harley and quailed under his scrutiny. 'Why are you looking at me like that?' she blurted. In her head the words sounded like mild enquiry, but came out abrupt and defensive.

'Sorry,' he said coolly. 'Wasn't aware that I was.'

Liar, she thought and he gave her a brief, sardonic look, as though he had read her mind.

'So,' Turtle said briskly. 'May tells me she's visiting for a while!'

At this, Harley's infuriating composure slipped. He glanced at Turtle and then darted a look at Stella, as though one of them might help him. But when he spoke his voice gave nothing away.

'Oh?' he said dispassionately. 'Not just passing through?'

Stella came to the rescue. 'No,' she said and drew her friend close. 'And we are thrilled.'

'No doubt,' Harley said quickly. 'I guess I'll be seeing you around, then. I should be getting back.' He moved his head in the direction he'd come. 'Y'all let me know about that porch door, Turtle? Catch you later. Take it easy Stella, good to see you.'

He turned and made his way back to Rob, who was chatting up a woman with a shining copper bob behind the bar, leaving May feeling bewildered and embarrassed. Anyone would think *she'd* been the one who'd brought everything crashing down, she thought angrily.

'Well!' Stella burst out as soon as they left the warm fug of Molly's and began the walk home. 'What the hell was going on there? Anyone would think you'd insulted his mom! And you looked as though you were about to burst into tears.'

'Stella,' said May in exasperation, 'I've been in a perpetual state of almost bursting into tears for the past six months. There's nothing unusual in that, I'm afraid, but Harley…' she paused, thinking about his strange, unfriendly manner. 'God that was uncomfortable.' She gave a huge sigh and Stella looked sideways at her.

'Okay?'

'Not really.' May smiled through tears. There's nothing like answering honestly to crumble all your defences, she thought ruefully.

'I don't remember him like that,' she said at last. 'He was never rude. He really wasn't very nice, was he?' She couldn't seem to stop talking, seeking reassurance from Stella without knowing why. 'Did he seem… uneasy to you? He seemed twitchy to me, underneath. Or did I imagine that in my paranoid state?' She laughed, a little hollow, and threw a quick look at Stella to see what she was thinking.

'Uh, no.' Stella was emphatic. 'I'm completely mentally

stable, May,' she deadpanned, her mouth flickering with a shadow of a smile, 'and I noticed it. Man's got the jitters.'

They made the corner of Main Street and Riverside drive and paused, breath frosting heavy and white in the night air. The sounds of Pete and his noisy posse of basketball pals echoed merrily off the empty roads from some way behind. Stella said, 'Ah, he's a big boy, he can make his own way home.' They carried on downhill towards the house.

'So,' Stella said with a naughty sideways look. 'Aside from being an asshole, I'd say Harley sure has aged well, wouldn't you?'

But May wouldn't lighten up. She thought about his dark, shadowed eyes and the tension at the corners of his mouth. 'I thought he looked a bit rough,' she replied. 'Tired. And he needed a shave.'

'Fuckin princess,' Stella reprimanded her cheerily as she fumbled with the key in the lock, but May barely heard her; she was remembering so vividly, she could hardly breathe.

She pressed a light fingertip along her swollen lower lip and smiled. Her skin held the memory of the rasp of his cheek where he had nudged and whispered at her, trailing and grazing over the sensitive skin at her throat, her belly, the dip between her shoulder blades.

'Where did you disappear to last night?' Stella crowed, as May walked into the dark basement kitchen of the house, the morning after. She felt light, her spirits free. She laughed as Stella greeted her with a lewd smirk, quickly answering her own question in a mocking high-pitched English accent. 'I'm just going to get some fresh air... With Harley Daniels!'

'You sound like Dick Van Dyke you stupid arse,' May said darkly, but she was unable to sustain her sneer and met Stella's smirk with her own smile. 'Oh Stella... Stella... Stella,' she chanted, sitting at the counter. 'That boy is... breathtaking. I don't think I've ever met anyone like him.'

That morning, he'd propped himself on one elbow, amongst his tangled sheets, hair all over, and watched quietly as she dressed. He'd reached a hand and stroked his thumb gently over a slight rawness at her hipbone.

'Is that me? I'm sorry… maybe I should shave twice a day.'

She'd smiled, remembering his mouth tracing along the curve of her waist and over her hip, their fingers had twisted together again as he'd drawn her back to the bed with an answering smile.

'Well, I'm glad you had fun,' Stella said turning from her towards the closely packed sink of dirty dishes 'Harley Daniels is a great guy, May. Really. Terrific. But don't hold your breath waiting for him to show his face. As far as I can tell, he doesn't have relationships he just sleeps with people. You cool with that?'

'Are you speaking from experience?' May asked Stella abruptly and felt stupid.

Stella stopped clattering about amongst the scorched pans and the orange dried-on residue of Kraft Mac 'n' Cheese.

'You're my friend, May Flower, and I don't want you getting hurt. I'd have said something sooner but I didn't know you'd move so fast.' She screwed up her face. 'I honestly did not mean that the way it came out. I swear-to-god there was no judgement. You're a grown girl. You probably know exactly what you're doing.'

Just as May was thinking that her friend had neatly sidestepped her question, hating herself for wanting to know, Stella said, 'And no, I was not speaking from experience.'

She turned back to the sink and was muttering something about probably being the only one in town who hadn't had the pleasure, when Courtney slouched in wearing an alarming towelling bathrobe that looked as though she'd hauled it out of a passing skip.

'Saw you hanging on the wall with Har-lee Daniels last night,' she sang teasingly. 'In fact… where did you get to?'

May shrugged, remembering what she didn't like about small town life.

'He's pretty cool, huh?' prodded Courtney.

'He's alright.'

'He's alright?' she said, outraged; May managed a laugh.

'I didn't mean to offend you,' she said lightly and took a swallow of her coffee.

'Yeah well, no one calls Harley Daniels "alright" and gets away with it. He. Is. Smokin hot.'

Courtney emphasised every syllable as she rearranged the filthy dishes with much crashing, before finding a bowl and rinsing it.

'Do you know him well, Courtney?' May couldn't stop herself asking.

'Hmm.' Courtney took her time. 'Just one drunken fling, never repeated, never forgotten.'

'That good, eh?' May forced a jovial note into her voice and tried to ignore the unmistakeable heave of jealousy that rose in her, tauntingly. Grow up, she told herself.

'Actually, I don't remember it all that well,' Courtney was saying. 'It was Freshman week.'

5

'You can't smell melted snow!' Stella was indignant.

'Of course you can,' May said, laughing. 'You just don't know you're smelling it.'

She was standing with her friend at the edge of the woods, where the trees met the pebbled, fast flowing water's edge. It was hard to believe that this dark and rushing, debris-filled soup was the same river she used to swim in; that in a few short months, she might again. If I'm still here, she thought.

'Just stop and pay attention a moment,' May said, taking a lungful and chasing away unwanted thoughts. The smells of the earth filled her, dense and spongy with last autumn's leaves.

'All I can smell is rotting vegetation.'

May snorted at her friend and paced back into the trees. She crouched, looking at the newly revealed forest floor, compressed and glistening, deeply dark, having finally emerged from long months beneath heavy snows. To her, it smelled rich and dark, pitchy and full of promise; she knew that soon she'd see fronds uncurling, testing at first, then confidently nudging through, pushing aside the covering of leaves and reaching for the light before the dense canopy of summer checked their growth.

'Come here,' she said, putting an arm around Stella and hauling her back towards the water. 'Look at all that, surely you can smell more than fetid leaves?'

Stella hooted. 'Still a *total* fruit cake! Most people say Open your eyes and see, but oh no, May wants you to take a look and smell,' she rumbled on, but she hooked her hands onto May's arm and looked out over the water.

The other side of the river bordered dun-coloured meadowland and endless, rolling fields, softly smudged and a little threadbare, dotted with darker swathes and blurs of yet more woodland. Pale blue skies were streaked across their heights with fragile, stretched out clouds and far across the meadows, against the still snow-capped backdrop of mountains, white and cream clouds, delicately shaded at the edges in misted, slate-blue, seemed weightier, their soft, expansive shapes hanging low.

The light breeze that had been stroking at her, picked up briefly then dropped again and May cried out triumphantly, 'There! That was it! You must have smelled that. That—that coolness, cleanness?'

Stella cocked her head and smiled slowly until she was grinning broadly. 'I get it!' she said sounding new and excited. 'That's so cool!'

They stood quiet and still for a while until Stella checked her watch and pulled a face. 'I have to get back and teach class.'

They turned towards town, through the birdsong and sunshine, weaving between trees and small moss-covered outcrops of granite.

'You know,' Stella said musingly, 'I don't know when I last took time just to walk out here. Thanks, Mayflower, let's do it again. Let's make sure we get plenty in while you're here.'

May stopped walking. I can't go home now, I can't. Not before the leaves and the green and the meadow flowers. And she remembered again the sensation of those summer days melting over her; of inhabiting herself utterly. I don't want to miss it, she thought. Not any of it.

May left Stella at her faculty building and wondered aimlessly along Main Street. It was a little before nine and she felt like the only person who wasn't moving purposefully towards a destination. She was just wondering if today was a good day to borrow Stella's car and explore when a voice startled her and she saw that she was right outside Molly's.

'How about that coffee?'

'Hello, Turtle, how lovely, I was just wondering what to do with myself!'

Turtle held the door open and, guiding May towards the bar, yanked a stool out.

'Sit!' He commanded and poured a cup of coffee, sliding it towards her.

'Are you not having one?' she asked as he leaned back against the wine rack and folded his arms across his chest.

'Uh uh,' he shook his head and gave her a bristly smile. 'If I drink any more coffee, *guaranteed* I'll start hallucinating. Cops called me at 4am to come and deal with the alarm and I've been mainlining it since!'

'Was everything alright?'

'Yeah, looks as though the alarm actually put em off. That's a first.'

The restaurant seemed different during the day, especially empty. An elderly couple lingered over some coffee in a booth at the back, but there was no one else. The place had a warm, siesta quality and looked spacious and gleamingly polished.

'So, what's up with you? Things haven't worked out for you in London? What's your story?'

'Oh I don't know,' she said wearily. 'I don't know. I'm so tired of myself, Turtle, I'd much rather talk about anything else. I've left London, left my job, the idea being that I take stock of my life and decide which direction to go.'

Turtle laughed. 'Okay, so not much going on with you then.'

'I tell you what, though,' May said, and a swift spike of adrenalin animated her. 'You're not hiring, are you? I'd love a job if you've got anything. I need to get some structure going, otherwise I'm in danger of remaining in the Pit of Despair.'

'Ahh...' Turtle sounded interested. 'You think you're going to hang out here for a while?' May nodded emphatically. 'Always hiring in a college town, May, you know that. We'd be glad to have you. How about a couple of shifts to start, to get you up to speed? See how we do?'

May nodded, caught out by how excited and scared she felt, all at once. She didn't want to mess Turtle about. Was she really going to do this?

'I hope it's like riding a bike,' she said. 'I haven't waited tables for years, I've been a high powered magazine exec you know, with a battalion of staff at my beck and call.' Her tone was self-mocking and Turtle laughed.

'And now you'll be at my beck and call. How the mighty fall.'

As she made her way back down Main Street, May had the feeling of having done something huge. She glanced into shop windows, not paying attention to what she saw, and thought about working at Molly's again after all this time. What had possessed her? She stopped for a moment, and told herself not to make such a big *thing* out of it. When did everything get so heavy? I never used to be like this, overthinking every decision. She gave herself a shake and was just about to cross to the green and head home, when something caught her eye in an estate agent's window.

It was a photograph of a dilapidated looking two-storey house in a rural setting, with a porch running its length. All the other featured properties had star-shaped cards attached at jaunty angles with exclamations making statements about them. *Waterfront property! Easy commute! Beautiful family home!* But this one said, *I just need a little love!*

Well, I can see that, thought May, peering closer to make out if that was a bunch of missing tiles in the roof or just a shadow in the photo. What intrigued her most was the hint of garden and woods. I'd love to see that place, she thought, and acting on impulse for the second time that day, ducked through the doorway. When she came out, she was clutching a few stapled pages of A4, on the front of which was a bad colour photocopy of the picture in the window.

She had been working at Molly's almost a week before she plucked the nerve to tell her sister she'd got a job.

'You're waitressing?' Lallie's voice skittered tinny and incredulous down the phone line.

'Yup! It's great; I'm really enjoying it.'

'Waitressing is not great, it's what you do when you're looking for something great.'

'Oh you just haven't worked in the right place, that's all,' May returned lightly.

'Oh and Arse-Fuck, Vermont is the right place?' Her sister was laughing now.

'Actually, half of the time I'm working behind the sandwich bar. It's like the backstage of the restaurant. Honestly, Lal, you won't believe it, they had to train me to make a sandwich.' Her sister laughed again as May chattered on. 'They're so enormous you have to fasten them together with a toothpick or they topple. Then, you have to put a flag on the top of each toothpick as a warning, otherwise you get sued by some over-excited porker who bites into it and punctures their palate!'

'Well I guess it'll stop you twiddling your thumbs while everyone's at work. And you'll be home before the novelty's worn off too I suppose… so no chance of you becoming mind numbingly bored.'

'Well it involves food and people,' May said brightly, ignoring Lallie's comment about her return, 'which as you know are of great interest to me.'

'Yeah, whatever—whichever way you spin it, May, you're still just making sandwiches and coffee and being friendly to idiots.'

Of course Lallie was right, it wasn't the most cerebrally challenging job, but she loved how it wore her out and that she could leave it behind at the end of her shift. She enjoyed the pace and people, who were mostly friendly and a lot of fun, in particular a graduate student called Amy.

'There was one other thing, Lal.'

'Mmm?'

'Is there any chance you could send my Sarah quilt?'

'Oh, May, that'd be incredibly bulky and expensive to send,' Lallie laughed lightly. 'Don't they have blankets at Stella's?'

May laughed obligingly but felt prickly. Why can't you just do it? For me. 'I'll pay for the postage, Lal. Can you just do it? I'd really like to have it.'

May sensed an instant coolness in the silence that preceded her sister's response. Her voice when it came was studiously patient and once again, May felt like a foolish child.

'Well, of course if it's that important, but when you come home it's going to be a pain in the arse to bring back. Surely you can manage a few months without?' She broke off and gave a sharp blow of breath. 'Whatever, fine, but you'll have to wait until I've got time to go traipsing over there, wrap the bugger and then get to the post office.'

'Oh don't, Lallie. You're right, I didn't really think it through,' she lied, trying to halt the rising irritation in her sister's voice and wishing she'd not said anything. 'I know you've got enough on your plate.'

There was a long silence.

'Lal? Really, it's fine...'

There was another pause before the warmth returned to her sister's voice as she said, 'I'll do my best, babe. Okay?'

6

May was up and out the next morning before the others and had taken Stella's car for an appointment at the old farmhouse. She slowed and glanced at the photocopied directions on the passenger seat next to her.

Left at the junction. What junction? The only way to find anything around here was to know where it was. Nothing signposted, just scattered houses and woods and fields along endless narrow roads. I'm going to have to go back to the bridge and start again. Count the turns more carefully.

'Three quarters of a mile after bridge turn left,' she read aloud, as though talking to someone a bit slow. 'But surely that's someone's driveway,' she muttered, turning obediently and slowing the car to a crawl.

The track led her to two houses spaced apart, their boundaries marked by dry stone walls and silvered split-rail fencing. She recognised her house at once and smiled at the marked contrast between the two. You *have* let yourself go she thought with instant affection.

She drove a few yards past the first house with its white and blue mailbox, red flag standing to attention and turned into a wide gravelled drive. What struck her, the moment she switched off the engine, was the bright, sweet, pipe and call of birdsong; it filled the clear spring air and she stood quietly listening, letting it fill her too.

She was early and the realtor hadn't appeared, so she wandered along the driveway and up the wide, wooden steps to a long, high, open-sided porch, across nerve-rackingly sagging boards, its white painted railings blistered and peeling.

She moved slowly along the porch, trailing her hands across the wooden railings, bump, bump, bump, until she got to the end and a flight of narrower steps that took her down to an overgrown brick and flagstone terrace.

Remnants of what might have been raised beds were set in geometric shapes, the wooden retaining edges rotted and splintering, one completely collapsed. May could see the angry rusted nails thrusting viciously from the corner.

Where the patio stopped, the hefty New England flagstones were embedded in the edges of a sweeping slope of green. Someone had used a mix of birch trunks and low dry-stone retaining walls at intervals, creating a loose terraced effect and the whole thing swept down for about a hundred yards until it stopped at more split rail fencing, giving onto pasture that rolled like great, swelling ocean waves, over fields and woodland until May lost it in the haze of clouds or... were those mountains?

It was coming to life, with mists of soft green spreading across the land, the memory of winter showing up in tawny smudges here and there like worn velvet. As the clouds tumbled and sped across the huge sky, the colours and shadows changed and she sighed expansively. This is unbelievable, she thought. I could never get tired of it.

For as long as she could remember, May had been drawn to stories and images, to places and things that gave her a sense of freedom, opened her up, and helped her loosen and throw off the ties of her usual urban environment. Standing here, in this peaceful and ancient place, she had the strongest sensation of life pulsing through her, of hope and promise.

She walked around the side of the house and with a flush of pleasure saw that the suggestion of woodland she'd seen in the photo of the house grew nudging and abundant right up to the boundary of the garden. The trees were already laced with unfurling green, dramatic against the dark trunks of the grand sugar maples and the luminous white of the golden birch's slender trunks. She would have followed the path into the woods if she hadn't heard a car changing gears and an engine revving, then slowing; she turned back the way she'd come and made her way towards the car, smiling at the woman who got out.

'You're early!' she was announcing as she thrust out a hand and gave May a wide smile. 'Jen Weisner.'

'I was afraid I'd be late. I'm still getting my bearings so gave myself plenty of time,' May answered. 'I'd forgotten how rural it is around here.'

'I know, right? Let's take a look.'

At five-thirty that evening, May sat in Lou's Bakery waiting for Stella. It bustled with life: diners clattering and thudding boots, which rang from the wooden floors. Voices murmured and shouted, laughter burst from booths and May noticed there was a disproportionate number of young faces, the insistent reminder that this was a college town.

She ordered an apricot nectar, for nostalgic reasons, and remembered sitting there years before, with shorts and bare arms, enjoying a hangover with her girlfriends, wolfing scrambled eggs and muffins dripping in butter, crisp bacon, and having the piss taken out of her accent, taking the piss out of theirs.

'May?' Stella's voice broke into her thoughts; she stood to hug her friend. 'How did it go?'

May leaned across the red Formica and chrome table feeling a pulse of pleasure and anticipation she hadn't in ages. 'It's lovely. A bit run down and very sparsely furnished. But absolutely begging for me to live there.'

'Damn!' Stella returned, banging her fist on the table with a laugh. 'Why?'

'Just so utterly full of promise,' said May, unable to explain quite what the pull was. Stella looked puzzled. 'My very own Secret Garden.'

'Ahh…' Stella smiled. 'I look forward to a tour. Why so cheap?'

'You mean apart from having to work out which are the

safe bits of the porch to walk on to get to the front door?'

'Yeah! Apart from that!'

'It's quite remote. And it needs a lot of work, it's falling apart at the seams. The owners have retired to Florida. They'll cut a break on the rent if the tenant repairs it.'

'Wait a minute, it is sound, right?'

'I suppose, how can you tell? Anyway, it's not as though I'm buying it. Presumably the landlords would be responsible if it fell down around my ears.'

Stella looked momentarily alarmed and May laughed. 'It's really not that bad, I'm exaggerating.'

Stella's face cleared and she sat back. 'So, you want to go for it?'

'Well, yes. I do.' May was hesitant.

'What?'

'Well, I'm not all that well versed in Zen and the Art of Household Maintenance,' May replied. 'I'd need help. Or to learn a lot. And that's another thing,' she rushed on. 'The one point I was adamant about was that I needed to be near enough to town to walk into work, and this place is so off the beaten track I won't be able to function without a car. That was the last thing I wanted. I don't want to have to start thinking about insurance and maintenance and all that other stuff that…'

'May, would you stop? What's the big deal about a car? This is America. Let's take a look at the place together; I can't even begin to help you with this without having seen it. I've got the afternoon off on Thursday. How about we take a drive out there after that?'

'That would be great! You really are a Top Bird, Stella.' They both laughed.

The waitress came up and asked rather pointedly if there would be anything else.

'You all set?' Stella asked her and May nodded.

'I'll get it.' She put a ten-dollar bill down on the table,

which disappeared almost instantly and was replaced with lightning efficiency by a small saucer holding coins. On their way out, Stella bought muffins and six huge chocolate chip cookies.

'Pete always gets snippy if I come in here without him and don't come back with—oh!' she said in surprise. 'Hi Harley!'

The tiny single file entrance to the diner was so narrow and crowded, May couldn't avoid being pressed against him as she moved to let him by. She looked down, avoiding his eyes.

'Hey, Stella. May. How's it going?' he said, sounding friendly, but he moved off towards the back of the diner without waiting for an answer. May's face flamed. She took a deep breath.

'So. Pete will eat all those himself?' she said cheerily, feeling slightly nauseous. 'The man's a human food vacuum and yet he doesn't seem to have an ounce of fat on him.'

'I know, bastard. It's always the woman who carries the load. Although you, my dear, if you don't mind my saying so, are still just a little too thin, which doesn't suit you and can't be all that healthy either.'

'I know, I know. Leave me alone.' But May smiled when she said it. She knew she'd filled out a bit since she'd arrived and certainly had more of an appetite.

They walked along Main Street in silence, until Stella said, 'Are you okay?'

'Yes. No. Weird.' Then she stopped and turned to her friend. 'I feel like an idiot every time I see him.'

'Harley?'

'No, Stella, the man in the frigging moon. Of course Harley.'

'Calm the fuck down, lady!' Stella said laughing. 'So, he still rings your bell, it's okay!'

'Oh don't be stupid, it's not that,' May said unpersuasively

70

and strode off, irritated. It wasn't okay, it was unsettling and embarrassing. Stella didn't know what she was talking about and anyway, what did her feelings matter when it was clear Harley was unfazed by her to the point of disinterest.

'Do you have any plans for tonight?' Stella asked, changing the subject.

May gave a hard shout of laughter, which brought a bewildered look.

'What did I say?'

'Oh I don't know, it just seems funny. I'm not very independent yet, am I? I mean, if I had plans for tonight, they'd involve you wouldn't they?'

'I guess so. Well, do you want to go out? Pete's got his basketball game and we could meet them, or we could go to Harry's. It's open mic night tonight which is kind of fun. Do you remember we used to go there when you lived here?'

'I do, and I also remember that everyone only ever seemed to sing Brown Eyed Girl, very badly.'

'That is not the spirit. It's just for fun, not to get a record deal! Anyhow it was just a thought.'

'Sorry, Stell,' she said mock-sheepishly. 'Actually, I'd love to go. It'll be a laugh and if anyone does Brown Eyed Girl you can buy me a drink.'

'How about if anyone does it more than once. It doesn't count if you're singing it.'

'As if. I don't do that kind of thing anymore.'

A couple of nights later, May was in Stella's warmly lit kitchen, stirring pale butter gently over a low flame, when she heard her cheery call through the back door.

'Who's in m'house?'

'Your dream come true,' she called back in answer and carried on stirring until there was only a shiny little oval island left in the golden liquid. She cracked dark, bitter chocolate into it and took the pan off the heat, stirring,

stirring, slowly stirring, loving the sound of the wooden spoon as it knocked dully. At last, the lumps were gone, and into the smooth, shiny pool she poured cups of white and brown sugar and stirred vigorously, listening for a slight change in the coarse, scratchy sound against the walls of the pan.

'Yo, girlfriend, if that's for dinner, you are my dream come true.'

Stella dumped her bag and a six-pack of Rolling Rock onto the kitchen table, pushing aside some unopened letters and several weeks of newspapers. May smirked.

'They're a sample for Turtle. He's asked me to do some for the deli because I told him theirs were shit. But he doesn't need the whole batch, we can have some.' She cracked eggs into the pot. 'You know, you can't get white eggs in England?' she asked, circling her wooden spoon around the edges of the pan, scraping and scooping at the bottom, jabbing at the yolks to get them to disperse and allow the thick chocolate mixture to absorb more easily.

'No, I didn't. Is that because you're a nation of health nuts? You all think you're eating wholemeal eggs or something?'

'Yes, Stella, we all think we're eating wholemeal eggs,' May said dryly. 'Make yourself useful and pass me that flour, will you?'

Stella did. 'Is Pete home yet?'

'I haven't seen him, but I've heard a lot of banging outside.'

May carried on stirring the thick batter, until it was glossy and not a trace of the flour remained to be seen.

'Where's my tin gone?' She looked about distractedly. Stella moved her bag and the beer.

May smoothed the batter into the tin, with the back of her wooden spoon, pushing it into the corners, ignoring its reluctance, and bent to slide it into the oven.

'So, Thursday still good for you?' Stella asked as she began sifting through the mail.

'What, to visit the house?'

'Yeah. I have a thing in the morning, but we could go any time after noon.'

'That's perfect. I'm off work at two. What thing?'

Stella gave her a contemplative look before going on. 'Oh just a thing, I'll tell you about it later if it's interesting. Honey, does Lallie know? That you're staying on?'

For some reason this irritated May and she answered a little testily.

'There's nothing to tell just yet. Anyway, she knows I've got a job, it's not as though she'll be expecting me home any time soon.'

'What's the deal? Sounds like I hit a nerve.'

May looked at her friend with a sweep of gratitude. 'You miss nothing,' she said. 'So perhaps *you* can tell me.' She sat opposite Stella, chin in her hands. 'Why am I scared to tell her?'

'Ahh… no, I *did* miss that. I didn't think you were scared, just very… secretive? No, that's not right. Protective.'

May thought, yes, that's it. I don't want Lallie getting *in* it. 'You know,' she said aloud. 'I love Lallie to distraction, so, so much. She's always been there for me. And I admire her and sometimes feel so awed by what she's achieved in her life…'

'But?' Stella smiled.

'I just don't want her bloody opinion about why I shouldn't be investing time and energy here, or in a broken-down farmhouse in the back of beyond that won't even be mine when it's all over. And why aren't I looking about to see what else is out there?'

Stella was laughing at May by the time she'd finished rushing all this out. 'Sure that's not what *you're* thinking?' she asked.

'You're so annoying,' May said with a laugh. 'Maybe I am but I just wish Lallie would leave me to it.'

'Nah, you don't really want that. You want permission and you ain't gonna get it. Might as well accept that, right off the bat. Your life, baby. Live it!'

'What even is that?' May teased. 'You sound like a sportswear slogan!' But she rather liked the sound of it.

Just then, Pete crashed through the back door, making them jump, staggering in under a pile of logs. He dumped them on the floor of the little utility room.

'Hey ladies!' he called out jovially. 'What's that great smell? We having cake for dinner?' He hugged Stella's head against his belly and sat. 'We sure are going to miss this when you go, May, I haven't eaten so well since I lived at home!'

'Get-the-fuck-outta-here,' grumbled Stella good-naturedly. 'Your mom can't cook to save a life.'

'Better'n you can, honey,' he said with a honk of laughter.

That night, May woke from a dream that left her uneasy and anxious. She tried to recollect the fragments as they melted and slipped away, lying in the darkness with just a humming silence. Something to do with the farmhouse, but she couldn't tell if it was fear of losing it, or fear of taking it on.

She got up and went to the desk to look at the specifications for the millionth time. She reached for a soft, cream-coloured, cashmere shawl that had belonged to Sarah and wrapped herself in it. Its whisper-fine weave murmured to her of nights long ago, when she used to sit huddled on her lap, and Sarah's soft voice spun golden images and stories to chase away May's nightmares.

As a little girl, perhaps five years old, she had been haunted by dreams in which she was chased by Medusa-headed harpies down huge geometric corridors of red and black chequerboard tiles. Sarah would sit by her bed stroking a light finger up the bridge of her nose to her hairline, over and over, slowly, slowly and talk, in her soft, high voice.

'Remember the picnic by Mole and Ratty's river, May-

May?' she would ask and May would pretend she couldn't, so that Sarah would tell her again. Her words were like her tapestries, beautiful pictures of vivid colour, and in little May's head, for a while, there was no space for the darkness.

She hugged the shawl closer. Even though she had washed it many times since taking it from amongst Sarah's things, it still smelled as she remembered; of wool and warmth and the faintest memory of Chanel No.5.

Sitting back in her chair, she ran her fingers into her hair and massaged at her scalp while she looked at the coloured photocopy of the house. Her eyes flicked over the written details, but she didn't take them in. She looked back at the image. It felt so familiar to her, as though she knew it, like an old friend. Would it be such a terrible mistake to take it on?

7

A spectacular rain coursed down the next day as May stepped off the curb, hurrying to the bank before it closed. The simultaneous screeching of a sustained car horn lifted her off her feet as she leapt back onto the pavement, heart banging in her ears and up through her veins.

'You stupid bitch! What the fuck are you doing? You could've gotten yourself killed!'

The driver leaned angrily on his horn again and drove off, water spraying from his car tyres and sheeting onto the pavement and over May's feet and legs. She stood rigid at the side of the road, heart pounding, and for the second time in two minutes leapt out of her skin as a figure darted into her field of vision and hauled her back into the shelter of Bentley's awning. Harley.

He grasped her shoulders and pulled her roughly against him saying her name, and repeating it in such a voice, May sobbed. It's just the shock, she thought, but she couldn't stop crying and he held her while she did, stroking her head and murmuring into her hair. 'It's okay... alright.'

He was so tender it made her cry even more until she thought she couldn't bear it and he drew her further under the awning, loosening his grip a little. Eyes lowered, she muttered at him, 'I forgot what side of the road you drive on.'

'Well, you said it's been a long time.'

She glanced up at him and saw a half smile before she lowered her eyes again, unable to meet his.

'Oh, May,' he said softly. 'Don't cry.'

He fumbled with her hair, pushing it out of the way, bending his knees so he could look into her eyes and it was as though he was searching for something.

They stood close, quietly, while May leaned into him, coming to herself, her forehead against his chest, and he drew her into his arms a little more closely. She felt him breathing her in, slow and deep and for a split second everything was as familiar as though she had never left. He had always done that; told her she was the only girl he knew who didn't smell like something out of a bottle. *You smell of your skin*, he'd say to her, *I hope you always do*.

'Okay now?' Harley asked, finally breaking the silence. He sounded a little shaky.

'Yeah. I'm fine. I feel really stupid.'

'Forget about it. Can I give you a ride anywhere?'

He straightened and taking his arms from round her, raked both his hands through his hair, which gave him a vulnerable look briefly while it was not sheltering his brow. She wanted so badly to say yes, just so she could be in an enclosed space with him and pretend, but she only had to cross the road.

'No. I'm fine. Thanks. I'll walk.'

Harley gave her a swift, questioning look. 'You know where you're headed?'

'I was trying to get to the bank before it closed.' She glanced at her wrist and remembered she'd left her watch by the sink. 'Shit. Probably too late.'

She started to straighten herself, still unable to meet his gaze, sweeping her hands under her smudged eyes and grimacing when she saw the mascara on her fingertips. Harley reached out and grazed a thumb over the bone beneath her socket and then, as though scorched, dropped his hand.

'You're okay,' he said.

'Thanks, Harley.' She attempted a bright smile. 'Sorry about crying. I feel really stupid.'

He looked momentarily uncertain as though he was about to say something, then just said, 'Well, if you think you're okay now?' He stepped back a little. 'Take it easy, May.' He turned and jogged off into the now misting rain, towards his truck.

She walked down Main Street with no thought of where she was going until she found herself by the lake that formed part of a somewhat incongruous golf course. In amongst that wild, rural woodland was a manicured series of undulating tightly napped greens. It was vast and she started to walk around it thinking it might help to keep walking, but gave up about a quarter of the way and slumped onto a carefully placed bench. She was oblivious to the soft and varied green of the unfurling leaves, dripping softly from the rain, the birdsong and sunshine, and she kept going over and over her brief encounter with Harley, trying to decode his behaviour, his sparse words. Something had happened. He'd felt it too, she was certain, but he clearly hadn't liked it. She closed her eyes and thought about the way he'd held her, so fiercely at first, and the way he'd said her name...

She'd spent the day picnicking with friends and they were standing around at the edge of town in the oppressive heat deciding what to do later. May felt sweat tickling her spine, the prickle of it on her top lip.

'What's going down tonight people?'

'Party!'

'Paper due tomorrow.'

'Open mic at Hojo's.

'No way Stella!' said Danielle, 'you're already all shitty, you may as well come to Hojo's and write the paper tomorrow morning.'

'No, write it tonight,' May put in, 'then we can all have a laugh tomorrow when we proof read it!'

'I'm going to take a shower. D come and get me if you do go out,' said Courtney, trudging slowly off into the haze.

May was thinking of Harley. She looked at her watch. Five twenty.

'Come into town with me?' she asked Danielle.

Rarely a drinker during the day, especially in this kind of heat, May was aware of the couple of cold beers she'd had acting on her senses and thought she'd take a chance and duck into the music shop where Harley worked.

She and Danielle walked slothfully along the hot pavement and May squinted against the angled sunshine, despite her sunglasses.

'Come up and see Harley with me,' she said, wanting moral support. Danielle smiled and raised an eyebrow.

'Sure,' she said.

The shop was through a narrow doorway and up a darkly carpeted flight of stairs. The banisters had been painted so many times they were heavily textured with tiny potholes. Coming in from the brilliant sunshine, the dark seemed extreme, the air thick and heavy and May could hear the slow repetitive sound of a guitar being tuned. She pushed her sunglasses up her sweat-slicked nose and onto her head and rubbed the back of her hand across her mouth.

'I didn't know Harley worked for Ethan,' Danielle said.

They came to the top of the stairs and the glazed door with Hartland Stringed Instruments etched on it, propped open in front of them by a Yamaha keyboard.

Ethan looked up from behind his desk and threw a friendly smile in their direction as he put a hand on Harley's shoulder. He looked up from the guitar he was stringing.

'Hey…' he smiled, before going back to his work. May felt herself deflate.

'You girls look hot,' Ethan said as he put down the phone. 'Harley? Cold drink for the ladies?'

'Thanks, so do you!' Danielle replied with a mischievous look. She went to stand in front of a rotating fan angled in the corner and had her eyes closed as the cool air played over her.

'So goood…' she said with a sensuous smile, accepting a tall glass of water from Harley.

'What's up?' he said lazily to May, giving her the other glass.

'Not much.' She felt tongue-tied.

'We came to see if you're up for open mic tonight?' Danielle said, to May's eternal gratitude. Harley looked at her, half smiled and raised a sceptical brow.

'Yeah?'

May flushed and went to stand with Danielle by the fan wishing she hadn't come. This was hopeless. Obvious and hopeless. Harley went back to stringing the guitar. May watched his fingers making swift, deft movements, turning the pegs lightning quick, then slowing until he was making small adjustments, plucking a string, listening then turning, plucking and listening again until he was satisfied.

'Come on,' she said in a low voice to Danielle. 'Let's go.'

'Are ya'll going to be at the house later?' Harley asked, looking up.

'At some point,' May said, tersely. 'We live there.'

'Cool.' He was unfazed by her sarcasm.

'Good to see you girls,' Ethan called after them. 'Swing by anytime,' he said, giving Danielle a wink.

They were about fifty yards up the road when May heard a shout. They turned and she saw Harley jogging towards them. Danielle gave a low laugh.

'Later,' she said, starting off again.

Harley loped up and as soon as he stopped, moved lightly from one bare foot to the other. May felt the heat of the pavement seeping through her flip-flops.

'Was I just an asshole in there?'

May felt her whole self melt and she smiled at him.

'Yes, a bit.'

'Okay.' He took her hands in his. 'Okay,' he said again. 'Shit!' he laughed and started hopping from foot to foot. 'Sidewalk's hot!'

He pulled her over to a bench outside the hardware store and sat, knees bent up, feet on the seat. May sat too, full of anticipation and getting a kick out of his smiling confusion.

'I'll come by the house and get you later. Don't go to Hojo's.'

'Why not?'

'We can do something. I don't know. Watch fireflies?'

On her way back to the house, May stopped by the small farmer's market and bought a fat bunch of tulips, the soft, pink shade of the inside of a conch shell that used to sit on the edge of the bath when she was a child. She smiled, remembering how she and Lallie used to pretend they were mermaids, and hold the shell to an ear, listening for the ocean.

She gathered an armful of root vegetables and a bunch of thyme, thinking about planting a herb garden at the house, in that space by the kitchen terrace. I hope Stella's home, she thought. She could almost hear how she'd react to her encounter with Harley. *You guys...* she'd say and shake her head, chuckling.

As she turned onto Woodland Drive she saw right away that there were no cars and her mood stalled and slipped, and sighing, she trudged inside.

By the time Stella staggered in from work, May was chopping the roasted vegetables into a pan of stock and squeezing the now soft garlic out of its oily, papery skin. At the back of the hob was a boiling pot of barley. May tweaked out a piece and bit it between her front teeth, smiled, then drained the lot over a bowl, dumping the tiny pearls into the soup pot. She felt herself open, her tension melt, but wasn't sure where to begin. The house? Harley? Oh, what did it matter, Stella's ear—or shoulder—was always a good start.

'Hi gorgeous,' she greeted her. 'Hungry?'

'Starving. That smells awesome.' Stella looked tired and pale.

'How'd your day go?' May asked, giving her a taste of the soup. 'Careful! It's hot.'

'Yeah, okay,' she said, voice flat.

May stopped what she was doing and turned to look at her properly. 'You okay?'

'I'm... you know what?' Stella looked wobbly and sat. 'I thought I might be pregnant, but I'm not.'

May sat next to her. 'Oh, Stella,' she sighed, pushing away the tangle of house and Harley, all the confusion and indecision she'd been nursing since she got home. She felt herself scrabbling to take in what Stella was saying. 'I'm so sorry, sweetheart,' she said.

'Yeah,' Stella's eyes filled. 'Pretty sucky.'

'Was that what your "thing" was? You said you had a thing and I never asked.'

'Wha... Oh. Yes. I was late, did a test and it was inconclusive, but I was definitely feeling... I don't know, different. Weird. So I was booked in to see my... well, it doesn't matter. Got my period in the middle of a lecture on Nathanial Hawthorne.'

'Gutting,' May hugged her closer.

Stella nodded. 'It's okay,' she said unconvincingly. 'I didn't think it for long.'

'I didn't even know you were trying.'

'Wasn't. But now that I'm not pregnant, I kind of wish I was.' She shrugged and smiled tremulously.

'Does Pete know?'

'Yeah, I called him.' Stella said, dismissive. 'He doesn't really get it. What about you? How was your day?'

'Oh, you know. The usual. Went to work, got drenched in the rain, came home. What do you mean he doesn't get it?'

Stella sighed. 'Doesn't get why I might be upset about it.' She peered into the pot of reserved cooking water. 'What's that?' she grimaced at the cloudy liquid.

'I'm going to make lemon barley water. Ever had it? It's supposed to be very restorative.'

'It looks like dish water.'

'Yeah well, you'll thank me for the dish water when you can jump over three storey buildings again. This is ready,' she said waving her hand at the soup. 'Shall we wait for Pete?'

'I think he has a game; we can eat without him.'

They moved around each other easily, Stella finding bowls and spoons, May slicing the warm bread and ladling the thick, fragrant soup.

'You made bread?'

'Only soda bread, although I'm surprised you recognized it. The stuff you call bread here is shit.' She sneered at her friend, who shot a filthy look back at her. They exchanged a smile, and May felt that now she might be able to ask a little more about Pete not getting it, when the back door opened so hard it slammed against the wall, making them jump.

Pete's voice boomed at them. 'Hey, ladies! Smells good, any left for me?'

'Masses,' May answered, vaguely uncomfortable at his slightly forced joviality; it highlighted Stella's uncharacteristic fragility. 'I thought you had a game?'

He hugged Stella in his customary way, but was scattered, distracted as he tossed a printed flyer on the table and got himself a beer from the fridge. 'We...ll... I thought I'd come and hang with you.' May saw him give Stella a searching look before he quickly added, 'You want to see any of these bands? Part of this big Irish Heritage festival they're putting on at the Roth.'

May got up to ladle the thick soup into a bowl. 'Sounds like fun. I love a live band.' Without asking, she cut a fat chunk of bread and put it in front of him, smiling at his thanks.

Stella looked at Pete with a watery smile. 'We should go. Can you get us tickets?'

Pete didn't look up from the flyer, shovelling spoonfuls of soup into his mouth. 'Man this is good. I don't know, it's selling out. I ran into Harley on my way home, he gave me this in actual fact, said he's doing the sound for the whole week and could sort us out. You want to go, May?'

'Yes,' she said wondering if Harley had meant to include her. 'Yes, I do.'

'Cool. I'll hit him up later,' he said, getting up and banging his bowl into the sink. 'Who's up for a movie?'

Stella leaned back in her chair and sighed. 'I think I'll take a shower and get an early night.'

May stood, smiling regretfully at Pete. 'Sorry, darlin,' she said. 'You're on your own. Early night for me too.'

May woke with a jerk and lay as still as she could, trying to stop her rushing breath from drowning out the silent sounds of the night. What had woken her like that, with such uncompromising emphasis? Was it internal, to do with the snatched fragments of dream that were even now slipping away? Something in the house? As her breath settled and the rigid fear ebbed, she was reassured by the familiar shapes of her desk, the chest of drawers, the chair at the window.

The gauzy light had a vague greyish tint, implying the morning side of midnight and she listened to the clock at her bedside and its rapid, quiet tic-tic-tic-tic. There it was again. The vaguest something. A chair moved? A whisper of wood against linoleum. A dull thump. Definitely a thump. And then a prolonged silence, but it was as though she wasn't the only person in the house holding their breath, waiting. She sat up as slowly as she could, knowing that upright she'd hear better, move faster if needed. Another stealthy, muffled shifting of… what, a drawer being opened? Shit, she thought, panic swelling in her throat. Someone's in the house.

Without warning she heard a bursting shout, an angry roar and a crashing of wood, furniture tipping, more shouts. She recognised Pete and another male voice. Then Pete shouting, 'Stay where you are! Stay where you are!'

May wasn't sure who he was shouting at, but before she had time to think, he was shouting again for someone to call 911. She acted instantly, barely registering what she was doing, but Stella had beaten her to it and she could hear her on the extension, talking to the controller.

She sat clutching her knees, her pulse fluttering in her throat. The noise from the kitchen subsided, punctuated by a burst of angry words from the unknown voice then Pete talking low and angry, repeating himself at intervals in a thrusting belligerent voice. 'Be still!' and with the last word, May could hear a grunt of emphasis from Pete, matched by a cry of pain.

It stretched as she waited, uncertain of what she should do before she became aware of blue flashing lights outside and started to get up, wrapping Sarah's pashmina around her shoulders and standing indecisively, listening with concentration to the cops shouting instructions and questions into the rapidly lightening dawn. Rooted, May felt a jolt of fear as someone rapped on the door of her bedroom, calling out in a self-assured tone, 'Ma'am? Everything okay in there? Ma'am, would you open the door please?'

Wordlessly, she pulled it ajar. A tall, uniformed cop was standing with one hand hovering over his holster. He didn't look at her at first, but over her shoulder, glancing swiftly about the room.

'It's fine,' she said. 'There's no one in here. I'm fine.'

He nodded briefly and then looked directly into her eyes, as though he thought she was hiding something. It was unnerving.

'Would you join us out in the kitchen?' he asked tersely and waited.

'Is everyone okay?' May asked somewhat belatedly, 'What happened?'

'Your friends are all unharmed.'

May followed him along the hall and seeing Stella in the kitchen huddled in her duvet, she felt an overwhelming urge to hug her. Stella clearly had the same idea at the same time.

Through the kitchen window, May saw the shapes of several officers marching a hunched boyish figure down to the patrol car. He was brusquely manoeuvred with a hand on his head into the back seat and driven away. Two cops remained waiting for someone from forensics to fingerprint the place and Stella made slightly limp jokes about the place always looking as if it had had a break in and everyone kept laughing a little too heartily. At last, they were finished and the police officers gave Pete a phone number, checked once more that everything was secure, then left the three friends to talk it over.

'So,' began May, 'let me get this straight, Pete. You just single-handedly stopped us from being murdered in our beds?'

She had meant it to sound over the top and funny, but her voice was trembling and she hugged her knees to her chest, wrapping her shawl around her more securely.

'No, no, no, no...' Pete raked his hand backwards and forwards through his fine, straight hair as he spoke musingly. 'No, nothing like that, he was just a kid.'

'Any idea what he was after? Who—did you recognise him?' Stella's voice sounded loud in the still emptiness of the dawn kitchen. She padded to where Pete sat and he drew her onto his lap, his arms circling her waist. He shook his head.

'Naw, didn't recognise him. But I sure would if I saw him again, the little shit.'

May shook her head, frowning. She kept thinking about the way the boy had kept incoherently crying out. From her bedroom, she had been unable to make out words, but the tone was clear and he had sounded desperate, pleading.

'What was he saying, Pete?'

'He was just crying like a mamma's boy because he got caught breaking into my home. They're all the same, these kids. Talking big until they get caught. Then it's all please-don't-turn-me-in. He was making out like it wasn't him—ha! Wasn't him! But it's his sorry ass I'm sitting on, so who the fuck is it?' He laughed aloud. 'Was probably high. Didn't know where he was or what he was doing.'

'You think?' May wondered.

'You just can't tell,' Stella said. 'You know, I had a kid in my senior class a couple of semesters ago who, it turned out, was doing Class As. Everyone was so shocked and his parents wanted to sue for negligence, but he just seemed a typical student. Mostly turned his papers in on time, turned up for class. You know, enough for no alarm bells to ring...' She trailed, her expression reminiscent. 'He was kind of interesting. I remember feeling real bad for being so out of touch I couldn't see what was going on in front of my nose. I wonder if his mom ever got over it. She was so mad at us. The college. She had trusted us to take care of her son.'

'Shoulda raised him right,' Pete said. 'Then he'd take care of himself.'

'Oh come on, Pete, surely you don't believe that?' May said.

'There's a hell of a lot of people out there who have no business having children,' he said bullishly and May winced and threw a look at Stella, whose still expression was unreadable as Pete tilted her off his lap abruptly and stood. 'I'm all in. Coming?'

May sat brooding after Stella went back to bed. When had Pete become so hard line?

8

May turned from greeting a table of six on a busy Thursday night a few days later, to see Connie leading another large party into her section.

'Could you put them with Amy?' she hissed. 'You've given me three tables in five minutes.'

'I thought they were friends of yours,' she drawled, turning and making her way back to her place behind the bar. May tried to swallow her irritation and reminded herself to relax as she approached the arrivals, smiling, unpocketing her notepad. She didn't recognise any of them, but one, a young girl of around twenty with a melting, anxious look, kept staring at her. It made May uncomfortable.

She didn't have time to dwell on it, though, it was a busy night and she soon forgot that they'd asked for her as she galloped down the stairs to fetch up an order of chicken wings for a rowdy table of college kids. She enjoyed their noise and laughter and they were a nice bunch; regulars who called her by name and tried to buy her drinks. She gave them a hard time if they stayed too late and they would tease her and chorus 'Yes, Mom.'

She was standing by, watching the last of her tables drifting off, calling out goodbyes and see-you-agains, or nudging up to the bar for one last drink, when she felt a firm, swift yank at the tie of her apron and the whole thing heavy with the weight of her float, pad, pens and keys, fell to the floor. May spun to see Amy laughing at her own cleverness.

'You're like a stealth bomber!' May cried indignant, laughing. 'Would you stop that?'

'You want a soda?' Amy asked blandly, face now composed, as she siphoned one for herself.

'Thanks.' May fastened her apron with a tight double knot.

'Amy, do you know that woman talking to Connie?' It was the young, pale girl from the mystery table. 'They keep looking at me. I feel like I'm at school again.'

Amy laughed. 'Maybe they think you're hot,' she said and laughed even more at May's expression. 'I've seen her in here a couple times,' she said. 'She works at the Paint and Paper Barn downtown, but I think she's a student too.' She started filling glasses with ice and setting them out on a tray.

'She seems to have had her beady eye on me all night. I wonder why? I hope Connie isn't saying anything horrid about me.'

Amy looked rather surprised. 'Why would you care what Connie says?'

'Oh… I don't,' said May expansively, waving an arm as though she was trying to dispel smoke. 'She just makes me feel a bit edgy, that's all. Doesn't matter.' She looked over at the bar again. 'Is it just me,' she asked, 'or does that girl look really sad?'

'So would you if the only person talking to you was Connie.'

The two of them went off into fits of giggles and Connie shot them a look as though they were naughty schoolgirls, which made them laugh even more, just as Turtle rounded the corner and reprimanded them sharply.

'I've got two tables wanting to know why they can't get their checks.'

'Sorry, Turtle,' they chorused and went off to their separate sections to appease the customers and try to salvage their tips.

It was a while before she finished her shift and Turtle kept her hanging around wanting to discuss the possibility of her making brownies for the sandwich bar on a regular basis. Even so, as she called out goodbye in the general direction of everyone and made to leave, she saw the longhaired girl still hovering at the bar. She caught May's eye and slipped quickly off the stool, heading her off at the door.

She was an eclectic mix of floaty scarves and a chiffon overdress skimming the knees of her faded skinny jeans; a cloud of pale blues and lilacs with a softness about her curved mouth. Her large, pale eyes swam with sadness.

'Can I talk to you?' She seemed nervous but determined.

May hesitated, but the girl spoke again before she could reply. 'I'm really sorry. I don't normally do this kind of thing.'

There was something wounded and a bit desperate about her.

'Do you want to go somewhere?' May asked, thinking quickly.

'Is that okay?'

'How about Peter Christian's, that's usually quite quiet.'

They fell into step, neither speaking, as they walked the short distance to the basement bar.

'I'm May, by the way,' she said as they settled into a booth.

'I know who you are.' The girl let this just drop into the space between them and turned to the waiter and ordered a beer. 'I'm Liv.'

She said it with a weighty significance and paused, but May, having no idea what she was supposed to infer, said nothing. A rush of colour flooded into the girl's face and she looked as though she was preparing to take a great leap.

'Harley Daniels is my boyfriend.'

'Okay...' said May slowly. What does she want, she thought, my congratulations?

'Don't play games with me,' the girl said and the clichéd phrase seemed to embarrass her as it came out.

'I'm rather in the dark here,' May said, feeling uneasy.

'Harley broke up with me. Out of nowhere. He said I was a great girl; that it was him not me and that he didn't want me to waste any more of my time on him. The usual bull.'

'I don't—I'm sorry to hear that, but I don't know why it

has anything to do with me.'

'My friend saw you two together.' She said it as though presenting a trump card, but for a moment May still failed to understand.

'Harley and I barely know each other anymore,' she said, feeling she ought to say something useful.

'Outside Bentley's. Together. She saw you.'

May's head began to pound as her mind slammed back to being in Harley's arms after the car incident. She felt an alarming surge of fury.

'I think you've been misinformed,' she said tersely.

'I don't think so. My friend wouldn't lie about something like that, why would she do that?'

'Your friend,' May said, heavily emphasising the second word. 'Has very badly misinterpreted something. Truly. Harley and I did go out when I lived here before, but that was a long time ago. There's nothing between us now, really.'

Liv's eyes spilled with tears and she scrubbed at them crossly. 'But Connie told me... why would he...' she trailed and seemed to be casting back.

Connie, thought May angrily. Knowing that she would probably regret it, May asked, 'What exactly did she say to you?'

Liv almost whispered it and May could sense the growing humiliation this poor girl was experiencing. 'She said that she's known Harley years and he... he's always been a player and always just moved from one girl to another and that she had seen you and him together and it all made sense. If it's not true, why would he dump me?' she finished pathetically.

May felt so angry, her heart pounding in her throat. She found it hard to keep her voice steady. 'Perhaps because he's a player?' she said, trying for irony, but sounding bitter. 'Liv, how old are you?'

'Twenty-one, why?'

'You are old enough not to listen to gossip. And you

certainly shouldn't listen to Connie, she's a shit-stirrer.'

Liv looked wretched, but mulish. 'She's my friend.'

'I hope she's not your only friend. She doesn't seem to be taking very good care of you.'

'She was just trying to help. You don't know what it's like. I'm crazy about Harley. I just want him back. I've never known anyone like him.'

'No,' said May thoughtfully, 'there's no one like Harley.'

Liv's eyes snapped back to May's, suspicion rising in them instantly. 'And there's nothing between you now?'

'Nothing.'

But, bizarrely, May felt as though she was lying.

'So how did you leave it?' Stella asked when they were discussing Liv at lunch the next day.

'Well, she kind of poured her guts out in a very adolescent way about how much she loved him and finished her beer and left. She kept apologising. I feel so sorry for her. But I'm mad as a snake at that fucking Connie. How dare she?'

Stella laughed.

'It's not funny. She's a cow. That poor girl. And not to mention spreading gossip about me. I could fucking kick her.'

Stella, who was clearly amused at May's ranting, broke in, 'Hang on,' she said suspiciously. 'What about this "misinterpreted" thing she saw. Come on, spill.'

May pulled a face, sneering at Stella in their time-honoured way. 'Oh piss off, it wasn't anything.'

But Stella knew May too well to be fobbed off and gave a great shout of laughter.

'Look at your face! Spill. Now!'

'Well to be fair to Connie, *which* she doesn't deserve, there was room to. I think she saw Harley with his arms around me, kissing me in the doorway of Bentley's.'

Stella nearly spewed her drink over the table. May managed a sulky smirk.

'What the! Okay, rewind and tell me what the hell is going on.'

May was quiet for a moment. 'Nothing really. I don't think it was anything. Just an isolated thing, suspended in its own context.'

Stella looked sceptical. 'Poetic,' she said dryly before adding. 'You're so full of shit. How can kissing Harley in a doorway be nothing?'

'I didn't say I was kissing him. He was kissing the top of my head.'

'Well, I hope you used protection!'

May laughed, and explained what had happened. 'So you see, it wasn't really anything, just pity for a stupid old tart who stepped off the kerb without looking.'

'Right,' said Stella, lowering her voice melodramatically and exaggerating her Missouri accent, 'or when Harley's guard is down, his heart takes over.' She hooted with laughter.

May felt a thrill when Stella said this, instantly replaced by irritation. 'No, Stella...'

'And he breaks off with his girlfriend right after?'

'That girl's a baby, he shouldn't have been going out with her in the first place. Harley's even older than me, you know. God he's pathetic.'

'For crying out loud, May, since when have you been the age police? Give em a break.'

'Anyway. That was ages ago. Really, for a small town it's quite amazing how long you can go without bumping into people.'

This prompted more laughter from Stella; the previous day May had been ranting about how irritating it was that you could not walk down Main Street without having to acknowledge someone who felt they knew you.

'Don't forget Sunday!' Stella touched May's arm as they got up to leave. May looked at her blankly. 'Our brunch party! Don't say you forgot; you're doing the food!'

May raised an eyebrow. 'We haven't agreed terms,' she muttered darkly.

'Pimms!' Stella called out and hurried back to work, laughing.

9

The Sunday of the brunch party dawned beautifully. Pete was in his element, busying himself filling the bathtub with crushed ice and burying bottles of beer and wine in it.

'Something smells good,' he called to May, as he staggered through the kitchen loaded with a crate of drinks.

She was spooning cornbread batter over the top of a huge roasting tin of chilli.

'Thanks, I hope it tastes good. How many people are coming, Pete?'

He cocked his head, considering. 'Bout forty. You can never tell. Especially as I keep getting drunk and asking complete strangers to come. Makes Stella crazy!' He grinned and continued through to the bathroom.

'Darn right it makes me crazy,' Stella said cheerily, putting out a pile of paper napkins, clearly not in the least bothered. 'He even invited that cop who came at the break-in.'

'You're kidding?'

'Nope. They ran into each other at a game and Pete told him to drop by.'

'Hellooo...' a woman's voice called. 'I think we're early!'

'Someone's gotta be first! And now you can meet my friend May-from-London at last,' said Stella and turning to May, introduced her to what quickly became a succession of smiles and handshakes and glad-to-know-yous.

The house was soon full. People spilled into the yard, from both the kitchen and the living room doors, which were flung wide. May looked up from hauling the roasting tin out of the oven and saw Stella talking animatedly amongst a hoard. She felt overwhelmed by the close crowd and the realisation she knew almost no one, but the heat penetrated the thick cloth of the oven glove, distracting her, and she looked for someone to help her clear a space on the table, wishing she'd thought ahead.

'Here, let me help you.' Amy was at her elbow and whisked a space for her just as May thought she was going to drop the pan.

'Where did you spring from, Aims?'

She just grinned and directed. 'What you need to do is scoop out the first spoonful, then people will think it's okay to dig in.'

'Thanks, party genius. Why don't you have the first spoonful, seeing as you're here?'

May handed Amy the plate and was scanning the room again with a fluttering expectant feeling, when she saw the casually dressed cop walk in with a couple she didn't recognise. He hovered just inside the doorway, his large frame taking all the space. The couple abandoned him instantly as they plunged through the crowd towards Stella, now in a rowdy huddle with Pete and a few of his basketball players. The noise climbed a notch and the cop spotted her.

He was much taller than she remembered and powerfully built. He had what her stepmother Sarah might have called the bring-him-home-to-mother look—fair, even-featured, relaxed carriage—but for something about his eyes May couldn't catch, that made him compelling, where otherwise he might not have been.

'Well, it's quite a crowd.' He smiled at her, showing strong, even teeth.

Once, she'd asked Harley why he didn't have American teeth and he'd told her, baring them and growling, that what he *had* were poor boy's teeth.

'You really think this is the land of milk and honey, huh, baby?' he'd laughed at her. 'Ev'body got a big car and a swimming pool? Stay here long enough and you'll realise there's no such thing as a free lunch.' And arms around her, he sang into her hair, chuckling at her a little more, *'there ain't no free lunch, no free lunch today... I'll buy you a steak, but I'll take it out your pay!'*

'Your friends are awfully rude,' she said to the cop. 'Abandoning you like that the moment they see someone more exciting.'

'More exciting? Oh. Well, I guess they're not my friends anymore.' Then he smiled and said, 'Really, I don't know them. We just happened to arrive at the same time. But I know you, Miss May Aldridge,' he said seriously and May felt a fleeting anxiety. 'I had to type your name up a few times in the incident report.'

'Oh! Of course. Well, I don't have your sly advantage. You're going to have to tell me yours, I can't keep calling you The Cop, it sounds like a really bad airport paperback.'

This made him laugh. 'It's Mark,' he said.

'That's incomplete,' she said. 'I'll need a last name too, otherwise you have me at a disadvantage and I can't have that.'

His eyes widened briefly. 'You like the field even, huh?' he said smoothly. 'What if the idea of you being at a disadvantage appeals to me?'

'I'd revise my initial good opinion of you.' She moved back a little, scanning the room again.

'Sassello,' he said swiftly, laughing. 'Mark Sassello.'

May relaxed and laughed with him. 'I think you need a drink, Mark, and maybe something to eat?'

He didn't want to eat, but accepted a glass of Pimm's, saying it was like a Long Island iced tea.

'It is a bit; I've never thought of that. Why no food? You're not one of those people who thinks it's a waste of good booze to mop it up with food are you?'

She gave him a stern look and he stepped back raising his hands in surrender.

'Mouthy, aren't you? You always say just what's on your mind?'

This surprised her, but she liked his confidence and gave his question thought. 'I've found,' she said at last, 'that when I don't, is when I've ended up in the most trouble.'

'Interesting.'

May took a sip of her drink and surveyed the room, skimming faces and bodies for the one she couldn't see.

'Do you know everyone here?' Mark was asking her.

'No. Hardly anyone. I know who they are,' she said waving over at Pete and Stella's direction. 'Obviously. Oh. And I know him,' she said abruptly, spotting Harley at last who was propping the wall up with Rob and looking as though he'd been hanging out for hours. They were shouting with laughter, Rob punctuating it with a final punch line.

'Old flame,' she said and realised with a start that she should have taken her own advice and eaten. Mark looked a little surprised.

'Uh… which one?'

May burst into laughter. 'Oh dear,' she said at last, trying to pull herself together. She probably wasn't making a very good impression. 'The sulky one,' she said, catching Harley's eye and tipping her glass at him. He jerked his head briefly at her, smiled and then stared at Mark impassively for rather too long, before turning back to Rob.

'Has he got a problem? You did say *old* flame, didn't you?'

'*Very* old flame. Long, long ago. So, Pete said you transferred from Boston. What brought you here?' she asked. 'There can't be much for a city cop to get his teeth into.'

'If I tell you that's part of its charm, will that satisfy?' he asked somewhat stiffly.

'Not really,' she said and drained her glass, before thrusting it under a passing jug of refills. 'You've just made me more curious.'

'Too bad,' he said blandly, grey eyes cool. May inclined her head.

'Indeed,' she said. I read that wrong, she thought,

uncomfortable. 'Well,' she said at last. 'I'm going to see if there's any corn bread left.'

'I'll tag along.' He smiled, surprising her again by his change of tone. She looked at him closely, wondering if he was always this hot and cold. 'Something wrong?' he asked.

'No. Yes.' She blurted. They both laughed and May said, 'I thought you were giving me the brush off.'

'You really do say what's on your mind. I was not giving you the brush off, I was absolutely not doing that.'

In their quest for cornbread, they'd ended up within earshot of Stella's group.

'The truth is,' Stella was saying loudly, to the several women gathered around her, 'Marriage is one big compromise. It's just about how and why you go about making which compromises. See, my problem with Pete, is his inability to stop joking when I need to talk. It's like he'll settle down when he's good and ready but until then it's all joke, joke, laugh, laugh. Ugh, I can't tell you how frustrating it is.' She gave a shudder as one of her companions picked up the baton.

'I know what you mean. If I want to talk about something, Jeff will either switch on the TV or kind of clam up. You know, with that tight-mouthed thing they do or…'

'Okay, okay, I've got one,' said another woman, excitable, 'Jim actually just walks out like he doesn't even hear that I'm speaking!'

'I hate that,' said a sleekly bobbed woman. 'How can they say they didn't even know you were talking?'

There was a general babble of consensus and Stella broke in again, her voice strong, assertive. May, uncomfortable again, heard the slightest welding at the edges of her friend's words and had a sense that Stella was probably much drunker than she appeared.

'But what do you make a big deal about and what do you just kind of shrug your shoulders over and say "hey that's just him, what's the big deal?"'

'Well, I don't know. I think if you let too much go, they just think they can get away with anything. I mean it's not okay to leave the garbage unemptied or expect me to always think about his sister's birthday or… I mean for crying out loud, she's his sister, not mine. When I married him, it wasn't in the marriage vows that I would take on all his personal family responsibilities!'

They laughed together. May muttered to Mark, 'I wonder how it would be if they heard the men talking about them like that.'

He didn't reply, just raised his eyebrows briefly and swept his gaze around the room.

'Do you know what I think?' she continued. 'I think that when women talk about their men like that, it's the female equivalent of men taking their wives to live in the country while they continue to work in town. You know, like a caveman knocking his mate over the head and dragging her back to his cave so no other caveman can have her. If you make out your man is so hopeless and useless, no one else is going to want him.'

'Interesting theory,' Mark murmured. 'And you don't think men should drag their women into caves?'

For a moment, May couldn't quite read his tone, but he smiled and reached into his pocket, pulling out a ringing phone. She moved off, but he stopped her, closing his hand firmly around her arm, shaking his head at her while he spoke tersely into the mouthpiece. She drew away and he smiled at her and snapped the phone shut, finally letting go of her arm.

'I have to go. Work. But I'm going to take you out sometime, okay?'

'Um… not sure…' she began to think up reasons she shouldn't go out with him, not knowing why.

'Don't argue!' he said lightly. 'We'll have a good time.' He turned to leave. 'Remember, I know where to find you, so you can't hide out!'

She walked out to the deck and saw him off, feeling strangely deflated after he'd gone. She'd enjoyed the bit of sparring and thought maybe it would do her good to go out with him. Take her mind off other things, she thought deprecatingly; Harley was heading towards her.

'Hello,' she said, looking away.

'Your new friend split?' he asked with a smile in his voice.

May bristled. 'It would appear so, why?'

He shrugged. 'No reason.'

'Then why ask?' She said, instantly flinching at how waspish she sounded.

'Well okay,' he said slowly. 'No small talk?' and he leaned back against the railings, looking loose-limbed and relaxed. May felt petty and sad. Here he was trying and she was snapping his head off. Wasn't this what she wanted? For them to be friends. Yeah, right, she thought. Who are you kidding?

'Where's Rob?' she asked and Harley laughed, a low half-stoppered sound. 'Talkin to blondes. Are we doing small talk now?' He twitched an eyebrow at her and she softened.

'Yeah, I changed my mind. How *are* you?'

'I'm good, May, how are you?' They laughed. May settled back against the railings and started to ask him what he'd been up to, when Stella came crowding out with her little posse laughing and talking loudly. She flung an arm around May and kept up her stream of chatter.

'I keep giving up, then falling off the wagon,' she was saying. 'Cigs,' she said, turning to May and lighting up. 'I need another way of destressing when I'm kvetching about something. You want one Harley?'

'Nah, I'm good.' He whistled to his black dog, Piper, who was lolling patiently on the deck. 'You need you a dog, Stella,' he drawled at her, flashing a smile. 'Makes you get out there, away from everybody who's tailin your ass...' he didn't finish, as Piper had jumped eagerly to her feet and was butting her head against his hands. He talked low and sweet to her, telling her what a great girl she was, then straightened to leave.

'Later y'all. Great food Stella, later buddy,' he said to Pete and strode after his dog, leaving May flushed and with that slightly edgy, incomplete feeling that happened whenever she saw him.

It was already dark and May was out on the sun porch. Courtney had filled a big plastic jug with beer from the tapped keg in the basement and brought it carefully up the stairs, managing to shimmy to the low beat of southern rock coming from the stereo without spilling a drop. She passed it through the open window to Danielle who was trying to coerce May into cards. They had been up till dawn the night before and May had been waitressing all day. Her feet were aching.

'You look haggard,' said Danielle with a chuckle.

'And I stink of burgers and onion soup,' May said. 'I'm going to have a shower.'

'Well be quick, I need to laugh at you some more.'

When May joined them half an hour later it was getting dark.

'Now you look haggard-with-makeup,' Danielle said, her voice deadpan.

May gave her the finger. 'Treat me right, gorgeous, cause I've got something you want,' she said.

'How do I know I can trust you?'

'Try me.'

'Okay English girl, you're bright, beautiful and you don't suck at cards!'

'Careful...' warned May, but she was already reaching a strong, tanned arm behind her into the open window and pulling out the bottle. There were whoops from Stella, hollers of 'We're gonna get Pimmed!' Their chorusing voices bouncing back at them from the walls.

'Party time!' sang Stella.

Courtney asked what they needed as mixer and headed off to the kitchen, the weak jug of beer forgotten.

Someone had pulled the speakers out onto the deck and the energy levels ratcheted a notch. Work and studying and hangovers forgotten, the night ahead was full of promise.

As the evening wore on and people came and went swelling the numbers, crowding the wooden porch and adding to the noise, card games were played, beers chugged and Danielle attempted to teach May some of her more funky dance moves to Sweet Home Alabama. The porch was uneven, full of splinters and sloped alarmingly towards the gutters; it wasn't easy.

Around midnight, May heard the clang of boots ringing on the iron steps of the fire escape. It was Harley. He hadn't been around for a while and she gave him a slightly challenging, quizzical look; he half smiled and shrugged a little. He joined her and the girls, sliding down the wall and into a crouch beside them.

'What are we all playing?' he asked and scooted towards May.

'We're trying to teach May to play poker, but it's not working.'

'It would appear that my poker face isn't,' May said with a laugh.

'What are we all drinking?' he asked, jerking his chin at the jug of Pimm's.

'What do you mean we?' demanded Danielle hunching protectively over the jug, but Stella nudged her away and poured a large plastic cup full for him.

'Pimm's. May brought it. Go easy. Tastes like Seven-Up, acts like vodka.'

Harley raised his eyebrows, lightning quick, and took the cup. He scooted over so he could look over May's shoulder at her cards and she felt the heat of his body, smelled his clean, warm skin. She took a deep breath and let it out slowly.

'Yeah… me too, beautiful,' he murmured so low, she almost thought she had imagined it.

He pointed at a card telling her to play it, telling her what to play next.

'Whose is that?' he asked, pointing at an acoustic guitar propped *against the wall.*

'House guitar,' Stella said, 'can you tune it?'

He picked it up and plucked, turning keys, twanging and wincing as he went.

'Man, when was this last tuned?' he muttered rhetorically.

The girls continued slapping cards down and shouting insults at each other and, after a while, Harley tested a little melody. May held her breath. *I know this*, she thought. *It can't be.* She didn't think anyone else knew it. She'd first heard it with a cousin in South Carolina and loved it because of the rhythmic, bluesy guitars and gorgeous, soaring harmonies.

She thought later it must have been the Pimm's, because she wasn't much given to singing on her own in front of people, depending always on Stella, but she picked up the thread of Harley's playing and sang the sweet, longing refrain.

'There's no way I can/ change the past/ or your pain...'

Harley flashed her a look of surprise, gave her a quick nod of encouragement then with an intensity she usually couldn't meet for long, he watched her as she sang. By the time they reached the refrain again Stella, who could pick up a tune in her sleep, had added her voice, harmonising with sweet power above May's strong, pure voice.

Harley played with confidence and sang along with them, low; a ballast to their buoyant voices.

May was euphoric and for a long moment, a feeling of deepest connection to Stella and this dark-haired boy playing in the night. When he was done, Harley put the guitar down, people clapped, laughed, talked and resumed their games. He leaned towards her, breath shallow.

'Let's go,' he said standing and grabbing her hand.

'There's another phone message for you from The Cop!' Stella called to May from the garden a couple of evenings later. The days were now uniformly mild and sunshiny, but at night the temperature dropped dramatically and it was a chill and dark evening as May walked in, tired and hungry after a double shift at work.

'I was hoping you were going to say Jen had called,' May said tetchily. She was feeling increasingly tense with worry that the real estate agent was continually out of the office and hadn't returned her calls.

She dumped her bag on the floor of the kitchen and wriggled out of her coat. Stella staggered in with an armful of logs and dropped them in a tumbling crash into the basket by the wood burner.

'The Cop called. Again. What's his name? Mark something? He's going to call back.'

'No doubt,' May replied, then grinned and took the glass of wine Stella offered.

'That's the fourth time he's called today,' Stella said. 'That's quite a campaign. Are you going to put him out of his misery?'

'Oh, why not? I haven't had any other offers.'

'Hmm…' Stella's eyes narrowed. 'Waiting on any *particular* offer?'

May burst out laughing. 'If you had a moustache, you'd be twirling it!'

Stella sat with her wine at the table, shoving piles of newspapers and unopened mail to one side. 'Answer the question, Ms Aldridge,' Stella said, enjoying herself. 'A simple yes or no will do! Are you holding out for a particular offer?'

May's defences slipped; she never could avoid Stella's scrutiny long. 'Maybe,' she said, and took a sip of her wine. 'I won't hold my breath, though.'

'Why don't you ask him yourself,' Stella asked.

'Ask Harley out?' May felt sick with nerves just saying it.

'Sure. It can't hurt. He's clearly still into you. It totally makes sense. Why not? What could happen? He'll say yes or no then you'll know.'

But it *could* hurt and May's sense was that he might well

still be into her, but didn't seem to want to be. She thought about it for a while, comparing his reticence, his holding back with the full-blown pursuit coming at her from Mark Sassello. It wasn't just phone calls. He had come into Molly's several times to check she'd been given the messages and had joked with her that he wouldn't stop asking until she said yes.

'He's very persistent. Mark, I mean,' she said, musingly. 'And it's rather nice to know you're wanted.'

'Since when did you date guys just because they were persistent?' said Stella; May flinched inside.

'Hey, May!' Amy yanked at her apron tie and it fell with a clanging thud of canvas and money.

'Amy, you will die for this!'

It was a busy lunchtime at Molly's, and May had three tables seated almost at once. There must have been some kind of event going on in town and May was finding it tough; she just wanted to finish and get to the realtors before it closed.

Why hadn't Jen called her back? May was gnawing with anxiety that someone else would get in there before she could and kept hoping for a lull so she could at least go and sneak a look at her phone to see if anyone had called her back.

'What's with you and our new cop?' Amy asked. 'Connie says he's been in a couple times asking for you.'

'Nothing,' May muttered as she scooped everything up and tied her apron back on.

'Oh yeah? He's kinda cute. Way to go.'

'Oh, I don't know,' she said vaguely. 'He's nice enough, but I just don't… oh I don't know,' she said again lamely; it was so ridiculous to say, I have an odd feeling about him.

Amy was laughing at her. 'Then pass him on. Single, straight guy. They're at a premium!'

By the time she sat in Turtle's office to cash out, her legs ached. 'Argh…' She exhaled. 'All I had all day were parties and parties of old people who wanted half a sandwich and soup. What's going on? I thought they only came out for leaf-peeping in the autumn.'

Turtle smiled and shook his head, murmuring something non-committal. 'Yup! Happens sometimes!' He swivelled in his chair to face her. 'So. May. How's it all going?'

'Good. I'm really beginning to feel I'm getting the hang of it. How am I doing would you say?'

'Mmm. Not bad. Not bad at all. You just need to remember to punch through everything as you get it, so it's staggered. When there's a rush, you still have a tendency to store it all up and that makes the kitchen crazy.' He smiled at her. 'Do you have any preferences, Deli or restaurant?'

'Not really, just as long as it's not too much of one or the other. Turtle, I do have something I want to discuss with you.'

He stopped writing and leaned toward her, his keen feral little face attentive, jutting forward. 'What's up?'

'Well, the thing is. I'd like to move. I've seen a place I really like… d'you know the Barton farmhouse out in Dover?' He nodded and she went on. 'But I'd need more work. I know you only took me on part time, but would you consider making me full time?'

'Interested in management, May?' he said, his impulsivity surprising her.

She felt a pulse of anticipation. 'That's never occurred to me.'

'Don't know why. You managed a team on the magazine back in the UK, right? So I know you have the skills.'

She was quiet a moment while Turtle kept his keen eye on her.

'Think about it. And while you're doing that, I kind of want you to think about helping me out with menu innovations. You've got quite a talent for putting it all together.'

'I think I'd really like that. Money's better, right?'

A slow smile shone behind his neatly clipped beard. 'And salaried. Well you could shadow me a couple days a week. See what you think then if we're both agreed I can put you up for a deputy manager's job. What do you say?'

May finally got away from work and just made it to the real estate agents before closing time. Jen was profuse in her apologies, 'I've been crazy busy.'

You still could have called me back, thought May, but wanting to give Jen the benefit of the doubt, she accepted her apologies and said, 'So, can I have it?'

An hour later, she stepped out into the street.

10

One of the things May had always loved about Stella was her ability to experience the mundane as memorable. Where some people might look on moving day as a necessary evil, Stella gave the impression she was looking forward to it almost more than May and insisted that May move on the weekend so that she and Pete could help.

'Road trip!' she sang as May emerged from the shower the morning of her move.

It was a bright, fresh day after a night of steady rain and everything looked rinsed clean.

'Come on girlfriend, let's get this show on the road!'

They set off in convoy; May leading the way in the little Honda Pete had helped her buy. Her friends followed in their four by four with U-Haul trailer attached, carting the few essentials May had picked up at the yard sales and bargain stores.

She drove over long, curving roads that rose and fell through the ancient broadleaf woods, and each dip and rise revealed more rolling farmland, dotted with a glimpse of a barn or house, and the black four by four with Pete and Stella bobbed out of sight then reappeared in May's rearview mirror over and over in steady time.

As she pulled in to the uneven, gravelled drive, puddled with water from last night's rain, her pulse leapt. I'm here, she breathed. At last, it's begun.

She left the car door open and hurried around the porch to look out across the wet grass and tangled clumps of shrubbery, disturbing a pair of woodpigeons who flapped, startled, up and away. From the branches of a black walnut at the far corner of the perimeter fence, a lone bird was calling a joyful, persistent welcome.

'May, this is fuckin boss!' Pete hollered from his window

as he drew up beside her car.

'Come and see!' she called.

It didn't take them long to unpack the U-Haul, but it was much harder than May had anticipated getting the bed up the stairs. Pete spent twenty long minutes trying to dissuade her from setting it up in the smallest bedroom.

'It's the wrong room,' he argued. 'Where's your storage? And it's half the size of that one.' He waved his arm along the hall.

But May was adamant. It was much smaller, but she preferred it with its windows at right angles to each other; they gave a more panoramic view of the garden. 'The light's right,' she said. 'And it looks out over the garden.'

Stella was laughing at her husband. 'Honey, you don't have to sleep in it so what's the problem? If May wants to live in a snug, that's her decision.'

'Well as it's just me, Pete, I can have a sleeping room and a dressing room.' Then almost to herself, she murmured, 'I wonder which window I'll see the moon from.'

She went over to the low, deep, window sill that looked out to the widest sweep of garden and pastures and sat.

As a child, she'd always wanted a window seat, loving the hidden, cocooning idea of it, and now she imagined sitting here with cushions, a blanket, a good book. She smiled and peered out. The neighbouring property had a number of outbuildings and barns and what looked like stables.

'Oh Stella, what if they have horses next door! I love the smell of horses.'

'May, don't get me wrong, girl, I love you, but you really are fuckin nuts!' Pete laughed.

The shadows were lengthening, taking on cool purplish, lavender tones and it was getting chilly.

'May!' Stella exclaimed. 'We didn't check that the furnace works. And what about lightbulbs? And food! You need food! You might have to come back to town for the night.'

But while May and Stella went to fire up the furnace, and to try to fix a dangling gutter up with string, Pete did a run to a convenience store in the next town and brought back sandwiches, a bottle of Freixenet and 14 lightbulbs.

'There's a bag of groceries on the counter too. Coffee, milk, nothing fancy, just enough to get you up in the morning,' he said, examining the work they'd done on the gutter.

'That's so thoughtful, Pete, thanks.'

He smiled at her. 'I can follow instructions, honey, but you're welcome!'

May mouthed her thanks at Stella as Pete continued talking. 'This isn't going to be safe for too long, you need to get this sorted right away. First storm, that's coming down.'

'I know,' May said. 'And the porch steps are really unsafe. I need to deal with them pretty sharpish, otherwise…'

'Isn't that something the owners should be dealing with?'

'The rent is really cheap. The deal is, low rent in return for me doing repairs and maintenance.'

Pete looked sceptical. 'Who's getting the deal here, girl?' he barked.

May ignored him and went in to get some cups and the sandwiches. She could feel it warming up and thought with relief that the furnace and heating must be working.

'Well!' Stella announced into the darkness, when the wine and sandwiches were finished. 'I guess it's time we headed out. Are you going to be alright all alone?' Her tone was jocular, but May could see her concern.

'I'll be fine,' she said warmly. 'I'm excited!' which was true, but she felt an odd little pang of something unidentifiable, which made her feel small as she watched their lights slowly recede along the drive, turn right onto the tarmac and disappear into the night.

The next few days passed in a relentless flurry of cleaning; of windows and woodwork; of cupboards and appliances and making notes of what she needed to repair. She worked hard all day, accompanied by her radio and sang loudly to all the songs she knew, making herself laugh at how many awful pop songs she did know the words to.

Once, as she ran barefooted across her yard to dump rubbish in the bins, she saw the figure of an older man, white haired but strong-looking and upright, fiddling with the light fixture outside one of the outbuildings, a Jack Russell terrier at his heel. As he turned to go back inside his house, he raised a hand towards her and she waved back, hoping he could see her smile as she ran inside. And one evening at twilight, as she was stringing some fairy lights from Stella along the porch, she was sure she recognised a black pickup truck parked at an angle in the neighbour's yard, but told herself with a beating heart it couldn't be him, loads of people around here drove those, and went inside to call her sister.

'How's the new place, May?' Turtle was working at double speed unboxing crates of bottled beer and racking them up on the counter, while Connie and Amy put them away. May was polishing the brass around the booths at the end of shift and was about to nip off to do errands for Turtle.

'Great. I love it,' she smiled and then rushed on. 'It's got the most fantastic old General Electric oven—my granny used to have one.'

'Perfect for keeping the deli in brownies, huh? Those GE appliances, they're your regular old workhorse. You lucked out!'

'It's the Barton place, isn't it?' asked Connie without slowing or looking up. 'It sure is a ways out of town. It's going to be hell in the winter if you keep that piece of tin you're driving.'

May shrugged and without looking at her said, 'Well I

have a while yet, Connie, it's only just proper spring.' She turned to Turtle. 'Do you need anything else while I'm doing the banking?'

'You could call by Harley's workshop for me.' May felt a sharp, hot, thrust of nerves. 'I've been trying to get a hold of him all morning,' continued Turtle. 'And his phone's switched off. There's a door hanging loose out back and I'm afraid it's going to fall off and hurt someone.'

Connie made an odd noise and May looked at her sharply as she gave her an exaggeratedly innocent looking 'What?' face before saying to Turtle, 'He only switches it on if he's going to make a call.'

May turned from her with a wave of frustration. Why was she always so antagonistic? Turtle walked over to the Main Street window and pointed out where she needed to go.

It was a beautiful spring afternoon with all the rough edges worn from the day. People were outside the bars and cafes soaking up the sunshine. She did the banking, then walked down Main Street to Harley's workshop.

Piper was curled on a cushion under the window, but immediately raised her head and wagged politely as May stuck her head around the door.

'Hey,' he said lightly, briefly looking up from an oak corner cupboard he was waxing. 'Come on in.' He didn't seem in the least surprised to see her.

He had cut his hair and the back of his neck looked vulnerable and inviting, its smooth brown skin a shade paler than the rest of him. May stood watching him a while, breathing in the scents of sawdust and linseed, and of beeswax and the warmth of Harley's skin. She was almost afraid to go any further.

Her gaze was drawn to his open shirt, and she saw that he still wore a piece of knotted leather tied loosely around his neck; one knot for each of his lost siblings. He'd told her years before about them and found herself wondering why she had never pressed him for more detail.

He had pulled the sheet off his bed and they were wrapped in it against the mosquitoes, under the apple tree outside his cabin. He said he wanted to go to South America and make documentaries and as he held May, enclosing her in a warm tangle of arms and legs from behind, his voice murmuring and vibrating gently through his chest into her back, she thought she could listen to it forever. She loved the richness and depth, the husky edges in his throat and the unexpected emphasis on syllables that still sometimes caught her out; she loved that he played a guit-ar, loved to hear the gliding over his vowels in certain words and the laughter that frequently sat behind his words when he was telling a story. He asked where she dreamed of going. Nowhere, she thought. This is enough. Right here with you.

'I want to go somewhere that has the biggest vastest sky ever,' she said, after he prompted. 'You know, those sharp blue skies that seem to have a kind of sheen? I used to read about them when I was a little girl in Little House on The Prairie. London always felt so grey and closed in and I read those books over and over, just to feel the light and the space... to be somewhere else.'

Just talking about it filled her with an expansive joy and she heard Harley's low response, a sigh filled with laughter.

'Okay, Prairie Girl.' He chuckled, kissing her through her hair. 'You could go there. Or you might find something like it in the southwest. Why'nt you try Arizona? New Mexico?'

'Is that where you grew up?' she asked, seeming to remember something of that sort.

'I lived there fo while.'

'When? How long for?'

He was quiet a moment, before saying, 'Ah... not for long. It was just after my mom wasn't around anymore. I guess I was around twelve.'

'What about your dad?'

'Long gone,' he said dismissively, then flippantly sang a snatch of

a song. 'Long, long gone, John…'

'Oh…' She leaned back against him and held his arms closer around her. 'Are you an only child?'

A very long pause. You'd think he'd know if he had siblings, she thought with an uneasy sense of stepping somewhere uninvited.

'No,' he said at last. 'There was me, my brother Stef and two little sisters, Libby and Pearl.'

'Oh sweet names! I love Pearl. Older or younger?'

'Me, I'm the oldest.'

'So what are they all doing now big brother? Do you have to keep an eye on them?'

He didn't answer, but stroked her hair, tangling his fingers into it, then smoothing it out.

'I can't answer that question,' he said at last, into the darkness. 'I don't know the answer.'

She looked sideways up at him twisting her head to try and catch his expression, then broke away from his embrace and turned to face him, drawing her legs up and hugging her knees.

'What happened?' she asked, curiosity and tenderness washing through her.

'Lost,' he said. 'Lost.' Then in a stronger more detached tone, added, 'I'm sure you're aware that if a kid ain't got no parents they get put into care and moved about a fair bit and well… people get lost. I had an aunt who took me in for a bit, just me. She moved around a lot for work. It's a big country, baby. I got lost too. But hey!' He put on a heavy drawl, exaggerating his gentle suggestion of the South, 'I saw a whole lot o God's chosen country and I got me a Southern accent!' They'd laughed together.

Which of them hadn't wanted to venture any further into that dark loss? She wondered. He'd had a family; sisters, a brother—where were they? Did they have families of their own? Harley might be an uncle and not even know it. Maybe he did. Maybe they had been reunited. There was so much she didn't know. And she wondered now, if she could go back, would she do it differently? Would she ask him how it had felt to lose his family? Probably not. She'd probably been scared of upsetting him, breaking the intoxicating but fragile bond that had sprung up between them. Did any of it even matter?

She finally realised she was going to have to speak. He'd always been this way, perfectly content with silence, rarely the first to speak. She gave him Turtle's message and with a rush of impulsive blood, unable to just leave, she said, 'That *is* your truck I keep seeing parked next door to the Barton's, isn't it?' she trailed off and felt herself flush.

'Probably.' He threw a smiling glance up at her and looked back down, concentrating on what his hands were doing, moving comfortably around the small room, reaching instinctively for tools and cloths. The late afternoon sun came in at a dazzling angle through a small window and picked out the dust in a delicate, shimmering shaft.

'You know the neighbours?' He smiled in her direction, without making eye contact. 'You know I'm living there now?' she was beginning to feel ridiculous.

'I figured it was you,' he said casually. 'There can't be too many English women running around Dover County in their bare feet.'

'Why didn't you come and say hello?' she asked, belatedly hurt now he'd confirmed it was him.

Harley stopped what he was doing and looked up at May, squinting a little into the sunlight. He ignored her question. 'You really need to wear somethin on your feet, May.' He chuckled to himself and added, 'Can't believe you've got old Matthew worryin about your bare feet and all them ticks and critters that might take a bite out of you.'

'Who's Matthew?'

'May! He's your neighbour. Matthew Burrows. How long you been moved in there? Two, three weeks? You should know your neighbour by now.'

'Two,' she said crossly, then added petulantly, 'Harley, do you know everyone around here?'

He just chuckled at her. 'I could ask him to call by?'

'I'm perfectly capable of meeting my own neighbour, Harley.'

'Evidently not.'

Something about his laugh, the way it sounded young and uninhibited, touched her. She smiled at him and his eyes locked onto hers for a moment, then darted away.

'Oh dear,' she said. 'I suppose I'm still a bit too "city". It'll come!'

'Yeah... I guess. Takes a while to adapt to a new place.'

'Well, it's not untested territory, is it?' May said. 'You may remember I lived here before?' She meant it to sound lightly humorous but something in the long look he gave her caused a rising tension to climb up through her.

'Of course I remember,' he said quietly and the temperature dropped.

He leaned back over his workbench, dabbing his soft cloth into a dark waxy paste with light, tapping movements. A faint smell of turpentine tanged at her nostrils.

'You see much of Pete and Stella now you've moved out?' He threw a quick glance up at her then focussed on the side of the cupboard, applying the wax in small circular movements.

'Of course I do. I park my car in their drive sometimes so I get a bit of a walk.'

'Say "hey" to them.'

Harley's face was frowning in concentration and he muttered something to himself, rummaging distractedly through a box on the bench by the window, his back turned to May, shoulders hunched.

'Okay, well I'll be off then.' She felt in the way.

'Seeya...' he murmured.

He didn't look at her and she slipped out of the doorway

into the evening sunshine.

As she turned the corner she glanced back and saw that he was standing in the window looking down the street towards her. She raised a hand, but he turned as though he hadn't seen her.

May and Stella were sitting beneath the stars and a hardy grape vine, in the garden behind Bentley's, a couple of cocktails between them, waiting for Pete and Mark to arrive. It was a lovely warm evening and it felt as though spring had truly arrived and settled in.

'So, what made you change your mind about the cop?' Stella asked.

May, wondering how honest to be, looked at her for a moment before answering as she usually did when it was Stella.

'I'm in need of a distraction.'

'Ouch! I hope you didn't tell Mark that!'

May pulled a face at her. 'Of course not, I'm not *that* hard!' She took a sip of her drink and sighed. 'So far it's not working. I'm obsessing about bloody Harley. Why do I keep feeling as though I just need to find the key?'

'Uh oh…' Stella looked at her, not a little dismayed. 'I'm getting déjà vu.'

May didn't say anything. Then, 'Mmm hmm. Old story. He's complicated. Says one thing acts another.'

'You mean he's fucked up!' They laughed together, just as Mark walked out into the garden looking about the place.

'Here we go,' May said and Stella kicked her under the table.

'Not nice,' she said firmly. 'Give the guy a chance.'

May raised her hand to catch his attention, resolving to give it her best. What did she have to lose? Mark's eyes registered he'd seen her then almost imperceptibly, hardened as he saw Stella.

118

'Hey, ladies,' he said, sitting opposite May. 'You brought a chaperone?' He laughed when he said it, but May was sure she heard an edge to his voice.

'You remember Stella?' she asked. 'I'd already arranged to see her and Pete this evening, so I thought—hope you don't mind?'

'Of course not,' he said smoothly. 'I'll take what I can get!' They all laughed.

It was May's turn to get the drinks and as she stood at the bar trying to catch the bartender's eye, she thought about how the evening was going. Mark and Pete got on fine, discussing baseball stats, and Mark's perspective on urban versus rural policing, but the interesting spark she'd noticed between her and Mark at the party was failing to ignite. At last, drinks secured, she turned from the bar and stopped. Harley was walking through the swing doors.

At first, he didn't see her, but then his eyes lit on her and he smiled a little self-consciously. Her heart was pounding so much she couldn't move; she felt slightly sick. What on earth was he doing here? Damn him and damn her impulsivity. She wished she could magic poor Mark away. Realising she couldn't just stand there, much as she wanted to, she tried to calm her breathing and made her way towards him.

'Hey,' he said lightly and glancing at the four drinks on her tray asked, 'Who's here?'

'Pete and Stella, Mark Sassello—d'you know him? And me. Come and say hello.'

The warmth had gone from his eyes. 'It's okay. Wouldn't want to tread on anyone's toes.'

'Don't be daft,' she said. 'Come and say hello.' She turned without waiting for an answer, wondering why she was insisting. Shouldn't I be trying to avert any awkwardness, not create more? She felt a wave of remorse about Mark, overlaid by the strongest need to keep Harley from leaving.

'Harley!' Stella called out merrily as they neared the table. 'Are you joining us?'

'Nah,' he drawled. 'I'm meeting someone.'

He put his hand out to Mark as May introduced them and they shook briefly. Mark gave her a scrutinising look, before shifting so that the only place she could sit was jammed between him and Pete. Safely corralled, she thought wryly, and stayed standing where she was.

There was a brief, awkward exchange of small talk until Harley said, 'Well, I guess I'll shoot.' Then, to her astonishment, he leaned in and kissed her. 'Enjoy your date,' he said in a low voice close to her ear and headed towards the bar.

She took a moment to still herself, closing her eyes before she sat, subdued.

'Any other surprises?' Mark asked coolly.

She looked at him apologetically. 'I'm sorry,' she said, putting a hand on his arm, still feeling the warmth of Harley's breath on her cheek. 'It's not what you signed up for, is it?'

He covered her hand with his and gave it a squeeze. 'You owe me, honey. Dinner. Just you and me.'

'Why not?' she answered. 'Sounds nice.'

Mark had gone to get their second jug of Long Island iced teas when Stella dug an elbow into May's side and smirked. 'You know what? I'd be pretty pissed off if the guy I was out with was staring at someone else across the room all night.'

May had been studiously avoiding looking over at Harley all evening, but now she followed her friend's look and saw he was watching them like a cobra. She felt a ridiculous thrill, which she instantly despised herself for and looked quickly away.

Mark returned with their drinks and she wondered if she ought to just tell him it wasn't worth his while, just tell him: that old flame? I'm still in love with him. Because that was the truth, wasn't it?

11

A few days later, May was making herself a pot of peppermint tea from an enthusiastic plant at the back of the kitchen door. She heard voices outside and crunching of gravel and went out to the porch.

'Hey, May,' Harley called. 'This is Matthew Burrows. Your neighbour?'

He gave her an ironic little smile that made her want to kick him and the neat, upright older man she'd seen next door extended his hand to her. He was a head or so shorter than Harley, with a thick head of white hair. 'Good evening,' he said with a warm smile. He had a Southern accent that made her think of her father. 'I'm pleased to finally meet you. I've noticed you puttering about, but wanted to give you time to settle in.'

He had an unruffled, contented air she warmed to, but what was instantly intriguing was how Harley seemed with him; boyishly affable and affectionate. She offered them something to drink and they settled on the porch, looking out on the distant farmland, over which swallows swooped and the late afternoon sunshine shed its gold and apricot light. May was keen to hear about what had brought Matthew up to this part of the world from his native Georgia; what had made him stay.

'I'm always curious about what makes a person leave their roots,' she explained.

'Yes. That is always of interest, but of course people pitch up places because they have no roots, too.' May thought he flicked a look at Harley, but couldn't be certain.

Matthew was a painter; he talked about coming up there as a young man and falling in love, both with the landscape that was so different to the one where he grew up and with a local girl, whom he had married.

'Work brought me here, and love kept me,' he said with a chuckle, drawing the word 'love' out, long and full. 'It's been five years now since Hope passed. We lived here together and raised babies and gardens together for forty-three years.'

'I'm sorry, Matthew. That must have been hard. My stepmother died recently, I know it's not the same, but to lose someone you love...' She trailed off as Harley shot her a swift, intense look.

'Was she your mama, this stepmother?' Matthew asked, surprising May with his astute question.

'Yes. Yes she was.' She looked at him with fresh eyes.

'I'm sorry.'

She nodded mutely and feeling Harley's unflinching look, said, 'What?'

He shook his head and looked away. 'I didn't know. About Sarah.'

He looked back at her and May thought she saw hurt in his eyes, but something else too, something tender that touched her.

After a moment she spoke to Matthew. 'What I'd really love to do is sort out the garden. It looks like it's quite something.'

She swatted a hand in the direction of the overgrown terraced borders that punctuated the sloped garden. 'But I don't know where to start. I don't feel I know the climate well enough or the soil or the animals that might want to eat my plants.'

'Well now, I think that's a fine idea.' He turned to Harley. 'You didn't tell me my new neighbour was a gardener.' Matthew was pleased.

'I don't think he knew,' May said.

Harley shrugged. 'There's a whole lot I don't know, Matthew,' he said, weary. 'But she always did love a thing that God or nature made, so I guess it don't come as no surprise.'

How does he do that? May wondered. Her heart aching.

Just say something that feels so intimate.

'Let's take a walk, young lady,' Matthew said, then turning to Harley he gave a little mock bow and added, 'We'd be glad of your company son, or you can go on home or wherever it is you'd rather be. We don't need you no how!'

Harley gave an affectionate laugh. 'Okay, Matthew.' He chuckled. 'I guess you can find your own way home. You're all grown now.'

'Get out of here, boy.' The old man smiled.

Harley hoisted himself off the porch steps and without looking directly at May, said he'd see her around. Matthew was quiet for a moment, as Harley's truck bumped slowly along the dirt track toward the paved road.

'Now I wonder what's gotten into him,' he murmured.

'Isn't he usually like that?' May said sulkily, adding unfairly, 'He seems to be whenever I see him. He's moodier than a teenaged girl.'

Matthew smiled, but said nothing for a while as he sipped his drink. The sun began to slip, imperceptibly at first but the quality of the light was changing, getting thicker and headier, the colours taking on more flushes of pink and deep, burnished golds.

'Now, would you care to talk gardens?' Matthew asked and they passed a very pleasant hour as May talked about what she had in mind.

'I've always wanted a proper garden of my own. All I've ever really managed in London was a few large pots of cherry tomatoes and some herbs.'

She looked around at the space and light, felt the soft tickle of the spring breeze on her arms and remembered the dank, concrete steps that ran down to her basement flat and the tiny west-facing garden that only warmed up at the end of the day.

'Now don't get so carried away with summer you forget everything else. You can grow beans to dry and pumpkins and onions and all kinds of good things.'

May hugged her knees and gave a shiver of excitement; the world seemed full of promise.

'What about some hens?'

'Well now. I keep chickens myself. Surely you've heard my old rooster raising hell?'

'Oh, he's not so bad.'

She leaned back, stretching her legs and raised her arms above her head, reaching back behind her, letting out a huge sigh. She was deeply contented as the sun warmed her and she imagined the months ahead in this beautiful, peaceful place.

Matthew broke the silence. 'It'd be a pleasure to help you out with the garden, if you'd like that. Maybe help you tidy things up a bit, see what's survived the winter. Fix up those raised beds out back.'

He waved an arm over towards the brick patio outside the kitchen.

'I would love that. Thank you.'

After Matthew had gone, and May was tidying the cups and plates from the porch, she stopped briefly to look out over the garden as it disappeared into the smudgy darkness. She pictured the raised beds they had talked about with a vivid clarity and imagined she could smell the earthy, sharp bruise on the air of tomatoes ripening under the pearly glow of a full moon. She remembered her father telling her about the importance of warm, soft air at night when you were growing tomatoes. They get tough skin if the night air is too chill, he had told her.

How is it that these unacknowledged, pointless little pieces of information came back to her at odd moments, so full of meaning and value? Her father had been a mine of them; unconnected, unannounced, coming sometimes out of nowhere and drifting off, unanchored by May's interest. And now, like so many dandelion seeds floating off into the air, they were settling. And why had he never minded? It drove her crazy when she felt un-listened to and yet he seemed to need only to express the thought.

Within days, Matthew had reappeared without prior arrangement and he and May spent several companionable hours plotting out the best places to build the raised beds.

'Matthew, I can't let you do this for nothing,' she said anxiously.

'Now you listen to me,' he said firmly. 'I like to keep busy since Hope died and this suits me just right.'

Each day, May returned from work with anticipation fluttering in her breast. Frequently, she would arrive home drained and tired, and her spirits would soar as she saw what Matthew had been up to. He built six long beds with narrow paths between them the width of his mower, so May could wander along and reach them without standing on the soil. They were to the side of the porch, facing towards the sweep of farmland that could be seen from the living room window. It was a little late in the season to plant some things, but Matthew had been generous with his plants, started off under glass earlier in the year, and helped her to set out tomatoes and peppers and various coloured courgettes.

Matthew persuaded her to dedicate a bed to sweet corn and another for salad vegetables, then spent an afternoon putting up gauzy protective netting over the tiny leaves, supported at the corners by posts like some great colonial bed, draped in a mosquito net.

'Keep these watered, missy,' he admonished her sternly. 'Every evening once the sun is off them. Don't want to scorch their leaves.'

Amongst all this, he had planted a riot of zinnias in hot, exuberant colours that had reminded her of the autumn dahlias in Holland Park back home in London.

May was more contented and filled with anticipatory pleasure than she had thought possible months before. What troubled her, though, was Harley.

Often, she'd arrive home and see his truck in Matthew's drive and hear laughter and voices from somewhere in her garden, but he always took off within moments of her arrival and never accepted her invitation to stop for a drink or a bite to eat. Clearly, he preferred to keep his distance and this hurt May, but she was aware too that while he was with Matthew during her absences at work, he was busy fixing things up at her place. Who was this for? Matthew, so he wasn't over taxing himself, or her? She wanted it to be for her, but there was no way of telling.

One evening, as she was clearing her supper things, she heard Matthew call out to her from the front door.

'Hello,' she said, feeling a swell of warmth at his smile. 'I'm just making some peppermint tea. Would you like some?'

'Oh no, I'm not staying. I'm in my studio tonight, finishing up a painting for my son and his wife's new place in San Francisco. I only wanted to ask you if it would be convenient for Harley and me to get to those porch boards that need doing, tomorrow. He's just called to let me know he has a whole day free and I'm like to getting a little antsy that we haven't fixed them up. Sure as night is night and day is day, you are going to stick one of those bare feet of yours through, if we don't get to it. Which reminds me. Put some shoes on your feet, Missy, this is not your English garden.'

'Matthew, you are so kind,' she said. 'Of course it's convenient. I won't be here, but let me know if you need any more cash for the supplies.'

'No, that won't be necessary, you gave me plenty a while back and I'm keeping a tab for you.'

He said goodnight and headed back to his studio calling over his shoulder through the darkness, with a chuckle, 'Shoes!' and she smiled.

She was gone the next morning before Harley and Matthew arrived and worked flat out on a double shift, only coming home at dusk.

The two men were finishing up by the light of a small rigged up floodlight and bickering and laughing as she pulled in to her drive. She sat a moment, letting herself arrive, feeling the gentle stillness of the early summer evening settle about her.

After a while, she got out of the car and stretched, calling out a good evening to them.

'We're almost done here, my dear,' Matthew called back.

It was hard to see in the growing darkness quite what they'd done, but she could feel at once how solid the porch felt beneath her feet. The place was littered with sawdust and tools and she went inside to grab a brush and pan and the big dustbin.

'This is unbelievable,' she said. 'How did you manage it all in one day?'

'Oh it's not quite done, but the rest I can do on my own when I have time.' Matthew answered. He sounded tired.

'Matthew, let me get you something to eat and a drink.'

'I'll pass, my dear, but thank you.'

Harley murmured something to him about finishing up without him and he almost shooed the old man home.

May began to clear up and Harley joined her, working quietly until the tools were put away, the deck swept and the off cuts neatly stacked out in the yard.

'Thank you so much for doing all this,' she said when they were done.

She'd brought out a couple of bottled beers in the hope Harley might stay; to her surprise he took one and sat on the swing seat that Matthew had dug out of his barn for her.

She looked at him, stretched in the corner, one arm slung over the side, scratching lazily at his dog's ears and took up the other corner. He smiled at her.

'No problem. I couldn't let that old man do it all by himself.'

May flushed. 'I don't quite know how I can stop him. He's so keen to help and…'

'I only meant my pride, May,' he broke in and nudged her foot gently with his. 'It's okay.' He smiled. 'I know you wouldn't indenture an old man.'

She smiled back, grasping with absurd pleasure at the idea that he might think well of her.

'Thank you,' she said, shyly, aware it was just them with the stars and the crickets ringing and less than a foot between them.

The quiet grew and Harley pushed at the floor with his booted foot from time to time, setting the seat to a gentle sway.

'I always wondered,' May said quietly. 'What did you do after…' She almost couldn't say the words. 'After I left? Where did you go?'

He looked at her. 'Well…' he began, but couldn't finish. He looked away and took a swallow of his beer.

'Did you make any films?'

'After a while. One or two. Mostly I just goofed off as a freelance sound tech.'

'Did you enjoy it?'

He shrugged. 'Enjoy? I don't know if I could call it that. It was tough.'

She turned herself so she was facing him more fully and tucked one of her feet up under her. 'Why?'

Harley settled back a little more and set the swing off again. 'Why?' he looked thoughtful and she waited. 'Tough places, tough stuff going on. And I wasn't in a good place myself, May.'

'Why was that?' she asked softly and he gave her a long and thoughtful look before ignoring the question.

'Money was great, though.'

May respected his wish not to answer, but was hungry to know everything about him since she'd left and couldn't stop herself asking more, wanting more; to fill the gaps and spaces; to picture him in the years between them; she wanted to know him again. She felt carnivorous and compulsive, but he answered, patiently tolerant, smiling a little ironically at her, a scepticism about his mouth in the pause before he answered. And there was always a pause. You really interested in all this? he seemed to be saying.

And what was she doing? Playing for time? Trying to stop him from leaving and not knowing when she'd have him like this again, so unexpectedly relaxed and open?

'And why did you come back?' she asked. 'I always imagined you roaming the world indefinitely. An itinerant traveller.'

'Now why would you imagine that?' he asked, looking out over the darkening garden. 'You think I didn't get my fill of moving about when I was a youngin?'

May didn't know how to answer, it was hard to say that she'd thought it was his habit.

'It makes less sense for you to come back, wouldn't you say?' he asked.

'Now why would you say that?' she asked mimicking his tone, a little nervous at the direction things might be taking.

He was quiet, cocked his head at her and started the swing up again.

'Well,' he said slowly, appearing to measure what he was thinking. 'I always understood you to have had your fill of small-town living, May.'

She felt a smart of something. Hurt? Irritation?

'Really? Show's how much you knew me, then,' she said a little acidly.

He nudged her foot again and smiled. 'Nothin wrong with that, everyone's ambitious when they're young, right? Tell me what you did? Did you go to college in the end?'

'No, and everyone was furious,' she said. 'But when I got back to London a friend offered me an entry job at a style magazine and I took it.'

He raised his eyebrows. 'After all that, you didn't even go to college?'

'All what?'

'The pressure your family was putting you under. You

130

blew them off anyway? I didn't expect that.'

Well what had he expected? 'I wasn't in a good place then either, Harley,' she said quietly, her heart beating hard.

'You and me both.' He looked her in the eyes. 'Well how about that?' He stood and walked to the edge of the porch, followed by his dog and May watched from the shadows, full of emotion, unable to find the courage to say what she was feeling. Let's do this. Please. Let's try again.

She didn't want him to leave, but she held back as she walked him to his truck.

'Thanks for staying, Harley,' she said. 'It's been lovely, I don't know, just talking.'

'Yeah.' He smiled. 'Sometimes I…'

'What?' she asked when he didn't go on.

He shook his head. 'Nothin.' He pointed into the open door and looking at Piper's expectant upturned face said, 'Get up,' and followed her scrambling backside into the cab. 'I guess I'll see you around.' He closed the door. 'Small town and all that.'

'And here, right? With Matthew, I mean.' She stumbled over her words, wanting to tell him to come and see her, but something held her back; an almost imperceptible sense he was withdrawing or shutting a door again.

'Sure,' he said, switching on the ignition.

May stepped back and said goodnight, before watching his truck disappear into the darkness.

Harley began to come to the house almost every night or found her in bars in town or house parties of mutual friends. And every time she saw him her heart sped, her temperature increased. He was unable to keep from touching her. His warm fingers played in her hair, restless, restless hands reminding her that they'd be alone soon. Sometimes, through the noise and laughter on a hot summer night, she would catch him looking at her with such tenderness her breath caught in her throat, she'd forget what she was saying and have to look away.

They were so hungry for each other it almost scared her; the way everything fell away in a kind of fury. Nothing mattered except him. They devoured one another the moment they were alone. But what she was beginning to find hard was how remote he could become.

'It didn't matter at first,' she was burbling to Stella one night after they'd finished a jug of Long Island iced teas. 'It was all just such a horn frenzy.'

Stella laughed. 'Yeah, I know, you're just so glad you're getting it on, the other stuff doesn't matter.'

'But now… I don't understand how we can talk the way we do and, you know, have sex the way we do without it meaning something to him.'

'Way, way, wait a minute, what makes you think it doesn't mean anything to him? The guy's obviously nuts about you, he's always around.'

But May was barely listening. She was thinking of the night before, remembering the creeping loneliness she felt while lying beside him in the darkness, with just the edge of his hand touching hers as he lay quiet and far away beside her.

'So I lie there thinking something's wrong that I've said too much or he's going off me or the finite lure of sex with someone new is reaching its sell by date and then he appears the next day or whenever-the-fuck he feels like it and we have these unbelievably intense times… oh piss off Stella,' she said to her friends wiggling eyebrows. 'The way we talk, there's this incredible connection. It really isn't just about sex.' She began to cry. 'Oh noo…' she wailed. 'Now I've drunk too much!'

Stella was laughing with affection and came around the table to give her a hug. 'Oh Mayflower! I don't know what to say. Fear of intimacy? I don't know. He's a great guy but I think he's fucked up.'

He was leaning against the porch railings smoking a cigarette and looking moodily out at the night when she found him. There'd been an altercation at a house party between a girl and a drunken jock; Harley had intervened, stopping it from getting ugly, but in the aftermath, he had become withdrawn and unreachable. Feeling shut out again,

May wondered with a deep sadness if this was how it would always be with him. She leaned quietly up alongside and he looked sideways at her, lifting his cigarette to her mouth so she could take a drag and looking closely at her as though trying to find something. She saw a deep well of weary sadness before his eyes took on a flat, opaque darkness.

The late summer night was warm and shadowed, full of the call and response of tree frogs, the whir and whip-peep of hidden creatures singing and luring, anchored by the constant faint jingle-bell, chime of crickets.

'You know, you can tell what the temperature is by how many chirps a cricket makes?' Harley said softly, sending a shadow of a smile in her direction.

He sat along the top step of the porch, one leg bent up, the other flung out in a clatter down the rest of them and rested his head on his knee looking like a small boy.

'That was... amazing what you did in there Harley, talking that guy down like that,' May said in wonder. 'It was all so counterintuitive. I would have gone straight in to defending the girl and telling him to back off.'

'Yeah and he would've punched you, or her, or something like that,' he said bitterly.

'But how did you know that?'

'Trial and error. Mostly error for the first four or five years,' he said, voice parchment dry. 'My mama had any number of assholes just like him paradin in and outta her life for years. You learn.'

May was beginning to know when to stay quiet if she wanted to hear more from Harley. She waited.

'When I was a kid, I used to come home from school and wonder who'd be whupping on whose ass. Wonder if my mom was going to be sober or beat up or swallowing a bunch of fuckin pills again. The only time I called 911 was if she'd swallowed pills, everything else I worked it out for myself. Sometimes it worked, sometimes it didn't.'

13

May was sitting at the bar after work, waiting for Amy to finish so they could join Stella and the crowd at Hojo's. She spotted Mark, off duty and chatting to Connie, but he came over to her at once.

'What you got there?' he said, eyeing a letter she was reading.

'Hello,' she said, slipping it into her bag. 'How are you?'

'Good. What was that?'

May looked at him for a moment. 'Curiouser and curiouser…' she said, smiling.

'I'm serious.' He smiled too. 'What were you reading?'

'A letter, Mark. I was reading a letter.'

'Well I can see that, but who from?'

'Mark!' She laughed nervously. 'Actually, not your business, is it?' It wasn't even private, but his pushy tone was annoying.

'Hey, take it easy, I'm just intrigued as to who or what could hold your attention like that.' He smiled, but his eyes held no humour. 'I just can't work you out,' he went on. 'You're an interesting puzzle.'

'I'm fairly straightforward. If you're looking for some kind of secret me, you'll be disappointed. It was a print out of an email from my old boss in London.'

'But you do have secrets, don't you?' The way he looked at her made her flush.

'Pot, kettle, black?' she said lightly, remembering how he'd avoided talking about his transfer from Boston. 'We all have things we'd rather not talk about, but it doesn't necessarily mean anything significant or sinister.'

Mark looked at her steadily before his face relaxed into a smile. 'Of course, you're right. So is your boss trying to lure you back?'

'Something like that. They're launching a new quarterly food supplement to the regular magazine, the one I worked on, and she wants to know if I'll be coming back to London. She wants me to do it.'

'Oh, a woman?'

'Yes, Mark. My former boss is a woman, is that relevant?'

'Sheesh, you're real touchy, aren't you? I didn't mean anything by it, just curious if it's a guy trying to persuade you. Ulterior motive and all that. You know what I mean.'

'No, I don't, Mark,' May said, feeling her hackles rise. 'I was a good production editor, that's why they want me back. And anyway,' she added just to wind him up, 'you don't know that *she* doesn't have that ulterior motive, hmm? Or me? It does happen you know.' She raised her eyebrows.

He flushed. 'I don't know how we got onto this,' he said in a muttered rush. 'Actually, the reason I came over was to ask you when I'm going to get that dinner date you promised me.'

'Ah, yes,' May said, wondering why she still felt she owed him. 'We're all going to Hojo's for open mic night, why don't you come too?'

'That wasn't the deal.'

'No, but that's what I'm doing tonight.'

'I'm not interested in spending time with your friends.'

'Well!' she said standing as she spotted Amy at last. 'Another time, then.'

'Sorry I took so long!' Amy looked flushed and bright eyed as she joined them. 'Hey, Mark, you coming too? I'd love to see *you* take a turn on the mic.'

'Not my thing.'

'Music isn't your thing?' she said incredulously. 'Well, you're trying to date the wrong girl, then,' she finished with a laugh.

'Music is fine, listening to other people screw up Eric Clapton isn't.'

'Harsh!' Amy laughed. 'I love listening to other people

screwing it up, myself, and it's May's guilty pleasure, isn't it? Cover bands?'

May laughed with her. 'I'm afraid so. There you go, Mark, you wanted to know my secrets! Come on,' she said to Amy. 'Stella will be wondering where we are. See you, Mark.'

'I'll call you,' he said.

'If you like,' May said in a neutral tone, not wishing to encourage him and headed after Amy.

The next morning, as she drank her coffee on the porch before heading off to work, May noticed that overnight a beautiful froth of blossom had appeared in the ancient apple tree down by the corner fence.

She picked her way through the dewy grass, watching where she placed her bare feet and as she got closer realised it was a rose that had clambered and tangled up and through and around and over, spilling in a great tumble on the sunny side of the tree. Great trusses of pale pink and white pompons arched down catching the morning sun. She stood on tiptoes to touch the blossom, but they were just out of reach. In the cool, green stillness, looking into that tangle of whip-like, thorny branches, May thought of Sleeping Beauty waiting, waiting…

She caught sight of Matthew far off in a corner of his own garden, the familiar pale Panama hat bright in the sunshine. He was stooped over weeding one of his flowerbeds, a wheelbarrow by his side.

'Morning, Matthew!' she called.

He straightened and raised a hand.

'I thought the apple tree had blossomed again.' She laughed.

He shook his head frowning, indicating he could not hear her and came through the grass to lean on the split-railed fence that divided their property. 'What's that you say?' May repeated herself while Matthew squinted over at the tree.

'The things I most especially enjoy,' he spoke musingly, 'are the ones that manage to surprise you every year. Every June this beauty comes back, disappearing before you can get used to it. If I remember correctly, that there is a Paul's Himalayan Musk rose and, in the evenings, you're going to smell something out of this world.' The words rolled off his tongue with relish.

'Is it okay to cut some, Matthew? It's so pretty.'

'Won't hurt.'

'Well I don't have time now; I have a morning shift. Do you need anything from town? I'll be back by four.'

Matthew, already ambling back slowly to his chores, shook his head with a smile. May, pausing only to sling her coffee cup into the kitchen, hurried off to work.

It was a ripe apricot of an evening with the sun just beginning to lick the edges of the sky to the merest hint of rose, when she returned that evening. The air sang and sighed, humming with contentment. As she stood looking out across the garden and over the pastures, May felt a moment of pure joy, her spirits lifted and elated at the beauty of it all.

She headed inside and spotted a large glass Kilner jar full of rose blossoms waiting by the backdoor, along with a box of the first salad thinnings, vividly bright and smelling earthy. She breathed it all in and smiled. Dear Matthew.

When she had told him she needed to thank Harley for sending him her way, he had chuckled, saying he'd have found her anyway and not to give that boy more than his due. It always made her smile, the way he called Harley 'boy'.

It didn't concern her that she had no way of knowing when Matthew would be there. His presence was unobtrusive, comforting. He had no schedule, and yet there was a gentle rhythm to his tending her garden, fluid and steady like the flow of a summer stream.

He always looked up at the crunch of her car on the

gravel, lifted his arm in a languorous greeting, and returned to tying in the beans or staking the tomatoes or hoeing the sweet corn.

Sometimes May went to chat, their conversation never predictable, often woven around the garden, each sharing bits of themselves slowly, revealing who they were. Other times, she went straight inside, stopping only to call out to him, 'Hey, Matthew!' as she climbed the wooden steps.

Now, as she felt the sun warm on her back and smelled the earth on the tissue-fine salad leaves, she wondered why she had chosen to complicate her life like this. For as long as she could remember, she'd been drawn to stories and images, to places and things that opened her up, that helped her loosen the ties of her urban environment, giving her a sense of freedom. Standing here, in this wild and ancient place, she had the strongest sensation of life pulsing through her, the feeling that she could breathe, really breathe, and as she looked out over the land, it tapped at some primal longing. And yet... why this quiet, tilt of sadness, the thought of home and Lallie and the sting of tears, rising through her?

May was just leaving work one evening, when her phone rang.

'Hi, it's Mark.' Her heart sank. 'Where have you been hiding out? Some people might think you were avoiding me. It's been a while.'

'Yes!' she said brightly, nervous. 'How are you?'

'What do you say we go for dinner?'

'I can't, Mark,' she said. 'It's been a long day and I'm tired. I'm just going to go home, have a bath and get to bed.'

'I won't keep you out late. You need to eat something, right? Let me buy you dinner.'

'It's really kind of you...'

'I'm not being kind,' he interrupted. 'I just want to buy you dinner.'

'Thanks Mark, but no. I really have to go,' she said. 'Thanks for calling. Take care.' She hung up, feeling restless and uneasy. Why was he so persistent? It bothered her that he wouldn't get the message.

She walked along Main Street to collect her car from Pete and Stella's and as she passed Bentley's she was startled by thumping on glass and muffled cheering. Stella was with Pete and Dougie and their usual crowd at a long table in the bay window that looked out onto the street; they were all waving at her and beckoning. May felt a weight lift as she saw Stella and laughing, pushed through the door and into the bar.

'May-Day! May-Day!' Stella called. 'Yay! Sit down. Drink margaritas!'

'I'm way too tired to drink margaritas tonight,' May said, already better just for having seen Stella. She ordered a Sea Breeze.

Stella had been in the middle of telling Dougie and another guy a story about how she and May had got lost in the fog in East London one November night during Stella's semester abroad, looking for a party. May took up the thread and was laughing so much as Stella kept butting in with irrelevant detail, neither could get to the end of the story.

'We'd just been reading a stupid book about the Jack the Ripper murders and managed to convince ourselves that he was out there somewhere, despite the fact that all that had happened a hundred years ago.'

Through her laughter, May saw Mark come into the bar and stride over to the table, his face serious.

'Hello!' May said brightly. 'What are you doing here?'

'I could ask you the same question. I thought you were too tired to go out,' he said evenly.

Everyone went silent for a moment then started talking quickly.

'Oh, I know. I'm sorry. I was. I am. I just nipped in for a quick one to see Stella. It was spur of the moment.' May felt flustered. 'Here,' she said, squinching closer to Doug and Stella obligingly scooted along the bench too. 'Sit down.'

Mark looked at her for a moment, then at Doug who smiled nervously.

'Hey Mark,' Stella said brightly.

Mark ignored her and addressed May in a low tone. 'Step outside for a moment, we need to talk.'

Feeling awkward and exposed, and in her desire not to cause a scene, she stood and walked with him to the door. Out of the corner of her eye, she saw Stella half stand then sit again.

Mark opened the door, and with his hand on her arm propelled her through so that they stood together in the confined space of the small storm lobby. May felt horribly short of breath suddenly.

'What's going on?' he said.

'How do you mean?' May shifted uncomfortably.

'You playing me? Is that what this is?'

'Playing you? I don't know what you mean,' she said nervously.

'Jerking me around, playing me.'

'Mark...' she began, but he cut her off.

'Because it sure as hell looks like it and I do *not* like to be played, lady.'

He thrust his face forward and the storm lobby felt extremely small and claustrophobic; there was no place to go.

'Mark,' she said, trying to sound calm. 'I am sorry if it feels like I've been messing you about. It wasn't my...'

'Save it! I've heard it all before a hundred times. Women like you, playing guys off each other...'

'Wait a minute!' May interrupted. 'I am not playing anyone off anyone else! All that happened, was I said no to dinner and then bumped into my friends.' She almost told him to grow up, but bit her words back when she saw the look on his face.

'You fucking that dirty tomahonky keeps hanging around your place?' May felt a shock of repulsion. It was the term

140

he'd used to refer to Harley, rather than the assumption of sex, that bothered her, but he seemed to leap on her reaction as some kind of confirmation.

'You thought I didn't know?' His eyes fired up and he laughed nastily at her. 'I'm a police officer lady, it's my business to know things. People talk to me. And I hate to tell you this and bust love's young dream, but everybody in town knows he just sticks it anywhere he likes, when he likes. You think he saves it for you?'

May willed herself to be as still as possible before she spoke, but her voice trembled a little, 'I'm going back in.'

She turned away and felt a sharp, adrenalin shock as he grasped her wrist hard, wheeled her round to face him and shoved her against the doorframe.

Her heart banged so hard she thought she was suffocating. Fear and the need to escape consumed her. His fingers dug painfully into her flesh as he grasped her upper arms and she cried out as he spoke in a low, threatening voice.

'*Don't you turn your back on me until I say we're done!*'

He seemed enormous to May and he spoke in such a quiet voice, his words coming through gritted teeth, it felt far more menacing than shouting. Her blood pumped erratically. Her friends were just on the other side of the double glass doors, couldn't they see what was happening? She tried not to whimper, understanding on some level that if he realised how frightened she was, it would make him worse, but he was hurting her.

'Mark,' she said as steadily as she could. 'Let go of me. You're hurting me and I really don't think that's what you want to do.'

'You superior, patronising little *bitch*.' He thrust his words at her.

May felt heavily queasy. Oh my god he's bloody nuts, she thought fearfully. Oh fuck. But something burned hard and bright inside her. You don't scare me she thought, trying to give herself courage, her heart pumping. You don't scare me.

The glass door opened behind her with a yank and the sound of voices and laughter swelled through.

'What the-Hey!' Stella's voice came forceful and angry.

Mark let go of May and stepped back breathing heavily. For a moment the three of them stood rigid, then Mark turned and slammed out through the door without a word.

'Shit. What the fuck was going on there?'

'I don't know,' May's voice came out slightly strangled.

Stella opened the door to the street and they went out together and sat on the bench outside. Stella put her arms around her and stroked her hair, but May shrugged her off, needing space.

'You okay, honey?' she asked. May nodded, but she wasn't sure. 'You want to come back in or go home?'

'Home I think, Stel,' she said, rubbing her arms where Mark had grabbed her.

The door from the bar opened again and Pete joined them, 'Everybody okay?' he asked, worried. 'Sounds like someone sure had *his* nose outta joint, you okay?'

May nodded and felt tearful. What a horrible, horrible man, she thought.

She didn't get home until after one. She had gone back to Stella and Pete's to get her car and then hadn't wanted to be on her own yet.

'Tomahonky?' Stella was saying with a slow shake of her head, as they drank tea in the kitchen at Woodland Drive. 'That's nasty. And in this day and age too.'

'Stella!' snorted Pete. 'Which land-of-the-free are you living in that you think people still aren't racist assholes?'

'What does it mean?' May asked.

'I only ever heard it once or twice before,' Pete said. 'But I think he's referring to Harley being mixed heritage. You know, honky as in white and tomahawk as in Native

American. Nasty,' he said again, discomfort on his face.

'You know what feels a bit creepy, though?' May asked them. 'How does he know Harley spends time at mine?'

'Downside of a small town, May,' Pete answered carelessly.

Stella gave her a long, thoughtful look. 'You okay to go back there tonight?'

'Of course!' May said brightly, looking at the time and standing. 'Pete's right. It's a small town, that's all, and Mark does seem to be very pally with my dear friend Connie, who knows *every*thing.'

By the time she got back, May was wound up and worrying. She knew she wouldn't sleep if she went to bed and what was really annoying her, was that the idea of Harley still 'sticking it anywhere' as Mark had so pleasantly put it, upset her. It wasn't as though she had any claims on him and it was true he never seemed to lack the company of women. But still, it would be nice to think he wasn't still just filling the void, as Lallie used to say.

She wondered restlessly, unable to settle. Not even the sounds of the crickets helped. It would be just after six am in London. Lallie would be at her kitchen table with her cup of hot water and a slice of lemon, planning her day, enjoying the quiet before the children woke. May had a strong need to hear her voice.

Her sister picked up the phone almost instantly.

'Good morning,' May said, choking up at the sound of her sister's early morning voice. She curled up on the sofa and listened to Lallie telling her all the news of the children, Sam, her work. She was very concerned to hear about Mark Sassello.

'Whoa. Not good. That sounds like a bloke who needs a very wide berth. I wonder if that's why he transferred from Boston. You always hear stories about racist police officers

143

over there and then they just get moved over. A bit like paedophile priests.'

May could almost see Lallie shudder.

'And Alex got in touch,' she went on. 'Wanting to know if she had the right contact details for you—have you not had any emails from her, May?'

May felt a twinge of guilt at her old editor's name. 'Mmm,' she murmured noncommittally. 'What did you tell her?'

'That I didn't know why you weren't answering and that I'd let you know. Get back to her May, you don't want to burn that bridge. She said she has something you might be interested in. Also, darls, have you booked your flight home for Christmas. You'll probably save a fortune if you don't do it at the last minute.'

It all seemed so far away to May, but she agreed she'd do it and rang off as she heard Tillie and Max clattering into the kitchen calling their mother.

'Give everyone my love,' she said before ringing off.

At work a few days later, May looked up as the door from the street opened and Harley stuck his head round. He smiled over at Connie, and looked around before catching May's eye and walking over to where she was just slapping a drink order down on the bar.

'Hey, y'all,' he said, then turned to May. 'Your tyres are all flat, what you been driving all over?' he smiled.

'What?' May asked stupidly. 'I've got a flat tyre?'

'Didn't you hear the man?' Connie said. 'Tyres. All of them. I told you, you were driving a heap of junk.' She laughed and turned away to fill May's order.

'Connie,' Harley said, shaking his head. 'Why'n't you pretend like you was raised right, just once in a while?'

'Don't pretend you don't like me like this!' she said over her shoulder. 'I know it makes you feel right at home.'

'Give me your car keys, beautiful,' he said quietly to May,

holding out his hand and making a swift beckoning gesture with his fingers. She rummaged in the pocket of her apron and handed him her keys.

May couldn't even thank him, she was so distracted, worrying about having left her tables so long and hoping Stella could perhaps give her a lift.

'If I can get a hold of Rob, we could see to them tyres for you,' Harley was saying.

'Harley Daniels, you're so cute I want to barf,' said Connie.

'Careful, sweetheart, someday wind's gonna change and y'all'll be stuck like a mean ol one eyed mule forever!' He winked at her, laughing. 'And your mama says you used to be such a pretty little thing!'

Connie laughed. 'My mother doesn't know shit.' She filled a glass with two shots of Jack Daniels and pushed it across the bar towards him. 'On the house.'

'You know I don't drink that stuff anymore, Con,' Harley said.

'Afraid of what might happen?' she said with a smirk.

May felt a twist of something ugly inside and headed back to her section, Connie's laughter ringing after her. How on earth did all her tyres go flat?

Over the next days, the weather became torpid and heavy, the muggy heat building to such an intensity there didn't seem space for it in the air. May felt sluggish and stupid. She was irritable and short tempered; unable to get her thoughts to connect and had a recurring sensation of having started a sentence and going blank. All this was intensified every time she thought of her car.

Harley and Rob had sorted the tyres for her, towing it to the garage and giving her a lift, but Rob had been convinced they'd been let down deliberately.

'There's too much of this shit going down around here,' he

said. 'It's going to be some of them kids from the high school or up at the home. They don't keep em on a tight enough rein.'

Harley wasn't so sure, brushing it off and reminding them that May's access road was a mess of potholes.

Amy told her to chill. 'Wherever you've got bored kids, you've got pranksters, don't take it so personally.'

May tried to let it go. 'It's probably this heat just addling my brain,' she said lightly. 'I'll see you tomorrow, Amy.'

14

Just before the bridge that took her across the river towards home, she pulled in on the verge and ran down to the river. The thick, heavy air was filling with more heat than it could accommodate. Surely it would break soon and maybe they'd get rain.

College kids were lounging on the floating decks, diving off, shouting, reading, laughing and teasing. She wondered down towards a shaded corner, still squinting in the harsh light that leapt off the surface of the river.

Slipping off her thin cotton dress, she dived into the water in her bra and knickers, without waiting to wonder whether it was a good idea. As she hauled herself out of the water, she realised with a shock she was crying and all she could see was a vivid memory of Harley flashing up through the water like a dolphin, his laughter ringing across the sparkle of river as the drops of water arced quicksilver bright like a meteor shower over him.

May found him standing on a huge granite boulder at the edge of the river in just a pair of cut off denims. He turned as she said his name and squinted, smiling into the late afternoon sun.

'Hey beautiful… where you been at?'

She held up a paper bag and setting it down slipped her arms around him from behind to kiss his hot back between his shoulder blades. He put his arms behind him holding her close.

After a moment he broke away and jumped down. He grabbed a bottle from the cooler, popped the cap and sat at the water's edge.

'I brought some fruit. There was an honesty box by a stall loaded with berries and peaches.'

May took a fat peach blushed and soft with a thick fuzz, which she rubbed off on her frock.

'I love those things; the idea that there's trust in the world.'

He glanced at her. 'Is there? How do you know there won't be an empty stall and an empty box when you next go by?'

'There won't,' May answered and she took a big bite out of the peach.

The juice ran down her chin and she wiped the back of her hand across her mouth. Harley looked at her with a soft expression that made her belly quiver.

'Ahh May...' He sighed, and turned back to look out over the river. 'Give me some of that, it looks good,' he said without looking at her and May reached her arm out and nudged the fruit against his mouth.

He laughed and bit, at the same time taking it from her and rapidly taking another bite so that the juice ran down his arm. For a moment May watched him, then scooted closer.

She held his wrist and starting at his elbow, licked the juice, working up until she reached his pulse. Harley was still holding the peach and she looked up into his eyes, tasted the salt of his sweat. He watched her, breathless and still.

'That has got to be one of the horniest things anyone's ever done to me,' he said.

'Really? You haven't lived much have you?' She chuckled.

Harley kept his eyes on hers and slowly put the peach down.

'When are the others coming?' he asked and May saw he was thinking what she was thinking. She reached out and moved her fingers restlessly on the back of one of his up thrust knees.

'Are you sure that's the horniest place you've ever been licked?' she asked, tilting her head.

'That is not what I said...' he replied, jumping up and shoving his jeans down over his hips and kicking out of them. He stood naked and erect, grinning at her.

'You got way too many clothes on, honey baby,' he said.

May pulled into her drive just as a long, low, rolling sound vibrated warningly across from the mountains. The birds set up a clamour, chitting and scolding and darting about the yard and she felt a thrill of adrenalin as she looked over the fields at the far away flickers of lightning playing about, luminescent across the sky. Still damp from the river, her clothes sticking to her from her impetuous swim, she sat on the porch steps to watch the storm.

There was a crunch of gravel and she looked over to see Harley making his way from Matthew's towards her. His left arm was curled in towards his body, his hand cupped protectively around a lithe, sleek cat the colour of the storm clouds. It had an alert watchful look, but was calm and settled in Harley's arms.

'Oh! Who's this?'

'Hey,' he said smiling down at her. 'I brought you some company.'

She reached out and massaged her fingers gently around the cat's cool, smooth ears.

'You brought him for me?'

Harley nodded.

'Hello,' she said softly. 'Aren't you a fine, fine fellow?' And then she laughed. 'What a splendid sound!' The cat had a rich and sonorous purr that belied his neat, sleek form. 'I didn't like to think of you out here on your own all the time,' Harley said. 'And Matthew said you couldn't have a dog on account of your working hours, so… a ferocious guard-cat will have to do. I have a box somewhere in the truck that might do for a bed for him.'

He was back in moments, carrying a bag of cat feed, which he dumped on the porch, and an old apple crate. Its dark wooden slats almost blackened with age, were smooth and satiny, with faded lettering that bore the name of some long-ago farmer.

'Where shall we put it? Kitchen?'

There was a breath of familiarity in this, she thought, and she wasn't sure how she felt about it. He had always done this; turned up at the house unannounced, unplanned, surprising her.

Once, after one of his unexplained absences, he'd held onto her fiercely and whispered in a furious rush, *I couldn't keep away*. It had brought out a tenderness in her, a longing to show him that coming back to her wouldn't hurt him. Now, she didn't really know if that was true, she just wanted it to be.

Harley crouched on his haunches in the kitchen, lining the box with what looked like one of his shirts. May lowered the cat into it and the feline stared at her for a moment before casually jumping out to stand briefly and then saunter off a short way. The cat stopped to splay in the middle of the floor. They both laughed and startled by the noise, the cat lifted his head and stared again, before cleaning his face.

'He looks quite young,' May said. 'Where did you get him?'

'He's been hanging round in back of my workshop a few weeks. I think someone dumped him—he ain't a wildcat.'

'Clearly not, he's very self-possessed. Has he got a name?'

'I thought I'd leave that up to you,' Harley said, straightening with a smile. 'He's your baby.'

A loud, splitting fork of lightning caught May off guard, 'Wah! Exciting!' she said with a jump. 'It might actually rain!'

'I always knew you to love a storm,' he said quietly and her pulse jumped.

The wind lifted, dropped, lifted again, hushing and sifting through the leaves, ushering a growl of thunder with it. The clouds moved in, close and thick, giving off a strangely purple light but instead of a loosening and cooling, the air swelled with heat.

'Listen to that purr,' she said, crouching and stroking the little cat's head. 'I'm going to have to call him Thunder. It's impossible to tell if it's him making that noise or the elements!'

Harley reached out and scritch-scratched the cat between

its ears; as their fingers nudged against each other he flicked his eyes up at her, before withdrawing his hand and looking quickly away, but May had seen the heat in his eyes and smiled.

He leaned back against the kitchen counter and looked at her with such an intense stillness it made her nerves jangle. What's wrong with me, she thought in frustration. I'm all over the place.

'Do you want something to drink?' she asked, wiping the sweat from her lip with the back of her hand. She reached into the fridge, pulled out a jug of iced water and poured out two glasses.

'It'll cool off in a while, just as soon as the rain gets here.' He took the glass she offered him and thanked her, before draining almost half of it in two long swallows.

'Let's hope so. Did you work today?' she babbled, unable to look at him. 'How was it?'

'It was work,' he said, sounding softly humorous.

He's laughing at me, she thought, sneaking a quick glance at him, and was startled to see a tender look in his eyes she recognised from long ago. It disappeared so swiftly, replaced by his more usual guarded expression, she wondered if it might have been wishful thinking.

He nudged himself from the counter and looked her lazily up and down. 'May,' he said with a chuckle, shaking his head. 'I have to ask. What in hell happened to you?' He picked up a bedraggled lock of her hair. 'You look like you've been in a rainstorm already.'

'Jumped in the river,' she replied, smiling and reached past him to flip the lights on. 'I'm surprised it took you so long to notice, I'm revolting!'

He gave a short laugh and then stopped. With a quick prick of unease, she saw where his gaze had settled and tried to ignore it, busying with another glass of water, mopping a spill.

She'd forgotten about the dark bruising where Mark had grabbed her. In the brightness of the lit kitchen it stood out uncompromisingly on her bare arms. She felt a wave of shame as Harley continued to stare, his eyes flicking to the other arm and the almost identical bruises.

'What happened there?' he asked, looking straight at her, all the playfulness gone.

'Nothing,' she muttered, turning abruptly to the door. 'I'm going back out, it's too much in here.'

He joined her outside where she stood leaning on the porch railings and taking her shoulders gently, turned her to face him.

'What happened?' he asked again, and ran a light thumb over the bruising, letting it rest there for a moment. 'Looks like...' he stopped, rubbed his palm across his mouth. 'Is that someone's *hands* imprinted on your body?' he stumbled over his words.

She didn't want this, this change of mood or bloody Mark Sassello getting in the way again.

'Harley,' she said in as reassuring a tone as possible. 'It's okay. It's over and it's okay.'

He just looked at her as though he couldn't quite understand. 'It's over as in until the next time...'

'No!'

'Or it's over because whoever did that to you is—what? Help me out here, May.'

'I did have a bit of a run in with someone, because I told them to get lost, but it's done, it's dealt with.'

He stood for a moment, flexing and clenching his hands a couple of times, his expression troubled. 'Okay...' he said uncertainly, turning his gaze out towards the coming storm, and it looked as though he might let it go.

'Because you know what?' he said, wheeling. 'That kind of a man, a man who does that to a woman? You can be sure he'll keep it up. Next chance he gets he'll be doing it again.'

'There won't *be* a next chance,' she said emphatically, but he answered forcefully.

'You don't *know* that! People always say that, but you don't know! And it just gets worse, every time, it gets worse, until next thing you know, you end up in the ER or—shit, May, don't tell me it won't happen again like you know something about it!'

She fought tears, angry at the shame she felt, and horribly aware of what lay behind his anger.

The wind had picked up, and the branches of the birches were flailing at the edges of the woods. Somewhere down in Matthew's yard, a repetitive thump, bang, bang of a door being blown open and closed startled Harley back from somewhere else and he rubbed at the back of his neck. 'May,' he said in a low voice. 'I don't know how else to say it. It freaks me out, you know, to think…'

'I know,' she said. She almost stopped there but something made her add, 'I'm glad you care.'

'I. Oh… of course I…' he broke off looking uncomfortable.

They were quiet for a moment and then, as another rumble of thunder rolled through the sky, The Warhorse barked excitedly and a man's voice responded, carrying on the wind.

'I'll go check on Matthew,' Harley muttered distractedly and May reached out to him, wanting him to stay. He flinched very slightly, but enough that she noticed and she couldn't hide she was hurt.

'I can't…' he shook his head. 'I need to go,' he said.

'Okay. I understand.'

He gave her a puzzled look before stroking her hair back from her face. 'Do you?' he asked her. 'Because I don't even think *I* do.'

'So don't go,' she said, and she held his warm hand against

her cheek, closing her eyes. 'Not just yet.'

He said her name with a deep sigh and she softened against him, raising her face, her mouth searching for his, but he let her go and stepped back and May felt a weight like an anchor dropping as they locked eyes and she saw the confusion and something like fear in his face.

'What's the matter?'

'Nothing. Nothing's the matter,' he said. 'I have to go.'

'Harley,' she said quietly. 'Why does this keep happening?'

A fleeting look of something softer passed over his face, but when he spoke, it was gone. 'Don't, May.'

'Don't what?'

'Don't bring all that up. It was over a long time ago and I can't—I don't want it.'

She turned from him wanting to hide, hurt and angry at the confused signals he kept sending, but in that moment she heard him sigh, a low, dark sound full of heat and longing and something flared inside; so he *can* lie, she thought. She wanted to make him sigh like that again, to hear him sigh like that up close to her, to feel it in her hair, for him to sigh like that into her parted lips.

'Harley, what do you think's been happening between us since I got back?' she said, trying not to shake.

'May.' He was tense, now. 'We had a thing. It didn't work out. Let's just leave it there.'

'What are you talking about?' she blurted. 'It wasn't a *thing*! It was more than that, Harley, and you feel it too. I *know* you do.'

Harley jerked his chin at her. 'The physical thing? That's all it is. We were always good there May. If that's what you mean then yeah... I *feel* it.'

Her face burned at his mocking tone, but she also felt reckless. 'I know it didn't work out, Harley, but we were so young. The timing was wrong.'

He almost laughed, a hard half sound. 'Oh please, May! It

wasn't the timing that was wrong. The whole thing was wrong. We were all wrong. I should never have gotten involved with you. I knew you were only passing through. I was stupid. And I'm not making the same mistake twice. Jesus, May…' he broke off, then angrily exasperated, added, 'Let's just *not* do this, okay?'

'What do you mean?' May persisted. 'How was it a mistake?'

'Don't make me do this.' Harley's voice rose, his face taut.

'I will! You can't just dismiss what we had as a mistake and then not explain yourself! Tell me what you meant by that!'

Harley jerked his head back. 'What I meant,' he snapped, 'is that I opened myself up to you once before and got burned. Okay? I got burned. That's it. That's all. I'm leaving now.'

He turned and walked to his truck. She went after him. Something seemed to have become uncorked and it surged through her. '*You* got burned? *You?* Harley! You were the one who started casually screwing half of Vermont, remember? You don't think that might have impacted on us? You don't think that maybe, possibly, *that* might have been your mistake? Has that ever occurred to you?' She hurled the words at him with all she had left.

He turned furiously and May faltered, taking a step back.

'It doesn't matter!' he shouted, his anger rushing at her. 'It doesn't matter! That's not the point! You *left* me!' His voice broke as though choking on his words. 'Without a word! You never asked me nothin, never told me you was leavin—you never said goodbye, you just disappeared. Gone!' he slapped an open hand across his palm and May flinched. '*Gone!*'

'What was there to ask?' She shouted at him, ignoring the pain in his voice, knowing only that this was all wrong, that he *had* to see things from where she stood. 'Harley! You slept with someone else! There was nothing to say, you'd said it all. You didn't want me anymore!'

'How do you *know* that when you never *asked?* I wanted

you, May, it was you who left.'

'You had sex with someone *else!* What else did I need to know, Harley?'

He shot her a look of defiant anger. 'Well, if I hadn't been so fucking sure you were going to leave, I might have done different!'

'*What?*' Anger rose like bile to choke her. 'Are you actually saying that it was *my* fault you slept around?'

'No! Of course not. I'm not defending that…'

'Well good!' she broke in. 'because you should know I never *looked* at anyone else from the moment I met you. It was always and only you.'

'And that puts you in the clear, does it?' Harley's anger intensified. 'You think it's all just about who you're screwing? You were the victim because you weren't fucking around? No, May! That's no good, because what you did to me was a whole lot worse.'

'What I did to you? What did I *do* to you, Harley?'

'That's not a serious question, right? You—you made me—I told you things. I trusted you.' He struggled and stumbled over the words. 'You tore me open, got right inside me, pulled everything out. And then you left me with my fucking guts hanging out!' He balled his fists against his belly.

May couldn't believe what she was hearing, remembering only how much she'd longed for him, how profoundly he'd hurt her. 'Harley, if you had given me one word, one sign that you wanted me to stay I would have done!'

'Don't say that!' he said. 'It isn't true. I heard you, everyone did. You were always reminding everyone you lived in London, that you were travelling, that you were going to go back and get some job in magazines and have yourself a cool little apartment. I'd have been a fool to have believed anything else.'

'Harley! I was nineteen years old and you…' May felt as though her heart was breaking all over again. 'You didn't want me,' she sobbed, desolate. 'My family was there; it was my *home*.'

He looked at her for a long, dark moment and May felt a buckling inside and her throat tightened at the expression in his eyes.

'*You* were my home,' he said, so quietly she nearly missed it. '*You…*'

May sat with her friends in Lou's. It was a dazzlingly hot day at the tail end of August and they were lethargic, reluctant to stray from the air-conditioning. May heard the jangle and scrape of the opening door and looked up to see Harley with Rob. He glanced in their direction and his eyes lit; he said something to Rob who laughed, and came sliding into the booth to sit close to May. He slung an arm around her neck and pulled her against him, dropping a kiss on her temple. He smelled good, of sunshine and warm skin and the leather from the knotted lace around his neck.

'*So, freshmen are arriving today.*' *Pete said.* '*That was me three years ago. Ah! So young, so green…*'

'*So what,*' *quipped Danielle. Everyone laughed.*

'*What are you gonna do May? Ever going to go back to the UK?*' *Pete asked, pulling on a bottle of Corona.*

'*Do you remember it?*' *Stella asked.*

'*Barely,*' *she said, feeling Harley tensing and shifting herself to accommodate him.* '*Eventually I'll go, of course. It's my home. And there's only so much mooching around I can do. Have to start real life sometime.*'

'*But you don't have to, right? I mean you're not going to be kicked out by the government, right?*'

'*No, I've got dual nationality, but I already deferred my place at University and my family are giving me a hard time about it.*'

Harley, shifted abruptly and May slipped. She darted a quick look up at his face, but he was looking impassively towards some distant corner of the restaurant.

'*What're you going to study, May?*' *Courtney asked, eyes on*

Harley.

'English with Journalism, but nowhere that good, so I'll probably end up waiting tables again!'

'Then why don't you just stay? Cut out the middleman!' Stella laughed.

'Or go to college here?' Courtney asked.

'Because it's not free, here,' May said to a cacophony of incredulous questions and demands for clarity.

'You should so blow off London though, May. Shouldn't she Harley?' Courtney pressed and May looked at him with a smile; she longed to know and had never had the nerve to ask him. Do you want me to stay? Just say the word.

'Don't drag me into this,' he said with a cool look, 'May'll do what she's going to do.'

May was stung. And angry at Courtney for pushing this out into the open so publicly; she was sure she saw something triumphant in Courtney's expression.

'Who did Mikey disappear with last night?' Danielle asked no one in particular. She was scribbling frenziedly on the back of a pizza box, chuckling to herself.

'Kristie.' Courtney quickly supplied the answer. 'Why?'

'Just doing a wrap up for the weekly news bulletin and I've decided it should contain more important things than stuff about house inspections and the cleaning rota.'

'Oh dear... be afraid, be very afraid,' Stella intoned.

'Scoot over,' Harley murmured to May. 'I have to get back to work.'

He left without a word, striding across the diner. May watched him stop on the pavement, light a cigarette, then lope in the direction of Hartland Strings. She kept thinking he'd look back, raise a hand, but he didn't.

May wasn't sure how long she sat there after he'd gone, her nose swollen and hot with tears, oblivious to the pouring rain and passing of time. She felt emptied and shocked. His words

158

lacerated her. How had she not known he'd felt that way? If she had only... Her head throbbed and there was a pinching pain in the bones at the nape of her skull.

The rain subsided and May listened to the clearing air, welcoming the cooler breaths across the garden. Thunder found her, pushing and pressing his soft grey head against her and purring loudly. She spoke softly to him as he padded upstairs after her and jumped almost silently onto the bed. She slipped under the covers, without bothering to undress and lay curled, her hand resting on the little cat, with a paw over his nose beside her. She stared out of the window, watching as the hammered silver moon sailed slowly up and through the backdrop of trees.

The dawn chorus was joyful as the edges of the sky drained the night, then coloured up. May finally accepted sleep would never come. She got up and threw off yesterday's clothes. She could smell Harley's warmth on her dress and pressed her face into it, inhaling, unbearably sad.

The day stretched ahead. May went to let the chickens out and feed them. She loved how they acted so nonchalant even though until the moment she got to their enclosure, they were insanely anxious to get out at the soft, fresh grass. She returned slowly to the house, feet cool and wet in the dewy grass, tremulous with anxiety and sleeplessness as her thoughts returned endlessly to last night.

Harley's anger unleashed like that had frightened and hurt her. She had never seen him lose his temper with such force and seeing him like that because she had hurt him was agony. She stared out of the kitchen window thinking she might cook something for Stella and take it round later as she had been off work with stomach flu. She gathered onions, celery, garlic and her knife. She drew the blade down the steel a few times and glanced up again as she heard a rowdy crowd of red winged blackbirds jostling on the lawn under the birdfeeder.

As the oil heated in the bottom of her heavy saucepan, she knocked in a walnut of butter and watched it sizzle and foam until it melted, then ducked out to pick herbs from the raised bed Matthew had built for her under the kitchen window. The warmth of the sunshine seeping through her thin cotton dress and cloaking comfortingly over her shoulders gave her a brief lift, a little moment of freedom, the soft beauty of the garden, and the chit, chit, chitting of the birds helped her breathe. She sighed and raised her face to the sun.

Back inside May turned the heat down under the pan and left it to murmur gently to itself while she went upstairs to have a shower. She wanted to cry when the heat of the water released Harley from her skin and he disappeared with the steam.

'Stella!' May called out as she slammed through the screen door at Woodland Drive a few hours later, simultaneously trying to balance a big, cherry-red enamelled pot and her bag.

She walked into the kitchen and put the pot on the table, as usual shoving heaps of papers and mail out of the way. She heard a distant call and busied herself finding a coffee cup in the heaps of unwashed dishes in the sink and on the draining board. She switched on the machine and cleared out the sink, heaping everything dangerously on one side as she ran the water into it, hot and foamy.

As May stacked plates into the dishwasher, Stella emerged in a towelling robe looking pale and drained, but managing a wan smile.

'Hey, girlfriend,' she rasped. 'You look great; I'll swap your life for mine.'

May grimaced and muttered, 'Perhaps puking for days would be preferable. How are you?'

'Yeah, better. I can keep water down now.'

May poured a glass of water from a jug on the counter and

sat at the table with her coffee. 'I brought you a chicken stew for dinner.' She waved a hand at the pot. 'You can freeze it if you don't feel up to eating yet.'

'Thanks. So, what's up?'

Stella leaned her chin in her hand and looked at May expectantly.

'Harley came over last night… he brought me a cat… for company… It's so sweet.' May felt her mouth tremble with the effort of not crying.

'May… what is it, honey?' Stella asked, her voice gentle.

'I'm tired.'

May's voice cracked and she felt her face contort as she tried not to cry.

'Sweetie, what happened?'

Stella's concerned expression was too much for May; tears streamed down her face. 'It was awful,' she sobbed. 'We had a horrible fight. I don't even know how it happened. One minute he was all over me, the next he was yelling at me.'

Stella balked. 'You guys…' she began and trailed off, shaking her head.

'It all seemed to be going so well. I even thought that, you know, we were kind of… something was beginning to happen between us after all this endless circling about.'

Stella looked inquisitive, tender, her soft, fair brows wrinkled, expressive as a puppy.

'I couldn't have been more wrong,' May went on. 'He just yelled and yelled at me.'

'All this out of nowhere?' Stella asked doubtfully.

May tried to fill her in but found it hard to find the words without crying.

'Ouch,' Stella muttered and made a sharp hissing sound as she listened.

May pulled a tissue out of a box on the sideboard and blew her nose.

'God, it was hideous—but Stella!' she burst out, 'I don't

remember it like he does at all! I remember feeling really close to him. I remember the intensity of being with him. We loved being together, couldn't keep away from each other.'

But then she remembered the fragility too. It was far more complex than she had allowed herself to think, through the long months of remembering and dreaming, of longing to be close to him again.

'I'd forgotten how insecure I felt. He was so unpredictable. And then he started sleeping around and that was that.' May was pensive, trying to remember, to grasp wisps of memory. 'He never told me how he felt about me or what he wanted from us. It was just so intense and physical and... I thought he loved me. I thought he loved me and that he knew how I loved him. Oh, Stella!' May cried again. 'Did I idealise it? Romanticise the whole thing?'

'Well yes, probably, in some ways. First love and all that but don't you think maybe the sleeping around bit was what made it start falling apart?'

May drew a deep, guttural sigh. 'If I'd known how he felt it could all have been so different. I acted all free spirited because I was afraid of crowding him and all the time he...'

'May why are you taking on so much responsibility for this? And excuse me but you *were* free spirited. There never was anything phoney about you. You grabbed life.'

'Did I?' May said, wearily rhetorical. She shoved her spread palms into her hair, massaging at her still tense scalp, trying to ease some of the terrible tightness. 'I'll tell you what's doing my head in, Stella. I never told him I was leaving and it never crossed my mind there was anything wrong with that.' But the moment she said it she knew that was wrong; shame and defiance flushed through her.

'I wanted him to hurt,' she said quietly.

15

It was late afternoon the next day and Matthew and May were sitting on her porch enjoying a cold drink. May had made fresh lemonade and Matthew was enchanted, claiming he had not had anything so good since he was a child in Georgia.

'You and Harley seem to know each other really well, Matthew.'

The old man smiled and rumbled a low chuckle in his belly. 'Oh we sure do,' he said. 'We sure do. But now you two...' He let his words hang in the air a moment.

'Did you know we were together before, Matthew?'

There was something calm about Matthew that made her want to confide in him, something safe.

'Sure I did, sweetheart. I can see you've got history, unfinished business.'

'Unfinished business?'

'Unfinished business,' Matthew said again. 'It'll always get in the way of now.'

She was embarrassed to find herself blushing hotly.

'How long ago was it that you two were together, honey?'

May told him and again Matthew nodded in that slow way, as though he was beginning to understand things that had long eluded him.

'That was around about when Hope and I caught up with him again. He rented a room from us for a while, till he got back on his feet and found his own place.'

'That must have been after my time,' May said, as she remembered his tiny little cabin in the garden of a house just at the edge of town. It had just about accommodated his bed. She had called it the Wendy House but Harley had not understood the reference.

'What do you mean again?' she asked, her brain hearing

something Matthew had said. 'You caught up with him again, you said?'

Matthew looked at May for a long moment. 'What do you know about Harley? His background, I mean.'

May felt he was testing her, but not unkindly.

'Well, I know he had a tough start, he and his siblings were fostered out separately because his mother couldn't cope or something, I was never quite clear and I know they lost contact.'

For some reason, even though she was aware that the two men were close, May felt disloyal talking Harley's business aloud. He had always been so intensely private. The glimpses he'd given her, the things he'd shared had always been at times of great intimacy.

'That's correct,' Matthew said. 'And the other important thing to remember is that they sure did move around a lot. He never was anywhere much before he was moved on again. Nowadays they do things a whole lot different, but Harley, he had a tough time moving on, moving on all the time. What I'm sure you know is that he was a real bright kid. Clever. And people noticed. He had a high school teacher who knew that there were active recruitment programmes for exceptional kids with difficult circumstances to get them into colleges like this one here in town. You know all this?'

May knew some of it, but the details were vague. She had not known, for instance, about the recruitment part. It had simply never occurred when she was younger to even think about how a boy with Harley's background could have ended up at such a hotshot university.

'Now here's where your Harley first came into our lives.'

My Harley, May thought with poignancy.

A movement at the far edge of the porch caught her attention and she looked to see a hummingbird darting from the feeder Harley and Matthew had rigged for her. The bright red sugar water showed up brilliant against the shimmering blue sky.

'Hope and I had a small livery business and we always needed help. Hope came home one day saying she'd found someone to help out, but we had to help him first. Now that was Hope all over. Always rescuing stray dogs and picking up birds that had fallen out of nests.'

He smiled softly, lost for a moment in some private place.

'Harley had flunked out of his first year of college and she had met him in town one day. He was bagging groceries at the food mart, carried her bags to the car... He was a drinker and thin as seed hay, but boy was he a hard worker. And he worshipped Hope. She turned that boy around. She fed him and he quit drinking hard liquor and he took over all the care of the horses. Did yard work and repairs for us and I taught him joinery and such like. Anything he showed an interest in really. And finally, he was ready to go back to school and finish up. Took him a while, but look at all he's made of himself.' Matthew sounded proud, as if Harley were his own son.

'But that was all before I knew him, right? I mean when I met him he was already a graduate.'

'I guess that's so.'

He was quiet for so long May felt he'd said all he was prepared to and wondered who he was staying quiet for.

The lowering sun had a short way to go now before it touched the horizon and was casting flushed licks of light and colour against the undersides of a few sweeps of palest duck-egg blue clouds. May sighed at its beauty.

'So,' Matthew picked up his thread and sounded solemn. 'Harley came back to live with us again for a little while the winter after you upped and went home, I guess it must have been. He was all broke up and Hope thought maybe he was always going to be a little that way, you know? The kind of fellow who'd run on all cylinders, burn out and need to take a little time to get himself together. She was sorry he was drinking again…' he gave himself a little shake. 'But well, he's doing fine. She'd be real proud of him.'

May went about over the next ten days gripped by an almost frightening anger that Harley should seem to blame her entirely, and deep sadness that she had hurt him so badly. It was exhausting and confusing. Matthew's words haunted her; she couldn't get the image of Harley lost and hurt out of her mind.

She was finding it hard to sleep long and got up each dawn weary, relieved that she could get up. She fed and watered the chickens and sprinkled the vegetable garden. Every few days, she replenished the bird feeder and weeded the borders. She hung her laundry out in the brilliant sunshine and drove into town to work shifts at Molly's. Her mind went over and over Harley's words until she felt she was going mad. *You were my home.*

What she couldn't stand was the idea things could have been different. If they had only had the courage to tell each other what they'd felt, what they'd wanted from each other. It was as though they'd been playing a game of first to blink. And now, having spent the past ten years pushing it away, she remembered with a horrible intensity that last time she'd seen him.

He came crowding into the bar with Rob and another girl and jerked his chin in May's direction, half smiling at her.

'Uh… oh…' murmured Courtney. 'The prodigal returns.'

May threw a look of irritation at her, swallowed her fear and fury and stood on wobbly legs, but Harley was already making his way over to their table.

'Hey…' he drawled at them generally. 'What's going on?'

'Just heading out, Buddy. It's late!' Pete said heartily. 'Who wants a ride?' he called around the table.

May looked up at Harley and as her friends hustled about,

shifting and gathering themselves, she sensed their awkwardness. The only one not embarrassed was Harley, who just slid into a vacant seat opposite May and ordered a drink from a passing waitress, who smirked irritatingly at him when he called her sweetheart.

As everyone left, Stella lingered indecisively with a look of concern until May mimed 'I'm okay' at her.

Harley had a smudge of a smile playing about his mouth and raised his eyebrows at her in an ironic, somewhat challenging way. Shit, May thought, he's been drinking and he's riding that fucking motorcycle.

'Where've you been?' she asked.

He continued to look at her and repeated her question as though he hadn't quite heard it.

'You just disappeared, again,' she said, wondering why he was stalling. 'For days. Why do you do this?'

He took a large swallow of Jack Daniels and ignored the question.

'Where were you?' she asked, disliking how she was sounding to herself.

'Around. No place special.'

May didn't know what to say next. He was silently pushing her, goading her; so much so she had the strongest sensation he was waiting to pounce.

'Harley. What's going on?' she said at last, tired and hopeless.

'What's going on? Ah... I don't... you tell me May. What is going on?'

What she wanted to say was, do you still want me? Why so cold? She couldn't speak; her throat was stopped up with emotion and pride. She sat back in her seat, knocking back the last dregs of her now warm beer. The bar thinned and someone switched on lights, scraping and slamming chairs up onto tables and sweeping the floor with bangs and knocks.

'You want a ride home?' he asked abruptly, sliding back out of the booth and stretching lazily up to his full height.

'I think I'll walk,' she said slipping out of her seat and finding herself very close to him. He turned from her just enough for her to

notice and looked out across the bar. She wanted him to say he'd walk with her, wanted everything to be okay.

'You should probably leave your bike here,' she said.

'I'm okay.' Harley rubbed his hand over his mouth and continued to look out over her shoulder.

She felt paralysed by her bewilderment, he was so alien and she had a horrible feeling that finally this was it. He was telling her without saying a word that he was done with them. It was as though he'd closed and locked the door of a quiet, far off, sun-filled room.

For a moment May felt blank, hollow. She reached impulsively and he surprised her by putting a swift arm around her waist and holding her close. She felt him press his face into her hair, felt his mouth gently kiss her and heard him breathe in deeply. As he shifted, the heat of him came through his shirt and she breathed in then thought she was going to choke or faint because he smelled faintly, undoubtedly, of sweat and sex and somebody's perfume.

She drew back, breathing through her mouth, her heart pounding so hard she almost sat down.

'Oh,' she said, desolate. And as she looked at him, he met her eyes unwaveringly with a challenging defiance. She turned and left without looking back.

May had just finished a shift at Molly's, and her mind was far away when someone spoke to her. She felt as though she was answering in slow motion, like an old vinyl record on the wrong speed. She and Lallie had spent hours screaming with laughter, repeatedly doing this with William's LPs when they were little girls until he came in tight lipped and silently furious telling them to stop destroying the records.

She was getting cash out of the hole in the wall and as she turned, she almost walked straight into Doug, staring at her with a look of puzzled concern on his face.

'Hi,' he said, putting a hand on her arm. 'Are you sick?'

'Hello,' she said, 'I am quite well. Just a little overtired, I think. Did you say something?'

He looked doubtful and hesitated. 'I was just wondering if you'll be at Molly's tonight.'

May stared at him for a moment before the blankness started to form into something.

'Oh Dougie! Happy birthday. Momentarily I forgot. Of course I'll be there.' She mustered a smile and said she'd see him later.

She didn't feel like going out at all, but as Doug bounded off, throwing his limbs all over the place, she watched him fondly as he disappeared into the dazzling sunshine and felt grateful for the friendships she had.

As she headed towards her car, she saw Mark and his partner a little ahead peering into a sloppily parked car. She turned sharply, not wanting to see him, and as she walked, remembered the party when she'd told him that she only ever really got herself into trouble when she didn't speak her mind. In which case…

May walked along Main Street trying to keep to the shade of the shop awnings and maple trees. It was breathlessly hot and the pavement shimmered ahead of her as she walked. It was as though the heat of the sun was leaching the colour from the pale blue sky, which faded completely at the edges.

It was incredibly quiet, the only sounds those of the crickets and grasshoppers like the continuous unreeling of a fishing line. Nobody was about. She took a deep breath, rolled her shoulders and knocked on Harley's door.

She had not thought what she would do if he wasn't there, or worse, if someone was there with him; the latter thought came slamming viciously into her mind just as the door opened. He stood, barefoot, wearing jeans and an unbuttoned shirt, sleeves rolled to his elbows, his dark hair roughed about, which gave him an unguarded air. Her stomach tipped with a double lurch of desire and anxiety.

'I'm sorry. You've someone with you?'

He stood tall in the doorway and looked carefully at her, wordless, while his hand strayed up to the knotted leather lace at his throat, fingering it briefly then dropping.

'No,' he said slowly. He was looking at her with a mixture of curiosity, and what she could only identify as discomfort. 'You okay?'

'Harley,' May began then stopped, feeling herself flushing. 'I'm sorry to just turn up like this and I won't take up much—look, can I come in? Just for a minute?'

'Sure.' He moved aside a little and said, 'I've got work in an hour, so…' He trailed off, told May to go on in, and shut the door.

She was in an open plan living area whose back door was propped open, allowing a light breeze to filter through the screen. *The Washington Post* and the *New York Times* were in various stages of post mortem about the place and Harley picked up a few sheets to clear a place for May to sit.

'Drink?' he asked.

'A glass of water would be great. Thank you.'

She felt forced and unnatural, her mouth dry and her manners formal.

Harley padded over to the kitchen and pulled a jug of water from the fridge while her heart pulsed in her ears. She wondered how to start, what to say first. He walked quietly back, gave her the glass of water and leaned against the edge of his desk, watching her closely.

I can't do this looking up at him practically from the floor, she thought with irritation. She stood abruptly, wishing his unbuttoned shirt and the warm sheen of his skin weren't so distracting. He closed the buttons, eyes still on her.

'I don't really know why I think it's okay to just come barging in on you like this, when you've made it quite clear that you'd rather not see me.'

His eyes flinched a little. He took a deep breath and put his hand over his mouth, rub, rubbing a slow back and forth movement, then dropped it down onto the desk again.

'I have spent the last week or so thinking a lot about...' she stumbled a little, then pressed on. 'Thinking about that last... ah... conversation we had.' Her courage faltered as he looked away, mouth tightening at the corners. 'It seems so pointless to explain or defend myself,' she said. 'I'm just so tired of explanations and "it's worse for me" and any of that, I just want to say I'm sorry.' She felt the hated tears pricking at her eyes and went on. 'I would give anything to go back and do things differently... anything. And to have had the courage to tell you what I was really thinking, how I really felt. Even if you didn't feel the same way, just to have told you.'

Harley looked away over her shoulder, his eyes flickering, before the shutters came down.

'More than that, though, I'm sorry I was a coward and didn't confront you, or at the very least say goodbye, tell you to your face I was leaving. I'm ashamed of that.'

He was unable to look at her and she went on. 'So in the absence of the ability to time travel...' He smiled at that. 'All I can do is say how sorry I am I hurt you. I did love you, Harley, the only way I knew how. I love you now.'

His eyes darkened and he looked away. She hadn't meant to say that and felt hot and miserable.

'I understand that you can't or don't... so that's it, really.' She trailed off. 'Really. That's it. And now,' she said briskly, turning from his impassive response, which was worse than anything she had imagined 'I. Will. Go.'

'May, wait.' His voice sounded stopped up. She turned her head and saw his hands held open in a gesture almost helpless. He dropped them to his sides, 'Thank you.'

16

'You heard about poor Harley, right?' Turtle's wife, Cathy, asked without looking around.

May was standing behind her, waiting to use the soda station. She felt a swift, sick roll of nerves. 'No,' she said, trying to keep her voice steady. 'What happened?'

'He got beat up out by the dumpsters a couple nights ago. Crazy!'

'Is he okay?' Her hand shook as she filled her tray of glasses.

'Connie says he looks rough, but he's okay.'

May distributed her drinks at high speed and strode to the bar, ignoring the voices calling for her attention. She jerked her head at Connie who came slowly over, wiping a glass.

'Hi Connie,' she said, nervous. 'Do you know what happened to Harley?'

Connie leaned on the counter top in front of May, her expression cool and a little wary.

'Couple of kids jumped him, they were waiting for him out back.'

'How do you know they were waiting for him?'

'They called his name.'

'Oh my god, that's horrible! Why would anyone do that to him?'

Connie shrugged, 'Not everybody thinks he hung the moon, May,' she said in her languid way. 'If you shit where you eat, eventually someone's going to take you out for it.'

May looked at her with disgust. 'What are you talking about?'

'Oh, I'm sorry, my talk too trashy for you?'

'Oh for fuck's sake,' May said, not quite under her breath. 'He's your friend, he's my friend,' she said, her voice clipped.

'Can we stop with the point scoring a minute? Are you saying some jealous other half beat him up? Is that what you're saying?'

'All's I'm saying is that it wouldn't be a surprise to me if that was it—I mean, you know the guy as well as I do,' she said with far too much innuendo for May's liking.

She turned on her heel and tried to focus on getting through her shift. It was almost impossible, distracted by images of Harley in a heap amongst the bins. She was terse and short tempered with a new waiter taking longer than normal to get the hang of the computer system. Turtle would wonder if she really was management material, if she couldn't be civil under pressure, she thought wryly, as she apologised to the poor guy.

While she and Amy cashed out they talked it over.

'What I heard,' Amy said as she sorted out her tips. 'Was he was in here steaming, after some kind of verbal bing-pow outside Bentley's with Mark Sassello. No one seems to know who started it, but it got ugly. Next thing, Harley was in here laying in to Connie, telling her she doesn't know what she's talking about—man, he was in such a shitty mood, he could've started a fight in an empty house—then he leaves by the back door and gets jumped.'

May's mind leapt to the hideous image of Mark beating up Harley. 'But, there's no suggestion it was Mark, he had just gone on desk duty at the time. How do you know?'

'Connie told me.'

Why, wondered May, had Connie even thought to check that?

'How's it going ladies?' Turtle poked his head around the door.

'Turtle, do you have a number for Harley?' May asked.

'Sure!' He waved a hand at the rolodex on his desk. 'It's under Maintenance. D'you hear what happened?' he grimaced.

'Have you seen him?' she asked.

'Yeah, he's still standing!'

Relieved but still uneasy, May wanted more; more information, more reassurance, but she wanted to see him herself too, or at least hear his voice.

'You'll be lucky if you get him, though,' Turtle said over his shoulder as he zipped out of the office. 'You know he never has his phone switched on.'

She gave up after the third attempt and tried to reassure herself by remembering how blithe Turtle had sounded about it.

For the first time since she'd arrived in Vermont, she felt uneasy walking out of work into the darkness of the parking lot behind Molly's. A prickle of nerves scuttled up the back of her neck and over her scalp and she glanced over at the dumpsters, piled high with black rubbish bags.

Half an hour later, she pulled into the driveway and saw Thunder perched on top of her mail box. He jumped down and ambled casually up to her, rubbing his cheeks against her legs.

'Hello, fellow,' she said stooping down to fondle him gently by his ears. 'How are you?' The light was on in the studio in Matthew's garden. 'Come on, let's go and see him, he'll know if Harley's alright,' she said to her cat and then laughed. 'Unless you can tell me, Stella says you're his familiar!'

Thunder looked disdainful for a moment, then condescended to accompany her just to the fence.

Matthew looked up from his drafting table at her knock and smiled as he came and opened the door.

'Well, hello there,' he said, putting a hand on her shoulder. 'How are you now?'

'Fine, but a bit worried about Harley.' She explained what

174

she had heard and he nodded a little as she spoke, his expression attentive.

When she finished he took a moment before he spoke. 'Well, now,' he said thoughtfully. 'What time do you have?'

'Eleven thirty.'

'Hmm... okay, he will have finished work. Come on in and set yourself down a moment,' he said, turning from her and going over to a wall mounted phone. He picked it up, dialled a number and threw a reassuring smile at May. She felt an unfair fizz of irritation; surely he knew phoning Harley was a useless exercise.

'Hello? That you son? Mmhmm... I have me here a young lady, who's a little concerned about you and says you may be in some kind of trouble.' He laughed a low belly chuckle and looked over at May with another reassuring smile. 'Are you sure?... mmhmm... oh *I* see... mmhmm... well sure I'll tell her, but you... I am *not* starting, sounds to me as though you're the one who's set on starting things you didn't ought to be starting...' He laughed again, this time making a swatting gesture with his free hand. 'Okay, I had enough. You're alright you say? Well, that's fine. I'll be sure and do that. Alright, goodnight, son.' He laughed again and hung up.

'Matthew,' May said, getting up off the stool and twitching with a mixture of relief, irritation and curiosity. 'How is it that you just have to pick the phone up and he answers and the rest of us get the disembodied voice of an autocratic woman telling us that the phone is switched off? Always!'

Matthew was laughing by the time she finished, 'Would you like a drink of something? A little night cap?'

'Thank you.'

Matthew reached into a small counter-top fridge and pulled out a bottle of apple brandy and poured them each a small glass.

He walked out to the small seating area outside his studio

and they sat side by side, facing the pastures.

'When Hope was very ill and having hospice care, Harley had himself a landline put in. He used to call me each morning around 8am, just checking in, to see what kind of night she had had, if we needed anything. After she passed, he just kept that old phone line going, so as I could get a hold of him if I needed to. I believe I am the one person in all of Vermont who has that number.' He chuckled. 'Well, me and the folks at AT&T!'

May looked at him incredulously. 'You have your own private line? You're like a couple of old despots, Matthew! Honestly, if you knew how frustrated people get trying to get hold of him...'

'A fellow's entitled to a bit of peace and privacy, isn't he?' Matthew interrupted good-naturedly.

'Hmm,' she said grudgingly. 'So he's alright? What did he say?'

'Not a great deal more than you already knew, but he said it's superficial. He knew the kids. Evidently he and Rob paid them a call...'

'What? You don't mean...' but she stopped herself. Harley would never... what? Rough someone up? How did she actually know that? Why did she keep thinking she really knew him?

'Now, May,' Matthew was saying with an almost sorrowful look on his face. 'You don't think for a minute that he would do anything like that?'

'Of course not,' she said hurriedly. 'Why did they do it? He's so well liked in town.'

'I know. Evidently someone had given them the idea that if they were to give him a fright, then some petty charges against them would be dropped.'

'You're kidding me, that's awful! And why on earth would they believe that unless...' she broke off, not wanting to finish the thought.

'What's on your mind, May?' Matthew asked her, pensively.

'Well,' She looked at him, wondering if he knew what she was thinking. 'Why would they believe that the charges against them would be dropped, unless the person asking them to rough up Harley was actually in a position to... to... to make that happen?'

'That is what I was wondering,' Matthew said.

17

'Honey, how are things with you and Harley?' May could hear several questions barely concealed in Stella's one.

It was the end of the week and the friends were preparing supper at the house in Woodland Drive. Some friends of Stella and Pete were back from Mexico and Stella was keen for May to meet them.

May carried on stripping the tiny thyme leaves from their woody stalks, chopping them swiftly before answering lightly.

'Interesting question. Not sure I can answer it.'

'What do you want me to do with these?' asked Stella, indicating the garlic cloves she had chopped into chunky slices.

'Oh, just tuck them in under the tomatoes—they need to stay moist or the heat of the oven will scorch them.'

May ripped up fat leaves of basil, loving the almost aniseedy waft of the mature leaves, so different from the very earliest summer ones. She poked them into the peppers, snuggling them under and into the cradling tomato halves.

'Why do you ask?'

'It's just that he and Frannie are real good friends and she asked me to have him over so they could catch up. They were going to see him another time, but tonight's the only one he's not working at the Roth for a while. I could put him off if you like. I don't want it to be uncomfortable.'

'Does he know I'm going to be here?'

Stella shot her a look and carried on poking at the peppers. 'I think so, I mentioned you when I asked him to come. Does it matter?'

'I don't know. Yes. No. I mean I want him to have agreed to come knowing I'll be here, rather than thinking I won't.'

Stella stopped what she was doing and turned to face her.

'May,' she said, laughing. 'You're not making any sense, honey!'

'I know! It's just I've barely seen him since we had that row and I'm not sure he even *wants* to see me. And then all that awfulness with him getting kicked in by those boys...' She gave Stella a hard look, then took the plunge. 'Stella, would you think I was mad if I told you I thought Mark Sassello had something to do with it?'

'No, but I'd hope you were wrong. Why?'

May explained and added, 'I'm scared he's more of a nut than we realised. I'm not saying it was him, but apparently Harley confronted him about that night he freaked out at me and grabbed me at Bentley's and not two hours later, he gets jumped by a couple of kids who are told if they do it, the cops'll drop a potential trespass charge.'

'Jeez,' Stella breathed. 'Have you talked to anyone else about it? Harley?'

'No, I told you I haven't seen him apart from once just after the row.'

'Did he call the cops when it happened?'

'I don't know. I doubt it, Connie was mouthing off about him not even having a doctor look at him. Maybe I will talk to him about it,' she said. 'I'm glad you invited him, I really would like to see him, Stella. I'd kind of like to just show him things can be okay—normal between us. It's probably better to have other people around actually. We always seem to get into some kind of *thing* when we're alone.'

'Okay. If you're sure?'

'Definitely. I'd like to see him.'

And if I can't have him, I want to be friends. She felt her cheeks flaming and looked down so that Stella would not see her face.

'Great. Now...' Stella seemed to sense her cue and moved swiftly in another direction. 'What do you know about Jesse and Fran?'

There was no way Fran had reached five feet in height and everything about her was rounded off. Her head was helmeted by an exuberant mass of burnt orange curls; she had a plump round mouth and a face of dimples and apples.

'Good to meet you at last!' She said heartily to May, her voice surprising in its depth and gravel.

May was handing Jesse a glass of wine, when the back door slammed open, banging against the woodpile.

Pete came crowding in talking loudly. 'Great timing,' he crowed, 'come on in, buddy.'

May's pulse tripped then restarted as she heard Harley's low response.

'Good to see you, Pete.'

'Whoo-wee!' Pete laughed. 'That is award winning, man!'

Harley raised a hand and gingerly touched his fingertips to the purple and yellow bruising on his cheekbone, 'Yeah,' he said self-consciously. 'Looks worsen it is.'

'Hey, Stella!' Pete hugged his wife's head against his belly before she had time to stand up. 'Everyone here?' He smiled broadly on the assembled company, 'Don't get up Frannie!' he joked as he leaned way down to kiss her on the cheek. 'May!' he boomed. 'Where've you been? You don't call no more; you don't bring me flowers no more! What's going on?' He gave her a huge enveloping hug. 'Harley, man, you know everyone. Have a beer.' He handed him a cold bottle of Bass from the fridge, and topped another one for himself.

Harley smiled at May, hesitated briefly then went over to Frannie, with an affectionate, humorous expression. May felt a moment of derision, mocking herself for thinking for one second she would be happy with simple friendship. She noticed his tanned, strong forearms, the muscles rising and falling beneath his skin as he held Frannie's shoulders in his hands and wished he would do that to her.

'Hey, Frannie,' he said, kissing her on each cheek, then looking her in the eyes with a smile. 'Good to see you back.'

'Good to see *you*, my friend! How *are* you?'

'Same old, same old,' he said wearily with a low chuckle. He pressed his hand slowly across his mouth as though rubbing something out. Frannie reached up and smoothed his hair from his forehead and May was both touched and envious. He shook his head and straightened.

'What on god's beautiful earth happened to you?' she growled at him. 'Who's been trying to rearrange your face?'

'Aw, it's nothin Frannie, just some kids.'

'Not any of ours, I hope,' she said sternly. 'I've got a pet project with you in mind and I don't want anything putting you off!'

May was intrigued but the moment was swept away as Stella announced, 'Dinner! Come on people! Sit anywhere you like. I've single-handedly made an amazing meal that May had absolutely *nothing* to do with and I don't want it to spoil.'

Everyone laughed. Stella was indignant. 'What! You think I couldn't do that?'

'Maybe, but only if May was directing you from the wings,' Harley said in a voice that warmed her belly.

'Sooo…' Jesse drew the word out absently, his focus on some candle wax he'd begun to work away at. 'Are you a cook, May?' He shot a piercing look at her then refocussed on what his fingers were doing.

'Sort of,' she replied, hesitantly.

'She devises the specials menu at Molly's and cooks like an angel. If I wasn't already shackled to Stella I'd marry May for her cooking. And she's not even my type!' Pete laughed delightedly at himself and Stella gave an amused shake of her head.

'You wouldn't have him, would you May?'

'Oh I don't know,' she mused, 'he's good for some things, like playing DJ.'

She raised her eyebrows and glanced in the direction of

the silent stereo. Pete took the hint, scraped his chair back and went to the stack of CDs.

'And what do you mean I'm not your type, you cheeky bugger? You shouldn't divide women into types,' she said, then drawled in a dreamy voice. 'If you *loved* me, you'd *love* me.' Everyone laughed.

Pete came and sat back down as Van Morrison began to sing 'He Ain't Give You None'.

'But guys, if you can make it to our Labor Day party, then you'll have a chance to sample some of May's baked delights. She's not allowed to come to the party unless she brings brownies! Right May?'

May smiled. 'So I've been told.'

'I can't believe the summer's nearly over,' Frannie said.

'You'll come won't you Harley? You can bring a friend.'

May scowled at Stella, wondering why she'd suggest he bring someone. Stella gave a 'What?' look and shrugged.

'So. Mexico,' said Harley, turning abruptly towards Frannie and Jesse who were sitting on either side of Stella and Fran started telling him about the orphanages they visited, something to do with a charity they were involved with.

'We needed to see for ourselves how the money raised is being used and if we could share some of our expertise with them. We'll be reporting back to the trustees right, hon?' she said to her husband, without waiting for a response. He murmured something affirmative.

'Is that your work here, Fran?' May asked.

'Oh no. That's an extra. My food-on-the-table job is social work.'

'I think,' Fran was addressing the table as Stella put a bowl of peaches and blueberries in the middle. 'There's a very reactionary climate out there when it comes to attitude toward people at the bottom of the social pile and a lot of what goes on is just some kind of holding pattern until these

182

kids can be passed on to another agency.'

'That's awful, Fran,' May said sadly. 'It seems so cruel to just toss these kids out to the wolves.'

'Well, it's hard when you have to function within the system. And you know, until we start addressing the root social problems, we're just going to see the same things happening with the same families. And they're so ripe for exploitation when they leave care—take those kids that decorated your face,' she turned to Harley and smiled. 'Who knows what their story is?'

'Come on!' Pete bawled. 'Does there always have to be a story?'

'Well yes, Pete, there does.' Fran said, brisk. 'Every one of us has a story. Even you, my friend! I imagine yours goes something like this: My parents liked each other, they stayed liking each other, we lived in a house that never got repossessed, I got educated at no more than three schools. I went away to college and met a cool girl I liked and she liked me back!'

Pete laughed with everyone else. 'So that's my story, huh? I never realised I was so interesting!'

Stella poured more wine into everyone's glasses, her face soft in the candlelight before turning to Fran. 'Tell May what you told me about our break-in.'

'I can't be too specific for obvious reasons, confidentiality and all; I'd have to kill and eat you all,' Fran said. 'But we were particularly interested in the case because the kid Pete caught was one of ours.'

She leaned back in her chair, shifting her back until she looked more comfortable.

Harley had sat up a little at the turn in the conversation and looked at May with a familiar dark intensity, his eyes glittering a little in the candlelight.

'What's this?' he asked. Pete filled him in briefly. 'You never told me someone broke in while you were sleeping.'

Harley's voice sounded hard and there was a split second of silence. May realised with embarrassment he was addressing her directly.

'No,' she replied slowly, 'I don't suppose I did.'

'Well get this, Mayflower,' Stella steered the conversation back. 'This kid was being kind of pimped by an older man. Oh! not for sex or anything heinous like that,' she said, as May looked at her in horror, 'but for housebreaking and petty thefts and things. Like a kind of modern-day Fagin. Can you believe it? So he scopes out places and then sends the kid in and in return he's like his protector; gives him a home, food, that kind of thing.'

'And,' broke in Fran, 'I mean, what he's doing is wrong but he's taken an interest in this kid who used to be in our care system and perverse as it sounds, he's given him a kind of security. He seemed to genuinely care about him in his own screwed-up amoral way. I mean it was clear there was no kind of abuse or neglect, he just taught him to rob.'

'And coerced him into incredibly dangerous situations. That's not abusive?' burst in Pete, 'What if someone had shot him defending their property?' He looked really uncomfortable. 'Surely you don't think that's okay?'

'Oh my god,' said May feeling sick, 'I forgot about your gun thing.'

Fran smiled a slow, tolerant half smile. 'Of course I don't think it's okay. I guess what I'm saying, Pete, or trying to say, especially at work and to the policy makers, is let's just try and learn something from this. These kids need better support on the other side; decent role models; someone who cares about what they make of themselves. They sure as heck need something we're not giving them. This kid was someone's big brother, Mom gone, Dad doing time for dealing drugs and he gets shunted out into the world without a safety net. Has to leave his younger brother behind in the care home. Anyhow...' She shifted again and her tone had a more light-hearted ring. 'That's my new pet project. Transitional mentoring program for our young people and here is where my man Harley comes in, I hope.' She glanced swiftly at him before going on. 'If we'd had something like this for Danny, instead of leaving him vulnerable to the Fagin of the county, he maybe wouldn't have ended up doing time for breaking and entering.' Her tone by the end had become almost bitter and she gave a tight-mouthed smile to the table.

'How come they're not getting this stuff from the families who foster them?' Pete asked. 'What's wrong with these people?'

'I know.' Frannie looked pained. 'Two things. One, there are more kids than foster parents. Sad, but true. So they have to be in care homes. And two, there's obviously something wrong—and this is a private view, guys—with the way we provide care in our homes. What do you say, Harley? You'll have far more insight into this than me.'

Harley shrugged and said tersely, 'Doubt it.' He reached across May and poured himself a glass of water. 'Anything I ever experienced is so long ago it's barely relevant. Hardly remember any of it.'

He flashed his teeth at them all before throwing a reproachful glance at Frannie. She returned an apologetic smile.

Without thinking, May reached out a reassuring hand and rested it on Harley's thigh. Uh oh, she thought. Red wine. She had barely formed the thought before he had grasped at her hand, his warm fingers curling round hers and holding them hard. She glanced sideways at him, but he was staring ahead into the flickering candlelight.

18

May arrived early for Stella and Pete's Labor Day party. She parked on the street close to the house and picked her way carefully round to the back door, carrying a huge tray of cornbread balanced precariously on an even bigger plastic box of her brownies.

'Hi, Stell, I forgot the brownies,' May began to tease as she kicked off her flipflops and shoved them over to the side with her foot.

'Get out!' Stella shouted back. 'No brownies, no entry!'

She was pouring sparkling lemonade into a beautiful old glass punch bowl that belonged to her grandmother.

'Grandmaw gonna be turning in her grave right about... Now!' she finished triumphantly as she poured in the Pimms.

'Where do you want this, Stell?' asked May, indicating the cornbread.

'Can you cut it up and put it out next to the chilli? Cover it with a cloth or something. The flies don't seem to realise summer's almost officially over.'

It seemed a distant prospect to May too, as she looked into the soaring blue sky and felt the heat of the sunshine. It felt as though it was melting over her bare arms and shoulders, through the cotton of her sundress. Stella turned up the stereo and as they worked, they bellowed along to Ike and Tina Turner; songs they'd been singing together all their lives.

'Come on, Mayflower! Give me some o your corny harmonies!'

May could never remember the words the way Stella did, but she sang anyway and it made her utterly, completely happy.

As the shadows lengthened, Stella went about putting out ashtrays on the deck and arranging cushions and chairs artfully. She poured another bag of ice over the bin full of bottled beer and checked the flame under the vat of chilli. May was dolloping thick soured cream into bowls and uncovering plates of grated cheese.

'I can't believe you bought ready grated cheese, Stella. You're unbelievable.'

'I can't believe you waste so much of your life using a grater. It's like you're Amish or something.'

'Is anyone coming to your party? Did you actually invite anyone or did you just assume Everyone Would Know?'

'May,' said her friend slowly. 'Have a drink. Shut up. Whichever order you like. Pimms?'

'Don't mind if I do.'

'Don't mind if I join you.'

The two friends sat out on the deck sipping, sunglasses on, joining in the music sporadically and making each other laugh.

'Hey-hey!' called Pete, joining them a few minutes later. 'Just like old times. If I squint, you look like teenagers again!'

The sun dipped and got lost behind the trees and Stella got up with a stretch and said, 'Help me light the candles, Mayflower.'

They had slung ropes of solar fairy lights around the balustrades of the deck and as the darkness edged in they flickered into life. The two women moved about, lighting dozens of votive candles Stella had set about the place in a collection of old preserve jars she kept just for this. The idea of her saving jars to preserve anything was, as May frequently pointed out, simply a joke.

The party was in full swing, loud and full of shouts of laughter, voices raised to join choruses of songs, people squashed on sofas and perching on laps, when May saw Harley arrive with Rob and a pretty blonde woman who she instantly felt anxious about; she'd forgotten that Stella had suggested he bring someone.

He smiled through the crowd, his eyes warm, and then disappeared, swallowed by bodies. The night wore on, a few guests left pleading early starts, but the rooms and deck remained packed. Stella looked delighted, beaming every time she caught May's eye.

As May went to the kitchen to get more wine, she saw Harley deep in conversation with Liv and her boyfriend, an overseas graduate student from Holland. Liv had introduced them at Molly's one night and he'd seemed sweet. She was longing to get near enough to speak to Harley and see if things were really okay between them. He had left the dinner the other night without a word about anything that had passed between them and to her disappointment had let go of her hand without a look or another touch.

She was wrestling with a corkscrew in the kitchen, trying to open another bottle of white wine. Just as she was about to fight her way back through the throng, Doug waylaid her. He was drunk and determined to tell her all about his summer on the Jersey shore. May's eyes kept darting over his shoulder; she felt certain that by the time she got back into the other room, Harley would be gone. She was relieved to see the blonde he had arrived with pinned against a wall gazing at Rob and laughing every time he opened his mouth. He's not that funny, lady, she thought wryly.

'Doug. Help me fill up some glasses,' May shouted over his loud monologue and she shoved one of the open bottles into his hand. She headed off purposefully, tailed faithfully by the ungainly Doug, who hadn't a clue what he was supposed to be doing.

'Mayflower! Come and meet...' Stella called from her perch on the arm of the sofa, then followed May's darting glance towards Harley and chuckled. 'Uh oh... okay... singing!'

Harley was now sitting on the edge of a chair intently

tuning an acoustic guitar, his bent head almost touching the body as he listened.

May pushed through the room, pulling Stella by the hand behind her. She saw Harley pass the guitar to Rob and pick up the twelve-string propped beside him. The two picked out old blues tunes and kept laughing and starting again while the blonde woman attempted to sing. May watched Harley's fingers as they moved on the strings. She felt a deep sigh well up inside her.

'Come on girls, we need you,' Rob called out to May, 'this sweet thing's givin it her all but she needs a bit of help on the harmonies.' He gave them a wink.

May smiled and sat on the arm of Stella's chair watching Harley who looked over at her, his hand pausing over the strings. He plucked a few chords and sang in a comic, croaky old blues man voice.

'*The way you love me/ you love me so/ I can't do my homework.*'

'*Any mo!*' Rob joined him loudly.

There was a general burst of laughter and then Rob picked out a tune that made May feel a low swoop of dread.

'You guys!' Rob called. 'You gotta remember this!'

Harley caught her eye, face still, before he shrugged, half smiled and joined Rob, picking out the sweet melody with its gentle, minor key. The noise level seemed to drop a little as though the room itself was trying to hear it better. May's heart filled; memory brimmed through her. She almost couldn't bear it.

Harley sang now, softly, almost to himself.

'*Some say that I wronged you/But I don't know how,*' he looked up at her and nodded encouragingly as he went on, fingers plucking sweetly at the strings. '*If I could make it right/You know I would/You know I would…*'

Rob layered on some chords.

Stella broke off from her conversation. 'Harley! You da

man!' she called out delightedly. 'Sing it, Mayflower.'

May sat taut, listening for the moment to come in and as she began to sing a hush shivered across the room as her voice joined Harley's, close and harmonic, rising above then swooping back down to tuck in alongside his.

May was surprised she could still remember the words; she'd been unable to listen to it after returning to London; it hurt too much and even now, the tenderness, longing and sweet poignancy of their voices soaring, brought her to the edge of tears. '*There's no way I can change the past / or your pain...*'

Bloody booze she thought, but she knew it wasn't that, and she stole a quick glance at Harley watching her intently while he sang, his fingers picking at the strings.

The company clapped and whooped, Stella hugged May and Harley passed his guitar over to someone else. He picked up his bottle of beer and tipped it at May before taking a swig. She couldn't take her eyes off him.

It was well after midnight and the partiers were still there, scattered. Rob was still twanging the guitar with an open bottle of scotch and the blonde lying on the sofa with her feet under his lap, still giggling loudly at everything he said.

Stella was sitting with a huddle of friends, discussing the merits and demerits of the new Star Treks and May was sitting on the floor, playing a game of dice with Harley and Pete, Doug and Amy.

Harley was sitting beside May shaking and rolling the dice, his long legs bent up; he was so close she could feel heat coming from him as he moved. May began to feel a rising sense of anticipation. She was acutely conscious of the slubby weave of his shirt; of his arm brushing hers from time to time when he leaned forward to roll the dice; the throaty warmth of his voice as he murmured and laughed. She wanted him so badly she felt distracted and clumsy.

'May, you're still shit at games!' whooped Pete.

'Pete, you idiot,' she clucked at him. 'You can't be shit at dice, it's a game of chance.'

Harley slid a swift sideways smile at May before swigging from a bottle of Bass. She was afraid he'd realise how close he was and draw away and she wanted it so badly; to feel him like this, so relaxed.

Pete roared as he won the last roll and called for another game.

'I'm done, buddy,' Harley said. 'I'm going to call it a night.'

May wilted. Was it always going to be like this, so tantalisingly close and then nothing?

'Okay if I leave my truck in your drive? I think I need to walk home.'

'Sure, man, just leave a key in case I need to move it. But you can crash here if you want. You can have May's old room.' Pete smirked.

'I imagine May will be using May's old room,' Harley replied pointedly, standing and stretching. He clasped his hands over his head, let out an exhalation and looked down at May with a thoughtful expression as though weighing something; it scared and excited her.

Someone started playing Proud Mary and a great chorus led by Stella started. May caught Harley's eye and an almost imperceptible jerk of his head, a flick of his eyes towards the open doorway before he reached out a hand and pulled her up. Letting go of her hand instantly, he walked towards the open doorway, saying something about needing air.

Outside, the night felt voluptuously warm. The whir of crickets and the low trill of the tree frogs filled it and May breathed in the scents of pine and eucalyptus from the backyard. She hopped up to sit on the porch railings and hooked her feet around a couple of balusters. Harley looked down at her and smiled, candlelight from around the deck flickering on his face.

'Lost your shoes again,' he said, glancing at her bare feet.

May smiled up at him. He shook his head a little and for a long time said nothing. Finally he said, 'You always sang so pretty, May.'

'So did you,' she replied and they smiled.

She reminded herself to breathe and held his gaze as he nodded. Her pulse was tapping away distractingly at her throat and she felt out of her depth wanting to touch him, a little afraid.

'Well…' he said and then stopped and just looked at her, before smiling so sweetly he looked almost shy. Then he leaned in and kissed her mouth, his lips slow and warm. A tight spot of tension she hadn't known was there, softened and began to melt across her shoulders and down her back. She felt his hand touch her face; his fingers hook and wind through a lock of her hair, then run down its length. She was tentative, afraid he might change his mind, but as his mouth opened on hers, she sighed, leaning into him trying to deepen the kiss. He moved back, momentarily confused and indecisive.

'What is it?' she asked softly, kissing him on the soft curve at the corner of his mouth. His breath came sighing warm and sweet, his lips mumbling against hers.

'I… all I do is… I can't sleep, May.'

Hope rose, floating through her. 'What's keeping you awake?' she asked, hooking her feet around his legs, drawing him closer.

He exhaled a long breath. 'I wish *you* would,' he said. 'You want to come home with me and keep me awake?'

Desire spread through May's blood and bones. 'Well, yes,' she answered slowly, wondering at how his words came so easy after all the clotting and staggering. 'Yes, I do.'

Harley kissed her again and May had to wrap her legs tighter around him to stop herself falling. God he feels so good, she thought, forgetting where she was and wanting to devour him right there. He made a low, throaty sound, burying his face in her neck. 'Come home with me,' he breathed. 'Just come home.'

It took them ages to walk back through town as they danced along a deserted Main Street together and stopped to kiss in shop doorways, until Harley muttered against her breast, his voice dark and full of laughter, 'I can't hold out much longer, baby. If we don't make it home soon it's going to be right here in this doorway.'

'Tempting.' She laughed, her head singing, full of him.

They almost fell through the door as Harley turned the key in the lock. He was pulling at his clothes, pushing the straps of her dress aside, kicking the door shut with his boot. His hands seemed everywhere; he was pushing her back and back until she felt the wall, cold against her hot back. They tangled and tore at each other and she felt the sharp rasp of his jaw, his breath on her skin, mouth hot and tender. Harley was yanking at his belt buckle and May, impatient and lustful, thrust her hand under his and deftly unbuckled it with a few curt moves.

'Nice,' he muttered with a low chuckle.

He was sliding his hands up her thighs, pushing the slipping skirt of her dress up, gripping her hips; his fingers hooked at the waist of her knickers pulling at them, pushing them down. May couldn't keep up with him. There was something incoherent and almost frantic in how his hands flew about her and his apparent inability to slow down. Her breathing had become shallower and she was unable to think now. She twined a leg around him pulling him closer, undid the last buttons on his fly and pushed at his jeans, sliding her hand inside.

'Now?' He rasped, pressing his face into her neck, nipping at her.

'Yes.' Her breath rushed the word out of her mouth and he muttered something, while fumbling with one hand and tearing at the foil of a condom packet with his teeth.

He didn't breathe at all at first, then he let out a long, low groan that seemed to ride on his out breath as he thrust himself into her. She held him close and then for a moment they were both breathlessly, utterly still. May, desperate to hold the moment, to capture it, thinking this might be it, I might never be with him again after tonight, and then, oh don't, don't spoil this.

She began to move against him slowly, slowly at first feeling his breath caress her face, hearing her own as though it came from somewhere beyond her while the sensation of it escaping her lungs in short, abrupt, exhalations felt heady and narcotic.

Harley held her hips still with gripping hands, whispered wait, wait, pulled out a little way, breathed then muttered 'okay' and eased into her again, his mouth opening on her.

'Oh god... I can't...'

May could feel how desperate and close Harley was to coming.

'Don't,' he gasped. 'Wait... wait...' His words rode on each breath.

'It's okay,' she breathed in his ear. 'Let go.'

May pulled him hard against her, into her, clutching at his damp skin, reaching down between them, fingertips teasing. His body quivered, went rigid, he dropped his head then threw it back with a short, hard, bursting shout, pulsed, gasped a breath.

Moments later, Harley's head lay heavily over May's shoulder and he was breathing hard, holding her with both arms around her waist. She held him close, feeling his heart pounding, her hands in his hair stroking him while her own breath subsided, kissing the soft skin of his nape, feeling an overwhelming tenderness. He nipped at her shoulder with his teeth and turned his head to kiss her deeply, before drawing himself out of her then holding her tight against him.

He was quiet and May was about to ask if he was okay, when he said, 'I can't remember the last time I came so quick, kind of left you behind. Sorry, baby.' He kissed her on the side of her mouth.

'Well, I can't remember the last time I had sex up against a wall.' She chuckled softly in his ear. 'In fact,' she said kissing him, 'It was probably with you.'

'You mean you've had sex with other people?' He gave a low laugh then added a little dryly, 'that's not quite how I imagined it when I couldn't sleep nights.'

'No?' May smiled, warming at the idea that he'd lain awake imagining having sex with her. 'How did you imagine it?'

'Oh, you know. I'm pretty conventional really.' He smiled at her disbelieving 'yeah right'. 'So mostly I imagined you in my bed. But not always.'

'Oh, so you imagined it more than once?' She smirked.

'You want me to count the ways?' he drawled at her. 'Hmm... on second thoughts better not. You might think I'm some kind of...' He was pulling away now, peeling his skin off hers and he looked her over. 'Baby, you look like I've pulled you off the street.'

'You did.'

He laughed and snaked his arms around her, nibbling and kissing her through her hair making hungry sounds, pushing her hair off her hot brow and kissing it.

'Have you seen yourself?' she asked, holding the waist of his unzipped jeans and giving them a shake so the belt buckle jingled. 'You too look uncommonly dishevelled!'

Then, in an exaggerated try at his accent, added, 'You wearin your pants so low you look like you in the state penitentiary, baby.' Harley laughed.

She slid her hands under his unbuttoned shirt, running them over his hot, damp skin, before he stepped sharply from her and stripped off lightning fast. He gave her such a smile, then, so sweet and open and heart-yankingly honest she felt as though she was the only one in the world who had seen that smile.

'Now you cain't tell where I'm from,' he said, shaking his head so his hair fell sheltering over his eyes.

For a moment she was quiet. Her heart was full and she wanted to tell him.

'Harley...'

'Come here,' he interrupted, drawing her over to the sofa. 'I think my legs might just give up on me that was so...' He stopped and his face grew serious. 'Just come here.'

They lay together for a while and May traced her hands over his body trying to learn it; trying to find what might be familiar to her, he held her in his arms, his hands roaming warm and restless over her.

'You smell so good,' he said, kissing her in the crook of her neck, his unshaven chin tickling and scratching. 'First thing I noticed when you came back. You still don't wear any perfume.'

'I sometimes do now,' she said and, in that moment, realised she hadn't, not for months.

'Well don't, just don't.' He ran the firm tip of his tongue warm and slick, up the pulse along the side of her throat. 'It's *you* I want.'

May moved over him and kissed his mouth, licking at it. 'So, that bed you keep mentioning. Is that all part of the fantasy or do you actually own one?'

Harley laughed and tipped her off him, standing and padding over to the kitchen.

'Through there.' He pointed at the open doorway to the side of his cluttered desk and said, 'Glass of water?'

She nodded realising how parched she was; it was a hot

night and she was damp with sweat. She got up and walked to the bedroom, hesitating on the threshold. She didn't hear Harley join her, but felt him kiss her in the crook of her neck from behind, the combination of his warm mouth the light graze of his stubble, the hot flutter of his breath making her sigh. He reached an arm around her and slid the cold glass with its pearls of condensation across her breast, then up towards her mouth, tipping it up so she could drink, then as she turned her head away indicating enough, he poured it in a fine stream across her body shoulder to shoulder, put the glass down as she gasped and cursed him, laughing.

Turning her to face him, Harley ran his hands down her arms and linked his fingers in hers.

'Let me look at you, beautiful.'

He had a hot, sleepy look in his eyes and dipped his head and ran his tongue over her, licking at the water, his breath audible, or maybe it's mine she thought as she felt her skin start to hum. He let her hands go and she held on to him as he began to stroke her, one hand at her breast, the other sliding down her back.

'You like to lay down with me, baby?'

May smiled. They lay on their sides facing one another and she looked into his eyes. She saw herself. He traced her face with a light hand.

'I can't quite believe you're here,' he said softly.

'Nor me.'

'You have no idea how wound up with wanting you I've been.'

'Of course I do.' She laughed, but she was wondering what had changed his mind. And, more unwelcome, had he scratched that itch? Oh don't, she willed herself to stop this train of thought, just… stop.

She floated her fingertips over his lips, the rise of his cheekbone, down his jaw, resting in the dip of his collarbone while he touched her in long, soft, sweeping strokes along her side and hip, her belly and thigh. Long moments passed while they gazed at each other, smiling, sighing, stroking skin and hair, breast and shoulder, everywhere, over and over, again... again.

May felt as though they were learning a dance together, instinctively. She breathed the heat of him, the smell of his skin, the salt of clean sweat, the leather lace knotted around his neck and found a tender spot just at the juncture of his hip and groin where the skin was so soft and his response so sharp she kept returning to it with light teasing fingers, substituting her tongue after a time.

And so they began again, this time with slow purpose, lingering and savouring and May felt time slow down then drop out somewhere. Harley's breath came in light, shallow huffs, through parted lips, a smile fluttering across them from time to time as she touched him, running her hands over his back and flanks.

He was more vocally responsive than she remembered and with each sigh, each word of encouragement her confidence grew.

She drew his hand up to her mouth to kiss the palm and bite along the edge, at the sensitive pad of his finger, and Harley clutched at her hand so the blue veins in his wrist stood out and May delicately traced her tongue across the paler skin there, watching for his response. His eyes flew open and she saw a hot flash of surprised recognition in the look he gave her and the bloom of a smile that spread across his face reminded May of something long ago; of sunshine and peaches and loving him by the river and how he'd been touched by her optimism and belief in the goodness in people.

Oh my god, she thought, feeling her throat constrict. Why do I want to cry? Why now, when I'm here?

Harley drew her down onto him, into his arms and held her close, soothing her, one hand in her hair murmuring, 'Oh,

May, what is it? Don't cry.'

'I don't know.' she was unable to say how much it hurt her to be there with him like this after so long. Afraid he'd misunderstand and think she regretted coming. 'I can't explain.'

'Yeah… I know,' he crooned into her hair. 'I know.'

May lay in Harley's arms, listening to the birds begin their clear sweet songs through the screened window and his breath slow and even; feeling his lips through her hair and his arms clasped tightly around her. This, she thought, is all I wanted.

'May?' he said quietly.

She was riding a swell of sleep so seductive it took a moment to answer.

'Mmm…'

He was quiet for such a long time she felt herself drifting again.

'You are staying, aren't you?'

For a confused moment, May thought he meant the rest of the night until he said, 'In Hartland.'

May cradled his face with her hand, kissing his chest where her head lay.

Aah… she thought. 'Yes,' she said and slipped off the edge into sleep.

19

May woke with a pounding head, her mouth dry, and reached for the glass of water on the nightstand. Eight o'clock. If she left now and hurried, she'd have time to collect her car from Stella's, get home, shower and get to work. She was on a late double shift.

The morning sun slanted under the half-closed bamboo blind, gilding the foot of the bed. The lower half of one of Harley's legs was exposed where the bed sheet had ridden up and there was something about the boyish way his foot was turning in that made a quick aching grab at May's heart.

He was lying on his belly, hair rumpled and pushed about, stark against the whiteness of the pillows. One arm was flung across her, the other tucked into his chest. His breath came slow and even and May took in the warmth of his tanned skin in the golden morning, the sweet thrust of a shoulder blade. She traced his fingers with hers, remembering how they'd stroked and coaxed and played her and slipping out from under his arm, leaned gently over and whispered a kiss into the hollowed curve between his shoulders, breathing in the grassy, musky scent of sweat and skin and sex. Oh if only you were awake, she thought as she slipped out of bed.

She wandered about finding her things; her dress from beside the sofa, her knickers twisted and rolled in on themselves, limp at the foot of the sitting room wall, and she scribbled a note telling him she hadn't wanted to wake him and wrote her mobile number at the bottom.

She let herself out, quietly shushing Piper and fondling her ears as she whistled and thumped her tail, then stood a moment on the quiet porch. Everything appeared the same as it had been yesterday. But nothing is, she thought, before stepping onto the dusty yard and making her way down the deserted back street, parched and dusty from the long, hot summer.

She should have been tired, yet as she walked, she felt vibrantly alive. She could see the colours of the birdsong as well as hear it; taste the slate dark tang of tar and dust rising from the road; feel the crowding colours of the vivid scarlet and fuchsia pelargoniums and heavy headed hydrangeas, bursting lilac and rose through white picket fences.

She walked down Main Street with all its bars and restaurants, the college bookstore being unlocked by someone pulling the metal security blinds with a rattling, clattering rush at the end. She passed the florist and gift shop and the owner who was throwing water from one of his zinc buckets, sloshing it in a sparkling surfer's wave in front of him and jumping back from the splashes and waving cheerily at May as he always did. She saw her friend, a manager at Lou's Diner, scuttling off with her hand raised.

May felt as though she was one buzzing hum, a singing tremor of life. Her fingers were tingling and she had the strongest urge to leap into that huge soaring sky. Oh, oh, oh! She trembled with the joy of the beautiful morning and the memory of last night and hearing his words as she'd fallen asleep. *You are staying… aren't you?*

At last. At last…

She broke into a sprint, crazy-fast at first, then her strong legs settled into a hard, rhythmic run until she'd broken a sweat and was breathing hard. She reached the end of Main Street and passed Woodland Drive, heading on down to the river.

At the water's edge she stopped, panting, swinging her arms like windmill sails and broke out into a huge grin. She ran her palms over her hot, sweating face shoving them up into her hair and got a sudden waft of Harley on her skin.

It's you I want…

She shrugged off her jacket and threw herself off the dock and into the river.

When May finished work, Harley still hadn't called. She tried his phone but it was switched off. She felt flat and stupid and the two hours of sleep she'd got the night before hit her.

She drove carefully home in the darkness, feeling the road as it undulated beneath the wheels without bothering to put any music on, wondering why she'd thought it would be different or what she'd been expecting. She felt like a schoolgirl who thinks she has a boyfriend because someone snogged her at a party.

It had been hard to leave that morning without seeing his face, without seeing herself in his eyes in daylight and now she wondered why she hadn't woken him. You should have just done it, woken him and faced it there and then. Coward.

Her thoughts lurched wildly back to the night before. Had she read it wrong? She couldn't have. *I can't quite believe you're here.* Perhaps that was all he'd meant. Can't believe it. Just that. She tried to conjure up his tone of delight and wonder, his tender voice, the warmth in his eyes, but it kept being crowded out, drowned by louder voices; the fact of his not calling.

What if in the cold, sober light of day he had decided that being involved with May was too hard? Assuming that had even been what was in his mind. What if for him last night had been about sex on a hot summer night, nostalgia, booze?

As she slowed the car and pulled into her drive, the sound of the engine lowered and the gravel crunched and prickled under her tyres. She switched off the ignition and lights.

There was a brief moment of nothing, then she leaned back in her seat and blew out a long breath; her shoulders slowly loosened, relaxed. Her ears, which had been roaring with the air, rapid and hot through the open windows, buffeting her hair, began to still, to clear. She became aware of the familiar, the welcome, the comforting sounds of a Vermont summer night.

She leaned her head back and heard the crickets ringing rhythmic, steady, sure. The languid heat, thick with darkness, slipped through the open window. She relaxed and smiled. This, she thought. This.

And tomorrow, I'll put my fingers in the warm earth and scoop it aside and plant out my lettuce seedlings and Matthew might come to tie in the rose.

Finally, she got out of the car, her scratchy, anxious mood softened. She moved to slam the door and a spike of fear forced everything else aside. Something dark and silent was slinking out of the far shadows of her garden, making straight for her. *A wild animal that has no fear, you want to keep out of its way*, Matthew had told her more than once. *Could have rabies…* May stood still and held her breath.

Then she heard a low whistle coming from Matthew's porch.

'Piper, get back here girl.'

May breathed again, feeling a mixture of rushing relief that she wasn't about to get attacked by a mad critter and a surge of nerves, because Piper meant Harley. She leaned back against the car for a moment before heading across her garden towards the party fence.

'Good evening gentlemen!' she called softly.

She heard Matthew say something and the two men laughed before Harley came out of the shadows and leaned on the fence while she walked through the dew-drenched grass.

'Hey,' he said smiling.

'Hey yourself,' May replied and leaned up close to him. She trembled with lack of sleep. Or maybe it was being so close.

'So…' Harley gave her a curious teasing look. 'Is that how you roll? Keep me awake all night, then disappear; leave me without a goodbye or thank you and just a fake phone number?'

May couldn't speak for a moment. 'Fake phone number?'

'I tried calling you. You left a number out I think. Should I read something into that?'

He raised an eyebrow, flashing a smile at her.

'You keep yours switched off,' she countered. 'Should I read something into that?'

He laughed, paused, then said, 'Y'all going to invite me over, or do I have to stand by this fence all night howling at the moon?'

May smiled and stepped back. 'Be my guest.'

He jumped the fence and joined her, slinging an arm around her neck, planting a kiss on her temple as they walked together up the sloping garden towards the house.

'Harley.' She felt nervous all over again.

'Hmm?' he carried on walking, but May thought she sensed a tightening in him.

'I—last night—you asked me if I was staying. Why? What did you mean?'

'Did I?' he answered vaguely. 'I don't know.'

He moved away from her and went to sit on the porch steps. 'May, pretty much all I really know right now, is that when I'm not with you I want to be, when I'm with you it feels good. So I guess...' He broke off and slid her a sideways glance, serious. 'I don't know what's going to happen? Do you?'

May felt uneasy, afraid of what he meant by this. She realised she wanted some kind of declaration, affirmation. She almost told him but her courage deserted her.

'Of course not,' she replied. 'Maybe even less than you. I left London without tying anything up. I didn't know what I was doing. The only important thing after Sarah died was to get away—No,' she corrected herself, needing him to know. 'I had to come back here. Wanted to. But I've left a trail of loose ends and my family and a good job...' She stopped, worried she'd said too much.

'If you think you're going back, tell me now.' He gripped her hand, pressing it against his mouth. 'Please.' His use of the word touched her deeply. 'That's not something I want to find out later.'

She looked into his face and found a fragile stillness. 'I can't imagine ever living back in London. But how can I know? And if I can't promise, what? Would that be it for us?'

'Shit, May.' He was very quiet. 'Last night—it's kind of stupid, ain't it? I guess I must have thought us getting together like that would give us all the answers.' He smiled at her and she felt herself relax a little as he put his arms around her, drawing her close. He smelled so good; warm and a little of fresh wood shavings. She kissed him.

'I'm so glad about last night.'

'Oh me too, baby.' He kissed her back. 'You want a do it again?' He gave a low chuckle.

She quirked an eyebrow at him and he laughed. Okay, she thought, pulling him to his feet. One day at a time. They headed inside.

PART TWO

20

The days had grown shorter and colder. Fallen leaves piled up in dank, dark heaps against walls and fences or were corralled by more careful, organised people than May into bins and compost heaps to turn slowly, meltingly into crumbly leaf mould and then returned to the earth.

For the past two months, when she wasn't working May spent long sunny afternoons walking out in the woods, sucking in the clean cool air, drinking in the extraordinary sight of so many leaves turned red, gold, fired up with the orange of a setting sun against the backdrop of sky vividly brilliant, which showed off the darkness of branches curling, twisting out and up. The whole world seemed to be singing a great gospel chorus of colour and sensation and May felt there was nowhere else she would rather be.

She found her way home with her arms full of flame-coloured maple leaves that she thrust into a blue stoneware jug, tucking in a few of the exquisite gold fringed fluttery white branches of birch, which grew on the edges of the nearby woodland.

It was odd, she mused, and wonderful, that no maple tree had the same red shade of leaves, as though they were consciously flaming to outdo one another.

As soon as the sun had set, the temperatures plummeted and it was easy to forget during the day that the nights could be so cold. There was always a fire in the grate after dark and May spent most of her time in the west-facing side of the house, soaking up as much wintry light as she could.

Harley worked incredibly long hours. The Rothko Centre had a full schedule of shows from around the country, orchestras, ballet companies and rock bands and he worked late almost every night of the week. Often, he came home to May after the show had finished.

Sometimes she was up, other times he woke her as he climbed naked into her bed and wrapped his chilled body around her warmth. She loved the way he burrowed into her neck with his face, murmuring and nibbling softly at her, how he wrapped his arms around her and held her.

'Ain't nothin in this whole world like coming home to you, baby,' he'd murmur and she felt it deeply.

He kept his joinery business going around these hours and as he was an early riser he was often up and gone by the time she woke for work. It felt strangely dreamlike to May. They spent few ordinary hours together and she began to long for something more. Having dreamed of just having his skin on hers, now she wanted more. She wanted him.

As fall became winter, the roads were frequently icy before the salt trucks came out and at Molly's one morning there was a subdued air as she came in for her shift. One of the bartenders had written-off her car trying to avoid a deer on an icy road after her evening shift.

'It's amazing she got away with superficial injuries,' Turtle's wife Cathy was saying, as May came up onto the floor. 'Seems it turned over several times.'

'That gives me the shivers,' said May. 'I still feel like I'm driving on the wrong side and those roads are so narrow in places that it seems there's nowhere to go if something's in your way.'

'Yeah, and most people drive so fast, you don't have much of a chance.' Amy had joined them, leaning slothfully back against the bar, waiting for her first table.

'I drive like an old lady,' said May, not entirely truthfully.

'No old lady I know,' said Amy grinning, and she did a mime of a crazed driver peering up and over the wheel, moving at breakneck speed.

'Come on people, let's hustle.' Turtle came bustling up from the kitchen shooing them all about before him like a flock of chickens. 'You think any passing trade is going to venture in here if they see a bunch of you in a huddle? C'mon now.'

On a rare night off, Harley sat reading quietly with May on the sofa. She had her feet up in his lap and he was holding one, rubbing at the sole with his thumb, slow and firm. She glanced up at him and watched his face as he read the paper, feeling a rush of warmth to see him there so relaxed and unguarded.

'Oh man.' He gave a low laugh and shook his head. 'Listen to this, a wildlife "expert" has said that the way to stop black bear fatalities from chocolate overdoses…'

'What…'

'Is to—can you guess? What does the wildlife expert suggest? You got it, stop leaving chocolate as bait. Clever guy.'

He shook his head again and lapsed into quiet. Every so often she'd look up to find him quiet faced, watching her. He smiled and looked back down. As they sat, the fire flaming and occasionally cracking, the phone rang. Without looking up Harley released her foot and tipped her legs off his lap. She got up and walked across the room. Lallie's voice skittered down the line, full of warmth and laughter.

'Hi Babe, how are you?'

'Lallie! How lovely!' cried May. She walked out of the warm sitting room, into the kitchen to potter while she chatted.

Harley looked up as she came back and sensitive as a whippet, put down his paper.

'What?' he said, with a smile.

May sat beside him on the sofa and swung her legs up so she was leaning back against him. He put his arms around her and nuzzled her hair.

'What?' he said again.

'She wanted to know my flight details for Christmas.'

'Oh,' he said in a carefully neutral voice and looked around her at the paper.

'Harley,' she said suddenly, 'would you come with me?'

'Ooh no.' His voice was emphatic. 'I don't do Christmas.'

'Well I do,' said May, wondering why he didn't.

'Then do it here.' His voice was light, but she could sense he was trying hard to keep it so.

'Oh I *can't*. It's so much more expensive for the four of them. Anyway, I already have my ticket.'

'How long for, again?' he asked. She felt a prick of irritation; she'd told him numerous times.

'A month. You know that.'

'That's not just Christmas, is it?'

'Well no,' she answered, trying to stay patient. 'There's a lot of stuff that needs doing. I need to see my old editor, there's Sarah's house, my flat. It's a long way to go and I...' It hit her hard. 'I miss my sister,' she finished quietly.

'Sure you do,' he murmured quietly, looking sad.

'Why don't you come for some of it?'

Harley released May from his embrace. 'I don't do London.'

'Oh come on Harley.' She managed a laugh; his try for a joke reassuring her a little. 'You can't "not do" a whole city!'

'Watch me.'

'Seriously, why not?'

Harley, with a fleeting look of irritation, deflected with a statement. 'Look, this is your thing. You're the one who wants to go, so go but don't drag me into it and act like I'm being unreasonable.'

'Harley, that's so mean! You make it sound like I want to leave you. I want to see my family. I don't want to leave you.'

'Then don't go.'

May felt trapped by his finality. 'I have to!' Fear and frustration came out as anger.

'Look,' Harley said, his voice curt. 'You go, you stay. Whatever. You're an adult now May, you don't have to do everything your family tell you to do.'

He flashed her a brilliant, slightly savage smile and got up to throw a log on the fire.

'Oi!' she said finding her voice. 'Don't you pull that on me, Harley. That sounds rather unpleasantly like emotional blackmail.'

She stood tall and glared at him and he straightened and looked back without flinching.

'Does it? Well let me think. The last time you went back there, it was supposedly in no small part because of pressure from your family. Now here we are again with you going back and you say it's because of pressure from your family.' May tried to break in but he raised his voice. 'All I'm saying is you're not a kid anymore so you get to decide. It's quite simple.'

He turned from her and looked around the room fitfully, lifting the parts of the paper and some cushions that had fallen on the floor.

May took a breath. 'It's *not* simple. I want to see them; I want to stay with you.'

'Well, I can't decide for you.'

'I'm not asking you to. I just want to... to... what are you doing?' she asked, panicked.

Harley had started out of the warm, fire-lit room and was halfway down the dark hall before he stopped, turning to face her.

'I'm going back to town,' he said, avoiding her eyes. 'It's late and I have an early start tomorrow.'

'Since when was that...'

'May!' Harley turned to her, face taut. 'You said...' He clapped his hand over his mouth paced away then turning back his voice came tight, controlled. 'You said you were staying. You said that.'

'Harley!' May was exasperated. 'I'm not leaving here; I'm just visiting them. That's what people do; they visit their families. There is a difference. How can you not see that?'

The moment the words were out of her mouth, she heard how thoughtless, how wounding they were and his face, stricken, confirmed it. So she didn't fight him, she reached out and to her intense relief, he moved swiftly into her embrace, held her against him fiercely.

'I can't,' he spoke into her hair. 'I can't...' But no more words came and the way he clung to her made her cry.

As they lay together later, she spoke tentatively. 'Have you ever thought maybe... your brother and sisters might be trying to find you?'

Harley sat up so suddenly, May nearly fell off the couch.

'No,' he said sharply. 'I have never thought that.'

The brittle, closed look on his face frightened her, but she pressed on, 'Why?'

'Don't,' he said emphatically and rose abruptly to stand by the dying fire.

After a moment, she screwed up her courage and joined him, putting a gentle hand on his arm. He drew her to him.

'Sorry,' he said quietly.

'It's okay,' she said. 'But...'

'Just forget about it,' he said brusquely, then more gently, 'sore spot. Let's just forget it, okay?'

Deeply uneasy, she agreed, unwilling to hurt him or push him further away, but forget it? She couldn't do that.

The night before she flew to London, May fell asleep in Harley's arms listening to his quiet steady breathing, loving his warm skin against her own nakedness, but she woke to find he was lying beside her staring out into the darkness.

'Mmm. Sorry,' he murmured softly into her hair. 'I didn't mean to wake you.'

May tried to see what was in his eyes. 'Are you okay?'

He didn't answer, but drew her into his arms, holding her hard against his body, murmuring into her hair, 'Can't get you close enough.'

He began to kiss her, one hand in her hair holding her head, the other skimming over her breasts, her belly, sliding warm and calloused between her thighs.

'Help me forget,' he mumbled against her mouth. 'Just fo a while.'

We should talk, we need to talk, she thought. But his hot mouth and coaxing, urgent hands were crowding out her thoughts and she let herself rise up and ride with him.

21

London, December

'My God! You look amazing! What's happened?' Lallie was crowing over May, letting her go then hugging her again, while the other passengers in the arrivals hall swarmed past. 'I can't believe how well you look.'

'I told you it was doing me good to be there,' May said a little smugly. Lallie gave her a playful swat. 'You look dreadful, what are they doing to you?'

They laughed together and headed towards the car park. Lallie kept an ongoing litany of questions and information until May stopped and said, 'We've got a month, Lal, slow down!'

But Lallie didn't and after only a few days, May was feeling breathless with it all.

Since her arrival, she'd been haunted at night by dreams of weeding endless gardens of all descriptions, totally ineptly, and woke so anxious on her fourth morning she found herself nervously checking the time and counting backwards, wondering when Matthew's day would begin. She knew he was an early riser—all old men are, he had told her—but she knew that this was really much too early and she would have to wait until she got back from her day out with Lallie and the children.

Lallie had decided they would spend the day at the British Museum. Tillie and Max thought it a boring idea, or rather Tillie pronounced it 'bor-ing.'

May couldn't help feeling a little sympathetic. The London visit felt to May as though everything she did was a catching up session; that somehow her sister was trying to sell her London.

They skated at Somerset House, went shopping at

Liberty and had tea at Browns. They walked in Richmond Park and fed the ducks in Kew Gardens. She loved being in the company of her fervent little nephew Max, in the throes of a passionate obsession with Nelson, insisting on buttoning his coat with one arm inside, and being shadowed by Tillie, whose assertive little voice, constantly questioning, forced May to think about why things were so, but she missed Harley so badly she could barely concentrate and his phone was never on.

Lallie seemed to be attacking this visit and the short block of time they had at a frenzied rate, moving swiftly from one activity to another, fearful of empty space and time. When she caught herself thinking like this, she felt guilty.

She snatched a sight of her sister's face darting quick, anxious glances at her, asking if she was having a good time and realised that for Lallie, this visit held great significance.

Max trundled around on his hands and knees pushing a Playmobil horse and cowboy in front of him, murmuring, 'It... will... be... bor-ing, bor-ing, bor-ing.' His singsong voice pitched just about right to be heard with absolute clarity. Lallie was not taking it well.

'Tillie, how many times...' she broke off exasperated and turned on Max, her voice wheedling at first, and pitched a little higher than usual. 'Maxie, it won't be boring...'

'Bor-ing, bor-ing, bor-ing,' he sang.

'Stop it! Max, just because Tillie says a thing...'

'It will though, Mama,' Tillie persisted. 'You have to be all walking, walking, walking or standing everywhere or...'

'For Heaven's—if you insist on being bored you will be and it's not just walking and standing, there are lots of really interesting things to see. Don't you want to see the mummies?'

Tillie was standing rigidly, her hands on her hips, staring at her mother.

'What is it?' Lallie asked, seeming to check her brusque tone.

'How rude,' Tillie said, her tone so exactly like her mother's May very nearly laughed. 'You got right inside what I was saying.'

'Mam-aaah,' Max was wailing. 'Listen. To. Me.'

Lallie flew from the room, chucking commands over her shoulder as she went, and they piled up on top of each other like a heap of unironed laundry. Evidently uncertain of which to do first, Tillie and Max settled on nothing. Max went back to his cowboy, singing a different libretto under his breath. Tillie came and leaned against May's legs, silent, mutinous and tearful and May felt such a strong connection to this little creature it made her throat contract. They did not speak. Tillie played with one of May's fingernails, fitting her small fingertip under then over, under then over. May smoothed Tillie's russetty hair; it was slippery and feathered and fell back straightaway, to where it had just hung, seconds before.

Tillie twitched a little. 'What mummies?' May felt the oddest start of recognition, as she tried to formulate an explanation. She remembered how her father had struggled pedantically with the pronunciation as May had tried to picture, without success, what they might find at the British Museum.

'Not Mommies, May. Mummies. They're Mummies.' But May couldn't hear the difference.

A room full of mummies. What would they be doing? Were they waiting to be chosen, like the orphans in Oliver Twist? She wondered now if her father had quite realised how odd it seemed to May at, what was she then, three? four?

Lallie swept back in. 'Right, coats on. Shoes on. We're going.'

May gathered her energy and stood, stretching and making loud yawning noises to make the children laugh.

'Come on guys,' she said, 'let's do it. You never know what we might find.'

Lallie and the children were sitting down to crumpets and cocoa that afternoon, after a thorough visit to the museum. They had not made it to the mummies. A Children's Trail had caught their attention and they spent the day following clues and prompts to find statues of men with elephant's heads and cats with gold nose piercings. May slipped off into the sitting room to phone Matthew, keen to hear how everything was, to hear his warm, somewhat quavering voice. He was sweetly reassuring and sounded amused.

'Don't think this old man can take care of business while you're away?' he teased gently.

'Well...' she said infusing her voice with uncertainty, teasing him back. He laughed, as she'd known he would, and heard another low voice in the background followed by laughter.

'Oh, you have someone with you, I won't keep you.' She hurried on, as Matthew joined the laughter.

'Oh that's just a fellow I know who's cutting up about his girl phoning me an not him.'

'Harley? Oh!' May was thrilled, then annoyed. 'Well if he ever switched his phone on he might get a call,' she said sulkily and Matthew laughed at her.

'You want I should put him on?'

'Only if he's up for it.'

There was pause and then Harley voice husky and low came to her.

'Hey, beautiful.' He sounded laconic and far away.

They talked a little awkwardly, each offering the usual vaporous niceties; May feeling shy and clumsy. Bloody phone, she thought.

'It's cold here without you,' Harley said and the smile that she thought she heard in his voice, gave her a little courage.

'I'll be home soon,' she said, with a smile of her own.

'That's good, because Thunder misses you,' he replied.

May put the phone down and joined Lallie on the sofa and immediately noticed a difference about her sister, a subtle chilliness.

'What?'

'Nothing,' Lallie inevitably responded.

May at once followed the prescribed route. 'Come on, something's wrong.'

'No. I'm fine.'

'Lallie, everything's cool, then I make a phone call and suddenly you're all frosty?'

Lallie took a deep breath. 'Please tell me,' she said almost nervously, 'that's not the same Harley who couldn't keep his fly zipped and broke your heart.'

May felt clumsy and stupid so she said nothing, but she burned with unspoken feeling at her sister's reaction.

'Oh no, *May!*'

May tried to put something into the complete blank of her mind and failed; she felt horribly trapped.

'Why?' Lallie asked. 'Why would you get involved with someone like that again?'

She got up and moved over to the kitchen area, cleared plates, crashily emptying them of their detritus and stacking them on the counter above the dishwasher. Tillie, sensing something unappetising, slid down from her chair and pulled at her mother's arm.

'Mama, can Maxie an me do a teddy school?'

'Of course Til, but don't use all the loo roll.'

'We won't because that's for teddy hospital. We want to do teddy school, don't we Maxie? And can we have it in your room?'

'Yes. Okay. But you *must* tidy up after yourselves. I want to be able to get into my bed tonight without having to fight with a million soft toys.' She gave Tillie a tender look. 'And let Maxie make some ideas.'

The two scarpered and Lallie turned to May as she came

slowly over.

'Cup of tea?'

'Okay,' said May, not really wanting one but willing to take the olive branch.

'I don't understand.' Her sister looked tearful and May felt confused.

'Well, nor do I. Why are you so upset?'

'I'm upset, May,' Lallie sounded as though she was talking to Tillie. 'Because you went back to Vermont in a vulnerable state and you've started seeing someone again, who treated you like shit.' Her voice wobbled as she finished speaking and she took a faltering breath.

'It's not the same,' May said, hearing how inadequate her words must sound. 'Neither of us is the same.'

There was a long silence before Lallie turned back to the washing up. May picked up a tea towel and began to dry.

'God I hope you know what you're doing,' Lallie murmured, wrapping the bread and putting away the jams.

'Of course I do. And I wish you wouldn't worry so much,' May said, but not quite meaning that. 'You don't need to. It's good, Lallie. We're working it out as we go along but it's good. I'm very happy there. You noticed yourself how much better I am.'

'How serious is it?' asked Lallie, not acknowledging May's point.

'I'm not sure how to answer that,' she said. 'It's serious to me...'

'Well wasn't that the problem last time?' Lallie seemed to pounce. 'You took it more seriously than him?'

'No.' May was emphatic. 'It was far more complicated than that.' But it gave her the shivers to hear Lallie reduce it to that. *How do you know?* A voice whispered insidiously. *What makes you think it'll be different this time?*

'But, May, what about us?'

'What do you mean?'

221

'Me? The family? Without each other...' she couldn't seem to finish and May reached to put an arm around her.

'We'll always have each other, Lal.'

'Not if you're thousands of miles away.'

'Distance can't break what we have,' May said, fervently believing it true. 'It is hard and I miss you too. A lot. But I,' she struggled to find a way of saying it that wouldn't be hurtful. 'I feel suffocated at the thought of living how I was.'

'But you wouldn't be! You don't seem to realise that you would have started to get over it—Sarah, all of that— wherever you'd been. It would've got better, you just didn't give it a chance, and now, I'm sorry if I've come at this all wrong, but what I'm also afraid of is that you'll waste a whole load of time and energy on a relationship with no future and it'll be much harder to plug back into your old life and more importantly, your *career* when you come home.'

Somehow, being spoken to as though she was Lallie's teenage daughter—a familiar feeling, she reflected—took the fight out of her. She looked at her sister a long moment. 'Lallie, I am sorry if this is hard to hear, but Harley or no Harley, home to me for the foreseeable future, is over there.'

'Yeah,' Lallie said. 'I see that. But I think he's got more to do with it than you're willing to admit and *that's* what I'm scared of.'

22

To May's initial relief, Lallie didn't bring the subject up again, but after a day or two, it began to feel like the great unsaid.

They'd left the children with Sam for an afternoon while they went to sort through more of Sarah's things and as soon as she got into the house, May could see her sister had done a meticulous job organising and sorting things.

Photographs, letters, and paperwork had been separated and put into boxes or files, with large labels. Textiles—finished, were in a large blanket box next to Textiles—unfinished, alongside a tool box labelled: Threads, Notions, Haberdashery etc.

'Sarah was never this organised!' laughed May. Then more seriously, she said, 'thank you for doing all this, Lallie. It makes it so much less daunting.'

'But I didn't really look at anything, so I think we need to sort through and decide what to keep and what to get rid of,' she said to May.

May was sifting through a pile of letters, when she heard Lallie sigh. She looked across at her sister, her sleek, tawny head gleaming in the lamplight of the early winter afternoon.

'What is it?'

She raised her head and May saw a complex look flicker across her delicate features. Her wide, grey eyes looked sad.

'Is it just me, or is this picture more illustrative of our family dynamic than any other?'

May drew a deep breath and reached out, wondering as she did if she would see straightaway what Lallie meant.

'Where...' she didn't need to finish the question; she could see at once where the photo had been taken; Stella's family place in Kent, where the two families congregated every summer. 'It's a summer at Redgate.' Not just any summer, though, she thought.

Lallie scooted across the floor and heads together, they pored over the photo.

'Look.' Lallie pointed at their father, moustached, floppy haired, roman nosed, eyes dark and owlish behind his heavy rimmed glasses. 'I look at this and I think, why did I ever wonder why I always felt you were my one and only? That it was us alone in the world?'

May felt a twitch of disloyalty. 'We weren't alone. Dad— Sarah, they were there for us. They loved us.'

But even as she said it, she was looking at the two little girls, herself at five perhaps, Lallie eighteen months older, perched on the top step of the sea wall, legs tangled together, heads close, grinning and squinting into the camera. Lallie fair and elfin, with her chin thrust out, May sturdy and dimpled, dark, crazy curls blowing across her face. They had their arms around each other, hands clasped.

Behind them was their father and his new wife, Sarah. They looked so intimate, so together, as though nothing could penetrate their oneness. The look on William's face was almost painful, the love so raw, and the camera had captured Sarah meeting that look with her own steady affirmation.

'God, they were so in love.' Lallie said with an aching sound in her voice. 'There was never going to be any space for us.'

'Is that how you felt?' May felt uneasy. 'I don't remember it that way.' But she couldn't tear her eyes from the image. 'I always felt loved by them, I thought you did too.'

Lallie made an impatient sound in the back of her throat. 'I didn't mean that,' she said. 'Of course they loved us and Sarah was the very antithesis of the wicked step mother. It's just...' She stopped and took the photo from May. 'I think they were always waiting to be alone together. They didn't need or want anybody else. We happened to be there already when they found each other.'

May had a rather startling thought. 'Do you think they wouldn't have had kids if he'd met Sarah before he met our mother?'

'Who can say? But they'd have had that time together without kids. They never had that. We were already there.'

'I hate talking like this,' May said. 'Sarah would be so sad if she thought we'd felt shut out.'

'No she wouldn't. She'd have understood.'

'You're always so sure of everything, Lallie.' May heard herself sounding harsher than she'd meant, but Lallie didn't seem bothered and grinned at her as stood.

'Come on, it's getting late.'

They came out of the tube at Kentish Town and began the short walk to Lallie's, past the Assembly House and up Leverton Street, walking in thoughtful silence, feet stepping in unison, a steady, easy march.

A gust of wind buffeted down a side street and May shivered and thrust her gloved hand into the crook of Lallie's arm.

'Blimey, gets right in your bones doesn't it,' she said with an exaggerated blowy shiver of a sigh.

'Don't whinge, isn't it cold in Vermont right now?'

'Yes and deep in snow and ice, but this damp cold is *whingey* cold!'

She bent her dark head into the wind at the very same moment her sister did and picked up the pace. With a warm pleasure, May realised that Lallie was beginning an old game from long ago and she smiled. She increased her steps, Lallie went faster, May edged up a notch—but no running; you run you lose—Lallie followed suit and then before she knew it, May broke into a run, dragging her sister. Lallie gave a triumphant 'Ha!' and they sprinted the last fifty yards to the front door, breathless and laughing.

'You can never hold out!' Lallie crowed. 'And your legs are longer!'

May screwed up her face, conceding. 'In the end, I just want to get where I'm going more than I want to win,' she said.

The next day, she and the children were sitting at the table finishing a leisurely breakfast and enjoying a game of consequences, when the phone rang. Lallie passed it to May.

'I think it's the States.'

It must be three in the morning there, thought May. If that's finally Harley calling he must be drunk. She put the receiver to her ear and Matthew's voice came through, sounding far away and hesitant, fragile.

'May honey, I'm calling you from the ER. Harley had a wreck this evening on his way home from work and he's in surgery right now. I didn't want to call you until I had something to say, but they can't tell me much right now and I started to feel pretty uncomfortable thinking there you are, not knowing.' He was stumbling over his words.

May was vaguely aware of Lallie hovering just at the edge of her periphery and she walked out into the hall as though that might help her get her head round what Matthew was saying. She tried not to panic, to ask calm questions but the inside of her head seemed to be screaming, full of white light.

'Is he conscious? What sort of injuries, Matthew?' She felt sick just asking.

'I was with him when he went in to surgery and he seemed to know me. But honey, he looks pretty beat up.'

'How did they know to call you?'

'Well, they didn't, but one of the ER nurses asked if there was anyone they could call.'

Thank God, thought May, at least he was lucid enough to give Matthew's name. She clung to this with the tenacity of someone drowning.

'Matthew, are you okay? Is he going to be okay? Oh Matthew, I'm so sorry!'

She started to cry and was vaguely aware of the warmth of Lallie's hand on her shoulder.

'I'll come as soon as I can. I'll let you know when. Matthew tell him… tell him… just tell him I'm coming.'

May put the phone down and sat still for a moment, then jumped up and started pacing the room.

'Lallie, I have to go home, I need to get home.'

'What's happened?'

'Harley's had an accident.'

May choked and put up her hand, pressing it white over her mouth.

'I'll come with you.'

May felt panic rising in her throat. 'I'll be fine. I just need to get back.'

Lallie sat as Sam came in looking from one to the other, quickly sizing up what was going on.

'Everything alright?' His tone was light, his eyes earnest.

May looked up at him imploringly. 'Harley's had an accident.'

'Your fella?'

May nodded, stealing a look at Lallie who said nothing.

'I'd like to go back with her, Sam.'

'Is it that bad?' Sam said, still addressing May, concern in his voice.

'She won't like it there Sam,' she said a little stupidly.

Sam came quietly over and sat on the arm of her chair, putting an arm around her shoulders.

'Doesn't matter. She likes you.'

He moved quietly over to the computer and was already looking for flights to Boston. They were discussing how to get from there to Hartland. Harley had driven May there so she did not have a car waiting. The idea of taking the bus was arduous and tormenting. She just wanted to get there as quickly as possible.

'I'll hire a car,' said Lallie. 'Sounds like you live in the middle of nowhere.'

'Good idea,' murmured Sam, 'bring me your license and then pack. I'm booking you both for tomorrow 11am. That okay May?'

She exhaled with relief that she wasn't going to have to hang around waiting for available flights and nodded. She felt choked with fear and was almost unable to think, her mind going over and over the brief phone call with Matthew. Come whenever you can, he had said and she veered wildly between imagining Harley dead before she could get to him and clinging to the reassurance that Matthew tried to convey when he had said that Harley was stable.

Max and Tillie did not seem in the least bothered at the sudden and imminent departure of their mother and aunt. They seemed only to be tremendously excited by the drama. Tillie came in to help May pack, which involved sitting in the edge of the bed fingering everything and trying things on. She was sliding a heavy silver bracelet up and down her thin little arm and chattering to May.

'Are you coming back again when your friend is better, because you're still in your holiday?'

'I don't think so, darling. I was going home next week anyway, so I don't think I'll be able to come back.'

'How soon will you come back?'

'Not sure, angel, but Mama is coming back in a week.'

'Oh Mama,' said the little girl dismissively, 'she always comes back.'

May smiled at her wonderfully callous sense of security. Lucky girl, she thought.

'Mama says you don't live there but I think you do because you always say "home" and you've been there about fifty years.'

'Is that so?'

'Mmm hmm. And Daddy says od-viously you live there,

228

because you live there and have a house and a job.'

Tillie seemed to think this was hilarious and giggled like mad. May smiled at her, grateful for something to take her mind off the horrendous images that kept threatening to invade.

'Well, missus, perhaps you'd like to come and visit me where I don't live? How about that for an idea? There's lots of lovely swimming and picnics and skiing in the winter. Oh! And did you know that where I don't live is where maple syrup comes from?'

Tillie's eyes grew wide. She adored maple syrup, possibly because it was one of the few sweet things her parents allowed her.

'I'm going to tell Max,' she said with solemnity and slid off May's bed and ran off still wearing the silver cuff and an oyster silk camisole of May's that she had put on over her corduroy frock.

Before she went to bed that night, her bags packed and sitting silently in the downstairs hall, May called Matthew at home. She left a message on his answer phone and then phoned his mobile, which switched straight into message mode. She repeated her message, saying she thought she would get to Hartland around six o'clock local time. She would call if there were any delays.

When she woke next morning, feeling as though she had fought her way through a tangle of vivid and disturbing dreams, she lay a moment wondering why she was so filled with dread. The weight of fear almost suffocated her as she remembered.

23

Lallie and May arrived after a heavy snowfall, but the sky and the roads were clear. They took turns driving the four hours to Hartland and as they drew nearer, Lallie asked, 'Do you want to go straight to the hospital, or home first?'

May was unable to answer and looked helplessly at her sister.

'May?' Lallie pressed her, then added gently, 'Don't worry about me.'

'I really need to see him.' Then suddenly a thought cleared the fog. 'When did you last see Stella?'

'It's been years. Her wedding I think.'

'Harley's in the local teaching hospital, it's less than ten minutes' walk from Stella and Pete's. How about I drop you and our stuff there and then I can walk down and see Harley?'

Lallie took her phone out of her bag and punched in the number May called out to her.

'Hey Stellissimo!' she crowed, laughing. 'It's Lallie! Put the kettle on, I'm five minutes away and I'm dying for a cuppa!'

May could hear Stella's voice screeching incredulously out of the phone.

'No I am not "shitting" you,' said Lallie with dignity, 'Now do as you're told.'

They pulled up in the driveway behind the two cars and Stella was already tumbling out of the doorway, laughing and hugging Lallie for all she was worth.

Pete and Stella had only returned from Christmas with his family in Indiana the day before so had not heard the news about Harley.

'Go, go, go!' Stella said. 'We'll be here. I'll take care of Lal. Go on.'

May hesitated and Stella looked at Pete, 'Honey?'

'Come on I'll walk you down,' he said.

But May didn't want anyone. 'I'll call if I need you,' she said and Stella hustled her out of the door with a quick, tight hug.

May was scared. Her pulse staggered at the base of her throat making it hard to breathe and she felt sick. Her head was pulsing with a swelling pain that made her head feel huge. Matthew had given her very little information. An oncoming truck had swerved into Harley's lane to avoid a deer and they collided.

'Seems as though Harley tried to avoid the truck and sure enough, it went right on into his side,' he had said in his warm slow drawl and ended on a low sigh, 'I guess he's pretty beat up.'

The hospital doors of the reception area opened almost silently. The place was festooned with tired Christmas decorations, striking an odd tone amongst the medical personnel and anxious or frustrated friends and relatives.

She waited in line behind a pale, shaven-headed and oil-stained young man in a dark blue boiler suit, clutching two curly twins with warm, dark faces, both wearing pyjamas and slippers. He began to speak, wondering anxiously whether he had a concussion and May had a memory of a time once before, when Danielle had got concussed at a party.

She had slipped in a puddle of beer, her slide across the basement floor broken by a dense metal pillar designed to hold the ceiling up. A party of them had galvanised and taken her to the emergency room, but all May could remember about it was Stella pretending that the sterile rubber gloves were balloons, while Danielle lay immobilised by a neck brace waiting to go into theatre for an x-ray.

She remembered how a nurse had walked in and given

them such a look of disdainful disapproval their friend Courtney had started snorting with laughter and sprayed a ghastly shower of spit and snot into the room. 'This is a hospital, ladies,' the nurse had said. 'If you are drunk you will have to leave the premises. At once.' Nothing had ever seemed serious then.

As the young father slunk away and took a seat, she moved up to the unsmiling, fed-up woman behind the desk.

'I'm here to...' But the minute she tried to say his name she felt her throat constrict. She took a deep breath. Her nose stung and she fought to push her words out through the choking tremor in her voice.

'Harley. Daniels.'

'Excuse me?' the woman said, her voice cool.

'Harley Daniels. I'm here to see him. An accident. He's had an accident.'

'Are you family?'

'He hasn't got family,' she said, feeling for the first time how unutterably lonely it sounded. 'I'm his girlfriend.'

'I'm sorry, only family.' The woman continued to look, purse lipped at her. Silence.

'Please help me.' May was beginning to feel slightly hysterical. 'I have just flown all the way from London. His friend. My friend. Matthew Burrows phoned me in London yesterday to let me know Harley had had an accident.' May looked helplessly at the woman as she started to look around her to call the next in line.

'Can you at least let him know I'm here? I don't want him to feel alone.' May could not control her tears. The receptionist softened.

'Mr Burrows is with him now. He's not alone. Let me just call up to him and see,' she said asking for her name again.

May's sick nerves came rolling back over her, leaving her

lightheaded as she stood outside the door to room 215. The fluorescent strip-lights along the hall became sharper and took on a blue intensity. Matthew opened the door to her knock and hugged her gently, stepping back to open the door a little wider as she slipped inside.

It took all her self-control not to lose it. Harley's eyes were swollen closed and he had cuts and bruises all over his face. Underneath the purple-red bruising and scabbed cuts, he was a startling greyish colour and he had a livid gash sewn with thorny black stitches across his forehead. May could barely take in all the tubes and bandaging, but the most shocking thing was that his head was shorn.

She started to tremble and had to sit down. 'Matthew,' she began, but Matthew put a finger to his lips.

'He's awake.'

'Yes he is,' muttered Harley thickly, '…can hear you.'

His voice didn't sound like his nor as though it came from that strange form lying there. May quickly stood and leaned over him.

'Didn't your Mama teach you not to play in traffic?' she whispered, kissing him on the side of his mouth, trying to find a place that wouldn't hurt.

'May?' his voice sounded so far away. 'You're in London.'

'I came home when I heard what happened.'

'You came home.' He repeated her words and May's heart caught in her throat as she saw a tear rise in the swollen lids and slip down the side of his face.

His breathing shuddered and he winced and said her name again, breathlessly quiet.

'I'm here, my love,' she whispered, 'I'm not going anywhere.'

'Need to feel you. Really you?' He muttered and she saw the fingers of his right hand reaching and grasping at the bedclothes. She slipped her hand under his and said again, 'I'm here.'

May wanted Matthew to go home and rest. He did not take much persuading, but seemed anxious that May should understand.

'He's sedated.' He told her in such a quiet voice she had to put her ear right by his lips. 'But I think the drugs are giving him hallucinations. I haven't liked to leave him.'

As he said this, May saw the old man properly for the first time since she had arrived and felt a shock of worry. He looked so tired and anxious, his face drawn, a terrible blanched appearance around his wrinkled eyes.

'Glad you came, May. I didn't doubt you'd come but...' He broke off.

'But he did,' she finished for him.

'Yes, he did.'

'Matthew, my sister,' she said helplessly and felt a sudden wave of guilt.

'Now don't you set to worrying, May. I'm fixing to go by that way and she can follow me in her car.'

With a quick hug, he left her, walking more slowly than she had ever seen him go.

She sat quietly in a chair, lightly holding the cool tips of Harley's fingers. Listening to his breathing, laboured but reassuringly steady. At times he whimpered like a sleeping puppy, or muttered words she could not make out. She dozed, waking herself every time her head jerked, wondering where she was in the now darkened room.

At some point, May had no sense of the time, a nurse came in, punctuating the strange, warm fluidity of the room with sharp, purposeful movements. She checked Harley's temperature, his blood pressure, adjusting his pain relief and monitoring the drip that kept him hydrated and nourished. Standing to stretch and find herself a drink of water, May peered down the blindingly bright corridor and saw a water cooler at the end. She glanced back at Harley asleep, but still she hovered, indecisive, in the doorway. The nurse's voice startled her despite its low warmth.

'What do you need, sweetie?'

'A bathroom.'

'Straight down the hall, towards the exit light. You go on. I'll watch him for you.'

In the starkly lit bathroom, May peered at her tired, drawn face, splashed it with water and washed her hands. She squeezed the last dregs of some travel moisturiser out onto the tips of her fingers and breathed in the creamy coolness as she rubbed it into her tight skin. 'I'm frightened,' she said, surprising herself.

Harley had not stirred while she had been gone and she thanked the nurse in what she instantly recognised as a dismissive tone, wanting to be alone yet ashamed at her abruptness.

'No problem. It's tough, the night shift, I know. They tell me you just flew in from London. Must be quite a shock to find him like this.' May nodded, not trusting herself to speak. 'The older gentleman that was here, is that his father?'

'No. He doesn't have any family.'

'Oh that's too bad.'

'But we love him,' said May, trying for brightness and failing miserably as her voice cracked.

'Sure you do. Now he's going to be just fine. It'll take a while, but he's a fighter, we can all see that.'

May let the well-practised platitudes wash over her like a soothing balm that did nothing to take the real sting away.

'And now you're here, that'll just give him the strength he needs,' she continued in her measured, well-worn tone.

'Do you really think so?' May asked, clutching at the straws anyway.

'Yes I do. Just so long as he doesn't get an infection, he'll go from strength to strength.'

May felt a shiver whisper through her bones. There's

always something, something more.

'What do you mean?'

'Infection. That's why we take his temperature. So we can tell if there's any onset.'

May slumped further down in her chair but almost instantly bolted back upright and her heart skipped as one of Harley's eyes opened a tiny bit and glinted in the darkness. May glanced up at the nurse, whose expression remained unchanged, then back at Harley. Perhaps she had imagined it.

The nurse left, promising to look in on them before her shift finished and May briefly smiled, a reflexive motion, a quick stretch of her mouth, nothing more. She hunched herself together, her hands clasped and twisted under her chin, a thumb pressed against her lips and peered through the dim space between herself and Harley. The low light seemed hazy and had the comforting quality of candlelight.

'Oh my love,' she murmured on a deep, low sigh. She needed to touch him and felt suddenly tearful, the tightening in her throat taking her from behind. His eye opened, the tiniest bit but unmistakably.

'Hello,' May whispered, unable to keep the joy from her voice. She heard a short rush of breath through his nose, saw his mouth twitch a little.

'How are you feeling?'

'Stupid. Weird. Don't know. Can't feel much.' His voice sounded low and parched, like ancient bark.

'I think that's the drugs. I wouldn't mind some myself. I'm feeling too much.'

'What day is it?'

'Thursday.'

'Thursday… what Thursday?'

'Christmas was Friday, it's the first Thursday since Christmas…' She trailed off. 'Blimey, Harley its New Year's Eve.'

'D'you have a better party?' he slurred.

'Loads. Get your coat.'

'Can't laugh. Hurts.'

'Sorry.'

'Can't see you.' His fingers grasped, reaching for her again and she twined hers in them terrified that she would hurt him. 'Like hearing your voice. Tell me something.'

For a moment she felt tongue tied. What would he want to hear, what did he need? She thought about what Matthew had said about the drugs and began to speak, hoping she could chase away the horror in his head, whatever might be haunting him.

'Well...' she began. 'I went skating with Tillie and Max at Somerset House.'

She tried to conjure the beauty and magic of the lights and laughter and their cold breath furring in front of their faces, but as she talked, she found herself remembering a winter night long ago on the Marshes in Kent when everything had been frozen and silently, softly blanketed in deep drifts of snow. The family had rented a cottage for the Christmas holidays and it had seemed to her as though all her favourite winter scenes from the books she read had become transposed onto the slumbering snow-covered orchards and sheep fields.

She and Lallie had taken Hessian sacks from the barn and made themselves beds on the frozen dyke, the very same one that they had caught tadpoles in on a previous holiday.

Lying on their backs looking up at the black night sky dotted over and over with tiny bright stars, they had giggled and talked, sharing little secrets and embarrassments, their voices and laughter echoing and flat over the frozen landscape in an unfamiliar way. It had been a full moon and they had watched it slowly rising and sailing dreamily above them.

They'd decided they would sleep out there, wanting the serene and tranquil beauty to remain. Eventually, though, the cold had seeped into their clothes, then their bones and finally Sarah had opened the door of the cottage, the warm lamplight flooding around her shape in the doorway, and called them in.

The memory of Sarah nudged further into her thoughts and made her smile, comforted her.

'When I was a little girl,' began May and she saw a little smile twitch at the corner of Harley's mouth.

'When I was a little girl, I fell in love. Five years old and Dad brought home this beautiful woman with a floaty frock and long, long hair and apple cheeks. She had the bluest eyes and sat me on her lap and gave me sips of her wine. I thought she was the most beauteous creature I'd seen. And I thought he'd brought her home for me. When she had to go home, I cried my eyes out. The funny thing was though, in a way he *had* brought her home for me, me and Lallie, and she always seemed to honour that or at least understand that I might think that, even though they were in love; besottedly in love.'

May stopped talking and thought of Sarah.

'She made quilts and tapestries. You remember? Beautiful, huge wall hangings. There was always one in progress on a wooden frame and she used to stand at it or sit, listening to Cat Stevens. We've each got one, and whenever Lallie asked her how much someone was paying for whatever she was working on, she'd say "oh, curtains for your bedroom," or "doughnuts for three months."' She was lost in thought, trying to remember Sarah as she had been. Not how she was at the end, a painful collection of bones and skin whimpering for someone to make it stop.

'The amazing thing about Sarah,' she said, 'was how inclusive she was. I don't know what it was—confidence in herself perhaps—but she never seemed threatened by other people. The first quilt she ever made me had some of my mother's scarves in it.' She stopped for a moment, thinking. 'I think she might have been the only person in the world who

understood that it mattered that my mother had existed.'
Yes, she thought. She might have been gone before I could
remember her, but she was once there and Sarah had
acknowledged and honoured that.

Harley's breathing was slow and steady and May
wondered how much he had heard. She slipped quietly out
into the hall to phone her sister.

24

When Matthew arrived the next morning, May realised as relief filtered through her seized muscles, that she had been anxious about the old man. Harley was awake but confused.

'Harley? I'm going to nip home and shower. Matthew will stay until I get back. I won't be long. Okay?'

He nodded fractionally and May heard the pillowcase rasping rough against his stubbled head. The dense, empty dark of his eyes made her stomach tighten and May wondered how much he was taking in. She moved about straightening chairs and lining up the water jug and plastic cup on the overcrowded bedside stand. As she reached out to smooth his sheet, Matthew's voice surprised her and she shot a swift look at him.

'Get on now, girl. We can do just fine without you for a spell. I'm fixing to read the newspaper to Harley here. Then we can argue about the economy.'

He allowed himself a little chuckle and May noticed Harley's mouth soften about the edges.

'I'll be back before Matthew's run out of things to say,' she said into the hollow of Harley's neck and made herself leave the room before she could look at him again.

The world looked startlingly bright. The snow was throwing glitter up into the thin blue air and she was a little dizzy as she picked across the slick, dark tarmac towards Matthew's pumpkin coloured pickup truck. She was anxious to get home and back as fast as possible and the swell of nausea as she turned the ignition key was more irritating than alarming. I'm just tired, she thought, pressing on.

The gritters had been out during the night and the road home was clear of traffic as she drove, tattered fragments of thoughts distracting her from familiar landmarks. What if he couldn't work or walk or think as he always had?

Lallie was hanging up the phone as May trudged through the side door, into the boot room.

'That was someone calling himself "Turtle." Hello,' she added, with a sudden sweet smile and came to help May out of her heavy, quilted coat.

'You know who Turtle is,' she said, trying and failing to keep her voice light. 'He's my boss at the restaurant. What did he say?'

'That he'd heard the news about Harley and not to worry about coming in next week. Were you planning to? He's got you covered any way.'

May's head stalled with all the information and she stared unseeingly at her sister.

'Oh! And he wants you to call and give him news on Harley as the hospital won't release any.'

'They're hung up on next of kin and he hasn't got any.'

'Really? He's got no family?'

'No.'

'Poor guy. No wonder he's fucked up.'

A wave of weariness swept through her. 'You know nothing about him Lallie. If you... oh God, if you knew you'd be amazed at how un-fucked up he is.'

'You're probably right, love.' Lallie soothed. 'How is he?'

'Not great,' May replied simply. 'It's hard when you first see him to identify any bits that aren't broken or torn. He can barely open his eyes, can hardly speak; he's got a punctured lung, broken ribs, shattered thigh and a laceration like Frankenstein on his face. Both his arms had so much glass in them that only his fingers are visible.'

'Christ, I didn't realise... I had no idea...' Her sister's face suddenly looked incredibly young.

'Neither did I.'

Full of tears, she looked away, out towards the snow-covered landscape. She reached a long arm out behind her and Lallie responded with a strong, emphatic hand, her fingers twining with her sister's own.

'You okay?'

May shifted back towards her sister, her breathing a little too shallow to be useful and took a gulp of air.

'I don't know. Tired I suppose. This all feels so…' she trailed, unable to reach words or even any thoughts to anchor herself.

'I'll go and have a shower, Lal, I won't be long.'

'What about a lie down, love? It'll do you good.'

'I can't Lal. I'll sleep tonight.'

Half an hour later, she was standing still in the doorway of the sitting room staring at Lallie. Her sister looked up and May noticed a fleeting fear pass over her face. For a split second she thought there was lightening in the room.

'May?' Lallie said, quickly rising and steering her to the sofa. 'My God, you're exhausted.'

May leaned forward, elbows on her knees and felt Lallie's hands rubbing slow, firm and rhythmic up and down the muscles cradling her spine.

'I'm all right now,' she said, her voice surprisingly far, and she thread the laces through the eyelets of her boots. Lallie murmured soothingly and May felt a brief moment of comfort followed by a wave of fear. She raised her head hugging her arms around her knees and sank into herself as she looked at Lallie again.

'What are you going to do today?' Her voice was small.

'I'm having lunch with Stella, why?'

'Will you come with me first?'

'Oh, May, my darling, of course I will.' Lallie's response was instant and decisive. She scooped her into her arms and May burst into tears.

Lallie looked deeply shocked on first entering the emphatic

white of Harley's hospital room. She hovered near the door while May moved carefully around the room clearing a space for her to sit. Harley was sleeping and the two sisters sat quietly without speaking, while the room hummed monotonously through the still air.

May felt coiled up inside, tight and tense and the moment Harley stirred, she moved swift and noiseless over to his bedside, murmuring his name soothingly.

'You're back,' he said, his voice swollen and so low she felt she was squinting to hear it. She sat, taking his hand and stroking his temple with the back of a finger.

She couldn't get used to his head so exposed. Now his hair was shorn he looked so vulnerable, as though he had been stripped. The rise of his cheekbones and swoop into the dip of his temple where his pulse throbbed delicately, brought May to the edge of tears again. His skin, drained of colour became paler still where it met his hairline and the severely shaved skull. She rested her fingertips on the stubbled regrowth, already thrusting, dark, through his scalp. It was so much softer than she had expected; not like the rasping sharpness along his jawbone.

At the edge of her consciousness, May was aware of Lallie shifting in her chair and sighing deeply. Anxiety nudged at her and she swatted it, refocusing her senses on Harley as he slipped back into sleep without another word. It was only when his grasp loosened on her hand that May got up, kissed him butterfly light on the edge of his mouth and went back to sit with her sister.

'He looks terrible.' Lallie sounded almost pleading.

'I know. But it's how stripped he looks that's killing me.'

'What on earth do you mean? With all those bandages, he looks mummified.' Lallie shuddered a little as she said it.

'They shaved his head. He had the most beautiful hair. Beautiful.' May's voice cracked and, struggling to control her mouth, she clapped her hand over it, pressing hard.

'Oh May!' crooned Lallie. 'You're exhausted, love. You really ought to sleep.'

She shook her head and said too loudly, 'I'm fine.'

Then she glanced at Harley as he muttered something incoherent and moved quietly back to lean over him, her voice soothing as she breathed him in. Lallie was at her elbow, holding her up and guiding her out of the door. Her sister's arms wound around her, May felt bewildered by having an incredibly heavy body and boneless legs.

'I can't smell him, Lal,' she sobbed. 'I can't smell him.'

'Oh, love,' sighed Lallie.

She found she was sitting at the far end of the long hallway under the exit sign, her sister crouching in front of her. She saw the tight concern in her face, her eyes full of confusion and questions.

'Mayflower,' she said gently, 'I'm going to stay an extra week. Sam can manage another week without me.'

'What about all your clients?' May sniffed.

'Let me deal with that. I know you have Stella, but let me just see things a bit more stable before I go.'

May nodded quickly. 'I'd like that Lallie, thanks.' She managed a watery smile.

They padded quietly back into the room and found a nurse they had not seen before. She looked up as they came in and May was struck by the contrast between the darkness of her hair, her honeyed skin, and the opaque, jade green of her eyes. She walked over to them so her quiet tones could be heard. She spoke her 'g's' as softly as though she was holding something fragile in her mouth.

'He is very a-*gi*-tated about something,' she said to them, putting the emphasis on the second syllable.

'He has been asking where something or someone has gone. Not you. But I am not able to understand what he means.'

She sounded far away from home to May, who could feel

something flickering from behind the uniform; something of the woman.

'Has he said anything else?'

'Not really. But I think he is hurt. Here.' She placed a hand on her breast in a gesture that hurt May. She gave a half smile and said, 'Oh!' Her voice caught in her throat.

May pulled a chair closer to the head of Harley's bed, and his eyes flickered open, unfocussed, then closed, but his fingers tightened, grasping May's hand. The strength of his grip made her pulse leap and drum in the base of her throat.

Harley opened an eye, squinting up at her. 'It's gone,' he said, bleak as a winter marsh.

'What's gone?' May asked soothingly, while her stomach knotted and twisted.

His silence seemed empty.

'Do you know what's gone?' she ventured. 'Something *feels* gone?'

She heard a tiny intake of breath from the far side of the room, but kept her eyes intently on Harley, afraid she might miss something. He turned his head from her into the meagre shadows, the corners of his mouth pale and tight.

'Something I always had. I had something. Can't remember.' He closed his eyes and his long, slow, breath was broken in the middle with a jagged, staccato expulsion of air and his face contracted with pain.

May murmured, reassuring, stroking his head. Long moments passed.

At last, Lallie spoke, her voice sounded loud and she and May both flinched. She began again, more quietly.

'Shall we go May? Stella will be waiting.'

May got up so as to speak more quietly. She glanced at her watch, realised she had not registered the time and looked again.

'Lal, would you mind going on without me? His mate Rob will be here in about twenty minutes and then I can come and find you.'

'Of course! We've got loads to catch up on anyway. It's Lou's, right? It's easy to find?'

'Really. You can't miss it. Just right out of the hospital then straight, straight...'

'Straight on til morning?' Lallie said and May loved her fiercely in that moment, for the childhood reminder, for leaving her with a bit of comfort as she left her alone.

She went back to her place beside Harley hoping to ask him a little more, but he was sleeping again. She looked over at the nurse.

'Did he say anything else? About what he's lost? I can't tell if it's some item of personal property or if it's a sense of something. Do you understand what I mean?'

May was not hopeful, as she was unsure what she herself meant, but the young woman came over to her, pulled up a chair and sat.

'You know,' she began in her soft tones, 'he is on a very strong medication. This gives sometimes, some hallucinations. Nightmares. Can I tell you, he is not himself when he is medicated like this?' She leaned close to May, looking her deeply in the eyes her head nodding very slightly as she spoke.

'It is too hard, it is difficult, to know what is real and what is the morphine. So you have to help him... remember.' She smiled, briefly showing beautiful, straight white teeth before she quickly drew her lips over them and lowered her head slightly.

'Remember?' asked May.

'Who he is. Who you are?'

'But he knows,' May knew she sounded panicked. 'There's no memory loss. The doctor said nothing about that.'

'No. I'm sorry my English is not always accurate. I am talking of remembering himself here.' She placed her open hand on her belly. 'A feeling of who he is. You must do it for him, until he can be himself again. I think you have patience; may I say this?'

May smiled and nodded.

'And we do not like to keep people on this medication for any more than is completely needed. The dose will be reduced and you will find him again. His hair will grow, he will get stronger. Maybe slowly. Maybe not.'

The nurse smiled and said, 'My name is Asha. Please ask for me if you wish it.'

'Thank you.'

Asha inclined her head a little and left her alone again with Harley.

She leaned to kiss him and as she did so his fingers grasped at her sweater startling her with their strength.

'Thank you. For coming back each day. Stops me going insane.' His voice made her insides go still.

'How bad is it?' she asked, a little afraid of the answer.

'Bad. I can't…' He gave her a watery smile and she sat again, thinking.

'Can't talk now,' he said and turned his head slightly. She was not certain, but thought he whispered something else as he moved. She crouched beside the bed, her face level with his.

'Harley, I love you,' she whispered fiercely. His eyes were closed but she recognised the trembling breath catching a few times as he breathed in and felt her own throat constrict, her nose sting.

'Did you hear me? I love you.'

'Yes,' he bit out, his voice thick. May felt a wave of despair wash over her.

25

The Georgia state flag wasn't flying by Matthew's porch, his sign that he was available for passing visitors, so May phoned.

'Matthew, I thought I might come by. Are you around?'

'Well I will be now,' he said, with the sweet little humorous inflection in his voice that May had come to love.

'Are you sure that's alright?'

'Sure it is sweetheart, I'll be in my studio.'

'Thanks Matthew that would be lovely.'

'Is everything alright?' he asked.

'Ye…es,' she replied, a little uncertainly, then she rushed on, 'I'm fine… Harley's fine. I just have a lot on my mind and…' She heard herself stumbling and confusing things and finished in a rush, 'You *know* him, Matthew.'

She closed her mouth tightly trying to breathe steadily through her nose.

'I'll be in my studio,' he said again.

Matthew had built a studio extension to his house and spent his time either there, or in his garden. Now all his shrubs and roses, sweeping beds of herbaceous perennials and climbers draping walls and pergolas, were dormant and blanketed in the great drifts of snow that lay soft and deep over the undulating farmland.

She saw him through the large vaulted window, designed to catch the light, foraging in a drawer. He glanced up, saw her, and his face softened into a deep smile. He walked over to the French doors, his slow purposeful strides steady and quiet. May stood watching, as Matthew turned the lock and opened the doors to his studio. His fingers worked with such economy of movement; it was mesmerising. He neither clattered nor fumbled; he just executed beautiful little actions.

'Hello, May,' he said. 'Come on in.' He stepped aside in welcome. 'Want to see what I'm working on?' She felt a little flutter of excitement, she had only ever seen finished works.

She leaned on the edge of a drafting table and watched him selecting a brush from an old preserving jar. This was the very type of jar with its pale translucent jade tinge and its cursive glass script with the trailing vine, which she remembered from her early childhood in London. It was the time after her mother had gone for good and before Sarah had come into their lives.

Every autumn, her father William had gathered his little girls about him in their dank basement kitchen and announced the arrival of Grandmother Aldridge's Apple Butter. They would sit fidgety and excited as he unwrapped the brown paper parcel and withdrew two glass jars wrapped in protective layers against the long journey from granny's kitchen to theirs. May felt as though she could taste the faintest whisper of the cinnamon and cloves, feel the thick, velvety texture in her mouth of the apples simmered long and slow, as she looked at the jar and wondered where its lid was.

Matthew was working on a large canvas and it appeared to be full of shadowy figures, their ghostly, fleeting forms, sometimes appearing on the canvas more than once.

'This is my wife, Hope,' he said, indicating several figures that appeared to represent the three ages of Woman. One emerged from the sea, laughing with two small children held tightly to each side. Another was clearly the same woman, but younger, standing thoughtfully gazing out over some golden, ephemeral farmland. It was like the tremulous, shimmering forms of reflections on a pond. May spent a long time looking, while Matthew painted in silence.

'Can I talk to you, Matthew?'

He continued selecting a brush from his jar, lifting one, turning it, looking at it, his head cocked, releasing it back into the jar and picking up another and murmured some encouraging sound.

'It's about Harley.'

'Ye…es,' he said looking appraisingly at his canvas.

'I'm really worried about him.' And I'm scared, she thought.

'Mmmhmm…' he said.

There was a long silence while Matthew painted and May fiddled with a putty eraser, rolling it between her forefingers, balancing it on its side, pushing it over, balancing it again.

She wandered around the studio, flipping through the stacks and stacks of stretched watercolours, stopping to linger every now and then over a particularly arresting image of shimmering August fields under hot skies.

'You like that one?' She nodded. 'Take it,' he said, just like that. 'Take it.'

He broke off from his painting to lift it out of the stack and lay it next to May.

'Oh no, Matthew! I couldn't,' she said, distracted. 'It's too much.'

Matthew shook his head. 'Now, May,' he said, focussing suddenly. 'Tell me all what you're worrying yourself about.'

May replied fretfully, 'He's so obviously not himself, which makes sense under the circumstances, but I'm afraid for him. I remember what you said about how he was when you first knew him and…'

'Now sweetheart,' Matthew cut in, 'that was a very different time.'

'I know, Matthew, I know. But I can't get away from this fear. It just goes round and round my head and I keep thinking of that poor waif you told me about.'

Matthew selected another brush and made tiny adjustments to a figure in the corner of the painting with little dab-dab-dab movements, each creating an infinitesimal difference.

'Honey,' began Matthew, and something in the tone of his

voice made her more alert. 'I have known Harley a long time. When he came back to live with us—he rented that little outbuilding down yonder.' He swept his arm over towards the door. 'It would have been right about the time you went home to your family. He came partly to help Hope. We didn't know it, but she was already getting sick; she was beginning to tire out real easy. But he came because he was heartsick too. Don't forget, he has no family, no home, nowhere to go back. When he needs to lick his wounds, where's he going to lay down? Hope was real concerned for him. He was an orphan, she said, and needed someone to love him and understand that loneliness in him, to stick by him. She always said he had so much to give if he got a chance.'

Matthew paused and looked at his canvas for a long moment. May felt as though her heart would break.

'You hold on there, sweetheart. Wherever he takes you right now, go with him. It was always you he was wanting.'

Matthew put down his brush and walked over to where May was perched on the edge of a tall oak stool.

'Could you use a hug from an old man?'

May nodded and let him put his strong bony arms around her and she rested her head against his chest. He smelled of clean laundry and paint and a faint whisper of Old Spice. For a brief moment she felt as though she would like to just slip into sleep right there.

'Thank you so much Matthew,' she said, standing and running her hands through her hair. He made a dismissive gesture with his hand and turned back to his canvas saying, 'You come on by any time, sweetheart.'

26

It was about ten days into Harley's hospital stay when May saw Asha was on duty again. It made her feel weirdly shy, raw and exposed and yet she was at once conscious of a sharp burst of relief. I'm here, she thought, I haven't completely frayed away. She smiled a little as she passed, murmuring a low 'hi,' as she continued on towards Harley's door.

'Oh! Excuse me!' Asha called softly along the hall. May turned back to see the nurse heading towards her. She smiled warmly as she got close and said, 'This is for Mr Daniels. I am sorry about this mistake.'

She was holding out a large brown paper bag, folded at the top and sealed with a white label, printed with Harley's details.

'He should have had it always, from his arrival.'

'I'm sure it's fine,' said May dismissively, 'Have you seen him this morning? How is he?' She felt she was playing for time and wondered why. She felt nervous and a pulse throbbed hard, deep behind her ribcage as she clutched at the bag.

Asha gave May a curious look, her green eyes softening as the edge of her mouth tipped a little. May looked away dartingly, and then glanced back as Asha spoke again.

'I have seen him.' The distinctive lilt lulled May a little.

'Is he awake?'

'He sleeps and he wakes. But it is you I am thinking of now. Do you sleep?'

'I'm fine,' May said sharply, not wanting her to think she could not cope, but embarrassed at her tone. She smiled a little sheepishly and said more brightly, 'Really, I'm fine. Just wondering how he is.'

'I can tell you that he heals well. I can tell you that he becomes stronger. I cannot tell you what it is for him to open his eyes in the morning. Only he can answer this question. If you go in, you can see him and tell yourself. How is he?' Then she turned from May to call back down the hall, 'Mr Anselm... Please do not go this way!'

She hurried off towards a steady, shuffling form.

May hoisted her bag onto her shoulder, settling it more securely and grasped the paper bag. She tapped at the door realising she had begun to dread this moment, the moment when she arrived in the morning uncertain of the reception, unsure if Harley would be responsive, smile or greet her, be awake or asleep or pretending. She felt like a coward. This is shit, she thought, and felt an urge to rush back outside, into the cold bright sunshine and sharp air. She's right, May thought resentfully, this is getting to me. She leaned her hand on the lever handle and allowed the door to swing open a little. Light from the high, wide window poured into the room filling the corners, illuminating the walls with merciless brilliance.

Harley was sitting upright, propped by the raised head of the bed. For a brief snap of time, May couldn't work out what was different. Then she saw. Nothing was attached to him. The area around the bed was clear apart from the chair and bedside cabinet. No plastic tubes, no clear fluid filled bag hanging precarious and crucial. He still had a shunt taped to the back of his hand and his bandages were all still there, but no tubes. His eyes flicked open and for a moment he stared at her. Then May saw him take a deep breath and he smiled as he breathed out.

'Hey...' she said, drawing the word out in greeting, returning his smile. 'They letting your motor run on its own?'

'Hey, baby,' he said, tilting his head a little. May felt a catch at her heart as she recognised the characteristic gesture. His eyes rested briefly on the paper bag, but at first he said nothing.

'Yeah, they're giving me a trial run. If I eat the garbage

they bring round regularly and keep drinking and peeing, they'll start thinking about giving me an honourable discharge.'

'Does it have to be their "garbage"?' May asked as she waved over at a carry out bag from Molly's. 'I brought you some from the Outside World.'

Harley shrugged and patted the bed beside him. His forearm was still so heavily bandaged that it was a curiously solid gesture.

'Today,' he said loudly, as May came over to perch on the chair beside his bed, 'Physio. Assessment. Then we'll really see how broken I am.' His voice was bright, hard, and May felt it pushing at her.

'Any idea what to expect?' she asked, keeping her own voice cheery and hearing in turn how brittle it sounded.

Harley shrugged again. 'Nah.' She saw the bedclothes ripple as he moved his feet. 'What's in the bag?' he said at last, glancing at her feet, where the bag stood. May started guiltily.

'Oh, it's your stuff. Apparently, they should have given it to you. You should have had it all along. It's your stuff,' she repeated.

'What stuff. I don't have any. I mean I didn't pack a bag to come here, you know, it wasn't a *planned* break. It was a real spur of the moment thing to come.'

He smiled a little and then looked suddenly serious, all the softness of humour replaced by the hard, bleak quality that was becoming familiar. May reached and picked up the bag, putting it clumsily on his bed.

'Well of course you had stuff. I mean I take it you weren't driving stark naked? Though I'd like to see *that*!'

Harley smirked. Then said rather darkly, 'Perhaps not so much anymore, though, hmm?'

'What do you mean by that?'

May was surprised by the comment, his reply surprised her even more.

'Well I'm not all that to look at am I? Covered in these fuckin scars.'

'Harley…'

'Don't,' he said tightly. 'I've seen em, I know what they look like. You don't want to see them. So, what's in the bag?'

'I don't know.' May felt frustrated. It drove her mad the way he opened something up and then slammed it shut like that.

'Your wallet? Pens? Phone?' she said, rather aggressively, feeling guilty instantly, wondering how she'd be if the tables were turned.

Harley tapped the top of the locked bedside cabinet. 'All that's here.'

May noticed him absently scratching his beard growth along his jaw line. His fingers slowed and stopped. And then, as though the sensitive pads of his fingers were reading Braille, his first two fingers traced his throat. May watched, fluttered a smile and saw Harley's fingers groping the base of his throat, searching. His expression moved from almost blank, through confusion, then quickly to panic. May saw him breathe a deep steadying breath and before he really looked as though it had done any good, he blurted, 'It's gone.'

Very slowly and with utmost care, May said, 'The leather?'

'I had it. I always had it. It doesn't come off. It's not meant to come off.'

Harley's hand dropped to the paper bag and he grasped at it, clutching the folded top, crushing the paper. May knew she was holding her breath. She wanted to tear it open herself and get the whole bloody thing over with, whatever that might be.

Harley's fingers tore clumsily, fumbling at the folded top. He plunged his arm in and rummaged around, pulling out a dark wool hat, thick padded ski gloves and a soft dove grey scarf, each of which he dropped at his side. At last, as May watched his face, she saw a look of relief melt over his features, and he drew out a stiff string of knotted black leather. It had a dark patina along the edges and knotted parts and held its curved shape, rigid. It had been cut just to the right of the middle knot.

May realised with a start that she had jumped up from her seat as she saw his face. His eyes were closed and he was sobbing. His body trembled and shuddered. She pulled him roughly against her, forgetting his injuries, and sitting in the space beside him, half on half off the bed, held him as close as she could. He sounded as though he was choking as he turned his head into her, against her, butting his head and pushing into her so that she had to brace herself with one foot against the floor. She could feel his breath hot and gasping at her neck, the rigid tension of his body and the tears.

May held him fiercely, while her voice soothed and slowly, slowly the explosive force ebbed and she could make out a word or two as he rubbed his rasping head against her. She heard him repeat something about it being all he had left. She ran her hand rhythmically up and over his skull, again, again, feeling the new hair bristle and spring softly under her hand.

'Ohh... God...' he said with a last shuddering sigh. His body limp, exhausted. Tentatively, May unbraced her leg and shifted, to scoot up next to him. The room hummed quietly around them and she noticed voices calling in the hall, the muffled, repetitive, ping, announcing the elevator doors opening, closing and the squeak-clang of trolleys pushed along.

Harley began to talk very quietly, and she settled closer to him, curving gently towards him, trying not to put pressure on his body. As she curled softly around him, she felt the low vibration of his voice through his back, into her belly.

He talked about being a boy in South Dakota and watching his family fall apart. He told May an old story she had heard from him before; of drunken violence, broken limbs and black eyes. And then he told her a story she had not heard.

'I used to ride my bike to and from school. Every day. School bus stopped so far down the road it made more sense just to ride. Not in the winter though... not then...

'It was a long flat road. Straight. So I could see from a long way off something was going on. I remember feeling like the road was growing, ahead of my wheels, and I'd never get there. I'd just have to keep on peddling and peddling and never... just not ever... get there.' He stopped a moment.

'When I did, I couldn't get beyond the gates of the trailer park where we lived.' Harley's voice was hypnotically low and even. 'But I could see... and there were all these fire-fighters standing around and that weird blue flashing... They make so much noise when they're coming, but it's so... more than silent when they're there. And then there's the static of the radios...' He was quiet for a time before picking up the thread again. 'So then... I see my mother's boyfriend... in handcuffs... stumbling along with a couple of cops, silent, stupid. I mean he was always stupid but I couldn't recall ever seeing him without a torrent of shit coming out of his mouth. Unless he had passed out, of course, then he could be pretty quiet. And then I saw my Mom.'

His silence was profound and May wondered if he would speak again. She felt so taut and sharp inside, that she was afraid it could hurt him through his back She settled her arm around his belly, kissing the curve of his neck softly, hoping he could feel the softness of her mouth more than the stabbing anxiety inside her. As he spoke again, she could feel the muscular tensing and un-tensing of his torso.

'So... she was just lying there... just lying there, real still, but in the most... uncomfortable position you can imagine. All... just... twisted.' He seemed to almost swallow the last word, choking it down. 'Just lying there on the hard earth, no grass or nothing. It gets real brown and scrubby in the summer. Hard. And the whole place stinks and the trailer is black and smoking and paramedics are just standing there waiting while the fire-fighters come out with...' he drew in a deep, difficult breath, expelling it with startling force and May felt her body flinch and freeze in horror at what he was about to say. He went on, his voice stronger, before it cracked around the edges again.

'They were three little bodies on stretchers covered in blankets... completely... even their faces... and... you know... I'd seen enough TV to know what that meant. And all I could do was count. One, two, three. One, two, three. Over and over again until I was shouting out 'Where's four? Where's four?'

Harley's voice broke ragged again and May felt the shuddering rigidity return to his body. She stroked the soft regrowth of his hair. She was crying now and drew a rough breath in and held him closer as he pressed on.

'Until that moment I had been invisible. And suddenly everyone's crowding me and fussing me and all I could do was say, "There should be four, where's four?" over and over again. I just kept saying it, May.'

She squeezed him as she heard her name and the bewildered tone in his voice.

'And I remember someone saying, "What's he talking about? There weren't but three children and the mama in there."' Harley stopped speaking again.

'It's took me all these years to understand... I was looking for me... I was saying I should have burned up in that fire with my brother and my little sisters.'

May felt as though she had emerged from a collision; light headed and as though a thread had come loose from her connection to the landscape around her.

She finally left the hospital after Harley slipped exhaustedly into sleep. She realised she too must have been close to sleep, as she was startled by Asha's soft voice asking if she was all right.

'What time is it?' May said, feeling confused and glancing about her as though the room might give her some clue.

'It is nearly eight o'clock.'

She slid off the bed and straightened herself out. Her clothes were twisted and felt stretched in all the wrong places. The young nurse was checking his chart, filling his water jug and taking his pulse. He did not stir.

'I think you can go to your home now,' she said to May in a low voice. 'He will not wake for many hours. May I ask? Have you someone? Something has happened, I think.' Her voice, so full of kind concern, hurt May.

She left, feeling as though she was abandoning him and as she walked, she cried so that her throat ached.

'Jesus, May.' Stella looked appalled.

She and May were sitting at the kitchen table at Woodland Drive. May had found herself there after leaving Harley and called in, too tired to make the drive home. She watched as Stella's mouth began to form words, stop, then try again.

'So that's why the leather? The knots are... what? Each sibling? Oh my God... How old was he?'

'Twelve.'

'Twelve? Oh man, that poor, poor kid.'

'I know,' said May, unbearably sad. She thought fleetingly about her father's death, just as Stella said, 'I was just thinking about when you and Lal lost your Dad. But...' and then she stopped, looking embarrassed. May blinked slowly and managed a short twitch of a smile.

'I know... at least we had Sarah, right? We had each other? My god... an Embarrassment of Riches. Harley was totally alone. He had no one. And he was still a child.'

'What happened to him?'

'We didn't really get to that, he fell asleep. Stella, I've never seen anyone so eviscerated. It was like he was being purged.' May stopped, thinking about how raw, how feral he had seemed. 'But Matthew gave me a general picture of him being shunted from one foster home to another, from state to state. Nowhere permanent, nowhere that was a real home. I always thought that was how he lost his siblings, that they were out there somewhere. Harley certainly led me to believe that. Anyway, I didn't want to interrogate him. I mean... I know what I used to know, but... somehow that seems irrelevant... might not be true.'

She tried to tack down her thoughts in some kind of order, feeling that she had known him by his story, as he had once told it.

She tried to explain this to Stella who was not having any of it.

'Look, May, it's not like he's told you a bunch of lies. He's still Harley, just with some more detail. I mean no one tells everything about themselves.'

May felt tired and knew she was beginning to sound petulant as she said, 'But it's such an *important* detail.'

'Sure it is, but my point is, it's always been there.'

May let these words settle and she sensed the ground stabilising a little more beneath her. It's always been there.

Stella pulled her elbows back behind her, flexing her shoulders and arching a little over the back of her chair. Yawning loudly and giving herself a little shake, she said, 'Do you want to lie down, May? Take a nap here instead of driving all the way back to yours? I can call Lallie, tell her to come and get you.'

May accepted gratefully; she was beginning to feel light headed.

The patches of mud continued to bloom through the snow

and Lallie couldn't put off her return to London any more.

On the drive to the airport, May told Lallie what she had learned about Harley's family.

Lallie listened in increasing silence.

'Oh that poor, poor boy,' she said quietly, when May had finished. 'It does explain a lot about him, though.'

May felt vaguely defensive, she hated Lallie putting on her work head and analysing people, but she managed a neutral tone, 'How so?'

'When someone suffers that kind of catastrophic loss,' Lallie said as though feeling carefully for her words, 'it's almost as though they are always waiting for the other shoe to drop; the next big loss. Oh May!' she burst out sudden and impulsive, 'you don't need a man like that!'

'A man like *what*?' May snapped.

'One who feels the world might crash around his ears at any moment. Dependent on you for any sense of security.'

'Lallie. You don't know him. Stop trying to fit your theories around him.' What if we need each other, she thought. Then said, 'Let's not fight. We've got such a short time left.'

At the airport, they held onto each other until the last possible moment, Lallie begging her sister to, 'Come home soon.'

May cried until she could hardly see as she drove off and had to pull over for a while. She couldn't stand this feeling of being pulled apart.

27

She arrived one evening to find Harley propped in his bed, eyes closed. The radio was on too low for her to hear what the two competing voices were saying, as they swelled and died away.

Her visits were now always at this time of day. Partly, she told people, to give her a proper working day, and it was true Turtle had agreed to schedule her day shifts only while Harley remained in hospital. But if she was honest, it was because she knew it was as the dusk drew in and the hospital bustle began to slow, that his spirits ebbed.

'Makes me crazy that I can feel so tired, sure that I can maybe get me some sleep and all I find is that the inside of my head's flipping like a fish on a hook and I'm awake with myself and only the dark for company.'

He had laughed when he had said this, but May had heard no mirth in it. So she came in the early evenings, bringing her supper.

Harley had been strong and healthy before his accident and was healing well apart from a slight infection in his lungs. His broken ribs made it hard for him to clear, but he was responding to treatment and on track to be discharged in a few weeks' time.

Despite this, May was uneasy. Even when she was in the room with him, she found herself unexpectedly overwhelmed by what she could only identify as a kind of homesick longing. He was frequently somehow far away, inaccessible and she recognised that this was something she had known before with him; a remoteness or withdrawal. It gave her a horrible foreboding.

At night she dreamed of walking barefoot along endless, stark corridors, her chest tight with anxiety, trying to run but her feet obstinate, defiantly staying heavily on the floor, her legs weighty and useless. Each time she got to his hospital room door, giddy with relief, she opened it and it was only another long, geometric white hallway, leading to angular turns and long, white walkways. At some deep part of the dream, she heard voices, laughter, some kind of evening piano music from a closed room and waves of relief pulsed through her. She found that without opening the door or passing through it, she was in the room, standing on one leg one foot resting on the other.

Sitting in a flickering, wash of firelight was a couple leaning towards each other, murmuring. The man started as though he had heard something and looked over at May. He had her father William's build and stature, but his expression was so blankly charming, it couldn't have been him. He shrugged elegantly and turned back to the woman and May realised he couldn't see her.

She woke feeling alone and cold, despite the cloudlike warmth and comfort of her goose down duvet. Harley had brought it to her from his apartment when the Vermont winter had started to close in.

'Stay in your skin under here with me,' he had said when she'd threatened to wear socks and pyjamas in bed. He had dragged the thing in from his truck one night after work, and insisted on demonstrating there and then, the magical power of a goose down comforter. In the dim chill of the early evening, before the fire was lit, he had stripped off to his bare skin standing triumphant and brave in the cold and invited her to see for herself.

They had spent that whole evening, into the night talking and making love, cocooned in the soft, pillowy warmth and May had happily conceded that she could 'stay in her skin' if the duvet stayed at hers.

'But what will you do when you sleep at yours?' she asked a little belatedly and Harley raised an eyebrow with wry emphasis giving her a long, slow look. It had been a long time since he had stayed at his own place.

'Storm on the way,' he said now, opening one eye.

It had been an unusual winter for the area. After the first snows there had been no more and the ground, hard and dead-bone cold had been swept by bitter winds, leaving large areas snowless and scrubbily dark. Everywhere May went in town, people were worrying and complaining about the lack of snow. Tourists were cancelling their ski holidays and the annual ice sculptures for Winter Carnival were in jeopardy.

'Hungry?'

'Can't tell,' he said, which seemed to be his more usual response.

The bones at his collar peaked sharp, his skin clung to the deep hollows at the edges and May noticed how his cheekbones thrust sharply beneath his smudged eyes. She felt again the fear creep across her back at the opaque density of his dark eyes. They reflected no light.

'Well I'm starving,' she said not entirely truthfully and poured soup into two bowls, tearing soda bread into chunks.

'May...' Harley's voice sounded softer at the edges than she had heard in a while. 'Is it hard to come here every day?'

She was surprised by the question and for a moment, wondered how to answer. She put down her spoon and glanced about the room, not taking anything in.

'Yes, sometimes,' she said at last. 'It is. But it would be a lot harder not to come.'

Harley was quiet and still, his breath audible as he watched her. 'Thank you,' he said.

And the way he said it, warm and sure, reminded her of something. What? She couldn't quite reach it, but she looked at him and he held her gaze and she felt a first touch of hope.

As they ate, Harley stopping after a few, slow, mouthfuls, May told him about work and Turtle; how accommodating he was being.

'He's good people. He dropped by this morning. In and out like white lightning.' Harley said, his words tailing with a breathless wheeze.

'Don't worry, baby,' he added, 'It's only when I try to talk and chew gum at the same time I can't breathe.'

She smiled, feeling a yank of irritation in her belly, at being unable to hide how easily she worried now.

'Well don't talk,' she said, adding emphatically, 'I'm going to read to you. Nothing too taxing but something of a favourite of mine.'

When May had first known Harley, she had learned swiftly that although he was razor sharp, any knowledge he had of literature, politics or film had been voraciously devoured and absorbed when he was no longer a child.

'Why do you call my cabin the Wendy house?' he had asked her once.

'You know…' she'd replied rather carelessly. 'From Peter Pan and Wendy?'

'Nope.'

'Everyone knows *Peter Pan and Wendy*! Children's classic!'

'How very colonial of you, May,' Harley had replied dryly, before going on, 'we never had any books the places I grew up.'

'No books. God how awful! We *ate* books. How on earth did you survive?' May cringed remembering her youthful self.

'Well… I suppose I was busy surviving other things.'

From what he'd said it became clear that not only had there been no books in the homes he had shared with his mother, but this was the norm wherever he found himself.

May tried to imagine such a thing. The house she had grown up in, the same static, always and still-there house she was now faced with clearing and sorting out, was packed with books.

William built bookshelves around doorways and in

265

alcoves and along undersides of cornicing and still there were stacks in corners and on tables and piled next to bedsides and sofas. Stella called it The House that Books Built.

'So how come you're such a reader now?' she'd wondered.

'Well,' Harley began with a throaty laugh, 'There was a substitute teacher called Lucy Carson at one of my High Schools...' he laughed as he caught May's eye and nodded. 'Mmm Hmm... Lucy Carson. What A Peach. We all thought she was hot. Anyways, she told me to read *The Catcher in the Rye*, so I did. It didn't make her pay any more attention to me, but that was the beginning.'

'God, Harley you're such a cliché!' May teased, covering up her ridiculous pang of jealousy of this far away crush of Harley's adolescent self.

She wanted to be the only one he had ever wanted, but knew, because he seemed to think it was no big thing, that he had been precociously, sexually voracious. Or promiscuous, May thought, depending on your perspective. She remembered her sister once saying that if he'd been a girl, he would have had a baby by sixteen. Filling the void, just filling the void.

May wondered what Miss Lucy Carson had seen in the young Harley that made her recommend that book. Was it just on the booklist, or had she seen his longing for connection along with his visceral impulse to pull away?

'God I loved that guy,' Harley said with a low self-deprecating laugh. 'Like I was the only kid Holden Caulfield spoke to...'

After that it was Hemingway, Harper Lee and John Irving; Harley read constantly and May had a game she used to play, where she'd try to find something she had read he hadn't.

She never could until she discovered he'd missed what she considered to be the most important books: the books of childhood.

So May had bought a copy of *Peter Pan and Wendy* and given it to him as a present. He had thanked her, put it to one side, and teased her that it was a long-winded way of explaining what a Wendy House was. The book that lay in her lap now was *My Friend Flicka*.

'This is the book that first spoke to my soul about the American landscape,' she said to Harley. 'The descriptions of Wyoming are so vivid. Do you know it?'

Harley shook his head. 'I know *of* it. Horses and a kid?'

'Yes, but it's also about love. Really. That's it. It's about love.' She smiled at his softening expression, lingering until he looked away.

As she read, Harley relaxed and leaned back in his pillows, eyes fluttering closed every now and again.

May, glancing up at the high, wide, plate glass window, was surprised to see that it was almost completely obscured by white. She stood and walked to the window, leaning her elbows on the insubstantial ledge, hands folded under her chin.

'Well, here's your storm,' she murmured, mesmerised by the swirling snow as it batted and scoured the glass. They were so well sealed inside she could barely hear the wind and the whole scene outside was as though someone had pressed the mute button and there was something eerie about the silent squalling; it was all rolling, turbulence with no sound. She turned back to Harley, but he seemed to be asleep.

Her skin started to feel alive and she was more awake than she could remember feeling in weeks. She tried to see out, to make out objects, but it was impossible. She couldn't even see the cars down below in the lot. I wonder if I'll have to stay in town, she thought. If this keeps up, I won't even be leaving the hospital.

She turned to look at Harley and he was watching her cat-like in the gloom.

'I love a storm.'

'I know. First time I met you was after a storm,' he said. He took a slow, trembling breath.

'I remember.' And she did. 'But it was a thunder storm.'

'You were soaking wet. No shoes.'

May couldn't help smiling, but why did it make him so sad? She wondered.

She walked back over to his bedside and sat down. She said his name and lay her head down next to his, kiss, kiss, kissing his temple, butterfly light.

'When I remember that I feel so happy,' she said.

'May,' Harley spoke with longing. 'I can't remember things like you do.'

For a moment May felt the freeze of fear that the accident had damaged him in ways they hadn't seen yet.

'How do I?'

'With colour.' He closed his eyes. 'It's like even though it didn't work out, you can still see the colour it had. For me it's all gone.'

May felt a quick stab of hurt, followed swiftly by immense sadness for him, his loss of these things, these nourishing, restorative memories.

'I know,' she said. 'I know...'

'Help me, May.' May climbed up alongside Harley.

'Scoot over,' she said and lay on her side in the little space at the edge of the bed. She curled one arm over his head and draped her other across his belly.

'Okay? Not pressing on anything I shouldn't?'

'Mm mnn.' He shook his head and shifted a little, settling into the pillows.

May talked, low and soothing about the long, hot, singing nights full of love and laughter and beer and dancing under the stars on the sun porch.

'And the music, Harley. Remember? Someone was always playing music on the stereo and dragging the speakers out of windows. And you and Rob with your guitars.'

She remembered friends banging on makeshift percussion of empty beer cans and upturned oil drums; the velvety, languorous heat, mosquitoes, cracked back yards and dusty sidewalks; dancing in rainstorms and swimming in the river as the sun set.

Harley smiled and closed his eyes. 'Go on,' he nudged.

'Do you remember how hot it was? It was unbelievable… *stiflingly* hot. And so humid.'

'Nah… I think you just weren't used to it.'

'I thought it would just keep on getting hotter and hotter until we all melted, like the tarmac on the road.'

'Tell me about when you came in the pizza place,' Harley directed her, voice muffled. 'With no shoes… standing there dripping wet… Tell me about that.'

May smiled. 'Well, we had just swum in a thunder storm in the river.'

'I never knew that. I thought you'd just been fooling around in the rain. Ya'll'd been swimming?'

May nodded. 'It's still all so vivid,' she mused. 'I remember the rain… I can still remember how it felt. These great drops of fat rain…' She heard the smile in Harley's voice as he said, 'Fat rain…'

'Really. And how it plopped into the dust like when you drop a lump of butter into flour when you're about to make a crumble.' Again, the slow smile bloomed, brief and sweet. 'I think Stella saw Pete in the window of Everybody's otherwise I'm not sure we would have gone in soaking wet like that. He and Stella were kind of fooling around a bit, not really a couple yet, but we all knew they would be.'

She recalled how they had burst through the door of the town's pizza joint, laughing and dripping all over the greasy brown carpet tiles.

'And that's the first time I ever saw you.'

She held him close, breathing him in, shrinking a little inside as she noticed he still smelled alien to her; all disinfectant and bandages and some other smell she couldn't place, something metallic.

'Tell me,' Harley whispered and he folded his arm up and held her forearm with his heavily bandaged hand. She could feel the springy crepe, thick and abrupt and his fingers as they emerged, curling over her arm. May thought for a moment.

'I didn't see you at first, it was so crowded.'

'I saw you,' Harley said quietly. 'The moment you walked in.'

May heard an aching tenderness in his voice.

'What was I like?'

'I can't talk May... not right now.'

He stopped and after a deep breath he said, 'Tell me. I like to hear your voice. You make it feel real.'

May longed to hear how he remembered her, but did not press him. 'Well, we were all trying to decide which house party to go to that night. And then... and then you said something and laughed.'

She remembered how his voice, low and slightly husky around the edges had come through the bubble of noisy voices. She had looked over and seen him. A boy with dark hair, sitting at a booth across the aisle, slightly slouched, turned halfway towards them, one long leg jutting out into the aisle, wearing faded jeans and heavy boots.

'You looked so unlike anyone else there. They were all so clean cut... brightly clothed... chinos and deck shoes kind of thing.'

'You saying I was dirty?' He laughed a little and kissed her arm again.

'Well, it didn't take long to find out that you were pre-tty dirty...' She laughed with him. 'But I mean you were all worn in, which was mmm... I don't know... just so attractive.'

What a lame word, thought May, thinking of the rush of blood that had surged through her when she had seen him, with his too long hair, curling over his collar, obscuring his brow, all rough and every which way; the way he'd tilted his head back fractionally and looked out from under his hair. And how the intense, searching look he'd given her had unsettled her and pulled her in.

'You seemed to know everyone, but... you weren't really with anyone.'

She remembered how occasionally a smile flashed through the stillness of his face with such spontaneous sweetness she'd been unable to tear her eyes away. It had made him look, if fleetingly, incredibly young.

May stroked his head and felt the buzz of regrowth against her fingers. She felt her eyes prick with tears and took a deep, steadying breath.

'I wanted more than anything else in the world, for you to look at me again. And you wouldn't! Everywhere but at me, damn you!'

Harley dipped his chin and brushed her arm with his lips. 'I couldn't,' he said, his voice a little lost, 'I...couldn't. You were so...'

'What?' she prompted gently, 'What was I?'

For a moment he said nothing, then he burst out, 'Alive! Oh May, you came in there just glowing with being alive and I remember that moment... feeling freaked out by it. Honest, I thought My God, I've been in a fucking coma. And...' he said softly, 'you just looked so beautiful to me.'

'Really?' she asked, her voice full of wonder. 'I just remember feeling really exposed.'

'That is because y'all mostly had nothin on,' Harley said with an exaggerated drawl and he smiled, eyes closed.

'No,' she said. 'It was something about the way you had looked at me that first time. And then you reached out and touched me as Stella and I were leaving.'

She closed her eyes, feeling again the strength of his warm grasp on her forearm as he'd stopped her from walking by; seeing how he'd searched her face with his intensely dark eyes.

'And you said, "so",' and May put on a deep, rumbling parody of an American. 'Will you be at the Decent Keg party?'

May remembered even now, the triumphant thrill. Harley shifted a little and stroked a finger on her arm. His eyes stayed shut.

'Nice,' he murmured. 'No wonder you slept with me first date!'

'Hmm… so that was a date, was it?' she said dryly, 'Good to know!'

'Where I come from it is,' he said with a half laugh. 'Go on, baby, I'm sorry.'

For a moment, May stayed quiet, stroking his face softly. 'Do you remember the party?'

'Not really,' he shrugged, 'but I remember kissing you on the porch and asking you to go home with me.'

They were both quiet and then Harley said, 'I didn't think you'd say yes.'

'Come on…' May was sceptical. 'You wouldn't have asked if you'd thought that.'

He shifted about a bit and said very quietly, 'You don't know.'

May stroked him gently and mumbled her lips against his temple. She felt again that haunting sense of loss and longing.

'I remember how you always used to cut the lights and engine of your bike just before pulling into the drive. You'd just coast in and I used to love watching while you sat and smoked in the dark before you came in to see us.'

'It was you I came for, May,' Harley said before croaking out the words of a Springsteen song, '*I came for you… I came for you.* I always think I don't remember things, but I do. I remember, but I get this tightness and I can't…' he stopped. 'You know I thought I was just scratching an itch. But it kind of didn't work out that way. Itch wouldn't go away. Just had to keep on coming around. Does that sound weird? I just couldn't forget about you. '

'Why did you want to?'

'I don't know baby, just easier that way.'

The silence expanded between them until Harley took a deep breath and began to talk.

'You know what freaked me out? Sometimes it was like you could see inside me. Right inside. You still do that May and sometimes...' He stopped and May kissed the hollow of his neck. She couldn't quite tell what his hesitation was about; was he concerned for her feelings or his own?

'What?' she asked gently, hoping she didn't sound challenging but sensing her own need to push him on.

'I... ahh...' Harley stopped. May waited. 'Maybe you won't like what you see,' he said at last.

She felt herself relax. 'I've always loved what I've seen, all of it; or found it compelling, or intriguing. I realised a long time ago that you didn't lie; you might not volunteer much but you don't lie and that was such a revelation. Precious. I grew up with liars. Careless liars, protective liars, lazy liars. You are so beautiful to me Harley. You always were.'

Harley was profoundly quiet.

'Thank you,' he said at last, his voice was warm. He paused before continuing, 'May? Tell me what we used talk about.'

May smiled at his question; he sounded like a child asking for a story he knew by heart.

'Everything. Ev...ry...thing. Your thoughts seemed to leap about all over the place.'

Harley smiled and exhaled at the same as she went on, wanting to fill the room with it all.

'I thought we'd talk forever. Never, never stop. And that I'd finally know you.' May felt wistful as she thought about her young self so full of hope and confidence. 'But I suppose that was to imagine that knowing someone was some identifiable point of arrival and of course it's not. And how was it,' May went on but feeling suddenly flutteringly scared as she began to voice the thought, 'that we got so close but couldn't, couldn't tell each other how much it all meant? Oh *why* didn't you tell me you wanted me to stay?'

'You *know* why,' said Harley, swiftly angry, 'you had a home to go to. What was I going to do? Beg you to stay?'

You wouldn't have had to beg, she thought and was filled with despair at the time they'd wasted, the hurt they'd felt.

'May, I never could use words the way you do. And now here I am and I'm full to the brim with it all and if I was still myself I'd show you... I'd show you... but I can't. I can't.'

He was so full of frustration and longing, it hurt May. She remembered again, that first time she'd felt he was showing her and how hopeful she'd felt; how naïve she'd been.

They were naked, sweating, fused, skin sticking, peeling in the heart-heated dark of the night. May was right at the edge, that moment where it felt like she was reaching, reaching and might... just... not... get it, when Harley broke their rhythm, stopped moving against her and curved away a little to look down at her with his hot, dark eyes searching, searching. May clutched him to her and he crept his strong fingers into her hair, cradling her head.

'May...' he whispered, hoarse, but he said nothing more and she felt his words fly away and out into the singing night, wanted to reach out her hand and net them back, press them back into his mouth and hear him say them. She'd have given anything to hear what they were.

She listened to his fluttering, trembling, breath, heard it catch in his throat and felt such an intensity of emotion, love, longing and urgency she could say nothing, just held his eyes, balancing on the edge with him until they again moved with each other, one against the other.

Harley clung to her in the darkness, whispered her name again, let himself go with a shout she'd never heard, profoundly shuddering until he was gasping out, Oh god... Oh god, sounding desperate and lost.

He kissed her all over her face, her lids, her cheeks, her mouth, with such gentleness it made her want to weep. And instead of springing away from her and flinging himself onto his back by her side as he always did, he held her in his arms, cradling her against him, stroking her while their breathing slowly became even and quiet, kissing her softly through her hair.

'I never knew...' he whispered as she drifted away on a rising swell of sleep.

The next morning May stood in the open doorway, looking out at the early sunshine filtering softly through the trees. She could see a pair of little chickadees flitting about from branch to branch on the apple tree and hear the first revving up of the cicadas. She heard the shower stop and the cubicle door open as Harley stepped out wrapping a towel about his waist. His dark eyes were full of tenderness and flickering heat and he hugged her from behind pressing his cheek against hers looking out at the new day. I love you, she thought, feeling as though she was standing on a cliff edge.

They lay together for a long time, while the room hummed and the light through the window changed from icy brilliant white to a rose tinged glow. Harley seemed to slip in and out of sleep and then as he began to croak sing softly and his voice woke her, May realised that she too had been sleeping.

'There's no way I can change / The past or your pain.'

May felt her throat catch at the words and his soft husky voice singing to her. Her mouth slightly muffled by Harley's chest, she answered back singing softly, 'I don't want to fight... Let's start anew now.'

'It was such an obscure little song that just meant a whole lot to me and you started to sing it,' Harley said, leaping in as though she had been following his train of thought all along. 'And I just thought fuck me, how is it that she even knows this, this part of me? I wanted to jump you right there. We didn't make it back to my room.'

'Well... we did.' May smiled softly.

'Well yeah, after a while.'

'First time I ever did that… out under the stars…' May felt warm remembering. 'There were a lot of firsts with you, Harley. I'd never been so happy,' she said quietly, remembering how brief it had been.

That far off morning, watching the sun dancing through the trees and the birds darting about, May had felt it was a turning point for them, that he was finally letting his guard down. Trusting her. Loving her. It had taken her a while to realise which way things were turning.

Harley turned to May and held her closer, kissed her tenderly on her mouth.

'I'd never been so scared.'

'Scared?'

'Yeah, May. I was scared.' He was quiet a while before saying, 'I knew you'd leave.'

'So you slept with someone else? Other people? How… why would that be the answer?' It was still so hard to understand.

Harley took a deep breath and May sensed his reluctance to finish. Finally, his voice hard, angry almost, he said, 'Oh for chrissake May, you trying to put some kind of rational spin on this? It doesn't make sense, okay? It just doesn't and I hate it, I hate that there's something in me that smashes things before they get smashed… like I can't stand the wait…'

'Well,' she said, wanting him to know. 'It broke my heart. I thought I'd never get over that hurt, and the loss of you.'

Harley closed his eyes and took in a huge breath. 'Oh baby,' he trembled, 'I'm sorry. I wish… I wish…' but he couldn't seem to finish. 'Fuck.' He scrubbed his eyes. 'Why do you make me do this?'

The ferocity of the snow was easing and outside the window, May could make out snowflakes and see dark sky and shrouded shapes down in the parking lot. They lay quietly together as the room hummed. May had only turned one light on when she arrived and the light struggled through the darkness. Harley's slightly wheezy breath became deeper and more even, until she knew he must be asleep.

28

Rob was sitting hunched on the front porch steps, ear buds in, nodding and tapping tack, tack, tack on the wood to some silent music, when May turned up with Harley's key.

He yanked the wires out of his ears when he saw her and stood up and stretched, exposing his lean, pale torso and the waistband of his underpants as the edge of his bright red down jacket and untucked shirt rode up.

'I've been waiting for you so long my ass is about froze right off!'

'I told you I couldn't get here any earlier than two,' May said mildly.

Harley had accepted Matthew's offer of his old room and was not renewing the lease on his one room apartment off Main Street.

Rob seemed to have forgotten that he had offered to get a place with his friend and had already moved in on another local girl. May was so relieved she had not minded having to spend a whole afternoon with him boxing up Harley's things and carting them to Matthew's.

It was a brilliantly bright day, with a soft breeze melting the icicles hanging from the eaves, making the drifts of snow delicately pockmarked and roundly contoured.

The air felt suspended and cold inside. May stooped to pick up some of the piles of leaflets and newspapers that had accumulated on the rug. She was surprised by how much there was considering that Matthew came and collected the mail every week.

Rob looked at her strangely. 'What?'

'I don't know… odd to be in here without him, I suppose. I feel a bit like we're trespassing.'

Rob screwed his face up. 'What the fuck you talking

about?'

May had only been here a few times and it would now never feel familiar to her. She looked around trying to take everything in, before she started dismantling it.

'How are we going to do this Rob?'

Again, Rob's response was of puzzlement. He was looking at May as though she was a bit mad, or he was afraid she was. 'We open up boxes, throw shit in, close the boxes.'

May sighed. 'Rob. We can't just "throw shit in". Look why don't you pack up the kitchen, I'll do his bedroom, then we can do this room together. Try and take care with his things.'

Rob shrugged and muttered something that sounded suspiciously like, 'Yes Mom' before slunking off into the kitchen area.

She wandered into the bedroom and sat on the edge of Harley's bed. After a moment she lay down and looked up at the ceiling, looking for cracks or patterns or something Harley may have watched as he'd lain there at night. She turned onto her side hoping to catch something of his smell, but all she could detect was washing powder.

The bluish green glow of numbers on the digital clock radio flashed rhythmically. The power must have gone off, she thought, maybe during that storm.

'Rob, check the freezer!' she called out. 'I think there might have been a power cut.'

He ducked his head around the corner and laughed at her lying there.

'Wasted already?'

He disappeared back around the door and May sat up, reached down behind the bedside table and pulled out the plug of the lamp. Coiling up the flex, she rolled it in bubble wrap and stood it in a deep cardboard box.

'Is it okay, Rob? The freezer?'

'No problem, he only had some ice and vodka in it.'

But he doesn't drink spirits any more, she thought. She

opened a drawer and felt a lurch. What if she found something he wouldn't want her to see; not compromising, just private.

'Harley, I hope you know that we're just going to pack, not look at things.'

He had been painstakingly shaving, leaning on a crutch, peering at himself in the mirror above the sink as though he didn't know who he was looking at. He had smiled.

'Ain't much to look at anyhow.'

'I mean it though. I keep thinking how twitchy I'd feel if I knew someone was going through my things at home.'

'Well... like you say. You're just packing it up... not going through it.' He met her eyes in the mirror. 'Right?'

His bedside drawer was full of pens, condoms, some pretty hard-core pain relief tablets and matches. There was an envelope of photos that she stopped herself looking at and a black A5 Mead notebook, stuffed full of scraps of paper, news clippings, postcards and almost three quarters filled with writing. She put it to one side. It seemed to throb and glow in her peripheral vision. She opened clothes drawers and put t-shirts, socks and underwear in another box.

Harley appeared to have nothing superfluous except for pens; they were everywhere in large numbers. Every item of clothing she folded and put away, she had seen him wear many times. All the fabrics were worn and faded and unusually for America, not a logo in sight apart from a Jack Daniels t-shirt. She smiled at that. Rob still sometimes called him Jack; it had been all he drank in the old days.

She started to take the things off his dresser. A pair of sunglasses, post it notes stuck neatly in rows with instructions and reminders of work, names of people to call. Liv's name and number leapt off one of them. Loose change. Some CDs: Curtis Mayfield, Dr John, *Exile on Main Street* and *Fisherman's Blues*, which brought a surge of longing; she had played that to him first, long ago.

She spent a few moments reading the news clippings taped up around the edges of a mirror, some funny, others not.

Area Man Wants 'Hell' Taken out of 'Hello', South Dakota County Suppressing The Native American Vote, Federal Agents Raid Gun Shop and Find Weapons, South Dakota Tribe Gets Grant to Establish Foster Care Programme.

Tucked into the edge of the mirror was a photo of him with Hope. Harley looked incredibly young and intense, but Hope was hysterical with laughter. He had her around her middle from behind and had lifted her off her feet, his legs astride, standing his ground in heavy boots, knees slightly bent. His hair was obscuring his eyes and he was jutting out his chin in a pose that looked like mocking defiance.

She took it out gently and another smaller photo fell out from behind it, face down. May picked it up and written in Harley's script, she read the words, *Harbor of my soul.* She turned it over, pulse suddenly banging.

It was a photo of her, perched on the railings of the sun porch where she'd lived with Stella and Danielle. She was wearing a very short frayed denim skirt and a fuchsia edged black swimsuit, under a white shirt that she knew had been Harley's, unbuttoned and fluttering in the wind. Her skin was tanned and her bare feet resting on the seat of Harley's motorcycle. Her dark hair was blowing about in the wind and she was laughing, looking directly into the camera. May looked at it for a long time. My god, she thought. I really was happy.

Back in the sitting room she started on his desk, stacking papers and journals and carefully writing each item on the sides of the boxes as she put them in.

Rob held up Harley's twelve string acoustic. 'I don't

suppose he'll be needing this for a while, his hand's too fucked. I better take it back to my place.'

May pounced. 'Absolutely not, you bloody vulture. Put that in the pile and behave.'

She started packing books into another box.

'He hasn't really accumulated much stuff, has he?'

'Yeah well, he was a war correspondent, wasn't he?' Rob flung at her in his careless way. 'They never have much, might die tomorrow.' He cracked out a laugh. May felt a jerk of surprise.

'Was he?' She turned from the ladder that Harley used as a bookshelf, a copy of *For Esme with Love and Squalor* held in midair. How had she not known this?

'Well, camera, sound or something. He covered shit in South America a while cause of the Latino thing, you know? When he was with CBS.'

She looked at him, blank. Rob carried on breezily dismantling Harley's desk and said, 'He speaks Spanish. His mom was from Nicaragua or Honduras or some other fucked up place like that.'

'No she wasn't. She was from South Dakota, Crow or Sioux or something.'

'Okay his Dad then, what's the freakin difference?'

'What's the freakin difference?' May mimicked Rob's voice. 'You're his friend Rob.'

He laughed, raising his little finger as he held an imaginary teacup. 'Aow,' he pronounced, in a strangled attempt at her accent, 'Oym sorry madame.'

Then he gave her the finger.

'Fuck off yourself.' She shot at him with a grim smile, and they resumed the stripping of Harley's home.

May and Stella were in Lou's a few days later when May's phone started to vibrate in her pocket.

'Sorry Stel, it might be...' she half said, looking at the

screen.

Stella stood. 'I'll go pay.'

When she came back a moment or two later May looked up at her unable to speak; She felt hot and raw inside.

'What?' Stella's voice was concerned as she peered at her friend.

'Well...' she said, swallowing, 'here we go.'

She felt tears sting her nose and her throat constrict.

'Harley's being discharged today. He's coming home.'

Harley was sitting in a chair when May arrived at the hospital, one long leg thrust out in front. He wore his own clothes for the first time in almost two months and it seemed that his gaunt frame was holding them up at the shoulders and hips rather than wearing them.

Somehow his over-lean, hollow appearance seemed more alarming to May than when he'd been in the pyjamas Matthew had bought. Now in his familiar attire it was as though she was seeing for the first time how physically altered he was.

Harley was holding the newspaper and talking to a young male nurse, striding about briskly from corner to corner, tidying things, coiling wires and stripping the bed.

'Hey baby.'

His eyes lit up as May came through the door and even as her heart soared, she realised that this was what she always looked for when she walked through the door, never quite sure if it would come.

'Hi love.' She came over and kissed Harley tenderly on his mouth. 'How about it? Feel like a change of scene?'

'Why not? I think I've taught them all I can.'

'Okay.' She grinned at him, excited and nervous. 'Let's go!'

And then for one insane moment she thought, I wish we weren't going.

In this cloistered room she had frequently felt intimately

close to Harley. They had shared things with all the polish sloughed off, with a raw tenderness that had sometimes hurt but felt vital. What now? What next? She wondered if they could sustain it. Would they even want to? You can't live at that level of intensity, she thought, as she took one last look around, can you?

As they got up to leave, the nurse called out, 'Oh, sir, you haven't packed your nightclothes.' He held up the neatly folded pyjamas.

'I'm done with them. Thanks.'

29

It was a beautiful day, bright and blue and crisp, but the drive home was difficult.

'Shit.' Harley hissed softly. 'Didn't know I'd hate to get in a car again.'

He threw her a slightly pleading look then closed his eyes and took a deep breath.

'Just say if you want to stop and we can pull over for a bit.'

He smiled tightly. 'Let's just do it, baby. Get it over with.'

May drove as smoothly as she could, pointing out a favourite oak tree, drawing his attention to a beautiful marbled, pearly sweep of cloud over the horizon, but aware of his fragile stillness. His mouth was tight and white at the edges and she reached out a hand and massaged the nape of his neck briefly while she steered with one hand.

As they drove on the colour slowly seemed to drain from Harley's face until he looked quite unwell.

'Okay…'

He nodded, mute, but May pulled over. He flung open the door and threw up on the verge, hunched over as though he was protecting something.

She rubbed her hand gently up his back, along his spine and down again until he shrugged her off and sat back, smiling weakly. He pulled at some of the tissues sticking out of a box in the well between their seats and wiped his mouth, chucking them out and slamming the door.

'Whoa…' he breathed and looked sideways at her. 'Quick thinking, baby, way to go.'

'That's okay. I'm sorry love, horrid for you.'

'Feels better. Let's go.'

He switched the radio on and fiddled until he found a station he liked and sat back, nodding a little while May sang along to the Rolling Stones's 'Slave'.

As she pulled into Matthew's drive, their old friend came out of the house to greet them with a huge smile on his face.

'Welcome home, son!' he called.

May saw Harley's responsive smile and felt a surge of warmth as she watched the two men embrace and hold each other for a moment. The dogs came wriggling and tumbling around the side of the house and Piper whined and whistled as she saw Harley before hurling herself at him. He bent over her crooning and roughing her ears about until she finally settled down.

'Coffee first, or you want to settle in?'

'Coffee's good, but let me just wash up first.'

Later that evening in the warmth of May's kitchen, Matthew laid a gentle hand on her shoulder and said, 'Thank you for dinner, honey, it was delicious.'

'Any time, Matthew. Really.'

Harley was leaning back, one leg thrust out, an arm hooked over the back of his chair, while he tapped a repetitive scale quietly on the table. He tipped a sweet, brief smile at her.

'Well that's real nice, May,' Matthew went on, 'I spend a lot of my time in my studio and I like to know I'll see a body to speak to from time to time. Seems to me eating around the table together is the way to do that. When Hope and I were raising our boys, we made sure we all ate together once a day. Keeps it family.'

Harley nodded slowly and gave Matthew a long look then put a hand out and tipped a finger under May's chin, 'Thanks, beautiful,' he said quietly.

Matthew stood to go back to his studio, as he frequently did before he turned in for the night, and May watched as he put his hand on Harley's shoulder, squeezed it gently then patted, once... twice. He said nothing but the two men exchanged a look.

After Matthew had gone, May looked at Harley's pensive face for a moment before asking if he was okay. He smiled weakly.

'You want to walk me home?'

Harley had his arm around her shoulders as they walked through the thick darkness, their breath frosting in short, fat, plumes. Their boots crunched the packed snow with short, high pitched, twisting squeaks as they made their way along the length of May's drive, turned into Matthew's and started their slow decent through his yard. Harley's room, a small barn conversion, was located near the old loose boxes that had been used for the livery business.

'Well… here we go,' Harley said, his voice tentative.

'About time.'

She pushed her head against him and put her other arm around his middle, hugging him as they continued their slow progression.

'The stars look so sharp tonight,' May said, wondering if he'd seen them properly while in hospital, wanting to soar up there; pull him up with her. We'd be alright up there, she thought, nothing to get in the way.

He leaned on her lightly with every second step, his left leg always lagging a little.

'Okay?' she asked again, worried about how tired he looked.

His hand drifted from her shoulder and he stroked her hair gently, but said nothing.

They arrived at the barn and Harley took his arm from around her to open the door, standing back a little to let her pass in front of him.

It felt warm and she glanced over at the wood burner, seeing the glowing, burnished ripples through the glass-fronted door. It cast long flickering shadows through the clusters of boxes still waiting to be opened.

He dropped onto the bed, swung his legs up and leaned back against the scant pillows, letting out a long sigh.

'Come here, baby,' he said sounding more like his old self. 'You like to lay down with me fo a while?'

He put an arm around her, snuggling her into his body, his other hand stroking her face and hair in slow, slow caresses. Until then, May had had no idea of how bone tired she was. She felt Harley's heat gently seep into her as she breathed him in and the warm smell of his skin comforted her, drawing her into a gentle place of tenderness, of hushed sanctuary.

She closed her eyes and saw the shadows flicker and dance behind her lids, felt him kiss her softly through her hair and as she rose and fell on a swell of sleep, she heard him murmur so softly it could have been a dream, '...love you so...'

The next day dawned rosily beautiful, chilled and icy, with a pale washed blue sky and a strange stillness.

Harley had been restless and unsettled all night, unable to get comfortable, involuntarily flinching and clinging to May every time she shifted or tried to accommodate his constant movements, so she had stayed as still as possible. It was as Matthew's rooster began valiantly competing with the full-throated dawn chorus that she felt him finally relax and slip into a deep sleep.

She sat up, head heavy, but despite her stiff and aching limbs, felt like dancing, her heart joined the singing birds as she looked at him lying among the pillows. You're home, she thought, oh you're home. She kissed him softly on his cheek and slipped out and up to her house to shower. Why had she said she'd work today? What an idiot.

As she was leaving, she looked in on Matthew who was already in his studio. There was a churchlike silence in the air.

'I left Harley sleeping,' she said, 'I don't think he had a

great night. Will you tell him he can call me at work if he wants?'

'I'll do that, honey. Y'all have a good day.' He looked appraisingly at May. 'How long are you working today? Looks like *you* could use some sleep, little girl.'

May smiled at him. 'I'm just in the office today, not waiting tables. I'll be fine. I'll be back around four.'

She went straight to his room when she got home from work, without stopping to drop her bag. She could hear a throbbing baseline through the walls and Buddy Guy yelling angrily that she was *Damn Right I Got the Blues* and was surprised that at her knock he called out an almost instant, 'Yeah!'

'What amazing hearing you have.'

Harley smiled when he saw her, straightened from the box he was foraging around in and turned down the music.

'It wasn't me,' he said indicating Piper who had come from her basket over to May and was politely wagging at her.

His room looked much more like someone lived there; stereo set up, books on the shelves at either side of the bed and the photo of Hope tucked in the dresser mirror. May wondered where the one of her was. There was a pile of flattened boxes to the side of the door. At the far wall the boxes with KITCHEN marked on them were unopened.

He came over to her, face soft, half smiling.

'Hey,' he murmured, tilting his head, 'how'd it go?'

'Alright. I'm bloody knackered, though. I hardly slept.'

'I'm sorry. I keep getting cramp in this damn leg. I should have sent you on to your own bed last night.'

'Your first night back? No way!' said May lightly, wishing she'd thought before speaking.

She reached out to him and he drew her into his arms, murmuring into her hair. 'Come lay down? I've been waiting for you all day.'

May took her time to settle in his arms, fidgeting to find a familiar position. Harley squinted at her from the corner of an eye, with a half-smile half-grimace.

'What?'

'I can't get comfy... wait... that's better.'

But it wasn't. He sighed and pulled her against his gaunt shoulder, settling further back into the pillows and kissing the top of her head.

'I kind of like your hair like this,' she said, making it stand up about his head in dark unruly peaks. 'I like seeing your face.'

Harley shrugged her hand off and shook his head, but his hair stayed up and out of the way.

'I can't get used to it. Never had a naked forehead before. It feels very ex-posed.' He drew out the final syllable in a long drawl, the gravel in his voice a little more audible. May loved the sound. She closed her eyes to block out how he looked and let the sound of his voice wash through her.

'You're so bony,' she said without thinking. 'We need to feed you up.'

Harley ignored her comment. 'Everyone behaving themselves at work?'

'Mostly... Brett's back after the baby... looking radiant and exhausted. Connie snarky as ever. Everyone asking after you, sending love.'

'Hmmph...' Harley exhaled with a brief smile, then restlessly sat back up again, looking around the room.

'Maybe I'll just get on. I'll see you in a little while.'

'Harley...' May began, not knowing what she wanted to say but aware of something heavy between them. 'I didn't mean...' She reached a hand out to touch him and his slight but unmistakeable flinch startled her. 'Sorry,' she said softly and a swift look of irritation passed over his face, before he took a deep slow breath and looked at her, his expression quiet.

'It's fine,' he said dismissively, but May felt that she'd

made a mistake, upset him somehow. She was unsure how to put it right.

That night at dinner, Harley was withdrawn. He pushed back his chair as Matthew started on the dishes and looked closely at his left hand as though it was a strange curio, cradling it in the palm of the other.

'Does it hurt?' May asked.

'Nah... yeah... sort of feels weird. Hurts if I stretch it too much, but...' He gave up.

'Are you supposed to be doing anything to help it along?'

Harley just gave a partial shrug, a frown and went to help Matthew.

'Son, does your insurance provide for physiotherapy? That hand of yours is your livelihood and you need it back in shape.'

'No? Really?' Harley replied dryly.

May looked at Harley with surprise; he was usually so sweet to Matthew even when he teased him. She watched as he clumsily finished drying a glass.

'They seemed quite happy with it at the hospital, Harley, didn't they?'

He nodded and made a vaguely affirming sound.

'Did they give you any idea how long until...' she trailed off, unsure of what she was asking.

'What? Till it's back to "normal".' He sounded grimly ironic. 'I'm never going to be the same as I was.'

May opened her mouth, but Matthew got in there faster, surprising her with unaccustomed sharpness. 'That's enough. You're here. You're alive.'

He turned his back on them and drained the sink as May and Harley exchanged a look and Harley raised his eyebrows at her. He got up and leaned on the counter peering around at the older man.

'You telling me to lighten up.'

'No, son,' Matthew made an exasperated swatting gesture with his arm. 'I'm tellin you to count your blessings.'

'Count my blessings?' Harley echoed, a ripple of irony in his tone.

'That *is* what I said, yes. Wreck didn't affect your hearing none.'

'Well, Matthew, I hadn't thought of that.' The cynical edge sharpened. 'Maybe I'll just give that a try. It might help when I can't hold my awl properly and I stab myself in my half good other hand. What do you say May? You think I should be counting my blessings?'

'Don't, Harley.'

She stood quickly and cleared the table of the last dishes.

'Thanks for making supper, Matthew, I'm so tired at the moment it was lovely not to have to think about it.'

Matthew put down his dishcloth and looked at Harley a moment with cool scrutiny. The atmosphere felt dense as though a storm was on the wind beyond the trees.

'May, honey, give us a moment,' he said gently.

Harley looked as though he hadn't heard and picked up another glass to dry.

An hour or so later, Harley called her name softly down the hall.

'In here!'

She'd found it hard to concentrate on her book, reading the same bloody sentence repeatedly without understanding it. She was angry that Matthew had dismissed her as though she were a child and ashamed that she was angry with him. She was upset that Harley's mood seemed unstable; that it was spoiling what she had thought was going to be a happy homecoming.

She uncurled and stretched as Harley walked in, smiling at him to hide her anxiety. His eyes appeared bruised with fatigue, his mouth pinched and white at the corners.

'Just wanted to say goodnight.'

Sweet, she thought. 'Okay.' She came over wondering what had happened after she'd gone.

'Everything alright?'

'Oh sure. He just wanted to set me straight. Told me not to be an asshole and I said okay.' He smiled self-deprecatingly and May relaxed, realising only then quite how tense she'd been.

'Matthew wouldn't talk like that,' she said doubtfully, half smiling.

'He doesn't need to. I know what he means.' Harley straightened and took a gulp of air. 'So, you get yourself some sleep. I'll see you tomorrow.'

She wanted to ask him to come up with her but something held her back and Harley said, 'I don't want to keep you awake for another night, May. You need your sleep. I'm told I'm not the only one who's been having a hard time.' He smiled sweetly and she held her tongue. 'Hey…' He put an arm around her and kissed her head as she held his gaunt frame. 'Sweet dreams, baby,' he murmured into her hair.

'You too.'

Feeling drab, May went on upstairs, wondering what she'd thought would happen when he came home. That night she dreamed of him as he had been. He walked into her room, stripped off and fucked her; uninhibited and joyous. She woke, breathless, alone in the dark.

'Honey, for someone so bright, you're pretty stupid sometimes.' Stella and May were sitting opposite each other in Lou's Diner, sharing a plate of fries. 'Seriously? Your feelings are hurt because he's not the same with you as he was before the accident? What the fuck?'

'Oh don't be *mean*, Stell. I'm so tired of all of this and yes I bloody *do* want everything to be like it was. I miss him Stella. One of the things I remember most and miss… oh it *hurts* how much I miss it… is how sure he was about his body. He couldn't always say how he felt, but he held me, he touched me like he meant it. And since he's come home… I can't explain but everything seems more fragile. I feel like he's reluctant to do anything more than hold me. Sometimes even that seems too much for him. I can't tell if it's me, if it's him, if it's just because it's another change to accommodate.'

'Honey it must be so hard for him. Don't you think? Pretty emasculating I would have thought, for a guy like him. It makes a lot of sense.'

'Does it?' May's voice was clipped. 'Not to me.' She wasn't sure why she was being so stubborn. 'Why?'

'Oh come on May. You guys had just started out, you go away and he's a horn dog and you're all loved up, you come back and he's flat on his back his hair shaved like Samson and you have to practically feed him!'

'I should never have gone to London,' May spoke despairingly and Stella looked exasperated.

'I know,' she said with heavy irony, 'then he never would have gotten in a wreck. You know what, May? I bet you stepped on all the cracks in the sidewalk while you were there! That was probably what did it—you're so careless!'

She tore open a little sachet of sweetener and poured it into her coffee.

'You shouldn't eat that stuff you'll get cancer,' May muttered crossly.

'I'm not a lab rat, May, but thanks for caring,' Stella said mildly.

'Look,' she went on, 'from what I can understand, he's the most insecure man in the universe and...' She stopped and looked at May as though wondering if she dared to say what had just occurred to her.

May looked at her with suspicion. 'What?'

'May, my dear.' May narrowed her eyes. 'Are you being entirely straight with yourself?'

'With myself? In what way?'

'You want things to be how they were? Is that because it's not just him that's feeling weirded out by his scars and shit?'

May felt a hot flush of shame. She sat wordless, not bothering to protest. Stella looked so tenderly at her, with such understanding, that May started to cry quietly right there in the diner. 'Oh fuck,' May muttered, staring rigidly into the aisle.

'Well, perhaps that's your problem right there. You're missing his old body too and he knows it. Dude's no fool, that much I do know about him. If you talked about it, you could maybe get through it together. Rather than just pretending nothing's changed.'

'And this from the woman who doesn't talk to her own husband about anything other than TV and sport,' May said nastily and felt instantly awful. Stella didn't seem in the least troubled and grinned at her.

'Might I say, that that uncharacteristic little outburst just tells me I'm right and you're uncomfortable about it, so,' she gave her the middle finger. 'Up yours!'

May, chastened, smiled at her friend, 'Sorry. Uncharacteristic, eh? I suppose I should be grateful for that!'

May was coming to the end of a long shift a few days later and was tired. She stood with her weight on one leg and looked appraisingly at the large group of eight young men spilling all over the place, with their hollered jokes and bravado drinking. Frat Bros, she thought, even if they're not.

'Okay, guys, can I get you anything else?'

'Ahh… yes,' said a bulky shouldered one, winking at her. 'Get me a side of slaw.'

'A side of slaw?' She was unable to disguise the scepticism in her voice.

'Ya huh!' He looked around the table inviting approval and got some smirking nods.

She was punching the order through the till, muttering darkly, when Amy came alongside and started shooting sodas into a tray of tall ice filled glasses.

'What up mad lady?'

'I've been trying to close out my last table for the past half hour and they just ordered a side of slaw. One. Even though they've eaten their way through the entire Tex Mex menu. And had desserts.'

'Bummer!'

'And Connie's making me nervous. She keeps looking at me while she's talking to people. I hate when she does that.'

She saw her light flash on and ran down to the kitchen, grabbed the slaw off the salad counter and taking the stairs two at a time, placed it on the table.

'Enjoy!' she said, reaching in to the pocket of her apron to give them the bill.

'You know what?' drawled a blond baby-faced boy, winking at his friends, 'I think I'll get a grilled cheese sandwich.'

'Grilled cheese? Okay.' She turned away.

'Oh miss!' The voice was heavy with look-at-me-guys humour. 'I need a brownie sundae. With extra whipped cream.'

'Anyone else?' she said with a smile she wasn't feeling.

There was a big show of trying to decide and then, 'I think I'll wait until I see his, then I'll know if I really want one.'

As she was just reaching the edge of her section, a voice called her.

'Oh waitress!' she turned back and the entire rabble of them was turned expectantly towards her. Mouths half open, grinning stupidly, one or two a little glassy eyed. She walked briskly back, her insides curling with irritation.

'Umm… on the brownie sundae…' the boy said as May looked quizzically at his upturned face. 'The cream, is it the kind you shake and squirt?' His voice was solemn, his expression too deadpan for May's comfort as he demonstrated with his hand in the air. Don't jerk off at me, you little fucker, she thought savagely.

Out of the corner of her eye she could see one of them beginning to lose control and start to laugh silently.

'It is,' replied May.

'Well then, can you bring it here and squirt it on in front of me?' There were some stifled explosions of laughter.

May struggled to keep a neutral expression onto her face. She was desperately tired and worried she was either going to lose her temper or cry.

'The kitchen does that,' she lied.

On her return, they began loudly shouting drink orders. She took them down and strode back to the main restaurant, slapping the order down onto the varnished wooden bar.

'Connie! Bar order!'

Connie looked over at May from the other side of the bar. She gave a small nod, then went back to her conversation, leaning gracefully over the bar, her burnished copper bob slipping forward and accentuating the angle of her fine jaw bone. She seemed to be casting pointed looks at May as she talked and the girl she was talking to looked delightedly shocked and stared across at her. She felt horribly uneasy just as she spotted Turtle and darted over to him before he went downstairs.

'Turtle I've got a tricky table. Can you nip over and take a look?' She didn't wait for his answer; Connie had rung the bell. Then, just as May was lifting the tray, crowded with drinks, Connie said, 'Hey... whole town's talking. Too bad the leopard couldn't change his spots!' She slipped across to the other side of the bar to fill the shouted orders from the post-game student crowd.

'*What?*' she snapped across the bar, but Connie played deaf.

May's head began to thud, pounding blood. She steadied the tray and closed her eyes, took a deep breath and headed off.

'Behind you!' she shouted at Amy whose section she was speeding through. Her friend stood still and May arrived at her table hot behind the eyes trying to remember who had ordered what.

'Right!' she said, breaking a cardinal rule of Molly's, 'I'm finishing my shift now, so if there's nothing else I'll get your check.'

She knew she sounded angry, but was past caring.

A couple of the boys went quiet. The one with shoulders made a low, 'Oooh,' and put his hand to his crotch making a quick, aggressive, jerking movement. May stood her ground and looked at him unwaveringly. You little shit, she thought.

'Excuse me, eloquent though that was, I wouldn't want to presume what you meant by it. Would you like to use your words?'

He shrugged his shoulders. 'What I do?' he said, all injured innocence.

'You tried to make my job harder than it already is.'

'How hard can it be?' he replied looking around at his friends.

There was a ripple of uneasy laughter before they began to talk animatedly all at once.

May reached the first drink onto the table, holding the tray high on the flat of her hand. Out of the corner of her eye, she saw the gleam of Connie's hair and turned her head sharply to see that she was leaning on the bar grinning and staring at May. She felt her hand drop and the tray dipped swiftly to one side. Jerking her hand to right it, she misjudged by a long way and the whole thing flipped up towards her.

Glasses flew up, crashed onto the table, the floor. Icy slush and glass smashed into her, drenching her, the shock and cold forcing a horrified cry from her throat.

People suddenly seemed everywhere, some clapping, and people over in the bar were cheering and applauding the noise. May stood rigid, eyes stinging from the liquor.

She shivered and dropped to her knees, picking up shards of glass and balancing them lightly in her hand.

'May!' Turtle almost snapped. 'Don't do that, go downstairs and fix yourself up. We're done here everyone!'

She passed the grill on her way to Turtle's office and Kevin, flipping a line of burgers called out, 'Hey May! Heard you finally got majorly baptized!'

She jerked a V sign in his direction without looking at him.

'Hey! You're bleeding all over the frickin floor.'

She looked down and saw that her right knee was oozing thick blood. For a moment, mesmerised, she watched as the blood collected and swelled in slow motion, then dropped and started to run down her leg. Now that she had seen it, it hurt, sharp and stinging, the knee throbbed where blood was seeping. She got into the tiny office where the first aid kit was kept and rummaged around uselessly. As her hand foraged in the green plastic box, her mind kept going over and over

Connie's words. Too bad the leopard couldn't change his spots… that was what she'd said. May sat in Turtle's swivel chair and felt a wave of nausea swell through her.

Amy came sauntering in, glanced at May's leg and drew in a sharp breath. 'Nasty.'

She sped out of the office coming back almost immediately with a bowl of steaming water and a cloth and she began to dab away at the edges of the cut. Overwhelmed suddenly with weariness, tears seeped from May's tightly closed lids.

'Amy,' she said quietly. 'Has Connie said anything to you about Harley?'

Amy stopped and looked slowly up into May's face.

'Oh,' said May, feeling extremely sick.

'I'm sure it's nothing,' Amy said, sounding full of bravado. 'Otherwise I swear I would've said something to you. Woman never got over herself after some one night thing they had.' She was talking very fast, her hand on May's arm.

'Oh, god,' May's stomach pitched. 'He's slept with Connie?'

'Jesus! May! Not since the Stone Age. It's ancient history, that's for sure. Everyone knows that. She always goes on about it when she's drunk, she's always bad mouthing him, but she'd have him in a heartbeat.'

'No wonder she's so vile to me.' *Everyone knows…* 'I feel sick.'

Amy, who was working gently at May's knee, stopped while May leaned forward and lowered her head. After a long moment she sat back slowly.

'Okay?' Amy asked.

May nodded and her friend dabbed a bit more at her knee.

'So. Tell me. What's Harley supposed to have done?'

'Really, May?' Amy looked painfully uncomfortable, her usually eager face closed and tight. After an awkward silence she said, 'Okay. If you're sure.' She folded up a piece of gauze, placed it over the cut and sat back on her haunches.

'Apparently when you were in London before he had the car wreck, he… uh… was hanging out with Liv again.'

It took May twice the usual time to get home and her head was a mess full of the day she had endured.

The fog was so dense she had to creep along the centre of the road, her headlights barely picking out the road markings. She was fearful of sliding down the verge, desperate to get back and speak to Harley, dreading it. Why, she wondered, was she assuming 'hanging out' with Liv had more meaning than the simple words? She knew Connie was a shit stirring gossip. She'd got the wrong end of the stick once, spreading the word about her and Harley before there was a her and Harley…

She wanted to ask him if he'd slept with Liv while she was in London but knew if he had, he'd say yes. Could she bear that? She realised she was breathlessly afraid of his honesty. She was overwhelmed by a powerful surge of something viscerally primal. I'm not a coward, she thought. This is worth fighting for. Nothing can undo what we've been through together since the accident. Nothing.

May turned onto the unmarked single-track road that led to the farmhouse and slowed even more, but she still almost managed to miss her driveway. She felt disorientated and unsettled. As she pulled to a stop, she felt her shoulders up around her ears, tight and tense. She switched off the ignition and everything fell into sudden, muffled darkness.

She tramped across the yard and up her porch steps, hearing the muted thunk each step made. Damp fog floated in eerie plumes towards the porch light and the air was filled with the scent of leaf mould, wood smoke and the damp, dense earth.

Harley's soft, 'Hey,' coming from somewhere behind her made her jump and she turned towards him. She felt a rush of love and then fearsome anger.

'You're so late. Why didn't you call me? You had me real worried, May. That fog is blinding.' Harley's voice deep with concern, tugged at her.

'Sorry,' she said and dropped her bag on the hall floor adding tersely, 'I need to talk to you.' As soon as she said it, her heart pounded.

In the sitting room, she slumped onto the sofa and jumped straight back up again, unable to keep still. Harley, crouching to light the fire, turned to look at her over his shoulder and gave her a quizzical look before turning back and blowing on the flames. He stood, leaned back up against the mantle and watched her while a coil of tension in the pit of her stomach grew tighter. His eyes dropped to her knee and back up at her. 'What happened?'

'I have had an absolutely shit day,' she said, 'Which began with a nasty bunch of frat bros grabbing their dicks at me and ended with me kneeling in a pile of glass after I dropped a tray of frozen margaritas.'

'Oh, baby...' he began, his voice soft.

'But that was nothing compared to being told by Connie, right in the middle of my shift, that you...' Her voice wobbled precariously and she tried to steady it by forcing her words out. 'You continue to play around with other women.'

'*What!*' And you *believed* her?' He laughed a horrible, hard-edged sound. 'Man, that's twisted. Is she the only one in town who doesn't know where I've been the last few months? That I haven't been able to sleep with my *own* woman never mind any other women.'

'She was talking about while I was in London,' May said quietly and all the fight went out of him. Harley sat in the chair opposite May and ran his fingers through his rough hair.

'Okay,' he said finally, his voice heavy. 'It's about Liv, isn't it?'

May's heart was pounding in her throat so she could hardly draw breath. 'So it's true.'

'What do you want to know?' He looked at her with a directness she appreciated, but did nothing to ease her fear.

'How about you tell me why people might be talking about you and Liv this way,' she said in a low voice.

'May, is that what matters here? What people are saying?'

'That's your response? Questions? You want me to think something happened?'

'You want me to tell you I didn't sleep with Liv? You want to hear that? Okay, I didn't sleep with her. That make you feel better?'

'No, it doesn't make me feel better. I don't want to feel better I want to know what the *fuck* has been going on.'

'But why does that matter? Isn't it us that matters? Where we are? Now? How we are? Intimacy and connection and… come on, you tell me. This is your turf, May. What else? What else is important? Trust? What about that? I think that's a favourite of yours, isn't it? I'm supposed to just trust you when you say your life is here, that you aren't going to go back to your life in London…'

'Harley! Stop it!'

He looked at her shakily as she began to speak. 'This is not about my values or whether you think I'm just here for a holiday until I get bored.' Her words came from her with unchecked urgency. 'It isn't even really about whether the minute you were alone, you fucked an old girlfriend. It's about whether this relationship is just going to be a repetition of all the shit we went through before. It's about whether we're capable of doing things differently and not hurting each other again in the same ways. Harley, I love you.' The words as they came from her brought her to tears, the tension and pain in her throat easing a little. 'I love you,' she said again.

He leaned back against the chair, head flung back, silent tears spilling down his face and for a moment she couldn't go on.

'I want it to be different,' she said at last. 'I don't want you to be so scared of love that you want to hurt me for making you *feel* it.'

She was crying and reached her hands out to hold his face, picked up his hand and held it against her cheek and he clutched at her, threading his fingers into her hair.

'Just give it to me, straight. Then we can sort it the fuck out.'

She crouched ignoring the pain in her knee and made herself hold his gaze. He relaxed his grip and his eyes dropped to the blood-stained gauze. Reaching his hand out, he stroked the skin around it gently with warm fingers. For a moment he was still, then leaned back, closed his eyes and stretched his leg.

'Okay…' he said with a deep breath. 'Okay.'

The fire let out a long hissing, followed by a cracking spit and May leaned back against the sofa, drawing her knees up and hugging them close. The gauze of the bandage, stained with blackish blood turned her stomach and she quickly averted her eyes.

'So,' Harley began, sounding tentative. 'If I tell you that Liv spent a night at mine, but nothing happened would that be enough for you?'

May was incredulous. 'You're joking, right?'

'Look. It's really hard. I don't know how much detail you need or want. And I owe Liv…'

'You owe Liv?' May almost spat. 'Harley. You were in a relationship with me when you spent the night with another woman. What do you "owe" me do you think?'

'Yeah. Okay. I'm sorry. It's just that sometimes the more you hear the worse it seems.'

He took a deep breath and looked at May. Their eyes locked. 'What do you want to know?'

'Why did she stay?'

'She got really wasted at Molly's one night. I was in there

304

having a drink with Rob, Connie was behind the bar and kept serving her, even though she was already pretty fucked up when she got there.'

'So is that what you do? If some girl is wasted in a bar you take her back to your place?'

Harley winced. 'No, May. Liv isn't just some girl… you know that. I care about her. I only broke up with her because you came back to live here and you know it. But don't you go misinterpreting that!' He flashed at her fiercely. 'Liv was cutting up about her boyfriend. They'd broken up that evening. She was really fucked up and threatening all sorts of things, really down on herself and saying how I had dumped her and now this guy and what was wrong with her and that sort of thing. So I said I'd take her home, but she couldn't find her keys and it just seemed to make sense to take her back to mine.'

For some reason May almost laughed. 'So where did she sleep?'

Harley looked uncomfortable. 'In my bed.'

'And where were you?'

He tilted his head back slightly, 'With her.'

May had somehow known he would say this but still her stomach tripped and flipped.

'All night?'

'What do you think I should have done, May?' he asked angrily. 'Turned her out on the street?'

'No, Harley!' she shouted at him. '*You should have slept on the fucking sofa!*'

He flinched. 'Yeah,' he said at last. 'I should have.'

May had a vivid flash of memory; the feel of skin, his skin, the warmth of it and the memory of his nakedness under the sheets and her breath caught in her throat.

'Harley,' she said struggling to her feet, a little light headed. 'I'm going up… I can't…'

'*No!*' His voice lashed out at her and he stood up too, his

305

narrowed eyes flashing dark. 'No. You are not going to do this.' He sounded deadly. 'I'm not going to let you open this up then leave it spilled all over the floor. You stay here and we'll do like you said and sort it the *fuck* out!'

May felt a jerk of shock at his reaction and something else; a flare of hope ignited in her belly. He's going to fight for this she thought and she stood tall and looked him in the eye.

'Okay,' she said with emphasis, feeling an unexpected rush of adrenalin.

'Okay,' Harley said. His voice was punchy but he stepped back a little. 'So. What's it going to be? You going to punish me for making a mistake? I should have slept on the sofa out of respect for you—for us—but didn't. I didn't and I'm sorry. But other than that, there is nothing, *nothing* that I did that night that could in any way undermine my commitment… Yes, May!' he jerked his chin at her, 'My commitment to you. And it was *before* everything we've been through with the wreck.'

May felt a moment of resonance. Of course that was significant, she herself had been thinking it all the way home in the car.

'But answer me this, May. If I *had* slept with her, would you leave me? Would you leave, after all that's happened between you and me? Everything we've been through? After we got so close it was like we were inside of each other?'

He reached out and held May's face in his hands tilting it up, making her look at him, searching her eyes.

'Tell me,' he urged. '*Tell me* that *means* something to you.'

He thrust his fingers into her hair, hands cradling her skull.

Unable to speak, she held onto Harley as though he might fly off, her fingers grasping him, forgetting her fear of hurting him. He pressed his forehead onto her upturned one and she closed her eyes.

'It means everything,' she finally managed. 'Everything.'

Harley sighed deeply and pulled her into his arms. 'Then we're going to be okay, May. We'll be okay.'

But May couldn't relax and she felt his body stiffen. He moved back a little, eyes searching hers with such disturbing intensity she wanted to hide and lowered her eyes.

'What? Baby, what is it?'

For a moment she couldn't say it, then she took a deep breath. 'Were you naked with her?' she asked, tears pricking at her eyes.

'Wha…'

'When you were with Liv, taking care of her, were you naked?'

His face cleared, but when he spoke he sounded exasperated. 'May, I told you. I told you nothing like that happened. Why would you ask that?'

'I know, I know!' she cried, feeling stupid and difficult and hating herself for circling back but she had to know; it would always be there if she didn't know one way or another. 'Because… because you *never* sleep in anything and I've been imagining you naked with her and it's doing my head in. And I wish I didn't keep thinking about it but I do.'

'Oh, May.' He reached for her and held her in his arms, stroking her hair and kissing her tears. 'No… no… no…' and he punctuated each word with a kiss. 'You're my woman, no matter where you are, and I'm not gettin naked with anyone else. Okay?' He made her look at him. 'Okay?' she nodded, mute, and Harley said, 'I never even took my frikkin jacket off.'

He held her for a moment longer then drew back and began to kiss her, tentatively at first, then as May leaned in to him, opening her mouth a little, he shifted and she felt his hands in her hair, his tongue beginning to explore, gentle, deliberate.

Then as May slipped a hand under his shirt, searching for the warmth of his skin, she was sure she felt him stiffen, his mouth halt. She dropped her hand, gave him a quick kiss and stepped back, watching a guarded look of unhappiness settle in Harley's eyes. She felt helpless. What, what had happened? He drew her into his arms and held her quietly before saying, 'I'm tired. I...' he drew back smiling wearily. 'I'll see you tomorrow.' He kissed her again and left, pacing quietly down the dark hall leaving May with the fire for company.

Her mind rolled over and over the events of the last few days. Everything felt so bloody raw. She felt wrung out, and just as she'd felt they were beginning to get beyond the rocks, they plunged backwards, flailing, wordless, letting go of each other's hands. And speaking of hands, how desolate to find that hands have memory too, she thought, recalling how hers had searched forlornly for the familiar muscle and strength, the supple warmth of him.

It was dark and chilly when she came out of work the next evening and a figure emerged from the shadows. A young, high voice said tremulously, 'déjà vu?'

Oh no, May thought wearily. Please no.

'Hello, Liv,' she said aloud.

'Buy you a beer?'

'I don't know. I'm really tired.'

'But I can't talk here, it's too...'

Right on cue, the service entrance of the restaurant opened and out came Kevin and a couple of kitchen porters.

'Night, May! Liv.'

'Okay, a quick one. Peter Christian's?' Déjà vu indeed, she thought.

It was early enough to be almost empty and May and Liv slipped into a dark wood panelled booth with a couple of bottled beers.

'How's he doing?' Liv blurted. 'He's out of hospital now, right?'

May felt wary, unsure of what Liv wanted, aware of the barely concealed shiver of nerves from the girl.

'Great! Yeah, he's doing really well. It was a long time and he was getting very…' May stopped. I don't want to share any more of him than I have to, she thought, angry. There was a silence while the clatter of glasses rang across from the bar.

'Connie told me you'd found out about the night I spent at Harley's.'

May snorted. 'I found out because she made sure I did.'

Liv looked up from the table top. Her eyes looked enormous in her small heart-shaped face and May noticed how pale and tired she looked.

'Well that's Connie I guess,' Liv murmured and looked down at her silver-ringed fingers.

There was a long silence and May sipped at her drink, not really wanting it.

'Harley was just trying to help. You know that, right? I would hate for you to think there was anything else in it.' She looked up at May. 'He's a good man.'

Tears sprang into her eyes and she lowered them again quickly. May felt her hackles prickle; she didn't need Liv to tell her Harley was a good man.

'Liv, I'm not really sure…' May hesitated, not wanting to hurt her feelings, but she was tired and felt the rasp of irritation. 'I'm not sure why we're here.'

Liv flushed. 'I know, I'm probably the last person you want to be with, right?'

'No! It's not that,' May rushed to reassure, feeling like a liar. 'It's just… Harley explained what happened. That you were…' She stopped, not wanting to embarrass her.

'You can just say it,' Liv said acidly. 'I was wasted. I was really wasted.'

May shrugged lightly. 'Yes. He told me. And about losing your keys and all that. So…' May suddenly felt exhausted. What, what am I doing?

309

'Did he say anything else?'

May again felt the discomfort of knowing there *was* something; Liv's tone, Harley asking her what she wanted to know, rather than just telling her. These things all added to her conviction that she had been pushing aside an intuitive sense that there was something else.

But he doesn't lie... he told me he didn't sleep with her.

'No,' she said looking directly at Liv. 'He told me nothing else.'

'I told him,' Liv's pale face was suddenly suffused with a mottled flush. 'I was going to take a bunch of painkillers.'

'Oh no,' May breathed out softly. 'Oh Liv...'

'Oh, I wouldn't have done it, really I wouldn't, but sometimes I just get so lonely and I knew he wouldn't leave me alone...'

But May was thinking of Harley, not Liv. She imagined him taking care of Liv, taking her vodka and stashing it in his freezer, slamming his bedside drawer on the potent painkillers and holding her in his arms, gentle and patient, holding her until she was soothed and he could be sure she was safe. A sudden tightness grasped at her throat. She was shocked by her protective, possessive rage; she wasn't used to feeling this way.

'We dated for nearly six months, you know, and then you came back,' Liv said bitterly. 'He knew me. I did... I have done something like that before when I was in high school. He knew that.' Her voice was so low it was almost inaudible.

'And did you know *him*, Liv?' May asked angrily. 'Did you know how that might make him feel? He had to deal with that kind of thing far too much as a boy!'

Liv was crying now. 'No!' she sobbed. 'No! He was always just so strong...'

May hadn't meant to be so harsh. She took a deep breath. 'I'm sorry. I'm so tired I'm not thinking straight. That really wasn't kind. I didn't mean to upset you.'

'I just wanted you to know what happened. For his sake. He's a good man.'

'I know that, Liv. Look, Harley and I can sort this out. We'll be okay.'

Liv looked up at May with such an obvious rush of relief that she felt even worse. Poor girl, she really does want to make it right.

'How are you now?' May asked, unable to just leave it.

'I'm okay. He called my Mom. I'm seeing my guy again. Doctor from home. It's okay.'

Driving home through the heavy darkness May's mind was turbulent. She pulled in to her driveway noticing light from both Matthew's studio and Harley's room. She felt heavy with fatigue and her head throbbed.

Someone had left soup for her by her cooker and a chunk of sourdough bread. Sweet, she thought. She tore off some bread and stood chewing, thinking over what Liv had said, before heading down to his room.

He opened the door to her knock and gave a relieved smile when he saw her.

'Hey, long day?'

'Yes,' May leaned up to hug him and nuzzled his neck. 'It was, but good and I love you.'

Harley leaned back, his arms around her waist and looked down at her with a sweetly puzzled smile. 'Oh yeah?'

'Yeah,' she echoed. 'You're a kind man.'

She kissed him on his mouth and drew back to look at him again. 'I just really love you.'

He pulled her close with a low chuckle and May felt a surge of hope and happiness, enjoying the tenderness of being in his arms, of his mouth mumbling kisses over her hair.

'I'm going to have a shower and go to bed.' She hesitated, hoping he might come with her or offer her his shower, but he didn't and she quickly finished saying, 'It's late and I'm on early tomorrow.'

He released her and smiled such a sweet sideways smile that May almost forgot her disappointment.

'Sweet dreams, baby.'

30

Spring was changing the air and light. It felt fresh and sweet and everyday it seemed, something was emerging from the ground, thrusting forth with varying degrees of confidence.

The days were taking on a certain pattern, which appealed to May. She worked shifts in town and Harley prepared an old outbuilding of Matthew's for a workshop. In a week or so, he and Rob would move his carpentry business from town.

Early one morning, May was grubbing about in the vegetable garden, following some instructions Matthew had given her about planting out some seedlings. Gradually she became aware of the phone ringing far off inside the house and she jabbed her trowel into the soft damp earth and ran inside.

She snatched up the phone and was sure whoever it was would have hung up, she had taken so long to get to it.

'May? Frannie Lieberman. How ya doing?'

'Yeah, good, fine, Frannie. Nice to hear from you.' May burbled thinking fast and suddenly remembering her from Stella's dinner, months ago.

'Pardon me calling you out of the blue like this.'

'No that's fine.'

They exchanged a few more expected pleasantries, Frannie asking how Harley was getting on.

'You know he and I were in film class together? In another century!'

'No? Really?' said May. 'What was he like?'

Fran chuckled a laugh full of rubble and sand. 'Terrific,' she said, her voice fond, 'the most authentic person I've ever known. You don't know how rare that is until you come up against the real thing at last.'

May felt light-headed and grinned like a fool. She wished Frannie'd been around when she had been trying to explain to Lallie why he exerted such a pull on her. It was this, this essential part of him that she needed to be close to. She was jerked back as Frannie continued, 'I've got something out of left field that you might consider and I'm going to find it pretty near impossible to take no for an answer.'

Whoa, thought May before saying aloud, 'Try me.'

She walked over to the sun-filled kitchen window glancing over towards the chickens to see if they'd been let out. Thunder butted and stroked her ankles with his head as she picked her way across the floor, listening to Frannie, trying not to step on the cat's little paws and take in at least some of the information being poured down the phone.

At length, she gave up.

'Umm… Frannie, I'm not sure… *stop* Thunder… I'm not sure I've quite got this so, sorry if I sound thick. You've got a boy leaving care and you're wondering if I can… what? I can't foster him, if that's what you mean.'

Frannie voice cracked with explosive laughter.

'Oh Christ! What do you take me for? You've got more than enough to be dealing with. Are you kidding me?' she was laughing so much, May felt foolish.

'He's got no life skills, May. Remember we talked about this when we met at Stella's dinner? I kind of had it in my head that you were on side, if you get me. I just wondered if you and Harley would consider giving up a few hours a week, a regular commitment for, say, six weeks, and teach him some. Basic cooking, grocery shopping, balancing a chequebook, eating as a family. Anything that will help him make the transition.'

May switched abruptly from feeling like an idiot, to feeling a bloom of possibility. She was excited. She broke the habit of a lifetime and asked for time to think about it.

'Frannie, you do know that I have a full time job at Molly's? I mean it's shifts so there are definitely times I can be here, but I'll need to have a word with Harley, obviously and

Matthew.'

'Of course. No disrespect to you, May, but without Harley it doesn't work. The one thing the kid has said he likes in school is shop, so I'm hoping Harley can do some carpentry with him. I can give you three days, but I'm in the process of putting together a proposal for the kid's transition programme. Help me out here, May, there's so little for these kids.'

'I'll do my best Frannie, but it really does depend on Harley. What age is the boy?'

'Seventeen. Do you have email out there? Good, I'll send you his details. Just remember they're confidential.'

At dinner that night, May brought up Frannie's phone call and gave Harley a print out of the email Frannie had sent. Matthew was the first to respond.

'Do you good, son,' he said his eyes full of smiles, 'what else are you going to do with that no good behind of yours.'

Harley smiled lazily and took another piece of sourdough, tore it and started mopping up the last of the pan juices from the platter in the middle of the table.

'Matthew,' he said. 'If a tornado ripped through town while you were stabbing at canvas with a paintbrush, you wouldn't know it.'

May laughed as Matthew sheepishly acknowledged this observation. 'So how do you know what all I get up to?'

'Your lady friend here lets me know...' He held up his hands as May spluttered an indignant protest. 'And we both think...'

'Matthew!' she yelped over the laughter.

'We both think that you need to quit lounging in the swing seat being fed fried chicken and buttermilk gravy.'

Harley laughed, pushing his chair out noisily from the table, he stood and started clearing the table. 'How would it work for you? With work I mean.'

'Well I'm queen of the schedules,' May answered, 'I can make sure I have my days off during the week and do some lates as well, so I can mostly be here till two. Anyway, Frannie made it clear you're the lure. As usual.' She caught his eye and he raised an eyebrow at her, lightning fast. 'Male role model and all that. Oh, and apparently you speak Spanish.' She finished with an ironic brow.

'*Si, mi amor*.' He winked at her. 'That is true. Let's do it. Let's see if we can help this kid out. Surely we can't be as bad as nothing.'

After dinner Matthew took his leave and padded quietly out of the back door towards his studio whistling softly as he went.

Harley moved quietly about and May found she was watching every move he made; she felt her pulse speed up a little and stood up, grabbed a towel and dried one of the draining platters. Harley looked glancingly at her and then, like a butterfly lightly resting, held her gaze for a moment. He smiled gently, cocking his head a little and May felt a warm drop of pleasure spreading beneath her skin. She smiled to herself.

Now that the evenings were warming up, if May wasn't working, they sat out on the porch after dinner. Harley had made a log burner from an old washing machine drum to keep the chill at bay and it was lovely to sit out on the swing seat listening to the night sounds and watching the sky. Occasionally, he went home to work on drawings or rest, but mostly he was with May.

'You know,' he said after they'd finished the dishes and May had brought a couple of beers. 'The hardest thing for me was the constant moving on, moving on. I'd arrive at a place, begin to get used to it then, "hey time to leave".'

It took May a moment to catch his train of thought.

'When you were a kid? In care?'

Harley nodded without looking at her and took the bottle she offered with a low 'thanks'.

'I started to keep my suitcase packed and that was noted as evidence of how disturbed I was. It didn't matter how close you got to someone, a family, teacher maybe or made friends in school, you'd still have to go on somewhere else. And they were always telling you how important it was to be personable, make sure people like you and you'll be okay...' he trailed off.

'Oh no,' she said softly, 'that could backfire in so many ways.'

'Judging from Frannie's email it would seem that this kid is one of the lucky ones.' Harley's voice was dry. 'He's never moved out of state and has been in the same school for four years.'

'Different from you, then?' May said, trying to sound more casual than she felt. Even now after all they had shared, she still felt she needed to tread with extreme caution when asking him about his childhood. Harley shifted.

'Come sit down with me,' he said and May settled herself, leaning back against the arm at the opposite end of the swing seat tucking her feet under his thigh. He picked up one of her feet and held it in his warm hands, rubbing his thumbs up its length.

'Mmm...'

'I was never in the same school for more than a couple years and lived in five different States in seven years.'

'Why did you have to keep moving? Didn't they try and keep you settled somewhere?'

Harley sighed again and May said quietly, 'You don't have to talk about it if you don't want to.'

'Come here,' he said and May scuttled across and settled back against his chest as he held her close. He had always done this; held her close in his arms while keeping her facing away from him as his conversation deepened. How had she not noticed the significance before? I want to look at him, I want to look him in the eyes and see him. He kissed her temple and said, 'I don't really know why. At first it was because I had an aunt in Colorado who said she would have me. That's why I didn't stay in South Dakota. But she moved around... a lot.' He pushed on the floor with his booted foot and set the seat swinging a little. 'That first year and a half, we moved from Colorado to Oklahoma, then through Tennessee, Alabama and wound up in Georgia where she handed me over. Social services stepped in.'

'Oh Harley, how could anyone have handed you over?'

He made a half-hearted snort and fell silent.

'Did... did you feel at home anywhere?' May asked.

'Once or twice, maybe. I don't know.'

May felt a sharp stab and Harley went on, his voice taking on a familiar low, neutral tone. 'Everyone says that you just want someone to adopt you, but I was always scared shitless someone would.'

'People weren't unkind were they?' May said, realising how naïve she sounded.

'Unkind? Well no one broke my arm.'

May winced at the flat way he said it, remembering the story Harley had once told her of a particularly violent boyfriend of his mother's—had it even been a stepfather?—who had broken his arm in a fury as he'd tried to defend his younger brother.

They both started as Thunder jumped down from the roof of the porch with a great thud onto the wooden floor. Harley gave a quick half burst of laughter.

'You're a cat, Thunder! Act like one!'

The shadowy, muscular form jumped up onto a nearby chair and settled himself like a hen sitting on a clutch of eggs, looking smug with his eyes half closed. His extraordinary rumbling purr started up and came in waves across the air to them.

Harley loosed his hold on May and sat up.

'Well... I guess I'm going to head on over,' he said standing and stretching.

May wilted inside. 'Must you?'

Each night it seemed to May, this was the place they always stopped. They'd get to just here, a place of growing warmth and intimacy and then Harley would call it a night and what she wanted was... what did she want? She wasn't thinking about sex right now, although she frequently did, remembering how it used to be, the heat between them, his constant need for her. But right now, she just wanted him not to go, to not have to spend another night alone. No. It wasn't that. May didn't mind being alone, she minded not being with him. And what of Harley? What did he want? She was unsure. She didn't doubt that he wanted to be with her; he sought her out and he was warmly affectionate but...

'Nooo...' he answered slowly, 'What do you have in mind?'

'I don't know,' she answered feeling her pulse speed up nervously. He smiled, wary. 'Get to know each other a little better?' she said quietly.

'Oh! Ha!' He jerked the sounds out. 'I didn't know you were all that interested.'

Uh oh, one nil to Stella. 'What? No! That's not fair. It's not that...' she burst out feeling a flash of outraged hurt, then stopped not knowing how to explain. He raised a prompting brow. 'It's *you* that... I just feel like, I'm hurting you when I touch you, or maybe you don't... that you don't...'

Again she stopped and May felt a wave of frustration that she could be so tongue-tied, so unable to express herself. They'd been lovers; there hadn't been an inch of his body that she hadn't known intimately, how was it so hard to say what she was feeling? She saw his expression move rapidly from cool irony to confusion and then he looked at her softly.

'You think I don't want you?' he asked, the tenderness in

his voice unstopping her. She squeezed her eyes closed feeling the sting of tears.

'Maybe. Sometimes.'

'Oh, baby.' He sat back down and held her close with a huge sigh. She closed her eyes, his response vaguely comforting but she was afraid of what he might say next. Maybe he really didn't want her. Everything had changed. Maybe what he felt for her was simply gratitude and affection.

'I've felt so broken for so long and everything aching and tore up.'

'I know,' she said plaintively. 'But every night it's the same and…' she was so full of everything she didn't know where to start.

Harley sighed into her hair.

'Want to know a secret?' May nodded. 'I miss you. Want to know another one?'

May nodded again, 'Mmm hmmm.'

He held her even closer, wrapping her up.

'I'm scared you won't like me when you see me. What if you don't want me?' he whispered.

Two nil to Stella. He had lived by that body; its virility and strength. He knew the power it had held. Of course he did.

'Harley…' Something in the look he gave her, the sweet tilt of his mouth, expectant cock of his head gave her a quick surge of courage. 'Stay with me tonight?'

'Stay?'

Harley closed his eyes tightly, breathing in sharply while he held her.

'Okay, baby,' he spoke so softly she nearly missed it. 'I'll stay with you.'

Harley looped his fingers in hers as she led him inside wordlessly, up the creaking stairs to her bedroom. She left the light off in her room; for herself, for him? She didn't know, but she had a strong need to protect him from something.

Her uncurtained windows framed the moonlit garden and pastures that rolled and swelled into woods and mountains. May undressed him, slowly unbuttoning his soft, flannel shirt, kissing his chest along his thrusting collarbone, the skin over his ribs, her fingers tracing the raised, red scar tissue that clustered and scattered like shot across his waist and left side, some sunken and pitted, where sharp nosed tweezers had plucked at him removing glass.

'Oh…' she breathed. 'Look at your battle wounds.'

'No thanks,' he said.

She dropped a few little kisses on them and wondered. Surely that would be a way to get used to them, their power to shock or repulse would fade like the scars themselves.

She slipped the shirt from his shoulders, stroking his arms, hearing the soft sound as it landed on the floor, undid his belt, the metal buttons of his jeans. He was still, watching her closely, his breath becoming shallower.

'Sit,' she said softly and smiling, she guided him gently to sit on the edge of her bed where she kneeled at his feet and pulled off his boots.

'Wait,' he said sharply and she stopped instantly. 'Thank you,' he said, voice gentle this time. 'Let's lay down, baby.' She smiled and stood.

'Wait.' His voice was low and thick now. 'I want to see you.'

Harley reached out and undid the buttons on her shirt, slipping his hands behind her and undoing her bra. She shrugged out of them and held his head, running her fingers into his hair as he dipped to kiss her breasts, her belly then her throat, his lips warm, his tongue thrusting along their trail. He held her close and sighed and she felt him reassuringly hard through the fabric of his jeans.

They lay together and Harley curled his half naked body around hers, one hand strumming quietly in her hair, the other nested at her breast. His voice came through the darkness, familiar and warm, and his breath bloomed soft on her cheek.

'Baby, you can't tell me that the way a person looks doesn't affect the wanting them. You know, that base... fucking... horny... wanting someone.' He seemed to lean on each word as he breathed it into her ear and May's own breath missed a step.

'At first yes, when you don't know them,' she replied, getting rid of her jeans with a little help from Harley.

'What are you saying?'

'Harley, do you remember when I first came back to Hartland?'

'Of course.'

'Tell me what you remember. What did you think when you saw me? What did you feel?'

His breath came out in a hard half laugh. 'Pissed off! I'm not sure—What are you asking?'

'Try and remember. Did you just think, oh hey, there's that girl I used to know or what, because I know that when I saw you again after all that time, I would have had you that very day if you'd called me.'

Harley laughed.

'Well if I'd known that!'

'No, Harley, you were busy avoiding me so I don't think knowing it would've made a difference at that point, but what I'm asking you is did you fancy me. Did it give you the hots to see me?'

'For sure, sweetheart; after I got over feeling so freakin mad that you were back, that's what made it so hard, but what...'

'Right!' she interrupted. 'Did you not notice I was scrawny thin and sick with grief? I had no tits, no arse, my body as you had loved it, was gone?'

'Well… sure I noticed you'd changed, you were different, but it… it…' He stopped and May waited, one beat, two beats. His hand in her hair, stopped. The one at her breast slid around her to hold her closer.

'It didn't make no difference,' he whispered. 'It was you.'

May felt a little kick of triumph and kissed the side of his mouth.

'I walked around for months thinking about it, you.'

'What did you think about?' she whispered, slipping her hand into the edge of her knickers and getting rid of them too.

Harley groaned on a long, low breath, pressing himself against her. 'How good you smell, your hair, your skin, the way it would feel on mine…'

She closed her eyes, and moved against him letting the sound of his voice roll through her. His words warmed her, filling an empty space in the cage of her ribs that had ached hollow, filling it with something that bloomed buoyant and steady.

'What else…' she whispered, stretching and arching her back against him, running a hand along his thigh, feeling his warm palm brushing across her breast and resting there for a moment.

'The sound of your voice telling me how I'm making you feel, the curve of you belly, your legs strong around me… oh god… how *good* it feels to be inside you, the way you'd look when you'd come.'

He drew the words out murmuring into the hollow behind her ear his lips nipping at her kissing her, his hand stroking along the inside of her thigh once… twice… again… again. '*All* of that…'

As he talked his warm hands roamed slow and restless, touching the places as he named them, then stroking her hair, her neck, up, then along the insides of her bare arms, resting on her cheek. He kissed her temple, his mouth so hot and tender a familiar suck of hollow longing bloomed in her belly. Welcome back, she thought with a small smile. Then she turned to him and held his face gently.

'Get them off,' she said softly and he smiled at her.

'I didn't come prepared,' he said. 'I wasn't expecting this.'

'I did, I was hoping.'

'You got some?'

'I'm on the pill, Harley.'

Still he hesitated and nudged his face at her throat.

'I ain't done it without a condom since I was a stupid teenager, you sure? I ain't been tested in a while…' But he didn't finish as a huge smile broke out on his face. 'But then there's only been you.'

'Same.'

'You didn't sleep with that prick of a cop?'

'Harley!'

'What?'

'No. I did not sleep with that prick of a cop.'

'Well then…' He flipped the covers back and slid under them shucking his jeans and boxers as he did so.

She rolled onto her back and stretched languid, cat-like and he reacted instantly, moving over her and holding her face in his hands kissing her long and hard.

They made love, his hip bones jabbing at her, hard, beating out his rhythm on her thighs. After a few moments he stopped and flipped onto his back holding her hips, bringing her with him, muttering darkly, 'Fuckin leg.'

Later, as she was drifting off beside him, he stirred and turned onto his side wrapping himself around her, murmuring something loving she couldn't quite catch as he slipped back into sleep. May wondered if he would ever say words like that when fully conscious and if it mattered. Not really, she supposed, she saw in his eyes his strength of feeling, but sometimes she thought, maybe just once, to hear the words; to know that he was hearing himself say them…

It was hard to drag herself away from home the next morning. The colours were sharp-edged and clean, with a purity that sang to May as she drove along the rhythmically undulating road towards town the next morning. It took her past acid and lime green woodland on one side and lush green pasture on the other. When had it turned so decidedly from the soft fawn and dun that the disappearing snow had revealed, to this emphatic, verdant grassland?

She was smiling from deep in her belly and a joyful optimism seemed to spring from her pores. 'Oh world! I love you!' she called as the wind whipped at her hair through the open window. 'I *love you!*'

Cresting a slight hump in the road that curved sharply around an ancient part of the woodland, May spotted a doe and her two small offspring. She was glad she had taken this part of the road more slowly, a habit. They sprang silently into the green and shadow.

After the lunch rush was over, she decided to take her paperwork home. As she worked through the specials menu, May mulled over Frannie's request. The idea appealed to her. She felt something like urgency telling her they must try if they could to help this boy and more importantly—if she was honest—thought it would do Harley good. He was restless without his work and this might give him something to focus on.

Glancing out of the kitchen window, she caught sight of Matthew and Harley down by the split rail fence that looked over the pasture towards the woods. Matthew was stooping, his knees slightly bent, hands busy at something May could not see. He was looking over his shoulder towards Harley, who was behind him leaning back against the rails. His hands were holding onto the top of the fence, his legs thrust straight in front of him and he was dipping himself slowly, rhythmically, down then up, down then up, while chatting to Matthew.

His dark hair, still not long enough to lie down, was sticking up about his head giving him a boyish, end-of-the-school-day air. May watched as he stopped and shifted, so he was now just lounging against the fence. She saw Matthew say something and then Harley threw his head back and laughed with unselfconscious freedom. He darted his foot out towards Matthew's, stooped behind and laughed again in response to something the older man said.

At that moment, May saw Harley look up towards the house and she raised her hand. She could just make out his smile, then he said something to Matthew who swatted him away and went back to work.

Harley walked up the garden, using as steps the moss-covered silver birch trunks that held the terraced growing beds in place. His gait was measured and purposeful, but his limp still discernible.

'Hey beautiful,' he said, leaning against the doorjamb. She smiled, never tiring of this familiar greeting. He had first used it before she really knew him and it had become something warm, intimate, far removed from the light and frivolous arm's length flattery it had once been.

'Hey yourself,' she returned, looking up at him. 'How's your leg?'

He shrugged and smiled, 'Worth it. You?'

He'd seen the bruising on her thighs as they'd showered together that morning.

May smiled back. 'Also worth it.'

She noticed, as she often did, that his clothes still hung from his lean frame; the pale, soft flannel of his endlessly washed and sun-dried shirt looked as though it belonged to another man, a bigger brother. The smudged shadows around his dark eyes made them appear a little hollow, but the opaque dense quality had gone. She saw too, that the white tension at the corners of his mouth was no longer there. Without thinking, she moved quickly to him and open palmed, cupped his face, her thumb softly stroking the edge of his mouth as if to rub out the last bit of pain.

Harley's face softened and he reached up to hold her wrist, closing his eyes, turning his head to kiss the inside. His mouth felt soft, warm and tears pricked her eyes.

'Hey,' he murmured. May looked at him, at his intensely dark eyes and moved into his embrace. 'I'm so glad you're here.'

'Well that's good,' he said with a quiet smile.

PART THREE

PART THREE

31

May woke early with the warm sun slanting across her back and shoulders, fluttering through a ripple of leaves onto her pillow. Her languid stretch was distracted by unanswerable questions about the boy from Fran's project.

Today they would finally meet him. Carlos. What would he be like? Would they be able to help? She tried to remember herself at seventeen. She'd had an eagerness, she knew, never wanting to appear morose or marked by the tragedy of losing her father so young.

Encouraged by Sarah to see the half-full glass, to see the rainbow, to find something, anything salvageable when life threw things at her, suited her temperament, but there were times when it was oppressive; she was a girl who felt things in Technicolor, her father used to say, and needed to express it. Lallie had told her that the drive to remain positive and cheerful during Sarah's illness had meant May swallowed everything else; no wonder she'd crashed so badly afterwards.

'Maybe it was because she'd just died,' May had answered dryly.

Now, as she worked on some planning for Turtle, she looked up and out through the kitchen door flung wide, its frame embracing the sunshine and the flickering, fluttering, fresh green and birdsong of a glorious spring morning. She could see the chickens grubbing about under the apple tree and hear their gossipy, exclaiming sounds as they strutted.

Unable to concentrate, May decided to see if there were any eggs and sloped barefoot down the garden, kneeling amongst the shrubs and grasses, slipping her hand into secret shady places while the sun warmed the back of her neck and melted down her shoulders. She didn't know how long she'd been at it when she became aware of a dark Ford parked up in the drive. Shit. I hope they haven't been there long she thought, glancing at her wrist to see that as usual she'd forgotten her watch.

She jumped to her feet and raised an arm in greeting at the two figures waiting by the car. She could see what looked like a slender young girl standing gracelessly awkward, holding onto the open passenger door of the car, looking in the direction of the pasture. Weird. Whatever happened to Carlos? Standing alongside was another, bulkier shape, but the morning sun was slanting at an angle that made it impossible for May to see clearly.

'I'm so sorry!' she called out breathlessly, 'got distracted by chickens!'

As she moved into the shadow of the house, she could see it was Frannie smiling at her. 'May!'

'Hi, Frannie, lovely to see you. I didn't know you were coming.' She held up her grimy hands. 'Ugh… not a great impression.'

They both laughed and then May quickly turned to introduce herself to what up close was quite obviously a boy. His jaw was sharp, with a little feathering of hair along the edges, his features finely drawn. He wore his hair as long and sleek as a teenaged girl, parted severely in the middle and it gleamed tawny-tortoise shell in the sun, shining clean.

'You must be Carlos.'

The boy nodded, unsmiling, but not unfriendly. His shadowed eyes an intriguing backlit greyish green, looked bruised with fatigue. He extended his hand to shake May's, holding it briefly. She saw that around the base of each thumb he wore wide collars of silver. The muscles at his jaw were rhythmically and swiftly tensing a staccato beat and May softened, realising that he was nervous.

'I'm not normally this scatter-brained,' she said ruefully. 'I hope you like animals, Carlos. We have quite a few about the place.'

332

He glanced at Frannie, as though she might answer and she nodded vigorously at him.

'I'll be back for you at two o'clock, Carlos. Make the most of it, these people are good to give you their time.'

'Oh, no really. It's nice for us to have a young person about the place,' said May, wishing she didn't talk in clichés.

She waved Frannie off and was faced with a whole four hours with this silent young man.

'So!' she started brightly. 'What have you been told about us?'

'Umm… Not a whole lot. Just that I have to come here and… you all are going to show me stuff.'

His voice was light with little variance in tone and his words slipped out between his lips; he didn't speak them. They were soft and unformed as though they had no edges, making it hard to tell where one word ended and another began. It took a moment for May's ears to tune in to how he spoke. She gave him a quizzical look.

'Well, not quite. You're going to have to *do* stuff. Don't look so startled,' she added and his face, which until that moment had looked nothing at all, briefly registered surprise.

'Would you like something to drink before I show you around?'

'I'm good,' he said.

'Well I'm gasping for a drink,' May said brightly, 'so we might as well start inside.'

Carlos walked alongside her, his gait dipping rhythmically as he moved. May showed him the bathroom and the sitting room, and as they passed the stairs on their way through to the kitchen she told him, feeling a little awkward, that upstairs was private. *Boundaries!* Frannie had told them. *Real important, guys…*

'Harley lives next door with our friend Matthew and I live here. We all eat together and you and I will make lunch for the four of us every day that you're here if I'm not working in

333

town. Otherwise, you'll be with Harley. Okay?'

Carlos shrugged. 'Sure,' he said, his voice neutral.

'Do you like food, Carlos?' she asked him, her voice gentle.

'I guess.'

'Well,' May said, 'As I understand it, you are going to be leaving where you're living now, and going to a new place where you're going to have to be able to prepare food for yourself, amongst other things. I would like to show you how to do that. Maybe we can also find out if you like food. Okay?'

The boy nodded slowly, his long eyes watching her carefully. He seemed to take an age to blink.

At that moment, Harley slap-slammed through the screen door of the kitchen. Carlos flinched and froze all in a split second, his darting glance seeming to measure up the space between himself and the doorway.

'Oh *man*, why did I say yes to that commission?' Harley exploded, 'that woman's a…' He stopped abruptly and raised his eyebrows, his face relaxing.

'Harley, this is Carlos.' May said.

He thrust his hand towards the boy and without missing a beat said, *'Hola, Carlos, qué tal?'*

'Bien.' Carlos answered instantly and May thought she saw the tiniest flicker of something in those long, slow eyes.

'Te trata bien?'

The boy looked uncertainly at May and nodded.

'Bueno! Mejor hablamos en Inglés. Otherwise May will think we're real bad mannered!' Harley laughed.

'Sure.'

May shot a searing look at Harley as he washed his hands at the sink.

'Nice,' she said.

As he passed her to grab a towel, he leaned close, whispered, 'Later, baby,' and chuckled softly.

All that first day, May spoke a monologue of what she was

doing and why, while Carlos shadowed her around the place.

By the time they were ready to sit down to a lunch of sourdough, salad leaves and an omelette with herbs from the garden, May had decided she needed to take him to a grocery store. The reality was, he was not going to be living somewhere he could gather fresh eggs or grow his own vegetables. Before he left for the day, she had managed to extract an idea of something he might actively choose to eat, rather than just passively shovelling in what was placed before him.

She sat with him at the kitchen table after they had cleared away the lunch things.

'Okay, so you like a meat sauce?'

'Sure,' he said.

May had gently led him through the things they would need to make one and made him write them out on a list. His writing tugged pathetically at May. It was cramped print, slightly back slanted and he held the pen in a claw-like grip curled around awkwardly so that he could see the words as they formed.

'Harley's left-handed too.' She smiled as she watched him write. He said nothing.

'Okay. So I'm going to ask whoever brings you tomorrow, to meet me at Purity Supreme and we'll do the shopping and come back together from there. Okay?'

'Sure,' he said.

At dinner that night, she asked the men what they made of Carlos.

'Have you noticed it, May?' Harley asked, rather opaquely.

'What?'

'He's been battered, is my guess.'

'Not where he is now, d'you think?'

Harley shook his head, but looked thoughtful and then

asked Matthew. 'What do you reckon?'

'Well, without a doubt he is very... careful, I would say.'

'Maybe he's just nervous,' May said, not wanting to think of it. 'New situation. There's a lot to remember.'

But even as she avoided it, she could picture the boy's still and watchful almost animal quality. And if anyone knew what he was talking about it was Harley.

He himself often exhibited the same very still, but hyper-alert quality when he was in a room with more than a few people. She had noticed it the first time she had seen him in the pizza joint.

'What makes you think so Harley?' she asked finally.

'He keeps his back to the wall.'

May raised her eyebrow. She thought about the way Carlos watched their faces so closely, the carefully neutral expression, the regular sizing up of where the door was.

'Frannie said his Mom was an alcoholic,' Harley said cryptically. 'Poor kid.'

May pulled into the driveway late one afternoon a few days on, after a non-stop, high-speed day at work. The familiar sound of gravel crunching under her wheels and the sweep of the garden down towards the pastures warmed her heart. Even before Harley and she had got together, the road home lifted her spirits. Putting miles between herself and town had a softening effect on the events of her day.

No one was about. She called out a hello and jogged up the porch steps and on into the house, the smell of sun on wood and hot, dry earth following her inside. No radio, no low murmur of voices, just the quiet hum of the fridge.

Thunder had stretched himself out on the cool tiles of the kitchen floor and he stretched even more as May came in and stood slowly, winding himself around her ankles.

'Hello, fellow,' she said softly, reaching to scratch him between his ears.

The disembowelled newspaper strewn across the kitchen table showed that Harley had been there. He straddled the two houses more and more and May liked this expansive spreading out. It felt gentle and comfortable.

The clang-chime of her keys sounded overloud in the silent heat as she dropped them in a ceramic dish on the counter top. Then, thinking absently about dinner, she mooched outside again to pick lettuce thinnings.

It was incredibly still. Not a breath of wind; even the birds had been shocked into silence, but nothing stopped the indomitable cicadas with their rasping, whirring cycle of sound. High up in the tree tops they wound up and reached a crescendo as she trailed languidly back inside. She took the stairs two at a time up to her bedroom and then regretted it as she peeled her work clothes off and flung them into the corner. God it was hot.

Half an hour later, still glowing from the shower and dressed in the lightest of cotton, her dark curls damp and clamped up on her head, she walked lazily down the garden, looking for the men.

'Don't you come walking down here barefoot, Missy,' Matthew's voice came low and urgent, 'there's all kinds of critters want to take a bite out of you!'

May stopped in her tracks and lifted a leg, poking her foot in his direction. He chuckled softly at her unlaced, heavy boots with their black leather tongues lolling out.

Matthew put a finger to his lips and beckoned quietly. She edged closer and climbed over the split railed fence, stopping to sit on the top as he held his hand up, halting her. May felt a thrill, an impatience to know what was going on.

'Scoot along, honey, then maybe you can see.'

She edged carefully along the warm, brittle wood, trying not to get splinters, then hopped down on Matthew's side. Through the open door of the old loose box, she could see Harley's back. He was very still, but appeared relaxed, leaning at an angle against the frame. Standing close, like a held breath, was Carlos. He had an almost preternatural calm and stillness as he stood there, none of the tremulous tension that made up his more usual posture.

Harley was murmuring softly, gentle and rhythmic and all at once, May heard the unmistakeable whoosh and snort of a horse.

She jerked her head towards Matthew but her words didn't come as he gestured again with his open palms spread, a patting gesture in the air. Without turning around, Harley's quiet voice came from the dark, 'you want to come and see my new girl?'

'Go real slow, honey,' Matthew said and May crept through the long grass, feeling its scratchy tickle on her bare legs, seeing the silent spring of hoppers as she moved along.

Inside the loose box, stood a towering dull-coated chestnut horse, dark with dust and dried sweat patches. Her ribs were jutting stark, through the matted coat and at the sight of May, she instantly cringed, rolled her eyes and laid her ears flat.

'Okay, girl...' Harley's voice soothed, 'not ready yet... oh...kay... all...right.'

May's heart contracted. That poor, poor creature.

Matthew gestured with his head and May followed him up through the prickling grass and on into his air-conditioned kitchen. It felt still, cool and dim and seemed to have a bluish tint to the air as though seen through a tranquil pool. Matthew poured her a glass of water and they sat down at his small kitchen table.

'So...' she said, excited and curious all at once.

Matthew smiled at her. 'Horse needed rescuing, boy needed a project.'

It still made her smile that he called Harley 'boy', but in that moment, she wondered which boy he was talking about.

'Well, I can't argue with that I suppose. Where does it

come from?'

'Oh down yonder,' he said, waving his arm vaguely out the back. 'Humane Society gave me a call. They do that every now and again, forgetting Hope and I aren't in business anymore... so, they told me they had a poor, crazy mare that needed a home but was scared of folks.'

'She's afraid of people?' May asked thoughtfully. 'I wonder what happened to her.'

'Harley always had a way with the crazy ones. The more battered an animal, the more tuned in he was. I figured that can't have changed so I told them to bring her on down and we'll see what we can do. Harley tells me you have some experience with horses. We'll work it out.'

At supper that night Harley was buzzing.

'Her name's Phoenix. She's been rescued from a breeding farm out by Mountview. Now sweetheart, don't y'all go too close to her until she's settled in,' he said, the country boy in him coming out in his voice as it often did when his emotions were heightened. His dark eyes reflected the warm light of the kitchen and glowed as he talked. May put her hands up.

'Harley, that horse is scary. I'm not about to go near her.'

'You're not afraid of anything, May.' He smiled gently. 'And don't you try and tell me those Southern horses you took care of were all genteel manners because I know it ain't so!'

May watched him thoughtfully as he cleared the table, wondering. It touched her in an unexpectedly tender place that he would remember a detail like that. She hadn't mentioned it in years. She saw Matthew's enquiring face. 'We used to spend summers at my granny's in South Carolina. About a mile up the road was a stable yard and for a couple of summers I worked there for free lessons. God it was hot! And actually,' she poked her tongue out at Harley, 'those horses were all Country Club. Very polite indeed, so

339

I'm not sure how helpful I'll be with a spooky horse.'

He opened his mouth, but the phone rang and he slipped out as she picked it up.

Harley had his feet up on the railings of the porch, his chair tipped back and was sipping a bottle of Bass when May came out to join him twenty minutes later. Piper was lying quietly alongside and he was absently fondling one of her ears while he read the paper.

'Hey beautiful. Did Matthew go?'

May nodded and sat down on the swing seat and leaned back with a sigh.

'Okay?'

'Yeah. It was Lallie.'

'How's she doing?'

'They're all fine. There's something wrong with the boiler in my flat and she wants to know if I think it should be…' She broke off and muttered something about it being boring. 'But, she says she and Sam are talking about coming here for their summer holiday.'

'Oh.' Harley tipped his chair down with a light thud and joined her on the swing seat. 'Just talk or…'

'No idea. But I hope they do come. I'd love them to see how we live here and I miss her so much.'

'Yeah… I guess you do, sweetheart,' he said quietly.

32

'Baby, you going in to town today?'

May was sitting on the fence in the early morning sunshine, watching Harley groom Phoenix. Her coat was still dull and matted, but improving, and she was less inclined to cringe and shy at everything.

'Mmm hmm... I'm meeting Carlos at the supermarket.'

'Could you pick something up for me? From Ethan?'

'Ethan! I haven't seen him since you worked there. Of course. Will he remember me do you think?'

'Will he remember you...' Harley shook his head slowly in mock sorrow. 'How could you ask that? I'll give him a call, let him know you're going to swing by.'

'What am I collecting?'

'Just some parts for my camera. Shhh...' he said with a wink as she started to ask what for. 'But hurry back if you can. I want to get that boy back in with Phoenix.'

He slapped the mare's quarters and said, 'Get!' backing himself against her gently and turning; she followed, her strong muscled neck curving around in the direction Harley faced.

'I don't want to push it because he'll do what he's told, but you saw him in the stall with her that first day.'

An hour later, May stood in the chilly, artificially lit vastness of the Purity Supreme. She waited patiently while Carlos painstakingly selected items from the shelves and chiller cabinets.

He was so careful and slow May wondered if he was scared of making a mistake. Or maybe, she thought, he actually has trouble reading. She couldn't tell and was anxious not to increase his obvious self-consciousness. There was something in the way he looked expectantly at her, so still, barely seeming to draw breath until she encouraged him on that made her feel intensely protective.

She'd noticed him doing it with Harley when she'd gone down to the workshop, the afternoon before.

She'd stood in the doorway for a moment watching them. Carlos was leaning up against the bench, sleek hair falling sideways, long cool eyes fixed on Harley as he explained something about the grain in the piece of maple wood he was holding.

'Go on, buddy, use your hands. You won't know what I'm talkin about unless you feel it yourself.'

Carlos hesitated until Harley put the wood on the bench and pushed it towards the boy. Then, with his eyes still on Harley, he rested his hand on it. Harley smiled. 'Stroke it like you want to get to know it...'

Carlos gave a bashful half smile and moved his hand across the surface.

'Now the other direction...'

Carlos smiled a little and Harley broke out into a full smile.

'See?' he said.

May watched the boy now, while he compared prices, and then checked them off the list they had written. She wanted him to be aware of what was in the processed foods he naturally gravitated towards and reminded him gently it wouldn't take long and would cost a lot less, to make a sauce for his pasta.

'It's not worth your money, Carlos, if all you're buying is sugar and fillers and scrapings from the abattoir floor.' His eyes winced when she said this and she nodded vigorously, laughing. 'I'm not making that up. And it's not going to keep you healthy and strong. You don't need sugar in your bread or your pasta sauce.'

She wondered whether he absorbed any of this.

'I have an aunt in South Carolina,' May went on as they stood in the line at the checkout, 'who used to love sleeping over at her little school friend's house because they always had a particular brand of sausage from a can. Canned sausage!' May said wryly. 'They were livestock farmers and they ate canned sausage. Anyway, my auntie said that she *loved* that breakfast sausage until she learned to read!'

May saw a light flicker across Carlos's eyes and he twitched a small smile.

'The moral of the story,' May pronounced with a flourish, 'is always read the label!'

'They wouldn't put that on the label though, anyhow,' he said with a short huff of gulped back laughter.

May laughed too, with freedom, and Carlos glanced furtively around as though nervous someone might see him.

'Well let's see...' May picked up a tin of Chef Boyardee beef ravioli from a special offer pyramid and started reading aloud. '*Cracker meal, high fructose corn syrup, textured vegetable protein, abattoir floor scrapings.*'

Carlos rolled his eyes, but May felt a light frisson of victory to see him struggling to keep a straight face.

They were packing the bags in the boot of May's car when she remembered Harley's request. 'Oh! Do you mind if we drop by Hartland Strings on our way home? Harley needs something collected.'

Carlos gave her a strange fixed look. May couldn't tell if he was surprised or uncomfortable.

'What?'

'Nothing.' His neutral expression swiftly restored. 'Sure. I don't... I don't mind.'

As she pulled into a space outside the music store, May asked if Carlos wanted to come up or not and again he seemed nonplussed. He slid a look at her and she smiled at him wondering; does he not want to go in? Is it the place or what?

'Either way is fine,' she said.

'Okay.'

They climbed the narrow-carpeted stairs and May called out, 'Ethan!'

'That you May? Your man just called!'

They walked in and Ethan's face lit in a crooked smile.

'Get over here girl!' he laughed and coming around the side of his cluttered desk he enveloped May in a huge, crushing hug.

'Look at you! Still kick ass!' He laughed. 'So! You and Harley? Took your fuckin time, huh? Couldn't find a Brit that measured up?'

'You have no idea how close to the truth that is.' May laughed with him.

May turned to Carlos who was standing in the doorway.

'Ethan this is Carlos. He helps us out during the week.'

'How're you enjoying it?'

Carlos replied in his quiet way shrugging, the words all merging together.

'It's cool.'

'Harley used to work here, Carlos. Years ago, when I first met him.'

'And you,' Ethan cut in, 'sold more vinyl records in a week than we'd sold in a year!'

May laughed again, remembering the fun she'd had with her stall out in the summer sunshine, making friends with passers-by, trying to stop the records warping in the heat and looking forward to Harley nipping down for a chat every now and again.

Ethan still wore a small goatee and a gold ring in his ear, but his messy black curls were now close cropped and shot through with silvery grey. Nothing else had changed though. The small top floor room was still crammed with Yamaha keyboards, guitars electric and acoustic lined the walls and the racks of vinyl records still divided the room in one long half.

'I know you,' Ethan said suddenly to Carlos.

A nervous shadow fluttered across the boy's face.

'You hang out with Maryanne and Bebe, am I right?'

Carlos nodded and May saw a flush spread up his throat into his cheeks.

'Great girls. They help me out here from time to time,' Ethan said turning back to May. 'Well,' he went on a little more tentatively, 'that Bebe… if she's not careful, she'll end up in a whole heap of trouble, am I right?' he gave Carlos a conspiratorial smile and to May's surprise, Carlos gave him a wry look. 'Yeah, she likes to party.'

May was fascinated. Frannie had said they weren't to ask about his personal history although he may choose to talk about it and Carlos volunteered nothing, not even about the life he led now. May had no idea how he spent his time or with whom, whether he had friends or a girlfriend or if he even liked girls, so this tiny peek into his world was a treat.

May looked at her wrist, saw she'd forgotten her watch and asked Ethan the time.

'We have to get back. Ethan you should come out and see us. Have a drink, a bite. You have someone you'd like to bring?' she added with a grin.

'I'm between someones at this time,' he replied, all heavy gravitas and dignity. 'But I'll swing by sometime.'

'Really. Do. Anytime. Harley needs a bit of fun I think.'

Ethan pulled a face. 'How's he doing?'

'Mostly great. Come and see us. Let's go,' she said to Carlos. 'Do you want to drive?'

Carlos looked at her as though she was slightly insane.

'Umm… me?'

'You have a licence, don't you? If you want to drive, you can. It's up to you.'

She had the strangest feeling that this boy wasn't used to being asked anything.

33

May was in the garden picking tomatoes and beans a few days later. It was only ten o'clock but already the hot sun was a bright, white, burning disc that bleached the blue from the centre of the sky. She hummed quietly as she moved steadily along the rows, her hands feeling softly amongst the velvety leaves, sensitive fingers tracing around and along until they found a stem. The murmur of bees was all around her humming and buzzing as they moved giddily in and out of flower heads. She felt serenely happy in the soporific heat.

At last May stretched and looked about her, feeling a little as though she was coming to from a dream. A tickling trickle of sweat moved slowly down from her hairline at her temple and she rubbed it away, dazzled and hyper aware of the sharp-edged colours about her.

Taking her basket, she made her way back down the long length of the house and into the kitchen to get a drink; Carlos would be here soon. He'd been coming now for three weeks and as she stood by the sink letting the cold-water tap run over the insides of her wrists, May idly wondered if it might be nice to mark the halfway point.

She sensed a slight movement just out of her periphery and turned to see the boy standing in the doorway to the kitchen waiting to be invited in. His skinny black jeans emphasised the slight bow in his legs and a loose black t-shirt with *Not Made In China* on it was hanging on his lean, tense frame.

'Hello lovely,' she said, beckoning him in and getting him a glass of the grape juice he liked.

'So, what are you up to today, do you know?

'Something for a lady's porch,' he said vaguely, then added with a little kick in his voice, 'then Phoenix.'

She saw a keen, unguarded expression for a brief moment

before he tucked it quickly away.

'Are you enjoying working with her?'

He nodded. 'Yeah.'

'Harley says you're great with her. He thinks you have the right temperament to be around animals. I'd take that as a great compliment coming from him. He wouldn't let just any one near that horse.'

He slid May a watchful glance, then started towards the door.

'Hold on, I'll walk down with you. I need to water the hens.' She laughed aloud at the image this conjured and said, 'Can you imagine how cross they'd be if I actually watered them?' She exaggeratedly mimed pouring out a large watering can.

'They'd sure be mad,' Carlos replied with a soft snort.

They walked across the tough, springy grass scattering a couple of Matthew's wide-ranging chickens, past the silvered green and purple of lavender shrubs and terraced banks of pearl white cosmos cut into the sloping garden, shimmering in the sunshine. May stopped at a block of sweet corn already grown above her head, whose flat swooping leaves fluttered in a half-hearted breeze and showed Carlos how to see if they were ripe yet.

'See?' she said showing him the pale delicate silk threads sprouting from the top of a cob. 'It's so soft and silky… like fairy hair, but when you see them start to dry out and darken and they don't shine any more, the corn is ripe.'

She gently prised apart the tightly wrapped husk of one.

'Look.' She smiled at him, showing him the pale, shining kernels in tight rows. 'Aren't they sweet? Like little baby milk teeth.'

Carlos's mouth puckered sweetly and he looked at her, eyes shining before he turned his head quickly away.

'You see things kind of funny,' he said.

'Do I? But they are!' She laughed and for a swift moment

she felt as though she'd found the key to the Secret Garden.

They moved on, past hovering, threading, mumbling, bees that made the air around the flowers vibrate in the hot sunshine and as they walked, May told Carlos her sister was coming to visit.

'Oh... I thought you were like him,' he said in his curiously oblique way.

'What do you mean?' May asked. 'Like who?'

'Like him,' he said jerking his head towards Harley's workshop.

'Like Harley? How?'

'No family. Why are you here if she's there? Don't you like her?'

May was startled by the question. 'Of course I like her!'

He shrugged and without looking at her said 'families should stick together.'

They had arrived at the fence and Carlos started to climb over.

'Yes, I suppose they should if they can,' May said to his receding back, wondering if she'd lost ground.

Phoenix was tied up along the shaded side of the low wooden building and Harley was brushing her down with long, strong, firm strokes. Better than any bloody physio, May thought, as she saw sweat beading on his forehead and the muscles in his back and shoulders tensing and relaxing. His sleeves were rolled and she could see the livid red and purple scars on his forearms where the stitches had been removed, leaping angrily as he worked.

'*Qué pasa?*' Harley said, looking up at them.

'*Nada...*' Carlos said quietly, picking up a red and white bandana from the bench just inside the doorway and tying it around his head pirate style, knotted low on his nape.

Harley transferred the brush from his left hand to his right, shook it out so his fingers flopped about and grimacing a little, flexed and unflexed his fist. He handed the brush over to Carlos with a few quiet words.

The moment he was in direct contact with the mare, his movements became looser, rhythmic and steady, confident. May saw his lips moving continuously as he spoke to her and her ears twitched back and forth at the sound of his voice.

The morning sunshine picked up the flying dust and hair and May rub rubbed at the end of her nose to stop it tickling as she perched on top of the fence.

'I talked to my boss at the Roth today,' Harley said, stretching and flexing his shoulders. 'Told him not to hold my job anymore.'

'Really?' May was surprised. 'I thought you liked that job.'

She heard a whistle of exasperated air rush through his teeth.

'I do, but they can't hold it open much longer, May, and it was making me antsy thinking I had to make a decision. I don't have the... uh... I don't have the strength yet to do it.' He stumbled a little over the words.

'Can you take a break from work for a while?' she asked, somewhat euphemistically, wondering about money.

'Well, I think I could take on some extra carpentry work now. And Frannie said that there may be a budget for an apprentice.'

Carlos looked up just as Harley glanced over at him and May raised an eyebrow. How amazing if Carlos could be apprenticed to Harley. She wondered if they'd talked about it, then thought, of course they had, Harley wouldn't speak in front of the boy like that if he hadn't; he just wouldn't.

Harley straightened and reached for the towel draped over the post next to May. She handed it to him and he rubbed his face, roughing the towel through his hair. Phoenix spooked a little at the appearance of the towel and Harley clucked at her soothingly, showing her the towel, telling her she was an old fool in the most gentle of voices, that it was nothing to be scared of. Carlos took the towel and draped it around his neck like a boxer and said, more to Phoenix than anyone else, 'She don't need to be scared. This here's just a old towel...'

'Take her on down now, buddy and we can get started on some real work!'

Carlos gave one of his gulped back snorts of laughter and led Phoenix off towards her paddock.

Harley came and leaned his forearms on May's thighs. He looked up at her squinting into the sunshine.

'Got some sugar for me, baby?' he grinned.

She thrust her fingers into his thick, dark hair, massaging his scalp with the pads of her fingers and kissed him.

'Oh! Lallie emailed again saying mid-August would suit them if it's okay with us.'

'You asking me? She's your sister, darlin. Makes no difference to me when she comes. I ain't going nowhere.'

But May noticed a swift evasive look flit across his face, before he slapped her gently on the thigh and turned towards his workshop.

Long after supper, May and Harley were leaning on the pasture fence, watching the dark shape of Phoenix grazing along the perimeter. It was becoming their habit; to wander through the darkened garden, past the slumbering chickens and the quiet borders no longer humming and vibrating with pollinators and say goodnight to her.

Tonight was warm, thick and velvety with a clean eyelash of a moon and low, singing stars. It was all so beautiful and tender.

'She needs a mate,' Harley said thoughtfully.

'She's got one.' May laughed softly, prodding gently at Harley's chest.

'One with four legs... although there might be some similarities,' he said with a lewd chuckle.

'You are a vulgar and delusional schoolboy,' May said, laughing at his disappointed expression, 'despite which I love you.'

He folded her into his arms and nuzzled her hair, breathing in deeply. 'May...' he sighed, 'You know... you know.'

They were interrupted by the phone ringing and May grimaced apologetically. Seeing Frannie's name flash up on the screen, she answered.

'May? Frannie. You any idea where Carlos might be? He isn't by any remote chance with you guys?'

Instantly uneasy, May said, 'No. He left at his usual time.' She glanced anxiously at Harley.

'Well,' Frannie continued, sounding tired and worried. 'He missed curfew and still isn't back so we're a little concerned. It's very unlike him.'

'I'm sure. Obviously you've tried his cell? Switched off... oh...'

'He hasn't mentioned anything to you out of the usual? I mean, any new friends come into the conversation? Names you hadn't heard before?'

'No, nothing like that,' replied May, 'but he talks more to Harley than he does to me about that sort of thing.' Harley was already reaching out for the phone. 'I'll put him on.'

After a few curt responses, Harley hung up.

'Well...' he said, sounding as though he was trying for light-hearted. 'He's probably just cuttin lose with Bebe and Maryanne. Forgot the time.'

The look he gave her was uneasy though and May understood, because it just felt so out of character.

She was yanked out of sleep a few hours later by Harley's phone. She heard his voice full of sleep as he muttered a husky 'yes?' into the mouthpiece and even in her sleep-fugged state, registered that his phone had been switched on; he must have been more worried than she'd realised.

May heard a woman's voice rattling words, clearly distressed, and her heart pounded. Please, please let him be okay. Harley was making low sounds and the odd comment but mostly listening. It was impossible to tell what was going on.

As he kept the earpiece clamped to his head he was getting out of bed, searching in the dark. He snapped on the light and started sliding things about on the nightstand. Finally, he scribbled on the flyleaf of a book on his bedside.

May, now wide awake, looked at him for clues.

'That's okay, I'll be there as soon as I can. No, don't worry she'll understand.'

He put the phone down. Harley's face was set and he looked distracted.

'What's happened?'

'Carlos has been picked up by the police at some house out on Reidville. That was his friend Maryanne. He asked her to call us. She can't get hold of Frannie and he's asked her not to call the night staff at the home.'

May had already thrust her legs out of bed and was groping about for yesterday's clothes.

'We don't both need to go, baby, get some sleep.'

'No! I can't. I'm coming with you.'

'May,' he sounded hesitant. 'Maryanne said he doesn't want you to know. Just hold tight and I'll call you as soon as I know anything. Get some sleep.'

'I won't be able to sleep.'

'Don't sleep then,' he snapped.

He drew in a quick, sharp breath, and she heard the heavy weft of his jeans as he pulled them on and the faint jingle of his belt buckle.

'Do you know anything else? Is he okay?'

Harley's voice came muffled and terse, through his top. 'Nope.'

He came and sat on the side of the bed where May was sitting, hugging her knees.

'Get under there,' he said, his soft warm fingertips playing firm pressure over her shoulders and upper arms. His dark brows were drawn together. 'Try not to worry, he's a good kid.'

'I know that.'

Harley left, promising to drive carefully, and May lay awake in the dark. What kind of a house, she wondered. A party house? A drug house? Although he'd never seemed the druggy type, if there really was such a thing, she thought, remembering wholesome Stella's devotion to spliffing during college and far beyond.

Finally, she got up, irritated by thoughts whirling pointlessly, and went into the kitchen to make a cup of something soothing.

It was several hours before Harley called and the sun was pushing through the trees, casting long sharp angles of light and shadow across May's garden.

'We're on our way. See you in around forty.'

So much for me not knowing about it, thought May.

She was forking a wheelbarrow of manure onto the tomato beds when she heard Harley's truck pull into the drive next door. The doors slammed and she heard the low murmur of voices heading away from her. She finished the load and tipped the barrow up, balancing it against the wall.

It was another twenty minutes before she saw Harley. He came up the back stairs into the kitchen and sat wearily down at the table. He looked as though he was holding himself carefully. It was a while before he spoke.

'Well that was my least favourite thing I did this week,' he said dryly. 'Particularly as I had to fight it out with your old boyfriend.'

'What old boyfriend?' May said irritably.

353

'How many you had here before me, May? That cop from Boston. Might have been better if you'd gone down there instead. I got the distinct impression he was giving Carlos a harder time because I was with him. What an asshole. What'd you ever see in the guy?'

May felt the urge to defend herself and started angrily to speak but Harley interrupted aggressively. 'He wanted to keep Carlos in for questioning, something about being an accessory or something. I managed to assure them that he wasn't going to disappear; we'd be responsible for him. Then Frannie turned up. He sure is a hard ass.'

May didn't say anything. She knew he was.

After a long pause, May asked, 'Accessory to what? What was he doing, do we know?'

'May. Do you remember Frannie telling us about the kid who broke into Pete and Stella's that night?' She murmured for him to go on. 'His name's Danny.' May remembered that Frannie had let that slip out. 'Well, he happens to be Carlos's older brother.'

'Ahh...' Small town, small world.

'It's unlikely that Carlos knows of that connection, but all the same.'

Harley's right leg was jigging rapidly and he got up abruptly and paced to the porch stairs, fumbled about and lit a cigarette, took a couple of drags, coughed, dry and choking and tossed the cigarette down, grinding it under his boot.

May was careering about in her head wondering what the hell all this meant and if Carlos was okay.

'Anyhow...' Harley went on, looking at May briefly before his eyes flicked away. 'It seems Danny was released from prison a couple weeks ago and Carlos wanted to see him. Because he's a looked after kid, the courts decide things like that on his behalf, and they say he can't for various reasons so he took matters into his own hands and somehow got a ride out to where Danny's been staying. With the same guy, incidentally, who had him robbing people's houses in the first place. May, this is so fucked up.' He seemed momentarily speechless with fury. 'Where in hell do they think he's going to go if his entire fucking family is incarcerated, fostered out to the four winds or dead?'

May stood and moved over to where Harley stood placing a light hand on his arm. He shrugged her off.

'And what kind of fool doesn't get that this kid is going to want, *need* to see his brother when he comes out?' He let out a growling snarl and thrust his hands into his hair. 'And your fucking cop is frightening him out of his mind making these insinuations about the apple not falling far from the tree and all. Dad's doing time, brother just out. It's only a matter of time yudduh fuckin ya. I'm telling you May, I felt sick listening to him.'

'Harley,' May said icily. 'Don't call him "my" cop.'

'How is it,' Harley said wearily, ignoring her comment, 'that all the wrong people are in the wrong jobs?'

He leaned back in the wooden chair, eyes focussed at some spot on the far corner of the floor.

'Harley, where is he now?' May was desperate to see Carlos and reassure him everything would be okay.

'I left him in my room. He hasn't had but a couple hours sleep.'

'I'm going to nip down and see him. I guess he's worked out I have to know...'

Harley's grim mouth softened and curved a little and he looked up at her briefly.

Carlos was lying on Harley's bed staring up at the vaulted ceiling when May quietly put her head around the door.

'Hello you lovely boy,' May greeted him gently. 'Can I come in?'

'Sure.' His voice was quiet and more amorphous than ever and he slowly swung his legs off the bed. There was something deeply poignant about his white-socked feet with the hole in one big toe.

He sat clutching the edge of the bed looking down and his hair hung straight and dull, without its usual lustre. He looked empty and crumpled and May could faintly smell the stale, frightened sweat coming from him.

'Can I sit with you?' May asked as she put some clean towels on the bed.

Carlos shrugged a little without meeting her eyes and she went and sat in a wicker chair Harley had angled in a corner to catch the light.

'I'm so glad you're safe. What a horrible thing to have happened.'

He looked up at her, his eyes uncomprehending, surprise flickering in their depths.

'What?' she asked him. 'Did you think I wouldn't care?'

'No...' he said uncertainly. 'Maybe... you'd be mad.'

'How could I be angry with you for wanting to see your brother?'

Carlos shrugged.

'Why don't you have a shower and come up for some breakfast? I brought you clean jeans.'

She shook out the Levis she'd brought and laid them over the back of the chair. She didn't tell him they were hers, but he would have been tripping up all over the place in Harley's. She began pulling open the drawers of Harley's dresser, found a few tops that might do and draped them with the jeans.

'Come on up when you're ready.'

She was just slipping out of the door when Carlos's voice stopped her.

'You don't think I'm like that do you?'

May turned to look at him. He looked so young and forlorn, mouth slack and eyes empty and hopeless.

'Like what, lovely,' she asked gently, feeling tearful,

knowing she mustn't cry in front of him.

'My dad.'

'Oh Carlos!'

May came back in and sat. 'I don't know your Dad; I only know you. You might be like him in some ways and in others not. But I know you're an honest, kind-hearted boy. You work hard and I think you're probably very loyal too. All I know about your dad is that he's in prison and that doesn't tell me anything about the kind of person he is, does it?'

'Doesn't it?' he asked, resentment seeping in at the edges of his voice.

'You've never talked about him,' she said, not answering him.

Carlos nodded like a little shadow. May stayed with him for a while longer, but he said nothing more. It took her a moment to realise he had leaned sideways very slightly into her, not touching but very close. May held herself still, not sure if he would accept any touch so she just stayed with him. At last she got up.

'I'll see you up there. And try not to worry. We're on your side.'

As soon as she got in from work that night, May could see something was wrong. Harley was leaning on the porch railings with a beer and a cigarette looking closed off and pensive.

'Hello my darling,' she said softly, hoping it was something she could help with. She dropped her bag with a jangling thud and sat on the swing seat. She stretched her tired legs out, flexing her feet trying to work out the tightness of having been on her feet all day.

'Frannie came to get Carlos and stayed a while,' Harley said wearily. 'Her manager has "sanctioned" Carlos for his little trip to see his brother.'

May felt a weight on her chest. 'What does that mean?'

'Apparently,' Harley continued, his voice heavy with sarcasm, 'the kids know the deal. Privileges are contingent on their toeing the line and sticking to the rules. Evidently, Carlos coming here was a privilege.'

He sounded angry and mocking.

'I thought it was a necessity!' interrupted May while Harley nodded emphatically. 'Part of their duty of care to prepare him. And anyway,' she raised her voice, feeling her blood heat up, 'he's not in a young offenders unit—what the fuck!'

'I know.' Harley's eyes were snapping with anger and the two of them sat in the heavy darkness, both seemingly at a loss. 'He's not allowed to come for a week. Bastards.'

May stood and moved over to where he stood.

'I don't know what to do with myself, May.' He turned a stark face to her. 'I don't know what to do.'

'Come on,' she said impulsively. 'Let's walk.'

Harley looked for a moment as though he would refuse then suddenly whistled up Piper and strode off and up through the moonlit garden towards the woods turning at the gate and waiting while she caught up. They walked in silence, but for their feet crunching the densely packed path. At the fork in the path, Harley took the one that headed towards Perch Hill. It began almost at once to slope upwards through the broad-leaved trees, their way lit by an almost full moon. May stepped out with strong confident strides and they fell into a steady rhythm, Harley's still discernible limp giving her a moment of concern before she brushed it away. He knows what he can do, she thought.

The path began to incline more sharply and May was starting to breathe hard as she leaned into the climb. Harley seemed locked away inside himself and she roiled inside with concern for Carlos and worry about Harley's anger and frustration.

It took them about forty minutes to reach the other side

of the wood and emerge at the foot of the hill. May stopped and looked out over the sweep of pasture that fell away on a swell of rolling grassland, mysterious and pearly in the moonlight.

Harley climbed a huge white oak whose branches stretched long and dark, like open arms. He stood on the lowermost branch and reached out to May.

'Come on,' he said and she shinned up, then eased tentatively along the branch in front of him until she sat far out over the grass, straddling the branch as though astride a great cart horse.

Harley scooted behind her, locking his arms around her waist, settling his scratching chin in the nook of her shoulder and her neck. He took a huge expansive breath. 'Oh May…'

As they sat, the night swelled and throbbed around them with the call of the tree peepers and the night jars and crickets, soothing, comforting, alive.

'It's hard to remember detail,' Harley said quietly, 'about people. Feels a little like trying to remember a dream. If you just let it drift along you might get something, but if you try too hard it's like they all start melting and you're left with even less than you thought you had.'

May remembered sitting like this with Harley many years before, under an apple tree, his words coming from close behind her, low and sonorous through her, into her, unable to see his face or his expression as he talked, but always hearing more than just his words.

'Do you remember your daddy, May?' he surprised her by asking.

'Very much so.'

She often thought of him; when the smell of tomatoes growing on the vine pressed through the thick hot sunshine, when Matthew pronounced apricot with a short 'a' or when she heard The Beach Boys on the radio.

'I have photos and letters that give me a sense of him. He

wrote very well. Like he talked, so now, if I read something he wrote, I can hear him. Tone of voice, the way he said a word.'

May wondered how he would look now, how he would have aged. She felt an undertow of sadness pull at her, at the not knowing.

'I sometimes wonder if I'd know him in the street. You know if he hadn't died, had just disappeared and then I bumped into him... would I know him?'

'Mmm hmm,' Harley murmured. 'I'd love to know how my little sister's would've looked, my brother. Would we get on, be close? I watch other families sometimes and how all they do is fuss and fight. Would that be us?'

34

The next morning, May looked up to see that instead of climbing the fence between the two properties as he usually did, Harley was making his way along Matthew's drive, through her gate and down the driveway.

She came to meet him smiling apologetically.

'I'm an idiot to have suggested that walk. You look so stiff. Does it hurt?'

She walked slowly alongside him and he slung an arm around her neck and leaned dramatically on her.

'I feel like I lost bad at the rodeo,' he said ruefully. 'Fuckin leg. I could barely stand first thing. But my head sure is clearer.'

Harley sat gingerly in a chair, long leg thrust in front of him. He took a sip of his coffee.

'Baby, how do you like your old man?' He sucked his lips in over his teeth and spoke in a high-pitched rasp. 'Y'all go on and fetch me ma teeth from yonder glass, I've a mind to bite you!'

May giggled and nipped him along his jaw line with her own strong teeth. He pulled her onto his lap before groaning.

'Ahh! No! I can't do this,' he tipped her off again.

'You should have had a hot bath and a massage before you went to bed last night' May said and Harley gave her a very hot look.

'That wouldn't work now?' he asked sounding hopeful.

'Too late. Damage already done,' she replied swerving adeptly from his swatting hand.

Then all at once the atmosphere dropped and May wondered how Carlos was, just as Harley said, 'we should call Frannie and see when he's coming back. I'm thinking Carlos needs a room here if he starts an apprenticeship. How would that be for you?'

May smiled, touched by how protective Harley was of the boy.

'It's probably a very good idea. Let's talk about it later though. I've got a double shift; I need to get going. What are you up to today?'

Harley stood and held her face in his hands, kissing her mouth emphatically. 'Matthew and me are going into the barn to find the bedsteads for your sister's visit. Come on home as soon as you can, we fall to pieces without you around.'

May smiled and leaned down to pick up a disgraceful rubber bone and toss it across the yard. The Warhorse tore off, followed by a slightly more ambivalent Piper and May headed off to work wondering and worrying about Carlos.

The moment she entered the restaurant, May could tell something was up. The atmosphere was fizzing with a nervous, excited energy; she felt as though she'd walked in on the tail end of a massive row.

Waiters were rushing about without making eye contact and she was acutely aware that when she was looked at, it was as though she should know precisely what was going on. She instinctively looked over at the bar, but Connie wasn't there.

'What did I miss?' she asked Amy, as she tied her apron and ran her finger down the staff rota to see who should be here.

'Oh, boy,' Amy intoned, and she gave a sort of cackle. 'Connie just busted Mark Sassello wide open!'

'Not literally?' she asked, thinking she could easily see Connie take a swipe at someone if the spirit moved her.

'Not quite, but I don't think he's long for these parts.'

She felt a confusing ripple of excitement and dread. 'What happened?'

'Amy!' Turtle's voice came sharply down the stairs. 'Number 7 waiting to pay, let me see you hustle!'

Amy threw her hands up and called 'just a minute!' Then, turning to May, added, 'we heard Harley's boy was arrested last night. Then Mark came in for a sandwich and was just shooting the breeze with Connie while I made it, and out of nowhere—*on my way, Turtle!*' she called out again. 'Out of nowhere, Connie's in his face over the counter yelling at him. Turtle comes running over, everyone's losing it, Turtle's reading the riot act to Connie, Sassello's yelling back at her, shut your mouth, you crazy, fuckin—you know the kind of thing—and suddenly she says, "*Officer* Sassello," like, icy-calm, "If anything happens to that kid that shouldn't, I'm going tear it right open? You hear me?" Man it was out of control. *Coming!* Gotta go, Turtle's going to have a shit fit if I don't hustle.' She ran upstairs two at a time.

May sat at the desk in the office, head spinning. Turtle poked his head around the door.

'Uh.' He looked swiftly about, and came in, shutting the door behind him, something he rarely did. He perched on the desk beside May and looked at her for a moment.

'Well, there's some pretty hot stuff going on around here. You up to speed?'

'Something to do with Connie and Mark.'

There was a knock on the door and May jumped.

'Yep!' Turtle raised his hand at May, telling her to hold on and Connie opened the door. She cocked her head slightly when she saw May. '*You*'re here.'

May half-smiled and felt her heart thumping. 'It would appear so.'

'Look, before you go getting any ideas, I didn't do this for your benefit, but I couldn't let him go on thinking he owns this town just because he wears the blue. He's not even *from* here,' she said and shot May a venomous look. She was talking very fast and almost defensively, not her usual, languid take it or leave it tone. 'The man's out of control and someone had to put a stop to it, okay?'

May was almost dizzy with confusion. 'Connie, *Connie!*' She had to raise her voice to stop the stream of words. 'I have no idea what you're talking about.'

'You don't?'

'Not a clue. Only that it involves Mark and you in some way.'

'Not me, except I called him on it. It involves Mark and you...'

'And *me?*' May's scalp prickled.

'Yeah, and we all just heard that he arrested that kid Harley's supporting and right away I thought that poor little fucker doesn't stand a chance, so when he came in for a sandwich I told him.'

'It seems Mark underestimated—no, misjudged— Connie,' Turtle broke in a little impatiently. 'Bragged to her about his little hobby and thought she'd...'

'That bat-shit, crazy asshole thought I'd think he was the big man, because he's been targeting Harley. He wants to make you pay for throwing him over for Harley.'

May jerked upright. 'What do you mean?' Her heart was beating so hard in her throat she had to swallow a few times, hard. She took a steadying breath.

Connie gave her an almost pitying look, but there was disdain in there too. 'How should I know?'

'Connie,' she said in a low voice and tried not to think of her as an enemy. 'Do you want to tell me what's going on, or not? I can ask someone else to fill me in.'

Connie threw a look at Turtle as though she wasn't so sure of talking in front of him.

'I don't think you ladies need me,' he said, taking the cue and leaving.

The small office felt rather smaller and a little oppressive. 'So Mark's got himself the idea I have a problem with you...'

'Well, I wonder where he got that idea from!' May broke in with a hard laugh. 'He'll make a detective now, for sure.'

Connie smirked then broke into an actual smile. 'I'm going to move on,' she said and May smiled back, liking the honesty. 'I guess he thought it would give him chops, or something, if I thought he had something to do with Harley being jumped, your tyres—all of that.'

'He was involved with that?'

Connie gave her best withering look. 'Why do they always say Brits are smart? You're so freakin slow on the uptake. He organised it!'

'That's horrible. Horrible. And illegal.'

'Duh!'

'What made it all kick off today?' May asked and was surprised to see Connie look uneasy.

'He came over to my place last night and...' she broke off and blushed. Nice to see you might be human, thought May. 'Did Harley ever say anything to you when he was in hospital, or after, about the wreck?'

'No,' May said, uncertain where this was going. 'He said he couldn't remember anything after the impact, until he saw Matthew at the hospital.'

'That's something, I guess.'

'Why?'

'Well, think about it.'

Connie sounded exasperated again and May jumped in, 'Connie, you haven't *told* me anything!'

'Last night, Mark got wasted and told me he saw Harley's wreck and... drove on. He left him there.' Suddenly Connie looked stricken and May almost reached out. 'The fucking asshole just left him there.' She blew her breath out, and sat down all at once.

May was horrified and full of rage, her head throbbing with it. It must have been so cold on that night on the deserted, icy, woodland road; she wondered what kind of a man Mark Sassello must really be. 'Oh my god... he might have died.'

'If it's true,' Connie said. That brought May up short.

'Don't you think it is?'

'Who knows? The guy's sick. He thought I'd find it a turn on.' She looked upset and it touched May despite her feelings for Connie.

May was quiet a moment before asking, 'What do you think will happen?'

'How should I know,' Connie snapped, caustically, then blew another breath and spoke more neutrally. 'He's on notice, though, I tore a fucking strip off him when he came in.' She laughed, hard and humourless. 'For a minute there, I thought Turtle was going to fire me on the spot. Do not pass go.'

'What did you say?' May asked.

'I don't know,' she said dismissively, but went on at once. 'That he was a corrupt bastard and should have known better than to show his sorry ass in here after what he told me. I guess when I heard about that kid being arrested, it worried me.'

For a moment, May rather admired Connie's shoot from the hip personality. 'I'm really grateful, Connie, thanks for saying something.'

'What are you thanking me for? I didn't do it for you.'

May flushed, amazed at the swift resuming of hostilities. Shaking her head at Connie, she said, 'You really are hard as nails, aren't you?' she stood to go.

'That's me!' Connie said with a wide smile.

When May got home, Harley was waiting on the porch and came down to meet her as she parked the car.

'Cops came by today, wanting to talk to me.'

May swallowed. 'What did they say?'

'They've taken Sassello off Carlos's case, as a precaution while they investigate a claim from "a member of the public". Any idea what it's about?'

They sat together on the swing seat and May kicked off her shoes. She filled Harley in, watching closely for a response, but he took it all impassively, prompting her to go on once or twice, but otherwise nothing.

'Were you able to tell them anything?' May asked when she'd finished.

'A little,' he said. 'But you know's well as I do that everything's just hearsay or a feeling you get. Still, I guess it helps to know he ain't in a position to fuck Carlos around.'

35

Carlos came back after a week and got stuck right in. As Lallie's visit with Sam and the children drew nearer, May's thoughts and mood ricocheted between concern for him, and excitement about seeing the family.

'I hope they like Harley,' she said to Stella while she was collecting spare bedding from Woodland Drive later that week.

'Or what? You'll dump him?' Stella giggled.

'Oh don't be a git, Stella. You know what I mean. Can you imagine how awful Lallie and Harley could be if they didn't like each other.'

'Umm… not really, honey. Stop worrying about it; it's going to be terrific. Can't wait to meet those cute babies at last.'

'Hardly babies anymore. Maxie just had his fourth birthday and Tillie will be seven in January. But how are you?'

Stella was pregnant, much to everyone's delight and Stella's relief.

'Great. Look fat rather than pregnant, but I'm sixteen weeks now so I feel safer, you know?'

May got up reluctantly and stretched. 'Must go, Stel. I need to find some brute strength to help me set up the beds for the kids. Matthew's lent me an old iron double bed and the sweetest little wooden bedsteads his kids used to have. I think they'd been in his barn a hundred years though, took me all fucking morning to scrub off all the bird shit and greasy dust.' She kissed her friend. 'Ooo…' she said giving her an extra squeeze. 'I do love you, Stella!'

'Love you too.'

Back at the farm, May dumped the bedding in the hall, checked all the bed parts had dried in the sunshine and ambled to find Harley and Carlos to help her.

The door to the workshop was thrown wide, letting in the light and sunshine. May stood quietly a moment or two.

Harley's video camera was set up on a workbench and plugged into a laptop and they were watching the screen in a companionable silence. Harley said something in Spanish, stopped the action, jotted a quick note, rewound and they watched again. Then to May's utter astonishment, Carlos laughed. It was a sweet, pebbly tumble of laughter like a small boy and he dropped his head to the side and gulped it back glancing furtively at Harley.

'You like that?' Harley said turning a smiling face on the boy.

May tapped on the open door.

'Hi there,' she said into the room.

Carlos stiffened and turned to face her. Harley didn't break a beat.

'Hey beautiful,' he said absently as he rewound something quickly. 'This bit? Right here, yes?'

Carlos turned to look and nodded, then said quietly, 'ah… no… a bit more.'

'Further back?'

He nodded again and Harley said 'talk to me buddy. Caint hear a nod.'

He put a light hand on the boy's back.

'Back more. There,' Carlos said softly.

May came over and put her hands on Harley's shoulders. He jabbed a finger on the keyboard, stopping the image again and flipped the screen down before May could see what it was.

He reached behind with both arms and held May against him, tipping his head back and puckering up exaggeratedly for a kiss. May, laughing, obliged. Carlos looked away.

'*Està bien hecho?* What about it Carlos, *bien?*'

'Mm hmm.'

'Are we going to tell May what we're doing, or no?'

Carlos looked trapped.

'Oh don't. If it's private that's fine,' she said, burning to know. 'I just came down to ask you guys to come up and help me with the bed frames for Tillie and Max. I thought I could do it, but it's definitely a two-person job.'

Harley spoke rapidly in Spanish, getting up and swiftly unplugging cables and winding them up, putting away the camera. Carlos murmured something back.

'Okay, buddy. It's your call,' Harley said.

May wished again she spoke Spanish and felt an ugly tug of jealousy.

Upstairs in the still and silent heat of the master bedroom, the windows were flung wide, bug screens in place but the light breeze moving about gently through the tops of the maples, creating a fluttering green and gold light on the oak floor that was unable to reach the air in the bedroom. She set the ceiling fans whirring.

'Carlos, can you open the window in the bathroom? Let's try to get a little cross breeze going.' She wiped a hand across her sweaty top lip and pushed her damp hair back from her forehead. 'Do you think it'll storm?'

'Sure feels like it might. Air's getting heavier by the minute.'

May shook out all the loaned bedding and looked at it with a slight grimace as Carlos and Harley began putting together the bed frames.

'Why does budget bedding always look like it got in the wrong wash?' she muttered looking at the grainy blocks and lines of grey tinged blues, lilacs and sage greens. She felt a sharp longing for just one of the lush and vivid tapestries that Sarah had made into cushion covers for her, one of her quilts with their rich colours.

'Oh I wish…' she said suddenly and stopped.

'What?' Harley looked up sharply with a quizzical look.

'I wish I had one of my quilts. From home. They'd add a bit of colour.' He shrugged and went back to bracing a corner of the bed. 'Lallie never did send one,' she mused.

She looked up at a sharp clang-clatter and Harley's shout of laughter followed by a quick, 'Sorry, buddy. You okay?'

May smiled to herself at the reproachful look Carlos gave Harley.

'Yeah...' he said bending to pick up a long white enamelled pole.

'Okay. Let's start over.'

Harley stood and stretched, looking around. 'Why you never used this room for yourself, baby? It's so much bigger.'

'The windows don't face the right way,' she said and Harley laughed.

'And which way would the right way be?'

'Sunrise way,' she said emphatically and he laughed again. 'Okay, we're done.'

She was standing on a stool screwing large brass cup hooks to the sides of each window at the top. 'Oh lovely! It looks like it was made for this very room.'

She looked at the beautiful old enamelled iron bed, fitted perfectly between the two windows that looked out onto the garden, pastures and on towards the wooded hills.

'Hand me that would you?' she said, pointing at the curtains she'd threaded onto doweling rods. Lallie and Sam might not appreciate morning light quite like she did. She balanced the rod on the cup hooks.

'Let's just hope they don't try to open them!' She laughed. 'Who's hungry? Surely it's time to eat!'

While May washed dishes after lunch and Carlos dried, the phone rang. She froze a split second and the room seemed to twang with nerves. Ever since Carlos's arrest, the sound of the phone freaked them all out.

'You want me to…' Harley looked at her and she nodded holding up her sudsy hands as excuse and Harley moved towards the phone. He lifted the handset, walked out of the kitchen and down the hall, his voice neutral as he answered, then suddenly sounding urgent and serious, 'Fran! What is it? Yeah, he's here, you want to—okay.'

Matthew started back on the dishes and talked a little to Carlos about the split rail fencing down by the paddock that Phoenix had kicked out again.

'You want to work on that with me tomorrow morning?'

'Sure.'

Harley's voice came closer as he walked back up the hall, but May couldn't make out what he was saying. She was a held breath of trepidation.

He hung up and exchanged a look with Matthew.

'Well, I'll get on now,' the old man said quietly. 'Look in on me later, son?' he directed at Harley and padded quietly out.

'Carlos,' Harley said, 'that was Fran.'

May couldn't finish the breath she had just begun; it was stuck above her voice box at the back of her throat; a fish bone waiting to choke her.

'She says, they've collected statements from everyone who was there and they all corroborate what you said; that you were just visiting your brother. Nothing else. Sassello's facing charges, though.' He broke off realising perhaps that this might be a lot to take in.

Carlos's face didn't even flicker and May wondered for a moment if he had understood. Harley walked over to the boy and put his hands gently on his shoulders, bending his knees to look him in the eyes.

'They won't press any charges. It's over.' Then, his voice very gentle, he added, 'Okay?'

Carlos crumpled as Harley pulled him clumsily into his shoulder and switched to Spanish. May could no longer

372

understand what he was saying but it sounded deeply comforting to her. She slipped out of the back door, tears in her eyes her heart aching at the two of them standing there quiet now, apart from the sound of Carlos's stifled sobs.

May walked slowly around the far end of the porch, allowing the relief to seep through her as the hot sunshine poured over her hair and shoulders.

The full splendour of the six rectangular planting beds, hot and riotous with colour, hit May anew. Zinnias, dahlias and clambering tomatoes in all their varying stages of blooming life were vying for space and attention and she felt their call; the singing, joyous colour pulled her in and May stepped into the vibrating heat and earthy scent, surrounding herself with buzzing, humming colour.

36

A few nights later, Frannie sat with May and Harley on the porch watching a slow and iridescent sunset. She had stopped by on her way home and ended staying for dinner as Jesse was out of town. They were talking about Mark. *Again*, May found herself thinking in irritation. She couldn't wait until he was out of their lives.

'So what's he being charged with?' Fran asked.

'Much less than he's done, in all likelihood, but they want to get a conviction. So all the weird stalky stuff they're not pursuing,' May replied. 'There just isn't enough evidence, and any good lawyer could show that he's a fantasist trying to impress a woman.' She gave a small shiver and continued. 'But he's charged with inciting to assault, I think that's what they said, and corruption.'

'Frannie,' Harley said a little abruptly as their friend lit a cigarette with a guilty grimace. 'We have a more immediate problem.'

Frannie sighed, coughed and shook her head at May as she offered her more wine.

'Carlos?'

'Yes.'

May sat down and angled her chair so she could see the western part of the pasture going down in a blaze of glory.

'He needs to see his brother.'

Frannie's face hardened. 'I know, Harley, but the family court is clear and you can't ask me to mess with that.'

'I'm not, but we need to do something. Otherwise, Carlos is just going to keep skipping out.'

'He only needs to wait another three months, then he'll be eighteen and not our responsibility anymore.'

'Listen to yourself, Fran!' Harley said tightly. 'He needs to see him. Three months to a kid of seventeen is a lifetime. Tell me what we can do, not what we can't do. This is your turf, Fran, help me out. Can we do supervised? Can we offer Danny something here? The kid's got a family and it's being cauterised.'

'I hear you, Harley, I hear you,' Frannie said soothingly. 'We could apply for supervised visits. You prepared to put yourself forward?'

Harley just snorted and didn't bother with an answer.

'Have you talked this over with May?' Harley looked momentarily furtive and Frannie went on, 'How do you feel about a convicted felon being around your home? Not to mention that there's history with that break in.'

'He's done his time, Fran.'

'How long do you think it will take to go through the courts, Frannie?' May asked.

'These things can take months…'

'But,' May turned to Harley, 'would it help if Carlos felt we were at least trying?'

Harley's face softened a little. 'Yeah… I think it might.'

Not to mention you, thought May.

'In no particular order, the problem is that Danny has no permanent address and no job,' Frannie said. 'The family court states that they would like to see some stability before they let Carlos spend time with his brother.'

'Are you saying that if he did, then Carlos would be able to see him?'

'As I understand it, yes.'

'Really, as simple as that?'

There was something unnerving about Harley's hard, pushing tone of voice.

'Yes.'

'*Then why the hell is no one doing anything to help him?*' he exploded furiously.

'I never knew him to have a temper,' Frannie said as May

375

walked her to her car.

'Nor me. It's only since the accident. Apparently, it's not uncommon. He'll grow out of it.' She tried to laugh. 'But, Frannie, surely you can understand his, our frustration?'

'Of course!' It was Frannie's turn to show temper now. 'But why am I the villain of the piece? I'm doing my best in a real tough situation and he's not the only kid I'm taking care of, May! It shouldn't all be down to me, us. Where's the freakin community? These are all our kids! I can take it, May, but jeez, why is nobody coming forward with ideas, apprenticeships, work? You, for instance!' she jabbed a finger at May. 'Don't you have some influence at that jumped up burger bar you work in? *You* give Danny a job! Start the ball rolling, kid!'

May was shocked. Frannie wrenched her car door open then stopped and started to laugh. She turned back to May. 'Please accept my apologies for that little outburst. And I didn't even have an auto wreck! I've got no excuse. You're good people, May. I know you guys really care.'

'Frannie,' she said, relived. 'I'm sorry we're on your case all the time.'

They hugged briefly and just as Fran was slamming her car door May said suddenly, 'Oh! My sister's coming with her family on Saturday for a couple of weeks. I'd love you to meet her.'

'Your sister? Great! Just say the word.'

She hurtled off driving, as ever, at break neck speed over May's potholes.

It was a quiet Wednesday afternoon at Molly's a few days later. May was trying to pack in as much as she could before taking some time off for Lallie's visit. The lunch rush had come and gone and May and Turtle were making the most of the relatively empty restaurant to catch up on a bit of housekeeping.

May was kneeling up on one of the windows polishing brass curtain rods, while Turtle counted out a delivery of paper goods.

'What's the policy about employing people with criminal records?'

'You got something to tell me, May?'

She laughed. 'I'm serious, Turtle, is there a policy?'

'Well, we don't as a rule. There's a question on the form and if you've got anything more than a driving offence then it's pretty much a no. We have so many people wanting to work here that we don't need to scrape the barrel.'

May filled him in with the bare bones of her concerns for Carlos.

'Is there any way we could give his brother at least a trial in the kitchen?'

Turtle looked uneasy. His ferrety twinkle damped as he gave her a long unreadable look.

'What do you know about this guy? Other than that he's a housebreaking dope head, I mean.' His voice was dry, but even so May heard the tiniest inflection of wry humour and she pulled a face at him before heaving a sigh.

'D'you know what, Turtle? I've never even met him. I suppose I should start with that really, shouldn't I?'

'Look, May,' Turtle spread his hands as though patting something down. 'I'm not saying outright no. I'm as willing as the next guy to give someone a chance to make good. But it feels kind of weird that you're asking me this and haven't even met the guy. We neither of us have anything to go on.'

They lapsed into silence and Turtle looked uncomfortable. May rubbed harder at the brass.

'Here's an idea,' Turtle said, brighter. 'Check him out, see what you think. Don't let sentiment cloud your judgment, then come back to me? Does that sound like a fair deal?'

'Thanks T. It sounds fine.'

An hour or so later, May and Amy were lolling about in

the office on a quick break between their double shift May had her feet up on the desk.

'Look at you, Boss lady!' Amy laughed. 'You need a stogie and a glass of bourbon!'

'Go fetch.' May pointed at the door, eyes narrowed.

Amy unhurriedly and meticulously gave her the finger. 'Hey, how's The Bleeding Heart project going?'

May shook her head slowly. 'Don't you coin Connie's phrase, you traitor.' She nudged at Amy's leg with her foot.

'Okay, so how's your adopted son?' Amy giggled.

'He's lovely.'

May felt a swell of pride thinking about how Carlos's confidence was gradually growing.

'But he's pining for his Big Bad Brother and I don't know quite how to help him.'

May shook herself and dropped her feet down and spun the chair in one smooth movement.

'I'm just going to have to meet Danny and make up my own mind,' she said. 'Come on old lady, we have Ivy League archetypes to service!'

'Eeugh! That sounds gross. Hey, when's your sister coming?'

'Saturday and I can't wait. Damn!' May stopped at the foot of the stairs. 'I meant to ask her to bring a quilt of mine.'

'It's three days away surely she's still packing?'

'It's in my flat. Different part of town to her. Damn. Oh well, won't hurt to call and ask.'

The friends raced each other up the stairs two at a time, Amy reaching out to try and unfasten May's apron. She was too fast and sidestepped swiftly, leaving Amy to stumble ahead with the momentum of her grab.

They were both laughing when they reached the restaurant floor and May managed to undo Amy's apron before she turned and strode off to begin her shift.

That night as she and Harley stood leaning on the fence watching Phoenix and chatting quietly, May asked Harley if there was a chance she could meet Danny.

'I don't see why not. What's on your mind?'

May told him about her conversation with Turtle. 'So I need to meet him in order to make anything happen.'

'Baby,' he said gently drawing her into his arms. 'You're an angel, you know that?' May gave a soft derisive snort. 'What?' he asked. 'You are. Let me see if he'd like a visit. He's a nice kid, but a little more... how to put it? A little wilder'n Carlos.'

'When have you met him?' May asked feeling a little strange that she hadn't known. Harley actually looked sheepish which made her feel better.

'I went up with Carlos a couple times—I had to,' he hurried on. 'Otherwise, he would a just gone by himself and maybe got into all kinds of trouble. I made him promise not to go alone.'

May was conflicted. She understood why Harley might do this but it worried her too.

'I hope you're not going to get into trouble with the courts over it. Frannie would be furious if she found out.'

'Well she won't, will she?' he shrugged irritably. 'What would you have me do, May? Just let him lose the last little bit of family he's got left?'

'Well of course not,' she said, annoyed. 'Don't be a git.'

He turned a quizzical, slightly ironic look on her. 'What does that even mean?'

She shook her head dismissively, not wanting this to become a fight between them.

'Just be careful. It's a relatively short time until Carlos leaves the care home and...' she huffed with sudden exasperation. 'Look! Shall we focus on my meeting Danny? I'm trying to do something constructive; I don't know why this has become a whole thing about Carlos losing his family.'

Harley burst out with such force that May felt it jolt

through her.

'*Because that's all it's about!* It's the *only* thing that matters! The only thing!'

'Harley,' she said looking him in the eyes, searching for some clue to what had just happened.

He rubbed his hand hard across his mouth; across and back. Then closed his eyes, took a deep breath and pulled her roughly into his arms holding her tight, mumbling into her hair.

'I'm sorry, baby. I don't—I'm sorry.'

She stroked him gently. Well, that's not just about having got whacked on the head, she thought wryly.

The next day, May was just coming to the end of her morning shift when Harley came clattering through the entrance door with Carlos hugging the space behind him.

'Hey man! Long time no see!' Turtle called from the bar and May hung back, feeling an odd sensation of shyness and pride.

It was so strange to see him in there after all this time. She realised Harley hadn't been in to Molly's since before his accident and it was so very much her own space now. She instinctively glanced at Connie, who had her back turned, busy with a customer. Harley grinned at May, raising his eyebrows as though questioning her reticence, then turned back to Turtle and introduced Carlos who was standing carefully beside him.

'He's my right hand man, helps me out. Made my recovery that bit easier.'

Carlos seemed impassive, but May saw the twitch of a smile about his mouth and the flush that crept up his throat. She loved Harley then, more than ever. She came and joined them at the bar where Connie was shooting soda into a tall ice filled glass for Carlos. She handed it to him with a smile and then leaned on the counter.

'How come we don't see you in here anymore, Harley?'

'It's not intentional,' he answered mildly. 'I've got plenty to keep me busy out in Dover.'

'Yeah well, all work and no play…' She smirked.

'Don't you worry, Connie, it's mostly play.' He turned to May who was trying not to feel too triumphant and said, 'you about ready to go, baby?'

She didn't want to ruin the effect by asking where they were going or what Harley was doing there with Carlos so she just nodded.

'Yep. Just give me two ticks while I put my stuff away.'

Once she was out in the truck, tucked between Harley and Carlos, she asked.

'You said you wanted to meet Danny?' Harley said. 'We thought we'd take you out and see him.'

It was a twenty-minute drive along rural unmarked roads and Harley had the windows down and the music cranked. The hot wind tore and whipped at May's hair and Carlos handed her a band from his wrist without looking at her. It was such a sweet, thoughtful gesture. She and Harley sang loudly along to *Willie and the Poor Boys* while Carlos tapped out a beat on his thigh with his hand and his head dipped in tiny rhythmic nods. May's spirits were up with the birds, soaring amongst the startling blue sky, dazzled in the sunshine.

Then without warning as they turned a bend in the road, she saw a brown cluster of isolated, single story buildings. They looked as though they'd been pushed to one side temporarily, along with four or five rusted vehicles piled up nearby. The front of the main building had a sagging porch running the full length, with a couple of tan sofas, spilling their foam guts out. Carlos seemed twitchy and put his hand over his throat, rubbing at his chin and lip with a raised forefinger.

Before the truck had even pulled to a stop, the front door

opened and a deeply tanned young man in a close fitting white sleeveless vest and very dark close-cropped hair came out grinning and raising an arm in a greeting.

He jogged barefoot down the porch steps and rapped an open hand on the bonnet of the truck. He had a dimple in one cheek and a barbed wire tattoo around his muscled upper arm. Peeking out from the edge of his vest, she could see the first half of some swirling copperplate writing, initials, the first one of which was a C.

Beneath the tan and the wide smile his face was nervy and a little drawn, his eyes not quite settling on anyone not quite reflecting the smile. But there was affection in them as he looked through the window at his brother. Carlos got out and they hugged, then stepped apart and May felt a shiver as she saw that they had exactly the same eyes; it was almost uncanny. They were so physically different, she wouldn't have believed they were brothers but for those long, slow, strangely lit, grey-green eyes. Whose were they, she wondered, mother or father?

'I can't invite you in,' he said. 'Everybody's still crashed, man. We should take a ride someplace.'

'You gotta say hello to May proper, Danny. Okay?' Carlos said quietly and May nearly choked.

She couldn't recall a time when Carlos had ever said her name. It had become such a joke that he only ever referred to her as 'she' no matter what the context or to whom he was speaking that Harley liked to have a little fun pretending that he didn't know whether the boy was referring to May or Phoenix.

'She says can someone move the truck,' Carlos would say.

'Who's asking, May or Phoenix?' Harley would ask, straight faced.

'No. Not Phoenix,' Carlos would clarify and then say nothing more.

Danny cuffed his brother lightly on the shoulder and thrust his hand out.

'Glad to meet you,' he said and winked at her. Carlos flushed and May smiled.

'Hello, Danny. It's nice to meet you too.'

He gave her such a saucy look she actually blushed and made a note that he was going to need close supervision if she did decide to give him a trial at Molly's.

Harley gave him a look. 'Knock it off, Danny, that ain't going to work on her, she's far too smart and English on top of it; if a Brit gets even a whiff of shmooze you've lost.'

Danny was unruffled and grinned at May, who laughed and asked if there was anywhere nearby to go.

'There's a diner a mile or so that way,' Danny said, indicating further up the road.

They piled into the truck and spent the next hour over coffee and sodas. The brothers ate plates loaded with sausage and hash browns, pancakes and syrup and May noticed how hungrily Danny ate and with what speed. He barely looked up until he was about a third of the way through and he caught May watching him.

'What?'

'I'm sorry,' she said, genuinely so. 'I'm fascinated by people eating. Everyone's different and I always think it tells you something about them.' She burst out laughing at Danny's frozen expression. 'It's probably a load of old bollocks anyway,' she said.

Danny laughed too. 'You know, he told me you say weird things. I guess he's right.'

Carlos looked horrified and kicked Danny hard under the table.

'You're a fucking liar, Dan,' he said and then looked even more embarrassed and muttered sorry to May.

'Just you wait until you see me and my sister together,' she said, but Carlos couldn't look her in the eyes and appeared almost tearful.

'What?' Danny said, grinning at him. 'Okay, so maybe you didn't exactly say that. I'm sorry, but he did say you say things kind of…'

Harley cut him off sharply. 'Quit!'

May saw him lock eyes with Danny and there was a moment of tension before Danny laughed and shovelled a forkful of hash browns into his mouth.

'So, you got a job for me?'

Carlos groaned.

'What?' Danny glanced back and forth between his brother and May then looked at Harley who was sort of smiling and shaking his head.

'He sure is a handful,' he said later to May after they'd dropped Carlos off at the home. 'You going to give him a try?'

'I'd really like to. But I have to think carefully about what job he could do and how to manage him. He seems quite impulsive and all that jokey, larky shit is hiding a lot of something else. It's amazing how different they are, isn't it?'

'Is it?' Harley mused. 'My brother Steff was kind a like that. Absolute fucking firecracker. Made my mom crazy.'

May slid a glance at Harley's profile but he was giving nothing away, his face calm and neutral as he kept his eyes on the road.

'I'll need to talk it through with Turtle before I can do anything. I don't think it's quite as straightforward as I was hoping. If it was Carlos…'

'Yeah, I hear you baby, you'd have no compunctions about standing up for him. Danny, he's a live wire. But he's a good kid at heart, he just needs the right breaks. May, I…' he broke off and overtook a trailer chuntering slowly along. 'I hate to keep things from you.'

'I know, but sometimes you just have to, right?' she thought he was referring to his previous visits to see Danny.

'Yeah, well… I want you to know he's a good kid, he knows right from wrong, just sometimes it's about survival, you know?'

'What do you mean?' she asked with growing discomfort.

'You remember the kids that jumped me?'

'Of course.'

'Danny was one a them. Sassello had him in his pocket since he first arrested him at your break-in.'

May felt the air go out of her. 'No!'

'Yup. But I don't want that to affect the way you treat him.'

'How can it not?' She was indignant.

'Because me an him are squared. And he's state's witness in the corruption case against Sassello along with Connie as it happens. I want us to be there for him, for Carlos's sake, you know?'

May looked at him, for a moment unable to speak. He had no idea, she thought, how much she loved his spirit.

37

May had spent the next few days making the final preparations for Lallie's visit. It had seemed so long in the planning and waiting and now here she was two days into the visit, clearing the breakfast things.

She stepped out of the kitchen door onto the granite flagstones of the terrace to shake out the blue and cream rag rug, with great flapping jerks, letting it fly above her against the soft washed blue of the sky. Crumbs and dust flew up and away over to the woods beyond the shady north-eastern edge of the garden, with its ancient ferns and delicate silver birches.

As she turned towards the kitchen, she saw Harley and both children emerge from around the side of the barn with Sam. She could hear their chattering, high, birdie, voices, Sam's clear, hard, abrupt speech asking lots of questions and Harley's low, reassuring murmur registering under all of theirs.

'Harley's been showing us about! What a place!' Sam called out, a broad grin on his fair, fine boned, face. Despite the short time since their arrival the bridge of his nose and his forehead were flushed reddish from the intense sunshine.

Tillie came galloping across the grass towards May, who threw open her arms and swept her up into a twirling hug, swinging the little girl's legs out like a fairground ride. She nibbled and burrowed her face into the warm, soft little neck, growling, making Tillie squeal with laughter and Max came running over.

'My turn… my turn… Eat *me*, now! Eat *me*!' He hurled himself at May's legs and wrapped himself round her thigh like a little monkey.

'Kids!' came Lallie's strong voice from an upstairs window. 'Stop mobbing your Aunt May, you'll wear out your welcome if you're not careful.'

May, breathless with joy and laughter sat on the grass with a thump and hugged both children to her.

'It's fine.' Then, shouting up over their heads, 'don't worry, Lal, it's fun! I'm fine. Come on,' she said, taking the hand that Harley held out to her and springing up. 'Matthew's making pancakes. Who's hungry?'

At breakfast, Harley suggested that they all go to an old watermill for a picnic.

'It hasn't been too wet nor dry this summer, so the river should be full enough and just fast enough to make it fun to slide down the rocks,' he told Sam.

'Won't that hurt your bottim?' asked Tillie doubtfully.

'Oh no, sugar. The water has been running over those rocks for hundreds of years. It's made them slick and smooth. And it's real shallow, only about so high.' He indicated with his hands a height of about a foot. 'And what you do, is you get yourself sitting down on those rocks and push yourself off and slide on down… it's about like this.' He added to Sam and Lallie, showing a gentle incline, with his forearm. 'After a little while, when you're having so much fun you wish it would never end, it turns a corner and slips into a swimming hole. And in you go!'

'Isn't it dangerous?' Lallie asked looking frowningly at Harley.

He tilted his head a little. 'Dangerous?'

'Yes. It sounds quite dangerous. They're only small, Harley.'

'Well, I can see that.' He smiled lazily at her. 'It's more what you'd call *fun*, but hey you're their Mama, so you'll make that call when you see it.'

'It used to be a working mill until quite recently,' he continued and turned to Matthew for clarification. 'Didn't y'all used to buy all y'all's flour from there Matthew?'

May caught his eye with a twitch of laughter. She was sure

he was deliberately exaggerating his and Matthew's shared vernacular.

'Oh sure, everybody round these parts did until about 1990 or so. Then they sold up. The Andersons. They'd run it for several generations.'

Matthew stopped and looked thoughtfully out towards the pasture. They were breakfasting on the porch and Matthew quietly leaned over towards Max, who was sitting on a pile of books on a chair opposite him. He laid his hand lightly on the little boy's dimpled one, raised a finger briefly to his lips and pointed to the bird feeder, hung on a branch they had collectively decided would be tricky for Thunder to leap onto. Matthew had helped Max to put out the seed that morning and he had been disappointed by the lack of activity. Now, a goldfinch was pecking at the seed and Maxie's face bloomed into a slow and contented smile.

'There, now. What did I tell you?' asked Matthew rhetorically and they shared a conspiratorial look.

Matthew declined the invitation to the watermill, saying he would get on with his garden and see them in the evening.

While they were getting a picnic together in the kitchen, Lallie questioned May about his presence.

'He's a very nice man, babe, but he seems to be here the whole time and at every meal and what about that poor little waif and stray? Carlos is it? Is that how you live?'

She gave an awkward half laugh.

May stopped chopping the hard-boiled eggs and turned to her sister. 'Lallie... What?'

'What, what?' Lallie looked a little flushed.

'"Is that how you live?"' May echoed in a close approximation of her sister's voice.

'Oh I don't mean it like that, but I can't quite work out who lives where or with whom.'

'Lallie, love, it's not a problem for me... and if you're worried if we'll get any sis time alone together, then don't, we will. Okay? Now grab some scissors and chop those chives for me, will you?'

She was surprised to find herself only mildly irritated by Lallie's line of questioning and it gave her a warm, lifting sensation. When did that happen? she thought. When did I stop minding quite so much what Lallie thinks?

Everyone was scurrying about finding swimsuits and sun hats and armbands. Lallie was shouting at Tillie and Max.

'You two are a disgrace. We've been here three days and you've managed to make the place look like a rubbish heap.' Her voice came in quick, light bursts while she moved about, punctuating her words with emphatically dropped piles of things, as she tried to impose order on the children's clothes and toys and floated out to the terrace, outside the kitchen, where the others were all having coffee before heading off.

'Your aunt May won't want us to come back if we just turn the place into chaos.'

May grimaced and looked appealingly at Sam. 'Oh, Sammy, don't let her say things like that! It's awful and it's not true.'

He gave her a look with a long-raised brow that made Harley laugh.

'What are you saying, buddy?'

'I pick my battles, mate.'

The two men laughed in a conspiratorial way.

May noticed how comfortable they already seemed with each other. They were in many ways alike, clearly sharing a dry sense of humour, both practical and unfussy. This had particularly struck May, when she had found Sam fixing the perimeter fence with Harley, first thing that morning.

She'd walked down to tell them breakfast was ready and they'd been working in quiet companionship. Sam was bracing himself and a long board, while Harley made holes for screws with a drill. The board had sprung away slapping

Sam on the leg and Harley had leapt up and away and they had both laughed like schoolboys, the sound echoing amongst the trees.

May thought back to those dark days when Harley had first had the accident and how Sam had, quietly and without fuss, sorted the practicalities out. She had never thanked him she thought, with a wave of remorse.

Finally, everyone was ready for the trip to the water mill. Sam and Harley went together in Harley's truck taking a giant inflated inner tube from a tractor wheel and the cooler. May followed in her car with Lallie and the kids. The heat was getting to them and they fretted and squabbled as Lallie strapped them in.

'Just as soon as we get moving it will cool down,' she said, smoothing Maxie's damp hair away from his forehead and handing them both a frozen bottle of water to clutch.

'Genius, Lal! I wish I had one of those,' May said enviously.

'You don't need one... you can delay your gratification.' But she took Tillie's bottle and rubbed it across the back of May's neck and shoulders, making her shriek with shock and delight.

She pulled up behind the truck alongside a woodland verge that led into dense broad leaf woodland and the men jumped down from the cab and began to unload. Lallie got out and stretched and Harley came over and leaned into the driver's window and gave May an enthusiastic kiss.

'Hey, beautiful,' he said, his eyes glowing.

He's happy, she thought, my family is here and he's happy. Oh joy!

He sloped off to help unload the supplies, Piper and The Warhorse scrapping around his legs.

Loaded with blankets and towels, picnic basket and cooler, May led them along a trodden path through the trees. Tillie and Max went ahead making their way carefully over the moss-covered rocks and springy forest floor. It was dark green and lush, solemnly quiet, but the dense heat followed them into the woods, trailing about them and May felt the sweat on her forehead at once.

'Listen!' said Lallie and they stopped. 'What can you hear, Maxie? Tillie, can you hear it?'

Tillie's face slowly bloomed and she said, 'Maxie! Water!'

A few steps further and there it was about ten metres across shore to shore, running through dappled shade and leaping light of glorious sunshine. Further downstream on the opposite bank, was the old mill with its huge wheel hugging the side of the small timber and granite house. She pointed it out to the children.

'It's a tree house!' exclaimed Tillie.

It really did have the look of a tree house with its porch on stilts over the water, sheltering the wheel.

They laid out their camp and May helped Lallie put sunscreen on the children's fair skin and blow up their armbands. Harley, wearing only a pair of jeans cut off at his knees, walked out to the middle of the shallow, swift moving stream and stood with the water breaking white and foaming around his legs. His fading scars were a purplish silver against the dark tan of his arms and the muscles in his torso tensed and sprang as he bent his knees a little, balancing on the slippery rocks. He raised his arms out to his sides, palms spread, and threw his head back, face to the sun, eyes closed.

'Hoo… whee!' he whooped.

May bubbled with laughter and he turned a flashing smile at her.

'The only way to decide if you think it's okay for your youngins, Lallie, is come see for yourself,' Harley called.

May picked her way carefully out to where Harley stood, accompanied by Lallie.

'Stay there with Daddy,' she called to the children. 'Sam, don't let them near the water yet.' It was quite slippery and the water felt stronger than it looked. Lallie reached out a hand and May caught it.

She could see far down a good stretch of sloping stream. The water was moving steadily over the smoothed surface of the granite. It undulated and rippled and there were sudden flurries of foaming white as the water hit a particularly shallow piece of rock bed. May could see where the riverbed dipped and got deeper and where it got shallower again. What was clear, was that it never got very deep, perhaps up to a seated adult's waist.

'Here,' said Harley, reaching out a hand towards Lallie. She moved hesitantly out to where he stood and he grabbed her hand.

Then Harley moved so quickly May almost missed it. He slipped a strong arm around Lallie's middle, scooping her up and off her feet, crouching then swiftly sitting down on the rock bed and pushing off in one smooth movement, Lallie seated between his bent knees, his arms around her belly like a seat belt.

'Hold tight!' he yelled.

May whooped, the children screeched, Lallie shouted, 'You *bastard*!' but almost at once her laughter echoed up the rocks and bounced off the water and they could all hear her whooping and laughing all the way down.

Sam, holding each of the children by the hands, picked his way out to where May stood and they watched as Harley and Lallie spun around and Harley yelled, 'Here we go!' as they were swept backwards, in to the mill pool, under and briefly out of sight.

Lallie surfaced, then Harley a little further away and she waved a hand and called out.

'It's amazing! Oh my God! You have to do this!'

'Phew!' Sam exhaled. 'I told him it might be risky—she could've gone either way. You never know with Lal.'

May gave Sam a long look. 'You knew he was going to do

that?'

'Might've done,' he said with a low chuckle.

There was a little spot further down where Harley hauled himself out on to the bank and reached out a hand to Lallie. They high-fived each other and May could hear their laughter echoing out and ringing amongst the trees. She felt pure, soaring happiness.

'Mama, you sweared.' said Tillie with great solemnity when Lallie made it back to the top.

'I'm sorry darling I did, didn't I? I was *very* surprised.'

But Tillie was no longer looking at her mother, but staring at Harley's torso.

'It wouldn't work, if there was a lot of rainwater coming down from the mountains though,' Harley was saying to Sam. 'Sometimes, it's real fast with the run off. I wouldn't try it then...' he trailed off and looked down at the little girl, his face softening.

'Tillie,' Lallie said sharply. 'Stop staring.'

'It's okay, sugar. You looking at my scars? They're pretty weird, huh?'

Tillie's little face was red and confused. She looked at her mother then back at Harley and nodded silently. She looked as though she might cry. Harley crouched on his haunches and said, 'Anybody tell you what they're for?'

Tillie shook her head.

'Did your mama tell you I was in a wreck?'

'A car accident, darling,' translated May.

Tillie nodded.

'Well these here are all the places that were hurt and are now strong again.'

'Will they stay forever?'

'Yeah, but not like this. They'll fade, get flatter. But they're pretty ugly, aren't they?'

Tillie nodded. 'Does it hurt?'

Harley shook his head and stood tall again. 'Nah...' he

said, looking out over the river. May put a light hand on his back and he draped his arm around her neck, pulling her against him. 'Not so much anymore.'

38

May and Lallie were counting plates and glasses as they set the table for supper on the porch.

'I'll give Stella a call and see if she can bring extras when they come.'

Sam was in the hammock, reading a collection of Mark Twain's writings he had found at a yard sale they passed on their way into town the day before. Matthew was in his studio and Harley was crouched beside Max at the edges of a raised bed, whose retaining walls were made from rough granite stones.

Their heads were leaning together and Harley was pointing something out to Maxie, his voice soft and low. Maxie still had his intensely blond infant colouring and beside Harley's dark hair, it was glowing like unripe corn silk in the bright sunshine.

Tillie rushed up and leapt on to Harley's back, throwing him off balance momentarily and he reached his arm around to steady her, bracing the other hand on the ground.

'Let me see! I want to see!'

'Well, hush and you might see,' he said. 'Look, that big ol grey spider has built her web right across here and—see if you can find her, darlin.'

The children fell silent and then Tillie pointed.

'What is she waiting for?'

'Lunch, Tillie,' said Max, 'isn't she, Harley? She's waiting for her lunch.'

Lallie, came back out from the kitchen with a couple of plastic jugs and planted the cutlery in them. 'You've got so many lovely things at home, May, I bet you miss it at times like this.'

'Not really.' May shrugged. 'It's just stuff.'

'But you're living like a student here, May, and you've

always had such beautiful things around you.'

'The only thing I miss is Sarah's textiles, everything else… well, apart from you of course… but everything else I don't even think about.'

'Hmm, but you're going to have to, aren't you? The flat needs dealing with and you're going to have to make a decision at some point about where you're going to live. You can't keep hiding from the world in this lovely limbo land.'

'I *live* here, Lallie,' she said, keeping her voice as gentle as she could. 'But the flat yes, I need to think about that.' May marched into the house to collect a pile of napkins. 'I'm thinking of selling,' she called over her shoulder.

She didn't know whether her sister had registered this and she became distracted by Tillie's voice floating up from the terrace.

'Are you Aunt May's husband?'

Harley laughed out loud. 'Something like that,' he said. 'Scoot on over buddy, I need to lift the rock so we can fix the wall. You see how it's leaning over there?'

'Then why don't you live in the same house as her?'

'Good question, sugar, I sometimes ask myself the same question. Now see here? We need to be taking it down before we can build it back up again. I'm going to hand them to you and you place them in a row, smallest to largest. Watch your fingers when you drop em down.'

May listened to the scrape and dull thud of the granite and Maxie oofing and puffing as he carried the heavy rocks.

'May!' Lallie said sharply, and then made a brittle apologetic half laugh. 'Would you bloody listen you little dreamer? How long do you intend to stay out here? Another six months? A year? You are going to have to come over to London if it's going to be that long, to help me go through Sarah's stuff. I am not doing it by myself and I'm not going to wait until you decide to come home before we deal with it. The sooner we do it, the sooner we can sell it.'

396

'Lallie, I can't think about coming over again so soon,' May said vaguely. Then as though her mind had suddenly heard what her ears already had, she added tetchily, 'Do you ever listen to anything I say? I'm not on sabbatical. I live here.'

'Are those *poison?*' Tillie's voice again.

'Now, sweetheart, why do you think everything's going to be poison?'

'Tillie! Max! Stop harassing Harley while he's working and go and pick up some of the stuff you've strewn all over the place.' Lallie sighed deeply and then barked out, 'Now!'

Harley stood and walked over and leaned his arms up on the railings of the porch.

'Hey, y'all.' He gave May a quizzical look and in a low voice asked, 'Everything okay?'

May nodded and looked away unable to meet his eye; she wondered how much he'd heard. He turned to Lallie. 'I sure could use those youngins of yours just for a while.'

He clenched then flexed his hands with a slight grimace.

Lallie looked flustered. 'Oh. Yes. Of course. It's just I don't want them to get in your way.'

'They're not in my way. I'll tell them to "get" if they are.'

Matthew appeared at the fence between the two yards and called out.

'Son! Come on over here, I like to talk to you.'

Harley straightened and ran his fingers through his hair, making it stand on end.

'You look like a scarecrow!' giggled Tillie, 'doesn't he, Maxie? Maxie an me think you look like a scarecrow.'

Harley pulled a face at them both and said, 'Come on, let's see what the old man wants.'

He strode over the grass, the children at his heels like two unschooled puppies.

May watched with love and longing, brimming, aching inside. The children's voices trilled and squealed, Harley's hummed and murmured and then there was a shout of laughter from him as Tillie said something; it was a pure, perfect moment. She leaned against the porch railings and watched. I want that, she thought with a little shiver of fear. What if he doesn't?

'May,' Lallie's voice burst in, 'you are driving me to distraction. You've *got* to *think* about it. We've got to talk about it before I go back and I am not doing it all by myself. You will come and sort through all that stuff with me if I have to drag you back. Do you understand?'

Her raised voice must have carried because Harley darted a look back and watched while the two sisters stood in silence before turning his attention back to Matthew.

May knew Lallie was right, but she found it almost impossible to attempt to think about getting on a plane to London. Was it because of what had happened to Harley, she wondered, dismissing it as superstitious nonsense while acknowledging it.

'Lallie, I can't...'

'Don't keep telling me what you can't do!' snapped her sister. 'I don't want to hear it. You left me with everything, May, and you promised you wouldn't.' She looked fretful and overwhelmed. 'It's so hard without you.'

'I'm sorry,' she said, horribly guilty and then, even more so at her huge sense of relief as Stella and Pete arrived and they had to abort the conversation.

Hours later, the children had worn themselves out trying to catch fireflies, Stella was picking at the collapsed remains of a Pavlova. Tillie sat on the bottom step playing with Thunder, trying to be as quiet as possible so her mother did not call bedtime.

Max had climbed onto his mother's lap for one last strawberry and fallen asleep. He was straddling her lap, his belly against hers, slumped to one side, with his little head thrown back, eyes closed, cherry mouth slightly open. May saw the damp brow, his hair clinging to it and heard his slightly congested breathing. She reached out and touched his smooth, plump, cheek, glowing rosily in the candlelight and her dark eyes met Lallie's soft grey ones, smiling.

Harley was plucking a little tune in the dark, while Pete and Sam were arguing about the tyrannies or uses of government.

'Your big government bureaucracy, it's *suffocating*. Entrepreneurs—innovators, they need freedom to do their business how they see fit. We've got regulations up the wahzoo and everybody knows all *that* really does is choke the life out of business. Right?'

Sam smiling a little said, 'But without it you'd have no courts to protect your innovations.'

'So speaks the lawyer!' Pete shouted, laughing triumphantly.

Harley's fingers stumbled a little and he put his guitar aside, clenching then flexing his hand.

'Do y'all play any, Sam?'

'In my head, like Eric Clapton.'

The burst of laughter made little Maxie startle in his sleep. Lallie stroked his head, smoothing the hair from his brow, letting the light breeze catch it a little.

'Lallie plays,' said May softly. Her sister looked over at her with a half-smile.

'Not for a long time.' She sounded almost dreamy. Harley held the guitar towards her.

'Any time, Lallie,' he said, his voice gliding over the first syllable of her name and almost dropping the last.

'Sammy, learn to say my name like that!'

Lallie laughed and May was surprised by Harley's shy, averted look.

'I'm serious, Harley.' Perhaps Lallie too had noticed it. 'You make it sound gorgeous. I've never really liked my name. It always makes me think of someone clatteringly posh saying "lovely."'

They laughed and May said, 'I *never* knew that Lal...' it filled her with a kind of wonder that she could know someone so well and still not know a simple thing like that. 'I love the idea that you'll never get to the bottom of the well. That there's always going to be something new to learn about someone.'

May smiled quietly and thought of her younger self, hungrily gleaning all she could from Harley, thinking she'd have it all one day and then, finally, have him.

'Really, May?' Pete broke in deep scepticism in his voice, 'You can't really believe that. Most people are pretty boring. You get to the end of them pretty damn quick. Present company excepted of course! But not everyone runs deep.'

'That's just cause you have the attention span of a Junebug, honey and you're scared of *getting* deep, you're afraid you'll get stuck there,' Stella said affectionately.

Sam stood and took the sleeping Max from Lallie's arms, whispering a little as the little boy stirred. Harley offered the guitar again to Lallie, who took it and very quietly started trying it out, fingers tentative.

'Come on, Tilster,' Sam called softly, 'bedtime.'

'Can I take Thunder?'

'Oh darling, Thunder doesn't like to be taken anywhere,' said May, 'but if you leave your door open, he's very likely to come in.'

Tillie came over and leaned against May's knees, her little thumb straying close to her mouth, eyes on her mother. May put her arms around Tillie's firm, warm little body and nibbled her lips over her silky hair.

'Goodnight, angel. Come and get me in the morning if you're awake before me.'

They rubbed noses. Tillie went to Stella and hugged her, allowed herself to be hugged by Pete, and then stood uncertainly one foot on the other, head cocked, looking at Harley.

'Come on over here, honey,' he said softly.

She walked over and he put springy fingers on her head and scritch scratched at her scalp as though she were a little cat.

'Sweet dreams.'

'G'night Har—lee,' she said and scampered up the wooden steps, screen door slamming behind her.

Lallie started to play *The Sound of Silence*, the old Simon and Garfunkel song they had all known as kids. May remembered lying at night in the large bay windowed room they all shared at the seaside house of Stella's mother, during the long summer holidays.

They'd drift off to sleep listening to the grownups laughing and talking with the music on the record player floating along the hall, over them and into their dreams.

Stella sung softly and May picked up the harmony, surprising herself again that the words and melody could come back so instantly, so perfectly.

May was glad the earlier quarrel seemed forgotten, but she knew also that it would keep coming up until Lallie understood that May was home now. Here, in this place. And she didn't want to fight with Lallie. Their time together was so short.

'Do you remember the parents playing that album over and over again?' Stella asked.

'Summers. That was the only time we ever heard it. I don't think Dad and Sarah owned a copy…'

'Of course they did. Everyone did!'

'Well if they did they never played it.'

'Yeah, maybe.'

They lingered a while longer, finishing a last bottle of wine while Stella complained.

'I can't believe I now have to be permanent designated driver.'

'Oh, Stella, the awful part is it goes on longer than you

ever think it will too,' commiserated Lallie, 'and by the time you take up all your vices again you've the tolerance of a sixteen-year-old.'

'Which I suppose has the advantage of making you a very cheap date as *well* as being easy!' Sam laughed.

'Not all sixteen-year-olds have a low tolerance. Yes, Stella, I'm looking at you!' May quipped.

Lallie whooped with laughter with her sister as Stella winced and their voices competed to tell the story of Stella at a Christmas party, drinking until three in the morning with May and Lallie's step granny.

'And she got to the point where she couldn't focus while she was trying to pour Stella another glass of champagne...'

'And every time you moved your glass to go under the stream of champers she kept moving the bottle...'

'And she was basically pouring a bottle of Dom up your shirt sleeve!'

As they laughed, May glanced at Harley, shadowy in the candlelight, his eyes flicking between the speakers, a smile playing about his mouth, a look of wistfulness in his eyes.

'That was such a brilliant Christmas, do you remember how packed in we all were? And Sarah and Dad just slung mattresses all over the place...'

'Mine was virtually under the Christmas tree. Best Christmas prezzie Santa ever left!'

After they had waved them off and settled back on the porch, May longed for everyone else to go to bed so she could be alone with Harley. He was quietly slipping away, withdrawing into the darkness and May wanted to catch him before he got too far.

'You're so lucky with this set up, you guys,' Sam said. 'I could be really happy in a place like this.'

'No you couldn't,' Lallie dismissed. 'You'd be bored within a month.'

'Why do you say that?' Sam sounded annoyed. 'I'd love it.

Imagine coming back to this after a long slog at work.'

'Well it's not real, is it? Anyway I wouldn't like it. It would drive me mad.'

'There you go again, Lal,' said May quietly, 'if you don't like a thing, you can't see how anyone else could.'

Lallie laughed. 'Are you saying I've got no imagination?'

May shrugged. 'No, but it's just weird that you spend your working life empathising with people, but can be so...' she trailed off, not wanting to spoil the mood.

She looked at Harley, sitting at the end of the porch, tipping his chair against the railings. How young he looked in the moonlight, his hair all roughhoused, balancing on his chair.

He banged it down and Piper jumped and trotted to the steps to wait. He stroked May's head briefly as he passed wordlessly by and wandered off into the night with his dog.

'What's up with him?' Lallie asked.

'Nothing probably. He does that sometimes,' said May, but she felt a little uneasy as it had seemed more abrupt than Harley's more usual drifting off. 'He likes his own company after a while.'

'I think I heard Maxie calling. I'll say goodnight. Cheers, May, another great day.' Sam held out a hand to Lallie. 'Come on, darling, you look tired.'

She pulled a face at him. 'I'll be up in a bit.'

Sam shrugged, said goodnight again and left them.

'So does he sulk a lot?' Lallie asked in a humorous teasing tone, jerking her head in the direction Harley had gone.

'Not really,' May said, thinking 'sulk' was the wrong word. 'I think he's been doing really well, don't you?'

Lallie refilled her glass with the last of the wine, took a swig and pushed it towards May. 'In what way?'

'Oh I don't know...' May said, wary about saying the wrong thing. She wanted to convey that he was accommodating everyone being here so well, but didn't want

403

Lallie to think it was an issue.

'Well, he's used to having me to himself.'

'Oh! Sharing his toys!'

May leaned back in her chair and closed her eyes, stifling a sigh. 'Lallie, does Sam never mind if you're all taken up with the kids or work or… me?'

'Of course, he's a bloke isn't he? I just tell him to grow up.'

May couldn't think of a more grown-up man than Sam. 'That's a bit unfair. Wanting to be with you isn't childish, Lal.'

To May's surprise Lallie didn't snap back a pithy response. 'No,' she said quietly. 'It's not.'

The air, rich and sonorous with the song of the katydids and crickets, swelled and pulsed rhythmically and the frogs called from the woods behind the house.

'These night sounds are unbelievable, May.'

'I know. I love it,' May said quietly. 'Best lullaby in the world.'

She stood and padded softly over to the edge of the porch, leaning out over the railings. 'I wonder where Harley's got to.'

She whistled a low two-note call out into the darkness and Piper came eagerly towards her out of the shadows then turned back towards the lower paddock.

'I'm just…' She turned to her sister who made a light, dismissing wave of her hand.

'Of course,' she said, with a swift smile.

'I won't be a minute.'

The dew had settled and the grass clutched soft and damp against May's legs as she walked sure-footed down the sloping garden. Tall airy windflowers glowed luminescent in the moonlight as she passed a border edged with silver birch branches.

Harley was leaning against the fence in the shadows of the apple tree and May could see the dark shape of Phoenix shrouded quietly in the darkness. He turned before May said a word and reached a hand out, drawing her into his arms, wrapping and holding her tightly from behind, his whole body in close, hard contact with hers, as unyielding as the boundary fence he held her against. May sensed a fierce sort of melancholy about him that roiled up her insides with a mess of love and concern.

'Where you been at?' he whispered as though it hadn't been he who had wandered off alone.

'With Lallie. Sam's gone up to bed.' She paused and held his arms around her. 'Are you alright, my love?'

Harley sighed and nudged his face into her neck, his cheek rough against the tender skin and thrust a warm hand under her top, palm spread across her belly. The hoarse sound he made as he exhaled seemed frustrated, hungry and May tried to turn, wanting to see his face. She felt a reflexive tightening of his arms before he loosened them and muttered into her hair, 'Baby, stay with me tonight. Please.' This touched her somewhere deep. 'I want to wake up with you.'

May held him close. 'I left Lallie on the porch.'

Harley let out a hiss of exasperation. 'She's had you all day.'

'Well… they're not here for long,' May said.

'Come up for a while anyhow,' he said, turning towards his room. He slung his arm around her neck and began walking up the garden towards the stile.

'May, your sister…'

'My sister what?'

'She's kind of rude.'

May bristled. 'How do you mean?' she asked, knowing precisely what he meant.

'All that "this ain't real" shit.' His voice was quiet but his words came out hard-edged. 'And every time she thinks I'm out of earshot, working on you to quit here and go on back to London.'

'I know,' May sighed. 'It does seem rude but I don't think

she means it to. She's just quite... sure of herself when she's trying to make a point.'

He stopped and turned to face her. 'What point would that be exactly?'

'Harley, she and I have always been there for each other and suddenly I'm not there anymore. It must be so hard for her.'

'She has Sam and the kids,' he said tersely and began walking again.

They reached his room and Harley flung the doors and windows wide, leaving the screens in place against the bugs. He was pouring glasses of iced water for them when he muttered, 'She don't own you, baby.' It sounded almost childish the way he said it.

'Right. No one does,' she said, equally so.

He stripped his shirt off and slung it on the back of a chair, switched on the fan that stood beside his bed before throwing himself down on top of the sheet and reaching a hand out to her. Preoccupied as she was, May felt a quick kick of pleasure at his unselfconsciousness. She lay down with him.

The air around them was hot and close, and each time the fan turned with its slow clatter from her head towards her feet, May could feel the heat settle across her as though the room was exhaling.

Harley settled her into the crook of his arm, his hands and fingers stroking her skin, slowly tangling and twisting through her hair, while the night sang through the open windows, steady and rhythmic. They lay together and May listened to the frogs call with their comforting chorus, remembering how years ago when she and Harley had first met, she'd asked him what the sound was.

'Tree peepers,' he'd answered, head cocked a little as though puzzled by the question.

'Tree peepers!' She'd laughed, loving the image this

406

conjured and made a gesture with her hands, putting them up to her face and peering out from behind spread fingers.

Harley's face had softened into a mixture of humour and tenderness.

'They're little frogs.' He'd laughed, making her show him again.

'Oh my god that's so sweet!' she'd crowed.

Harley's mood had changed again and he seemed resigned, thoughtful.

'Y'all have so many stories.'

It took May a moment to catch where his thoughts were. 'Stories?'

'Y'all share so much. Stella, you, your sister. Old stuff. Memories. You none of you seem to remember them the same but still… seems kind of nice.'

'We're lucky to have had all those summers together, I suppose. Our parents were friends from forever.'

'I don't know a soul from before. They're all long gone. Never knew anyone for any time to speak of. Furthest back anyone goes is Matthew I guess. Rob. Ethan. And of course you.' He kissed her through her hair. 'Ain't no time really. Sometimes it's like…' he stopped and May held her breath. He gave a short, embarrassed sounding laugh. 'Sounds kind a stupid.'

'No,' said May, cupping his palm to her mouth and filling it with kisses. 'Tell me.'

He squinted down at her and smiled. 'Nah… it's okay.'

'Go on.'

'I don't really know what I'm trying to say.'

She heard his reluctance and let it be. Harley was quiet and May's thoughts turned towards Lallie on the porch waiting for her; Tillie waking in the morning and coming to find May as she'd done every morning since her arrival. Oh, it hardly matters, she thought, Lallie must have gone up by now and Tillie thought they should live together anyway. That made her smile.

'When I was listening to all your stories tonight, I got to thinking about that old philosopher's question,' Harley said, throwing her off balance again as she tried to catch his train of thought. 'About if a tree falls in the woods and no one's around to hear it?'

'What, you mean did it make a sound if no one was there?'

'Yeah.'

She hesitated, wondering if he would go on. Finally, he said, 'I told you I don't quite know what I'm trying to say. But sometimes, especially when y'all are freestyling, I think I got no one to say if I made a sound or not.'

How lonely it must be, to have to rely on only one's own memory to know that you had had a life, what would it be like to have no one to check in with? You could make things up or wipe them from the slate and there was no one to pull you up or reassure you or say you weren't alone.

'Anyhow,' Harley went on, 'I flunked Philosophy 101. I don't think that's quite the analogy. It's more like there ain't no one to confirm the footprints in the sand I left are mine. Told you it sounded stupid,' he finished with a huff of self-conscious laughter.

'I don't think it does.' May said thoughtfully. 'Now that you say it, it makes a lot of sense. We seem to spend so much of our time telling stories and there's definitely a comfort in it. It's reassuring. It's annoying too.'

Harley squinted down at her. 'How so?'

'Well, you can't escape. You become defined by what other people choose to retell.'

He laughed a proper laugh then and pulled her up onto his belly.

'You trying to say I'm lucky I got no family?'

'No. Just that it has its downside,' she said with dignity. 'Anyway, you've got me.'

The look he gave her warmed her through.

'Yeah… I do. I don't forget it.'

'Harley,' May said impulsively 'when they've all gone, will you come and live with me?'

'And leave Matthew?' His voice was quietly outraged and she believed it until she saw his teeth flashing a smile in the darkness.

39

Quivering, misty shafts of sunlight filtered through the trees as May woke early the next morning to the sound of the shower and Harley singing snatches of an Appalachian folk song. *'Cornbread and butterbeans and you across the table.'*

She smiled and stretched enjoying the ache of her muscles, running her hands slowly over the places where his had been. He came dripping back into the bedroom rubbing himself with a towel, flung it over the bedpost and threw himself down next to her.

'Yuh da duh and makin love as long as I am able,' he sang pulling May into a warm, damp embrace. His hair was wet and his dark lashes spiky with water.

'Hey, beautiful,' he said, shaking his head like a dog.

'Ugh!' May tried to avoid the water, but he held her fast, 'I was going to say how nice it was to wake up here!'

'Sorry!' He grinned at her.

'No you're not.'

'No.' He showed his teeth wolfishly. 'I'm not.'

He propped himself on an elbow, squinting through the open door into the sunny yard. 'Beautiful day for a party. You're a sweetheart to do this all for her, baby.'

'It's a very efficient way for her meet all our friends! Any way I've always loved an excuse to get everyone together, you know that. Did Carlos say whether he was coming or not?'

'Yuh huh... and he's bringing those girls he hangs out with!' He flashed May a naughty look that made her laugh.

Maryanne and Bebe. She was intrigued.

'I am dying to see what kind of friends he has. I hope they're nice. Good to him I mean,' she said with a protective rush.

'They're kind of cute. They mother him more than anything from what I can make out.'

May was about to ask where he got his information, but he rolled onto her and looking at her from under lowered lashes said, '*All* the girls like a Lost Boy, it seems.'

'Harley!'

'What?' he chuckled. 'You're crazy about that boy.'

'Whoa…' Lallie said later that morning, as she and May sat on the porch shucking corn. 'This is a lot of corn, how many people did you invite?'

Matthew had set up his rotating sprinkler in the garden and May could hear Tillie and Max counting, 'one… two… three, go!' Then shrieking and squealing with laughter. She cocked her head at her sister.

'Well, I don't know exactly. You know how it is, you start inviting people and then think of someone else and then there's everyone at work.'

'Oh honestly, May!' Lallie said incredulously. 'Why would you just invite everyone you know? That sounds insanely stressful.'

'Relax, Lal,' May said mildly. 'It doesn't bother me if I don't know exactly who's coming. It's part of the fun!'

Before either could say more, May was distracted by a car door slamming and high, excited voices calling out thanks. She got up and walked to the top of the porch steps, squinting into the bright sunshine to see who it was.

A tall, big boned girl wearing shorts, Birkenstocks and a loose sleeveless t-shirt was standing out in the hot sun. Her shoulder length hair, cut in choppy layers, was various shades of fuchsia and she was standing very close to a flaxen haired girl, all gleaming willowy-limbs and floaty bits of white muslin and scraps of denim. They hung back a little indecisively until May called out to them.

'Hi! Are you Carlos's friends?' She padded barefooted down the hot, dry wooden steps. 'I'm May.'

The fuchsia haired girl, who had looked quite severe,

smiled and it transformed her face into a radiant, openness that was all the more endearing because it was so unexpected. She held out a hand to May and said in a strong voice, 'Maryanne.'

The other girl put her hand out. 'Bebe. It's so cool of you guys to let us gate-crash!'

'Not at all. Carlos should have his pals here for the party!' May turned to her sister and called out, 'I'll just take them down to find Carlos. You want to come... or?'

'No-no.' Lallie said airily. 'I'll get on with those corn cobs. See you in a minute.'

'I won't be long, Lal.'

May led the way, making small talk, asking the girls about school and how they knew Carlos.

'We all just graduated high school together.' Bebe said all her words in one long breath that left May feeling like she had to catch up.

'Oh! Did you have a prom or something like that?'

Bebe giggled, 'Maryanne and Carlos didn't have dates so they went together.'

May looked quickly at Maryanne who had gone the same shade as her hair and was studying the ground in front of her as she walked.

'Now... where could they be...' she murmured, shading her eyes against the slanting sun and smiling quietly to herself. 'Ah,' she breathed as she glimpsed a coppery gleam and swish of a tail in the dappled shade of a huge Black Walnut tree that stood at the furthest corner of Matthew's property.

May whistled and Harley emerged from the other side of Phoenix's sleek high quarters. She could see the flash of his teeth as he smiled then he rubbed his palm across his mouth a few times. Harley said something in Spanish to Carlos who was obscured by the horse and walked round the back of the mare, extending his hand towards the girls.

'Hey! Maryanne? Bebe? Harley.'

The girls smiled and chorused hi, Maryanne's smile lighting up her face and transforming her serious expression once again.

Bebe ran her fingers through her long hair and pulled her shoulders back a little, letting out a light, giggling laugh. Harley slapped Phoenix on her quarters. 'Get on.' She grudgingly moved a few steps before dropping her head almost at once to start grazing again.

'Carlos,' called Harley, 'throw that maple branch over the fence. She probably won't touch it but its poison to her.'

The boy tossed the branch and then came over to May and the girls.

'Hey,' he said quietly, smiling and showing his small crowded teeth. He allowed himself to be lightly hugged by first Maryanne then Bebe, one of his arms coming hesitantly up around each of their waists briefly, before dropping down by his side.

Bebe gave a little shimmy of her hips and let out an excited exclamation, 'It's beautiful out here!' she said, 'no wonder you don't want to leave, Carlos.'

The boy looked furtive but Bebe's words gave May's heart a glad lift. He stood awkwardly a moment and then she said, 'Show the girls around. We'll give you a shout to come and help later. We're going to be foil-wrapping many numbers of corncobs to put in the barbecue pit later.'

The girls laughed and Carlos's shoulders relaxed. He stood a little straighter and the three walked off together, Carlos leading Phoenix, down towards the paddock gate. Bebe's high, excitable voice sounding out across the garden as May and Harley turned back up towards his room and the house. He draped a hot, sticky arm around May's neck.

'Mmm... I love when you smell of horse,' she said.

Harley laughed and pulled her against him, 'That's not horse, that's me.'

'I know the difference between you and horse,' she said emphatically.

'Well, I'm about to go and wash it off. You want to come and take a shower with me, baby?'

She looked at her wrist, saw her watch wasn't on it and caught Harley laughing at her.

'I don't know why you look, it's never there. What time did you tell folks to get here?'

'Any time from four.'

Harley cocked his head at the sun and squinted.

'Come on,' he said, sliding her a sly look. 'We got time.'

May loved that wolfish look of his; it made her limbs feel molten, as though she'd just taken a large swallow of Jack Daniels. Then she thought of Lallie waiting for her on the porch. He caught her look and she saw his eyes narrow briefly.

'What?'

'I better get back to Lallie, I left her shucking corn on the porch.'

'Nah uh...' Harley shook his head slowly and right there in the middle of the garden with the sun searing onto them, the squeals of the children laughing and everyone just pottering about, he kissed her and kissed her and kissed her. The smell of him was intoxicating and May felt heady with the heat and his mouth, hot and open on hers as he snaked his arms around her, his skin sticking to hers as he walked her backwards through the garden to his room.

May joined Lallie on the porch nearly an hour later.

'I wouldn't mind but you keep saying you won't be long then you just bloody well disappear,' she said as May apologised again. 'I feel like time is slipping away faster and faster and we're not making the most of it.'

'Oh, but we are, Lallie!' May cried in protest. 'We've had some wonderful time together. Haven't we?'

Harley came whistling up from the paddock with Carlos and the girls and gave them a wink as he headed round towards the barn.

'God he's smug!' Lallie burst out, startling May. 'He's just rubbing it in. I'm going to have a shower.' She stalked off leaving May guilty and cross. It wasn't until the sun was setting across the faded hayfields, through wispy stretches of flushed and glowing clouds, that she was able to fully relax again.

Clusters of people gathered, huddled and spilled about the place. The constant buzz of voices rose and fell, swelling louder and peaking to be punctuated by the sound of a punch line delivered, shouts of laughter, low exclamations of disbelief or delight. Music poured out from the porch over the garden, loud enough to drown out the sounds of the crickets.

Turtle suddenly called out 'Chow time!' to a great chorus of hungry cheers and he began expertly to pull the pork and pile it onto platters that Cathy and May held out for him and again he hollered, 'Come and get it while it's hot!'

May sat on the porch steps with Harley and a handful of their friends. She sat back contentedly, breathing in the smell of hickory wood smoke and crackling, mingled with the faint smell of marijuana, citronella candles and the night-scented stocks that ran down the fence from Matthew's back porch.

'Who's smoking weed?' asked Stella wistfully.

'Don't know, don't care, just as long as it's not those underage kids on my front lawn.' May replied breezily, then she leaned forward and looked a little more closely at them. 'Do you think he knows?' she asked curiously.

'Who? Knows what?' Harley asked nudging himself up from his comfortable looking slouch against the railings and leaning in towards May. She nodded towards Carlos and the girls.

Ethan made a low rumbling in his throat. 'Did you ever at

that age? I'm still in the dark half the time now!' He laughed shooting a stealthy look over in Amy's direction.

'What are we talking about?' Harley asked.

'Does Carlos know that Maryanne's so into him?'

Carlos sat cross-legged on the grass, skinny back curved over a deck of cards he was dealing with astonishing speed and dexterity. Behind him sat Bebe in her frayed denim hot pants, slim, tanned legs gleaming in the firelight, bare feet planted either side of his narrow hips. She was plaiting coloured threads into Carlos's hair, her delicately boned wrists with their assemblage of beads and woven coloured string twisting and moving in the firelight. Her fingers moved deftly down the sleek lengths as fast as she talked over his head at Maryanne.

Every now and then, Bebe had to stop and disentangle a skein of her shining, chamomile yellow hair from the silver spiral that grasped her upper arm, squealing her complaints until Carlos turned and said something that made her remove it from her arm and try to put it on him. He appeared to flinch as she touched him, then smiled briefly.

May watched as Maryanne, whose eyes were riveted on Carlos, dipped her head swiftly when he glanced up at her from his cards.

'No he doesn't know. For sure,' Harley said emphatically.

May and Amy both turned to look at him and he chuckled.

'How do you know?' May asked with suspicion.

'Because if he knew, they'd be A Thing already.'

May was incredulous.

'Harley...' she said dangerously.

He began to laugh even more. 'What?'

'How do you know?'

He winked at her. 'You're not the only one around here he talks to you know.'

They all laughed and Stella said, 'He talks? I wouldn't be

able to pick his voice out in a line up!'

'Tell me! How do you know?' May poked at Harley and he put his arms around her straightjacket style, nuzzling her neck and whispering below the laughing, rollicking voices.

'Tell me you love me and I'll spill…'

May kissed him below his ear and whispered what he wanted to hear.

'I know,' he said laughing and May felt a delicious sense of satisfaction; she thought in that moment that nothing could give her more pleasure than his certainty.

'So. What has Carlos said about Maryanne?'

'I can't tell you that! Let's just say that he *only* talks about Maryanne. Barely mentions Bebe.'

'Well that might be because he wants Bebe so bad he can't stand to talk about her,' suggested Amy.

'Nah…'

'Or that he thinks she wouldn't be interested in him,' said Ethan.

May looked over at the three kids again.

'Poor Maryanne. She thinks Bebe's got it all.'

'Bebe thinks Bebe's got it all,' said Ethan laconically. 'Who needs another beer?'

'So hang on guys.' Amy said putting hers thumbs up and smiling at Ethan. 'Are you saying that if one of em just said something…'

'It's never that simple, is it?' May felt Harley's hands briefly tighten on her arms and his lips touching her temple.

Amy shifted about and leaned back on her elbows; her legs thrust out in front of her.

'Have you ever been in love with someone and they didn't know it?' she asked.

'Hasn't everyone?' May answered. 'At some point? More interesting would be have you ever been in love with someone and you *yourself* didn't know it?'

'Never been in love,' Rob put in with pride, making a

comical prang of chords on the guitar resting on his knees.

'I rest my case,' May said in a stage whisper and everyone laughed including Rob. 'I bet you have,' she added briskly. 'You just won't admit it!'

'Nope! I'm too smart,' he replied.

'Too sad!' said Stella.

'You should give it a go, Rob, you might just like it.'

'No way, sweetheart, I'm doing great without all that mess. You hook up, you have a good time, party's over. Move on. Perfect recipe. Right buddy?' He nudged Harley whose face creased into a wry look.

'Don't look at me, man,' he said tightening his arms around May. 'I'm enjoying the mess.'

They all laughed and May felt happier than she could remember.

'Look at them two young'uns.'

Harley jerked his chin towards the perimeter fence and May softened inside as she saw Tillie and Max leaping and running in short bursting movements, darting about, suddenly changing direction and shouting excited directions and exclamations at each other.

'This holiday's the first time they've ever seen fireflies,' May said. 'Wouldn't it be wonderful to see a firefly for the first time again?'

'Oh, baby, you know what? I bet you do. I bet when you see them come out again first of the year it's like the first time for you all over again!'

'You make her sound like she's got the memory of a goldfish!' Stella said. Harley gave her the finger with a grin.

'You *know* what I mean, Stella "meh" Freeman,' he said, adding tauntingly, 'What's it like, honey, to have lost your childlike wonder?'

'Boom!' laughed Pete. 'Shots fired!'

'I won't be lectured by The Cynic of the Century!' Stella grumbled good-naturedly.

'Not me, girl, I'm born again, I believe!'

May smiled up at Harley, then peered back through the flame lit darkness.

'I can't see Lallie anywhere. I'd better go and make sure she's alright.'

'Sure,' he said, releasing his hold and smiling back at her, his eyes full of warmth and reflected light.

She found Lallie talking shop with Frannie and her sister drew her closer as she talked and put her arm around her.

'Hey-hey!' Frannie greeted her enthusiastically then turning back to Lallie she asked, 'Do you have any idea how wonderful your sister is?'

'Of course,' said Lallie defensively, but she smiled.

Frannie, swigging from her bottle went on. 'She's been a godsend for that boy and I thought it would be all Harley! Excuse me, but I did,' she said with a throaty chuckle in May's direction. 'See I didn't really know her, but they've formed quite the bond! He's very attached to her and that's what he needs you know.'

May smiled at Fran. 'He's a lovely boy Frannie. We both feel we're the lucky ones.'

'See.' Frannie leaned in closer to Lallie and was really warming to her subject. She seemed to be stimulated by the fact that she might be speaking to someone who understood what she was talking about; that and by her beer, thought May with a little smile.

'We're all about trying to find ways for our looked-after kids to form a healthy, permanent network of relationships.'

Lallie nodded and gave May a strange look that she couldn't quite catch in the dim light.

'Sure,' she said to Fran, 'but that's precisely what I feel uneasy about. And please don't take this the wrong way, but...' she hesitated. 'Don't you think it was a little rash to connect the boy with someone who doesn't live here permanently. I mean, May's lease will be up on this place next spring and then no doubt she'll come home. Where does that leave that young man?'

May pulled away from Lallie sharply. *'Lallie!'*

'What? That's always your trouble May, you don't think ahead. You're so impulsive and that can sometimes do more harm than good in circumstances like these. Fran, you know what I mean don't you?'

Frannie had gone rather quiet. 'I think you might just be mistaken,' she said. 'Don't you talk to your sister?'

'We talk, she just doesn't listen,' May muttered.

There was a horrible silence then May blurted out unthinkingly, 'Anyway I do think ahead. Harley's moving in. When the lease comes up for renewal, we'll be signing it together. So you see there's no danger of Carlos being left out on a limb.'

She heard Lallie's suck of breath. 'You're kidding me?' She sounded hollow.

'No.'

There was no time to say more as Max came running over through the darkness crying, followed by Tillie, both children calling out over each other. 'Mama! Tillie won't let me...'

'I didn't, Mama, but you said no more brownies and Maxie was having more under the table.'

Frannie laughed, 'I can't think of a better place to eat a brownie than under the table little guy! Only safe place, right?'

Lallie crouched to sort out the children and Frannie and May stood awkwardly before moving off together towards the porch. May's heart was pounding. Shit, shit, shit. She felt terrible for Lallie and anxious to reassure Fran.

'Frannie, I'm sorry...' she began, but her friend broke in.

'May! Not a problem. Seems your sister doesn't like that you've relocated. I get it.'

'It's more of a problem than I realised actually, but

whatever. That's for tomorrow.' May felt less confident than she sounded, but willed herself on. 'Tonight let's enjoy the party. Ethan!' she called. 'Where's your harmonica?'

May saw his smile in the flicker of candlelight and he patted the belt loop of his jeans.

'Well what's it doing in your trousers, get it out!' she said with a laugh.

'If that's how she talks to you buddy, you're a lucky man,' Ethan said with a chuckle to Harley. 'It's been so long since someone told me to get it out, I wouldn't know where to start.'

'I find that *very* hard to believe,' Amy said and they all laughed.

Ethan jerked himself up from leaning against the railings and thrust his hand out towards Amy who took it with a broad smile.

'In that case let me introduce myself.'

There were general sounds of hooted encouragement and laughter. He lounged back against the railings but May met Amy's sparkling eyes and grinned.

The Doobie Brothers' *Long Train Running* began belting out from the speakers and Rob instantly picked up the rhythm on his guitar.

'You're up man!' he called above the music to Ethan who obligingly put his harmonica to his mouth. Stella sang in her joyful, unselfconscious way, slinging an arm around May and holding her beer bottle up to their mouths as a mic. May laughed so much she could barely sing.

Later, May was sitting on her favoured porch step with the last stragglers, Harley one step above, holding her snugly from behind. The warm faint smell of his skin came to her through his shirt and her thoughts flashed swift and vivid to earlier that day in the shower; water sluicing down his hot, slick skin as he braced with one hand against the shower wall, the other on her shoulder. She smiled to herself, looking forward to everyone being gone, being alone with Harley again.

She sighed and Harley slipped a hand under her hair, moving it aside to drop a tender kiss on her neck. Life is sweet, she thought, and then caught sight of Lallie making her way across the garden carrying Maxie, Tillie trailing alongside looking sleepy. May felt guilty and wondered whether the weave of her sister's walk was from the weight of her child or one drink too many. If only Lallie could understand, could want all this for her.

'I'm going to put these two to bed. Pour me another one of those,' she said, indicating the plastic jug half full of Pimm's at Frannie's elbow. 'I'll be down in a mo.'

She was back quickly and sat opposite May on the same long step, leaning back against the stair rails and putting one of her bare feet in her sister's lap. May picked it up absently and rubbed it.

'You live in town?' Ethan asked Amy, standing and shoving his hands in his pockets. 'I'll give you a ride home as long as you don't mind, we drop Bebe and Maryanne off first. I told their moms I'd make sure they were home safe.'

They mooched off into the darkness and May chuckled.

'What're you laughing at?' Stella asked.

'Ethan,' said May feeling a swell of affection for him. 'I think he's trying it on with my friend Amy. Hope it works.'

'Isn't he a bit old for her?'

'What does that even mean?' May replied. 'Maybe. Not really. He's a good bloke. Isn't that what matters?'

'Does anyone even know how old Ethan is?'

Everyone's heads turned to Harley, who laughed.

'I ain't tellin. Older'n me, younger'n he looks, good enough for Amy!'

More laughter. May leaned back against Harley and was about to ask her sister if she'd enjoyed the party when

Frannie said, 'Harley's been telling us about an idea he has for the kids on my programme. I gotta say it sounds pretty interesting.'

'What's this?' Lallie asked.

'Oh, just an idea I have about helping them create audio visual… ah… scrapbooks, I guess you might say.'

'Oh yes?' Her tone held something of a challenge.

May felt Harley's fingers tap a repetitive piano scale on one of her shoulders. His knees tightened around her and she shifted uncomfortably.

'Well I'm sure May's told you something about my somewhat undocumented past,' he said ironically.

The atmosphere hovered then stilled about them. May was unsettled by this cooling in the air, the hostile tone that emerged from the shadows in their voices.

'Yes. A bit,' Lallie replied.

'Well, I been thinking a lot about how to kind of mitigate some of that not knowing, or not remembering. You have to document things really and families do that with their drawers full of photos and get-togethers and what have you. I like the idea of seeing if anyone wants to put something together with me. Carlos and I started on something of his…' He broke off and spoke directly to May. 'That's what you saw us doing on the laptop, remember? He wanted to wait and finish and show it to you.'

May remembered the way Carlos had laughed in that startlingly unguarded way before he'd realised she was standing there and the guilty prang of envy she'd felt at how much more relaxed he was with Harley.

'I think that's an incredible idea,' she said.

'We've been back to his old street, found old haunts, tried to see what he remembered. We talked to his brother, recorded them talking. Something like when y'all are all together. Carlos found old neighbours who knew the family before things started to go wrong and they talked real nice about his mom and dad. That was good for him.'

'Physician... heal thyself,' Lallie said dryly.

Harley straightened sharply, dropping his hands from May's shoulders. May tensed. Shit she is drunk, she thought.

'*Lallie!*' Sam said, low and embarrassed.

'You saying that's what I'm trying to do, or what I should do?' Harley asked testily. 'Quit with the riddles, Lallie. I kinda like you better when you're out and out rude.'

Frannie shifted uncomfortably and Jesse stood and went to fondle Piper who at the sound of Harley's raised voice, had come clacking enquiringly across the porch from her place in the corner.

'Sorry,' Lallie said, sounding hurt. 'I didn't know you found me rude.'

Harley stood and said irritably, 'Forget it.'

Before anyone could say anything else, there was a shout from the drive and Ethan's voice came out of the darkness.

'Hey, buddy, you got any jumper cables? My truck's stalled a little way down the road.'

Fran and Jesse started making leaving noises and Harley gave May a frustrated, vaguely apologetic look before going off to help his friend.

May felt twitchy and tense, her recent contentment already in another time zone and all at once she and Lallie were alone, standing at the foot of the porch steps.

The music had stopped and high, swift clouds kept sneaking across the moon then slipping away, obscuring then revealing the dips and hollows of the garden.

'May...' Lallie began and stopped. Standing there in the scudding moonlight, she looked small and more vulnerable than May could remember.

'Lallie, I'm sorry I told you about Harley moving in like that,' May tried to pre-empt.

'Why is it you who has to give everything up!' Lallie burst out. 'Why can't he come to London? It's not as though he has any family or ties to this place.'

Oh, where to start, thought May. Frustration flashed through May. 'Lallie. Once again, you're forgetting that when I *chose* to live here, it was nothing to do with him. Nothing. And as for his having no family… Christ that's low!'

'Why low? He doesn't. I'm not saying it's his fault. Obviously it's a bloody tragedy, but you do and that's not your fault either. I know you really care for him and I can totally see why… he's got some lovely qualities and incredible charisma. But May…'

'Incredible charisma?' May laughed, hollow. 'God Lallie, you make it sound like I'm some kind of swoony teenager!'

Lallie didn't stop. 'I know you. You need stability and commitment and I know you want a family…'

'What makes you think I couldn't have all that with Harley?' May asked and was shocked at how frightened she felt as she said it. She felt perilously close to tears. Was it Lallie's doubt or her own that she'd managed to bury deep inside?

'May-May…' Lallie said in a gentler voice. 'Has he ever given you any reason to think that you might? He clearly *needs* you… you can see it in how possessive he is… but you should never mistake that for love or commitment.'

May felt so rigid with denial, she trembled. He does love me. He does. 'Lallie, you don't know… you don't know what it's like between us. You want me to be happy? With him I'm happy! Here, I'm happy.'

'Yes! But it's the future I'm worried about! I can't see how a man who never had a mother's love and whose father abandoned him can give you what you need. It would always be you giving and giving.'

'Lallie! What the hell has happened to you? You of all people whose life's work is possible because you have hope and belief that people don't have to be trapped and defined by their past. What's happened to you?'

425

May wasn't sure if she was more upset by this revelation about the sister she thought she knew, or the fact that her old insecurities about Harley could be re-ignited so easily. Then all at once she felt her scalp prickling as a frozen look appeared on Lallie's face.

May looked over her shoulder in the direction of her sister's stare and her breath came like a choked hiss as she saw Harley standing in the yard transfixed.

He stood a moment longer staring then started forwards and, seeming to ignore May, he strode past her until he was so close to Lallie that she took an unsteady step backwards. The energy coming from him was frightening; he was incandescently angry.

'*You. Don't. Know.*' He wrenched out the words in a voice May had never heard. 'You don't know.'

Lallie started to apologise but Harley cut across her.

'Lallie,' he said, breathing hard. 'You have got to stop this. Your sister and me, we got a life here together…' Again, Lallie tried to speak but he raised his voice. 'No! You can't keep messing with that. She loves me! Your sister loves me! And that's what matters here, what May and me want. Not what you want. You *got* all you need. *Leave us be.*'

Lallie tossed her head up and asked him with some defiance, 'What about your feelings for May? You say she loves you, but what about you?'

'It's none of your freakin business what I feel for her,' Harley burst in angrily. 'That's private between her and me! I don't got to declare myself to make *you* feel comfortable. I don't need your *blessing* Lallie to have a relationship with your sister, but lord it just about breaks my heart that she does.'

Lallie looked shocked, then as though mustering one last effort she said angrily, 'Of course it's my business, she's *my* sister! *You* really think you know her and what she wants? Really? I've been through more with her than you'll ever know. There are things about May that you don't know and you could never understand. You don't know her at all!'

'Well sure enough, sweetheart,' Harley laughed bitterly. 'You've known her longer'n me and you spent all that time *telling* her what she wants and what she should do and not listening to any of what she's been busy hollerin at you!'

May let out a cry of fury. '*I'm here!*' She flung her arms out. 'I'm right here. I can speak for myself! What is this a fucking custody battle? *Stop!*'

May was furious and even more so when she burst into angry tears.

Harley turned slowly then, as though he really had forgotten that she was there and Lallie's face clouded with shame like ink spreading slowly in water.

May felt what it was to burn with anger. Her face was stinging with heat and her heart pumped in her chest so hard she found it hard to take a really deep breath.

'I have to make my own life. I have to.'

Harley moved swiftly towards May but she wanted no one. As she turned and strode away from them, she heard Harley's voice filled with disgust. 'Shame on the both of us, Lallie.'

40

May never fell into deep, sound sleep that night and lay, unable to cool off, on top of the sheet, moving from her belly to her side then flopping with exasperation onto her back. Her thoughts circled, by turn angry then defensive. She grew hotter and more restless hefting and twisting, hopelessly trying to find a cool spot on her frustrating sheets.

At breakfast the next morning, there was a subdued air when Harley appeared, poking his head around the door he looked absolutely exhausted, his mouth tight at the edges his eyes bruised with fatigue.

Sam was his usual relaxed self, so May assumed Lallie hadn't told him about what had happened. Her sister fussed around the children while Sam sat back with the paper Matthew had just brought in.

'Hello,' May said coolly from across the kitchen.

Harley managed a brief smile, but was preoccupied, hovering indecisively in the doorway.

'Morning,' he murmured.

'How's it going?' Sam grinned up at Harley, then with a smirk said 'how's your head? I think everyone had a bit too much last night and this hot weather's no good with a hangover, mate!'

Harley smiled slowly rubbing the back of his neck a couple of times.

'Uh...' He began, but thought better of it and accepted a cup of black coffee from May. He was staring at Lallie. After a moment she noticed and gave him a tight, enquiring smile. He tried again. 'I'm thinking maybe ya'll might like a last trip to the mill?'

Lallie's smile lost some of its tight edge.

'I think that's a lovely idea,' she said brightly. 'When could we go? We've hardly any time left and Stella and Pete are coming for The Last Supper tomorrow.'

Harley shrugged. 'Anytime. Might be nice to go late afternoon. Sunset picnic's always nice.'

Tillie and Max were beside themselves with excitement at the prospect of going back to the mill and the added promise of picnicking in the evening was almost too much to have to wait for.

'*But when?*' came Max's plaintive question for the seventy thousandth time, as Tillie put it. '*When* can we go?'

Now they were sitting at the water's edge on smooth granite boulders that still held all the wonderful warmth of that summer day and there was a soporific beauty in the golden evening air. May felt as though her limbs were moving slowly through warm water, but her thoughts were still troubled and she hated her unsettled feeling. Unresolved, she thought, everything felt precarious and unresolved.

Sam and Harley were talking quietly, laughing and sipping beer. May had had no time alone with Harley and she wanted to know how he was. He was holding something of himself back and she realised that although it was strikingly familiar to her, she hadn't experienced it from him in many weeks.

May had Max in her lap and Tillie was standing in front of her talking about the pebbles she'd gathered.

'Darling, move a fraction this way,' she said, indicating with her hand. 'Then you can be my sunshade.'

Tillie giggled and hopped on one foot.

'Well stand still you noogoo!' May said in mock exasperation. 'It's right in my eyes.'

She squinted exaggeratedly into the sharply angled setting rays and Tillie cackled delightedly, her bright, clear voice flying over the water and bouncing back.

Lallie was standing at the water's edge, talking over her shoulder at May.

'It's amazing how the water picks up those incredible colours. It's like it's actually coloured water. Ooh! Remember the coloured fountains in the square in Minorca?'

May mumbled a lazy affirmative and stroked Maxie's hair from his rosy face, planting a sudden kiss on his plump cheek.

'Oh you are so delicious!' she growled and he wriggled away with a sweet, belly laugh.

Looking up, May saw Harley was standing next to Lallie shoulder-to-shoulder, face turned towards the sunset. She couldn't hear what he was saying; he was talking in that low way he had, that meant only the person right next to him could hear what he was saying. Her heart sped up and she strained to hear but all she got was Lallie saying, 'okay.'

The two moved off along the edge of the water. Harley glanced back and raised a hand in May's direction, but the sun was now slanting so directly into her eyes she could only see his silhouette; there wasn't a chance of catching his expression. Lallie turned and called cheerily.

'You alright with them for a bit?'

'Sure!' May replied, wondering, nervous. Sam came and sat beside her.

'Go and see if you can collect enough stones to build a fort for the tree sprites or elves or whatever it is that lives in there,' he said to the children and they scampered off towards the edge of the river.

'You alright old lady?' he asked without looking at her.

May breathed deep. 'Mmm… hmm.'

'Pants on fire.' He squinted at her, then looked away. 'You were all at each other's throats under my bedroom window last night.'

May felt herself flush. 'Maybe… it was kind of brewing wasn't it?' May said, then turned impulsively towards Sam saying, 'What am I going to do?'

He looked genuinely surprised.

'Do? Nothing. You don't need to do anything. It'll be

alright in the end and she probably just needed to get it all off her chest. She's wrong about Harley anyway, anyone can see that. She'll come around.'

But it wasn't Lallie May was worrying about. What if Lallie wasn't wrong?

Sam put a light arm around her shoulders. 'But you've got to promise to visit regular like,' he said putting on a Just William schoolboy voice, 'otherwise I won't be able to cope with Lal—love of my life though she is.'

The sun had slipped over the edge of the world by the time May heard voices and then Lallie calling out, 'I'm starving!'

May stood and called the children who were busy building their castle of granite rocks at the edge of the river. 'Grub's up!'

Lallie came to help her unpack the cool box and Harley, looking tired but more relaxed than he'd been all day, put his arms around her and lifted her up off her feet walking a little way off with her, his face in her neck.

'You know I love you,' he said.

'What?' she said stupidly and pulled back.

Harley cocked his head and squinted at her, saying nothing.

He held her close again and May, crossing her arms around him and pushing her hands into his hair, pulled him against her until she could feel him everywhere and she filled her lungs with him relief filtering through her. I know, she thought. I do know.

'I love you,' he said again, 'But you know it. Thank god.'

The children were in bed. Sam and Harley had gone to see Matthew in his studio and May and Lallie sat on the porch, sipping cups of mint tea and talking. May wanted to know what had happened that afternoon by the river and Lallie seemed to want to give her the details.

Harley had apparently suggested a walk, saying he wanted to try and understand why Lallie was so hostile towards the relationship and that she needed to explain herself if any of them were ever going to get some peace.

'He was pretty angry at first, but I really do admire him for making it happen.' Lallie gave a short hard laugh. 'He said it again,' she said cryptically. 'About not needing my approval to have a relationship with you.' Lallie stopped and looked at May with a gentle, searching look. 'And that his heart breaks when he sees how much it matters to you. My approval.'

May couldn't say anything.

'Is that true May?'

May felt tears well up in her eyes and her throat closed. It had never occurred to her that Harley was that aware. Still so much I don't know. At last she said, 'I suppose it is.'

Lallie looked sad. 'Why?'

May didn't know how to answer. It just did. Or had.

'It doesn't matter as much as it used to,' she said. 'I mean I still care. I still want you to be pleased with me. But I don't think I'd make decisions based on it anymore.'

'Did you ever?' Lallie asked and then let out a small sigh. 'I was always afraid something would happen to you. Dad was always saying, "look after your sister, she's all you've got."' May sucked in a breath and took her sister's hand. Lallie squeezed it.

'Do you remember what it was like when he and Sarah first got together? I don't suppose you do... you were so young. But I do and they were so tight, so into each other there was no way in and it really was just you and me.'

So she had felt it too. All these years, she'd never known, not asked.

'Well...' said May with a grin. 'I *can* remember suddenly having amazing food, not just cheese on toast,' they both laughed a little. 'And that Dad started to smile and wasn't angry all the time anymore.'

'It's odd, isn't it, how you can live the same moments and experience them so differently?'

They were quiet for a long moment until May couldn't hold out any more.

'Lallie,' she pressed. 'What happened with you and Harley? What did you talk about?'

'We talked about the whole thing about him not having experienced any love as a child.' May's insides cringed. 'Oh god Lallie! No! You don't understand... poor Harley.'

She tried to imagine how much it must have hurt Harley to hear Lallie say that.

'Don't worry. He put me straight. He was absolutely fucking livid. Good for him, really.'

May managed a smile. 'What happened?'

'He held me by my shoulders and he said...' Suddenly Lallie looked as though she was going to cry and May's pulse skipped. Lallie took a long slow breath and went on. 'He said that every day his mother was alive, he was loved.'

May let out a long sigh. 'Oh Lallie.'

'I know.'

Lallie was almost as good a mimic as May and added, gently teasing, 'What he actually said was, 'mama'; every day my mama was alive was a day I was loved.'

May smiled a little and could hear how he would sound saying it. She wished she'd heard him say it herself. I want him all, she thought.

'But you know,' Lallie went on. 'I felt so ashamed because I remember when I was doing my training and I shared that my dad had died and some trainee kept going on about me having issues with men because I'd never had a father's love. And I finally got up the chutzpah to say, um hello actually I might have "man issues", lady, but it's not because of that, it's because I did have a father's love and I...' Lallie stumbled on her words so suddenly May reached out to her without conscious thought. 'I... lost it. It was taken away suddenly and with no warning and I was too young.'

When Sam and Harley finally came cautiously through the garden to join them, the sisters were holding hands, swaying gently on the swing seat. May had her head on Lallie's shoulder and her sister was stroking her hair gently.

'Weather's beginning to turn,' Harley said, as a much cooler breeze than they'd had all summer picked up and ran across the porch from one end to the other, causing the wind chimes to clang and the birdfeeder to swing crazily like a pendulum.

'Ready for bed, my love?' Sam asked and May shifted so Lallie could get up.

She hugged her sister tight and whispered in her ear, 'I love you.'

'Me too.'

41

May and Lallie were picking beans for their last supper together before the family left for the flight home to London the next day. They were arguing over what size to pick them.

'Well not *that* small, Lal,' said May, exasperated. 'And not those ones with lumps where seeds are forming. They'll do for next year's planting.'

'How do you know all this?' said Lallie, her small, fine boned hands fluttering amongst the leaves, trying to locate another bean.

'Matthew, mostly, but didn't you listen to *anything* Dad said?'

Lallie smiled. 'Well, he just used to drone on and on...' They both laughed. They had always called him The Quiet American; they'd had to winkle anything out of him.

Lallie slipped between two long rows of beans, the scarlet flowers brilliant against the lush green of the heart shaped leaves. She was like a small, lithe tabby cat.

'You can't hide in there!' But Lallie, shorter than May by four inches and much slighter of bone, could disappear as a child might amongst the foliage.

'Mama! Mama!' Tillie's bird high voice came trilling at them as she ran up the garden.

'Wait for meee Sissie...' Maxie's voice wailed. 'My legs are taaa yid!'

Tillie carried on running and calling. She saw May at the edges of the beans and stopped.

'Hello darling, what's so exciting?'

'Where's Mama?' Tillie asked, all news forgotten. May waved a hand vaguely into the jungle.

'In there somewhere. She's hiding because she's been very naughty.'

Tillie's eyes widened and May remembered too late, how

literal little people can be. Max came trotting up, face red and his normally serene and sweet expression mutinous and tearful. May crouched and stroked his damp hair from his forehead.

'Maxie,' she said in a low voice.

'Did Tillie tell?' He trembled at her.

'Maxie, I can't *find* Mama,' his sister said firmly and she looked suspiciously at May and then peered into the beans. All at once she screamed with laughter and her feet beat out a staccato dance.

'Maxie! Maxie! Mama's in there!'

'Don't come trampling in here, Til, I'll come to you,' came Lallie's voice and Max in his little white plimsolls and shorts, bent at the waist and peered into the green gloom until he saw her. His giggle rose up into the trees.

'Mama's hiding,' he crowed with delight.

Lallie crept out and Tillie reached her arms up to her.

'Were you naughty?'

Lallie picked her up.

'Ooph! You're getting too big for me. Come on, legs around or I'll drop you.'

Tillie obligingly wound her legs around her mother and tried to look her in the face.

'Were you naughty, Mama? Were you?'

'I'm never naughty Til, you know that,' she said, laughing and then pulling a serious face.

'Ma... *ma*! Aunt May?' She looked at May, holding her arm out in a gesture of appeal.

'Well darling, I was joking, of course she wasn't... but she can be, *very!*'

Tillie giggled and May said, 'Later on I'll tell you about the time she threw all my knickers out of the window... just tipped the whole drawer out!' and May mimed it very speedily and Tillie pealed with laughter while May and Lallie laughed so hard they cried.

'Well, ladies' came Matthew's warm voice, 'I see we're all going to get scurvy if that's the best you can do.'

They all looked down at May's basket.

'Bit pathetic,' May conceded, noting the handful of slender pods lying at the bottom.

'Now Missy,' Matthew continued, voice stern, 'They'll all run to seed... get picking!' Tillie looked solemn until he winked at her and smiled and she relaxed and winked back, her entire face screwing up with the effort.

'So what was all the excitement about Tillie?' asked her mother, 'What did you need me for?'

'Maxie an me want to go with Harley and Matthew and Caaarlos, don't we Maxie? Harley said that they've got a friend for Phoenix and we want to go with them and fetch him, don't we Maxie?'

He nodded.

'Wait, wait, wait!' commanded Lallie. 'Can we just hear this from a grown up, Tillie?'

May looked down towards the stable and could see Harley's back bent as he picked out Phoenix's hooves, Carlos moving about just beyond with a barrow and pitchfork.

'Maxie, go down quietly to Harley and ask him to come up for a coffee and a chat when he's done, would you darling?'

Maxie nodded and Tillie bounced up and down. 'I'll go! I'll go!'

'I need you here with me, Missy,' said Matthew. 'We have to fill the bird bath and you know I need you to steady the pitcher for me.'

Tillie smiled tolerantly at the old man and took his outstretched hand skipping along three steps to every one of his.

'What picture, Matthew? What picture do I have to keep steady?'

'Maxie!' called Lallie, 'Don't forget to be in front of the horse! *Always*!'

437

Maxie nodded as he trotted.

'Yes Mama!' commanded Lallie.

'Yes Mama,' came Maxie's voice jerking out in time to his feet.

Harley stopped what he was doing as Maxie reached him and nudged at Phoenix's high quarters until she swung haltingly away from the little boy, then he crouched in front of him.

Max, looking animated, reached out a hand and steadied himself on one of Harley's knees as he lost his balance in his excitement to pass on his message. Harley reached out and drew him into a loose embrace, listening attentively, head nodding every now and then. In a moment he stood, turned towards Carlos and said something, then turned back to Max. Carlos ambled over and hoiked the little boy up under the arms and onto Harley's shoulders in one smooth movement and May could hear Maxie's giggles and shouts as the three of them made their way up the garden towards her.

'Harley really is awfully sweet with the kids, May.'

May looked at her sister a moment before saying, 'That's the first unqualified nice thing you've said about him.'

'Don't be daft,' Lallie said unconvincingly and smiled.

'Humane society called,' Harley called out as he neared them, holding Max's hands and pretending to drop him backwards. 'They have a horse they think might make a companion for Phoenix. Young'uns might like to come and collect him with us. Your man says he's cool with it if you are.'

Lallie started to say something, stopped, then looked quickly at May, her expression uncertain.

'It's okay Lal,' May said, understanding. 'Harley'll take care of them, won't you?'

He smiled. 'Of course.'

'Well...' Lallie looked as though she was struggling. 'I don't know. What kind of place is it? Are there lots of loose animals, farm vehicles? They're very small, Harley.'

Harley lifted Max off his shoulders and leaned forward against the porch railings.

'Why'nt you come along Lallie? Put your mind at ease.'

As he spoke, May saw Lallie stand a little straighter and give him a bright smile.

'No, no. I'm sure it will be fine. Just make sure...'

'Like they was my own, okay?' he said and May felt a sharp contraction in her throat as she caught his swift sideways look.

So Carlos and Harley hitched up the trailer to his truck and Sam hopped up into the cab with Matthew and fastened the children in.

They got back almost two hours later with the most enormous piebald carthorse May had seen.

'He's absolutely vast,' she said to Stella over dinner that evening. 'And so sweet and gentle it seems incredible that anyone would give him up.'

'The owner died, baby. It's not such a heartbreaker as my Phoenix. He was loved until the end; he just out lived the old fellow who'd had him.'

'Who died?' Tillie asked, trotting up the steps and leaning on Sam's knees. 'Who died dada?'

'No one you know Tilster. The owner of the horse we collected.'

'Drum,' she said. 'He's name is Drum isn't Harley? He's name is Drum, Dada.'

Harley smiled and scratched her head gently.

'That's right, sugar. He's name's Drum.'

The need to be alone with her sister had intensified over the evening. She'd felt herself becoming increasingly anxious it would be one of those nights where everyone stayed up till the bitter end. But then, just before midnight, they'd all sort of melted away and May felt a warm swell of love and gratitude that both Sam and Harley seemed, without obvious consultation, to have decided it was the thing to do.

Lallie came and sat with May on the swing seat.

'Would you listen to those crickets?' she said, loud in the still night air and May knew that Lallie too was feeling the looming departure.

'It's been so lovely having you Lal.'

Lallie grimaced. 'Even though?'

'Even though. I'm sorry I've been wrapped up in myself. I really do feel terrible that I just left you after Sarah died. I will come and help you sort it. I promise.'

'You better,' Lallie said. But her voice was gentle and held a laugh. 'I know you will, May,' she went on. 'It just won't ever be soon or long enough for me.'

For a moment May felt the reactive flash of anger behind her eyes and then, just as swiftly it subsided. It's fine, she thought. Why on earth would I want her to feel any other way?

'Oh Lallie,' May said with a huge sigh.

Lallie hugged May against her side. 'And the worst of it is that the kids have had such a bloody good time, they'll probably leave me as well and set up a commune here with you!'

The next morning, as Lallie and the family packed the last things in their hire car and the children hovered, getting in the way and too hot in their travel clothes, May held her sister for a long embrace, throat aching wanting to get the goodbye over, not wanting her to go.

'May, think about coming for Christmas,' Lallie said as she finally pulled away. 'Harley!' she called out to him to where he stood on the porch. 'Christmas. Come.'

He just smiled and jutted his chin at her.

42

The mornings were now cool and misty with soft, washed blue skies pearling at the edges. As the sun started to throw light up over the eastern reaches, the colours changed from rose to opal and gold and edged into palest blue. After the fierce and heavy heat of the long summer, with its heady, saturated colour and light, May found that smudged softness soothing; it was delicious to walk on the damp ground and feel the tenderness in the moist air as it touched her cheeks. Some mornings it took a while for the chill of the cold nights to dissipate and in shady corners of the garden, the air felt still and cold.

One sharp October night Fran and Jesse came for dinner. It was a deep black night with only a whisker of a moon, but even so the stars were prickling attentively. May gazed up at them while they settled out on the porch after dinner. The log burner was fired up and they were wrapped in blankets, breath furring into the darkness. She sighed, deeply contented.

'So you know what I'm going ask?' Harley said to Frannie, voice dry.

May threw a glancing look up at him. She sat cross-legged with a pumpkin propped up in front of her, drawing a detailed design with a Sharpie pen, a Stanley knife by her side. He had his attention on Frannie.

'I sure do, cowboy, but you can hold your horses cause I have news!' she cracked out her laugh gleefully.

May saw Harley almost twitch with anticipation and she grinned at Fran.

'Okay…' he said slowly. 'What you got for me?' There was something endearing in the way he was trying not to smile.

'Finally, finally. You can have your boy. They've agreed a decent budget for him to get an apprenticeship with you. You have a year.'

May and Harley both whooped at the same time and they all laughed.

'Give me more,' Harley said. 'When can he start?'

'Well, he turns eighteen early November and then he'll be leaving our care.'

'May and me want him to come here. If he wants to, of course. We talked about this, right Fran?' Harley sounded slightly nervous.

'Sure, sure. I know. But you do understand that it's different from having him here daily?'

Harley gave Fran a withering look.

'Frannie... please.'

She shrugged.

'I have to say it. I'd be outta line if I didn't.'

'He's ready for it, Fran.'

'And what about that brother of his?'

May laughed when she thought of Danny. She was already fond of him, even though she had to keep a close watch on him.

'He's working at Molly's in the kitchen. Still living in that awful place, but he can't seem to find anywhere else. The conviction, you know?'

'Is he a good worker?'

May considered for a moment. 'Yea... but he's a bit of a corner cutter and thinks he knows it before you show him. And, oh god! He is the most unbelievable flirt.'

'Probably the only way he got by,' Fran murmured.

May nodded. Now that Fran mentioned it, there did seem something very functional about the way he turned it on; anyone in authority, anyone who might put a good word in felt the full force of his charm.

'He's genuinely sweet though,' she said. 'And he couldn't be happier that he and Carlos are near each other. He's thanked me a couple of times. Said that without the job he'd probably have left the state.'

'Fran says that happens *waaay...* too much.' Jesse spoke, as usual, without looking at anyone. His attention was on the lead foil from the bottle of wine as he fashioned it into a miniature wind instrument. 'The ine...vitable drift,' he said, poking tiny holes with a toothpick from his Swiss army knife, 'I guess that's what happened to your family huh, Harley?' He threw an unseeing look up, then refocussed on his sculpting.

May's breath slowed. Her hand stilled, poised over the pumpkin.

'What actually happened to them?' Jesse asked, without looking up. Then it seemed he became aware of the silence and stopped what he was doing. 'Sorry... Should I? Sorry, should I not have...' He broke off and looked at his wife, as though for guidance.

Harley began to say something, then stopped and May moved softly back leaning against his knees. She felt his hand slip under her hair and she reached up, holding it gently against her neck.

'They died,' Harley said quietly, then cleared his throat and spoke a little louder. 'When I was a kid. In a fire. Arson, in fact, seeing as we're going all out.'

'Oh my lord,' Jesse said, obviously shocked, a look of embarrassment on his face. 'I am so sorry. I didn't mean to...' he broke off with another helpless look at his wife.

May exhaled and took Harley's hand squeezing it tightly.

'Harley...' Fran gasped, half standing up then slumping back in her seat. 'I never knew. All this time I thought they'd got swallowed up in the care system.'

'I know.'

'And the weird thing is,' she went on with some urgency, 'I just never could square the guy I knew, with this idea that you'd accepted they'd disappeared, never tried to find any of them. It was a puzzle piece that didn't seem to fit.'

Harley took a long pull of his beer and exhaled loudly. 'I

appreciate that Fran. Means a lot. Really.' His voice sounded a little rough and May wanted to hold him. Does it get any easier? She wondered. Tenderly, she kissed his palm.

That night brought the first snows. May lay in her bed, their bed, back curled against Harley's naked warmth as he held her in his arms and she watched the soft, thick flakes against the black sky floating slowly down, weightless.

'Harley…' she whispered.

'Hmm?' He shifted a little, snuggling around her.

'Was that okay? Telling Fran and Jesse?'

He sighed. 'Don't know if I'd do it again, but it's okay.'

'I think it was brave.'

Harley snorted softly. 'I wish Matthew had of been there, though.'

'Do you want to tell him?'

'Yeah. No. I guess so.' He huffed, frustrated. 'I don't want to have to bring it up, but… shit May, sometimes being with you is like opening Pandora's Box the whole fucking time.'

She might have been hurt, but he held her closer.

'Sorry,' she said.

'Don't be sorry, baby. It means I'm alive, right? I'm alive.'

The next morning dawned sparklingly beautiful. The sky was a clean and vivid blue.

'Hey, baby, I'm taking the dogs up to Perch Hill.'

May looked up from checking through a pile of invoices and was almost blinded by the sharp sunshine pouring around Harley's silhouette as he stood in the kitchen doorway. The melancholy that had settled about him the night before seemed to have shifted.

He crouched to tie a bootlace and was mobbed by Piper and The Warhorse.

'Quit!' He laughed as he lost his balance. 'That mutt's leading my girl astray,' he muttered and gave his dog a stern look. 'Get.' He growled at her.

Piper sat back on her haunches and cocked her head at him, but The Warhorse continued to scamper around in circles as though the frost had got into his veins and he was going crazy with it.

'Can you take a break?' Harley took May's outstretched hand and hoisted himself up, a great bundle of coat and boots and muffler.

'I'd love that.'

They walked in peaceful silence at first, up the gentle slopes through iced woodland, their steps muffled. May's eyes followed the quick yellow flash of a goldfinch and flutters of tiny wings as it led them on and through, always a little ahead, while the dogs hurtled off, circled back then ran off again barking joyfully, their voices echoing through the slumbering trees.

Harley whistled sporadically as he walked, throwing a stick for the dogs, jogging after them, then slowing a little as May caught up with him. He flung an arm around her neck and kissed her temple.

'Carlos has found a college course that he wants to do next fall. After he finishes his apprenticeship with me. We'll have to help him out with all the financial aid forms.'

'That's fantastic. What's the course?'

'Forest management or tree surgery.'

May had a vivid image of Carlos in orange helmet and harness, abseiling down a tremendous oak tree. She smiled to herself.

'Did you see that coming?' she asked.

'Not at all. But he seems really psyched. But now, of course, he's scared he won't get on the course. You'll help him, won't you baby?' he asked rhetorically.

Harley hurled the disgustingly slobbery stick ahead of the dogs once more.

'So...' he said, giving May a sidelong look. 'If he moves into my old room in November, he can help Matthew take care of everything here if I come to London with you for Christmas.'

May felt a kick of joy shoot her and she leapt at him, throwing her arms around him.

'Shit, May! You and the dogs! Quit knocking me around!' He laughed, scooping her up in his arms and swinging her around.

The path took on a sharp incline as they emerged from the woods and climbed Perch Hill. May bent her head a little as she strode out.

Then she stopped walking, cheeks hot in the cold, sharp air. 'I am so unbelievably happy you're coming with me... you've no idea.'

He flashed a great smile at her.

'Sure I do.'

43

London, December.

It was mid-morning a few days before Christmas and the sky looked like dirty paint water; there was a flat oppressive quality to the damp, chill air.

May glanced about her as she and Harley emerged from the tube station at the far end of Shepherd's Bush Green and she felt a slight trip inside her. She took in the sheen of smooth, red brick at the Job Centre, the black stippled façade of the Shepherd's Bush Empire and Mohammed's corner shop, piled high outside with ugli fruit and plantains, yams and coconuts.

At the end of the scrubby, apologetic green stood a large, rather sheepish Douglas fir, covered with coloured light bulbs, knee deep in windblown newspapers and bright takeaway boxes.

What an odd place to put it, it looked as though it was waiting for permission to move along.

The noise of the cars and buses single-mindedly vibrating by, was distracting and it took May a moment to get her bearings. She turned to Harley and saw he was watching her, face still, eyes clear, expectant.

'Okay?' he asked, face softening into a smile.

May nodded. 'Ready to see where I used to live?' She smiled back at him.

Harley caught her hand loosely and looped his fingers in hers as they walked past terraces and side streets of polite houses and tightly held front gardens. Some had wreaths on their doors and the couple of corner shops they passed had gold foil banners with Merry Christmas in red and black gothic font below their awnings.

May looked about, scrutinising the cars and front doors for some indication that she'd been gone, that something had changed in some way.

As they turned right onto Stanlake Road, the edge of the sky along the hard line of pitched roofs took on a sudden silvery brightness, lighting up the undersides of a small flock of birds that sped high above. May stopped walking and watched the brief flare of icy white as they turned on a beat, then melted into the clouds.

'Well, this is it!' she said.

Harley stepped back a little and May led the way down the sharp-edged concrete steps into the dim, mossy basement. She felt nervous all of a sudden. She knew the last tenants had just moved out, but all the same she felt like an interloper.

'Feels really weird to be here.'

At first, she couldn't get the key to work and for a brief moment felt like throwing in the towel. Finally, she managed to lift and turn the key in the old way that used to come automatically to her, and the door eased silently open.

The passageway was cramped and dark, but the dryish green smell of the sea grass matting felt welcoming; a familiar note tingling at her nose. Harley shut the door and it seemed to May as though the ceiling became very low, the walls contracting around them. It was very quiet.

They walked down the narrow hall, past a tiny windowless bathroom and into the low-ceilinged, open living area. Amongst the soft mossy greens and putty coloured furnishings, a few vibrant objects leapt out. Harley appeared to take a step back and let out a soft breath.

A huge mirror almost filled the entire wall behind one of the two long, low sofas, its jagged, mosaic frame singing out of sunflower fields and endless Mediterranean seas or Aegean skies. Beneath and reflected in it, were two crazy patchwork quilts of silks and velvets in saturated jewel tones, lying over the backs of the sofas. Amethyst and fuchsia, emeralds, sapphires and garnets were softened and grounded by gentler, earthy toned calicos and fine-ribbed baby cord like miniature ploughed fields.

'There's only three things in here that could possibly be you,' Harley said.

He walked over to one of the sofas and gently fingered the cloth of one of the quilts. 'Sarah make this?'

May frowned, trying to make sense of them being there. 'She did.'

May came over to him and stroked her hand across the fabric, feeling the soft nap of silk velvet, the rough scratch of the gold thread.

'Something wrong?' Harley asked, concerned.

'I've been asking Lallie to send me one of these ever since I left…'

'Can't you just take one now?'

'I could, I suppose.' How to explain though? May didn't feel she could, it felt complicated and petty all at once. 'Too bulky to take on the tube… but that's not the point. Lallie doesn't want them separated, I think. They're companion pieces.'

'*Lallie* doesn't?' he said and the question hung between them in the air. 'Do they belong to her?'

May flinched, irritable. 'No, they belong to us both and she's probably put them here to "sell" the place to the next round of potential tenants. It's fine.'

She didn't want to step on Lallie's toes this time; she was grateful that her sister dealt with all this for her. 'I just thought they were in storage, that's all.'

She held up the edge of one and slipped her hand under, feeling the weight, its many layers, the beads and buttons, the hundreds—*hundreds*—of stitches that on their own were weightless but together, reassuringly, satisfyingly heavy.

'Did you know that every piece of fabric, every button came from something someone we knew had worn? Mostly us, but some of it—look, this.' She drew Harley closer and indicated an intensely violet irregular triangle of silk charmeuse. 'This came from a jacket of my dad's.'

Harley raised a sceptical brow.

'I did not see your old man as the Purple Rain type at all.'

May laughed.

'Only by stealth… it was the lining of a beautifully cut, very sober suit jacket.'

She kneeled on the edge of the sofa and scrutinised the fabric, running light fingers over the different textures, turning her hand so the back stroked slowly along the smoothness of satin, the spring of dense cotton velvet. Then as she lifted the quilt and bent her head, she heard the tenderness in Harley's gentle huff of laughter as she laid her cheek on the cool satin of an ivory and navy scarf.

'This was my mother's.'

'The one she blotted her lipstick on?'

May went still inside.

'You remember that?' she asked, incredulous, laughing to stop herself from crying and she wondered why this should still surprise her about Harley, touch her so.

'What? You think I don't listen to you baby?'

'No… it's just I told you that a hundred years ago.'

'Oh yeah… I forgot there's a time limit,' he said and laid a light finger on the corner of her mouth. She kissed his palm.

May walked across the room, down a wide shallow step into the one light part of the flat. The roof was conservatory glass, the space filled by a heavy oak table. She opened the French door that led out to a garden the size of a small bedspread and stepped out into the damp. It smelled of cats and earth and wet brick.

'Hmm,' mused May, looking around. 'I don't think the tenants enjoyed gardening, do you?'

Harley gave a short laugh and seeing him standing hesitant in the open doorway, May was aware of how out of place he seemed. Of course that's because this is someone else's space now, she thought. If we lived here, we'd make it our own. But she couldn't imagine Harley in this compressed and colourless place. She couldn't even picture herself there. How had she done it?

'Come and see!' she called, climbing the brick steps up to the patch of lawn. Harley came with his quiet, strong stride and joined her. No limp. She smiled.

'I used to love sitting out here with the papers and a coffee. You get quite a lot of bird life you know.'

She looked up at the white painted brick façade of the house and at the flat above, whose occupants she didn't know, but whose bath had flooded her once, long ago.

'Remind me why we came?' she asked, suddenly glum.

'I don't know... just to see, I guess. Help you make a decision?'

May squinted at him thoughtfully, hugging her arms around her belly.

'Harley,' she took a deep breath and swallowed. 'Could you ever live here?'

Harley looked startled, before his face shut down swiftly.

'I thought...' he blurted, then voice cool he said, 'I didn't think that was still on the table.'

'It's not, really, but I just wondered. If we're never going to live here, it would make sense to sell it, wouldn't it?'

Harley leaned against the open doorframe and laughed a short, ironic sound.

'Yeah, it would, but that is *not* my call.'

That night back at Lallie's, as the family were busy with last minute preparations, May came in to the sitting room her arms full of presents. Harley was standing in the bay window by the Christmas tree, examining the ornaments.

'Sarah's everywhere,' he murmured without looking up. May put down the parcels. He was looking at a plump, silk-velvet heart the colour of old roses. Tillie's name and birthdate was embroidered in curled, gold silk thread, the whole embellished with tiny seed beads of iridescent opal. He rubbed his thumb slowly across, then back over the textured surface.

'She didn't make that one.' May felt strangely shy. 'I did.'

'You?'

'I wasn't just a passive observer you know,' May said lightly and Harley chuckled.

'I never figured you were,' he said, moving closer to her.

May held up one of a group of trapunto hearts, in softly faded cottons. 'She made everyone a new decoration each Christmas. That's such a lovely tradition, don't you think?'

'May, I…'

'Harleee… Maaay?' Tillie came bursting in. 'Mama says supper is ready now, not yesterday!'

Harley blew out a breath.

'What were you going to say?' May asked him, holding Tillie's shoulder gently and giving it a squeeze. He wrinkled his nose and shook his head.

'It'll wait,' he said turning away.

May felt a rush of impatience then realised it was only with him she felt this urgency; so often in the past the moment was lost and she had never known what he would say. But that was then. She took a deep breath. It'll come, she thought. It will come.

After dinner, in the confusion of clearing away and preparing for tomorrow's Christmas lunch, Tillie called across the room to Harley.

'What?' he called back with a smile. The little girl came over and putting out a hand, pushed at Harley's hair, complaining she couldn't *see* him, then stood wobbling on one leg as she talked. Harley pulled a face at her and shook his hair back over his brow.

'Why are you going back before?'

'Before May you mean?'

Tillie nodded.

'Why are you?' She hopped onto the other foot and Harley reached out a steadying hand as she teetered about.

'I have to get back to work and look after my dog and make sure everything's okay.'

'But me and Maxi don't want you to go, do we Maxi?' she turned her head towards her brother briefly. 'We don't want you to go.'

Harley threw a helpless look at May.

'I know angel,' she said, counting off forks as she set them on the tray for tomorrow. *Seven, eight, nine.* 'But you'll come and stay with us again and we'll be back for visits.' She moved over to a waxy, pine corner cupboard and opened it, looking for Lallie's collection of fancy glasses and said over her shoulder, 'And think of all the stories we can tell each other.'

Sam came clattering in from the small back garden with a box of white wine.

He put it down on the table with a shiver of glass and called out, 'It's not really cold enough out there Lal! I'm going to have to shove it in the fridge.' Turning back, he said to Harley, 'So I'd no idea your audio whatsit project had grown so much. Sounds great.'

'Yeah,' Harley said musingly, putting his hand over his glass and smiling briefly up at Sam who was now trying to top him up. 'It's good. I like it. I think they get something out of it.'

'It's actually really important, what you're doing,' May broke in.

She polished the glasses, handing each one to Tillie to place on the table.

'He's given up so much of his time, Sam, taking them on journeys back to the streets where they were born, back to their old schools or tracking down people to talk to. It's very sensitive stuff, but he's done a beautiful job.'

'May!' Harley blew out a dismissive breath.

'But all those hours! Listening to them talk and coaxing out little vignettes…' She mouthed a thank you at her niece as they finished with the glasses, then carried on talking to Sam. 'Then he pieces and patches them together, *making* something with them, creating this collection of memories.' She stopped, sensing Harley's discomfort, feeling a bit crass. It's his story, she thought. 'I'll shut up now.' She laughed and Harley cocked his head a little and gave her a sweet, relieved smile as Lallie came in with a tray of mince pies and clementines.

'What are we talking about?'

'The importance of patchwork quilts,' May quipped.

Harley laughed and Lallie looked confused, but said with an exuberant flourish, 'Mr Daniels, I give you… ta da! Mince pies!'

She thrust the plate under his nose and he picked one up, explaining to Sam who was looking at him enquiringly, 'They're not A Thing where I come from.'

May felt a catch in her throat as he said it. *Where I come from*; to her sensitive heart it sounded as though he wasn't talking simply location. She wondered what traditions, if any, he had memories of.

She was still thinking about this later that night after everyone had gone to bed. Standing in the window of the spare room she and Harley were sharing, May watched the moon; how peaceful it would look on her snowy garden in Vermont. She missed it with an ache. She could picture the stark contrasts; the velvet dark sky and skeletal shapes of naked branches even darker against it and longed to be there. She imagined Christmases there, lights in the trees, adorning the porch and gathering friends around the fire, making their own traditions and rituals.

Harley came in and put his arms around her, resting his

chin on the top of her head, then kissing her through her hair. They stood for a quiet while, and May felt herself gently moving, swaying with the slight and whispered current coming from Harley.

'May,' he said quietly. She murmured an encouraging sound. 'You know this is not a place I feel all that comfortable in.'

'I do know, Harley,' she sighed, wondering sadly if this would be the only time he visited with her.

'But I'd do it. If it was a choice of you or no you. I'd do it.'

May turned around in his arms, her surprise total; having had no idea what he was going to say, she realised this was the last thing she'd imagined. Harley held her face in his hands and went on.

'I don't think you'd be much happy here either. You looked like a bird with her wings clipped in that tiny little apartment a yours. But if you need to be near your family, maybe we can find somewhere together. Y'all're supposed to be world famous for your countryside but I ain't seen none yet.' He smiled.

'Harley,' May put her hands over his, searching his eyes, wondering how it was he continually surprised her. In that simple offer, it felt to her as though some hidden conditions had been stripped from her decision to live in Hartland and she felt it deeply.

Later as they lay together, Harley stroking her bare skin with warm, gentle hands, he said he had something for her. 'It's after midnight so that makes it Christmas already.'

He flipped on the low bedside lamp and fumbled in a drawer by the bed before handing her a small, flat package of white tissue. For an instant she hesitated, holding the moment close, then she slipped a finger under the tape and unfolded the paper. Glancing up at him again, she saw he was watching her closely, his smile tentative.

On the bed of tissue lay a choker of three twisted strands of fine, supple, dark leather, onto which were strung two small, bead knots fashioned from silver. She threw a look at the leather around his neck. He'd replaced the old one, once again tying in three knots to remember Libby, Pearl and Stef.

'What a lovely thing,' she said, deeply touched. 'Help me put it on.'

She felt his hands move her hair aside and feel about, and she put her hand up to finger the knots where they sat at her collarbone. Harley touched first one, then the other.

'Could be you and me,' he said, 'or here and there... I don't know.'

He reached out and switched off the light, before taking May in his arms again.

'May.' Harley's voice was low.

'Hmm...'

He said nothing. May stroked his hair, gently teasing her fingers through the thick lengths. Finally, he said, 'This is for keeps, right?'

May's pulse sprang and began tap-tapping away at her. 'How do you mean?'

'Ten years from now. Twenty. Do you see us together?'

'I like to.'

'You like to?'

'Yes. I like to. I like to think that we are.'

'So... you think we might...' he paused, shifted a little and said, 'May, I want a family. I want a family with you. You think we might do that? Raise our own babies?'

In the darkness she couldn't see his expression, but his voice was filled with a warm urgency.

'Oh I do!' she said fervently, hoping he could hear how much she meant it.

'Okay...' He sounded as though he was trying to collect himself. 'Okay. I just needed to know... that you did... I didn't want to assume. I didn't know.' He trailed off abruptly.

May began to speak but he shushed gently.

'Not now. Not here,' he said, then as she tensed he added, 'Let's wait till we get home. Is that okay?' He held her close, curling around her drawing her back against his chest and belly. She relaxed against him and held the precious warmth of later close.

'Of course,' she murmured. 'Of course it's okay.'

He kissed her. 'Thank you.'

May found it so affecting, the way he said it. It touched a hidden part of her and she thought back over the times when he'd said it before in that quiet, powerful way. She had a sudden thought that made her insides quiver.

'Harley...' she stopped, not sure how to ask. 'When you say thank you like that...'

'Mm hmm...' he mumbled, then added, 'Like what?'

'Like you're saying... You sound so loving.'

Harley chuckled and held her closer, spreading a warm palm across her belly while he cupped her breast with the other.

'I am, baby.'

'It's like you're telling me you love me.'

'Well... I do.'

44

Sam and Harley came stomping in from a Christmas morning walk with Tillie and Max as May was whisking gravy in a roasting dish on the hob.

'Are they late?' May asked, wondering when Sam's parents would get there.

'No, they always come at the last minute, it's fine. Keeps things from getting overworked.'

'Harley says it's got snow where you live. Does it? Does it have snow where you live?'

Max came running and talking over to May as she whisked.

'Hello darling, good walk?'

'Yes, but does it have snow where you live?'

'Well if Harley says it does then it must do,' she teased.

'But *does* it?'

'Yes, my sweet boy, it does. I've sent you pictures haven't I—pass me the jug Lal—haven't I sent you pictures of my garden in the snow?'

'I don't know,' Max's birdlike voice piped.

'Get your muddy boots out of here!' Lallie yelped. 'And stop cluttering up this kitchen.'

Max's face went pink and he scuttled out to the hall. May could hear Harley's low murmur and Sam laughing as she poured the steaming gravy into the fat blue and white striped jug.

'I'm bringing the roast beast out!' called Lallie. 'Make sure there's a hot plate down for me. Sammy, have you opened the... Tillie for heaven's sake stop with the bleedin accordion... The wine Sam? *Sam!* Wine?'

Harley leaned up against the kitchen door and May caught his eye. He was looking at her with a suppressed smile, his dark eyes warm.

'Lallie?'

She shot out a quick, 'What?' then glanced over at him.

'Pass me something on over here, I'll take it through.'

Lallie smiled tightly and threw a tea towel at him before handing him a hot dish. 'Thanks.'

May smiled at Harley who gave her a wink as he went back out to the sitting room where Sam had set up a table. She stepped out into the hallway with her gravy and a ladle, just as a loud knock rapped out on the front door. Max and Tillie shot past her followed by Sam who opened the door over their heads.

'You made it!' Sam's warm voice sounded delighted and he stepped forward to hug a tall balding clean-shaven man of about seventy.

'Darling, you always say that as though we have to cross the Khyber Pass to get here!' said a cut glass female voice.

'Hallo you two,' she said stepping into the hall and hugging the children. 'Did Father Christmas bring you coal or presents?'

Tillie giggled. 'Hello Granny! Granny, I got a cordian, what did you get?'

'Definition of a gentleman?' said Sam's father, and Sam finished for him, 'Someone who can play the accordion but doesn't.'

His father laughed loudly, '*Can* play but doesn't! Ha ha!'

'Where's Lawrence?' Sam asked looking back at the door.

'Coming—just parking. Your street is awfully popular Samuel. There wasn't a space left. Not a space,' said his mother, giving herself a long, cool look in the wall mirror and lightly combing at her fine, blonde and silver fringe with her fingertips.

She finally looked over at May who was stuck behind everyone with her gravy and smiled brilliantly.

'May darling! It's been such a long time you look absolutely wonderful. Come here and let me look at you.'

'Annabel, you look amazing as always. Let me just put this down if I can get through here. Hello David, be right back.'

May slipped quickly into the sitting room, plonked down the gravy hoping it might keep warm and turned back to give David and Annabel a warm hug each.

'I'm trapped in here, Bel,' called Lallie's voice, 'come and say hello.'

Annabel disappeared, the door banged again and Sam's brother Lawrence appeared.

'May, *you're* here,' he said hugging her 'nobody tells me anything. If I'd known I'd have scrubbed up a bit.'

'Lawrence, you dog,' said May laughing, 'you look absolutely dreadful what have you been doing?'

'Thank you, darling, I've just returned from China to have Christmas with my children and their facking mother has taken them to Gloucestershire without telling me.'

'Loz, you didn't tell her you were coming til the last minute, you get what you deserve,' said his mother coming serenely down the hall carrying a pile of plates.

'Ma, you're supposed to be on my side,' he said petulantly, grinning at May.

'Not,' she said, fixing him with a stern blue eye, 'if you behave appallingly.'

She continued, turning to May. 'I did not bring him up this way but he insists on playing the part of a wayward black sheep. And my goodness, look what St Nick's gone and left by the chimney!' she said as she swept into the sitting room.

May wished she could see Harley's face at that moment and she nipped in quickly after Annabel hoping to at least catch a glimpse.

Harley was standing in front of the fireplace unscrewing a cork from the bottle opener. He put out his hand to shake Annabel's, looking a little dubious, but then he smiled.

'I'm here with May.'

Maybe it was because of the clipped, crisp vowels of Sam's

parents, but his accent sounded more noticeable.

'How divine!'

'Watch out, old boy,' said Lawrence, slouching in. He grinned in a slightly challenging fashion at Harley. 'She'll have you for breakfast.'

'Lawrence!' said his mother sharply, 'you are unutterably vulgar.' She turned back to Harley. 'Once again I find myself apologising for my son.'

May made a quick introduction.

'Absolutely delighted,' said Annabel smiling at him.

'So,' said Lawrence loudly, snuggling up to May, 'if we can get my mother to distract your boyfriend, how about a quickie before lunch?'

'Loz, your manners are appalling and you're not funny,' May said, laughing. 'I'm sorry Harley, he's an absolute disgrace. You can see why his ex-wife left for the West Country the moment his plane touched down.'

Harley had that still, controlled look that told May he was feeling anything but and she was about to go over to him when Sam leaned in close to Harley and said something low in his ear that made him break into a huge smile then a laugh that he tried to suppress.

'Sam...' he said looking at once slightly appalled and enormously amused. He left the room shaking his head and laughing, saying he was going to help Lallie.

'What did you say?' May asked.

Lawrence looked suspiciously at his brother.

'Oh,' Sam said breezily, 'I just told him that Loz talks like that as a front because he's got erectile dysfunction.'

May and Annabel shouted with laughter. Lawrence looked furiously red-faced.

'Darling, you absolutely deserved that,' said his mother.

When Harley came back in, with Tillie on his back and Max clinging to his front like a baby Bonobo, he shot a mirth filled look at Lawrence who scowled momentarily, then laughed. 'You win, I apologise and I will do my utmost to keep a civil tongue in my head from now on, scouts honour.'

There was a final frenzy of seating and Tillie wanting to move next to May then Max wanting to as well and then Lawrence saying it wasn't fair *he* wanted to sit next to May.

Then Sam tapped his spoon on his glass and a hush fell over the room.

'Just a few quick words,' he began, 'to welcome everyone to this, our fifth Christmas in Innismar road and to thank all of you who travelled far to be with us.

'Here, here!'

'Loz, glad you could make it.'

Lawrence bowed his head briefly and smiled. 'Harley, mate, really glad you're with us; it's been quite a year for you, I know.'

Harley smiled too.

'And let's raise our glasses to the chef.'

'Chefs!' shouted Lallie and thrust her glass towards May.

'To family!' called out Sam.

'Family!' chorused everyone. And May looked at Harley who met her eyes and held them before taking a quaff of his wine.

'So, to what was Sam alluding? What has made it "quite a year"?' Annabel asked, turning to Harley.

Harley threw a slightly helpless look at May and muttered that it was really nothing much.

'Harley had a hideous accident this time last year,' called Lallie down the table. 'He was in hospital for weeks. Took you quite a long time to get back on track, didn't it, Harley?'

'My god! Darling, how simply awful! But you absolutely cannot tell,' she said, eyes fluttering briefly over the silvery scars visible beneath his rolled shirt sleeves.

'No but show her your gold medal scar, Harley.' Lallie leaned over and pushed up his hair to reveal his forehead. Harley flinched, shrugging Lallie off.

'God's sake Lallie, leave the poor man alone,' Sam said, with quiet disgust.

'It's nothing to be ashamed of,' Lallie said airily and brandished her knife with a flourish, before she began to carve the turkey.

'Well you appear to be in robust good health,' said Annabel. 'Your recovery seems to have been a howling success. And now you have the requisite erotic flaw!'

There was general laughter.

'So now you're recovered do we get May back?' Lawrence asked shoving a forkful of turkey into his mouth.

'Unfortunately not,' said Lallie with a sly smirk. 'Harley's going to take her back to her genetic roots and keep her barefoot and pregnant in the kitchen, aren't you?'

May groaned inside. Harley looked tense around the mouth.

'Oh my god, darling the poor man! Do stop!' Annabel said. 'Aren't families awful,' she asked him rhetorically and poured him another glass of wine. He turned towards her and said something quietly that made her chuckle and lean in closer to him, then he glanced quickly across at May.

His mouth softened and he looked as though he was sharing a secret with her, his expression telling her, 'I'm okay'.

It was Harley's last day. In the pale blue and cream hallway of Lallie's house, just as Harley and May were heading out to the airport, Harley put his bag down and took hold of Lallie's delicate shoulders in his hands. Looking down at her upturned smiling face, he said, 'Thank you Lallie. Thank you.'

He kissed her forehead and May saw her sister's eyes swim with tears as she said, 'You are welcome. Take care of her.'

At Heathrow they held each other tightly at security, the air squashing with a slow hiss from the down jacket he wore.

'I'll see you in a week,' May said.

'I'll be there,' he said kissing her once, twice, again, lingering then pulling away to hold her one last time.

45

'Come on,' Lallie said briskly. 'We can't look at every photo we come across, you're only here another week and I'm going to make you stay until we're done, ticket or no ticket.'

'Argh!' May bared her teeth. 'You are the bossiest person I've *ever* known, Lal. I promised Harley I'd be home next week and that's where I'll be.' Then she threw a smirking look at her sister. 'I have to go and get barefoot and pregnant in my kitchen.'

Lallie laughed with her and they continued to work quietly together for long minutes until May said, 'La...leee.'

Her sister responded by echoing exactly the two notes from high to low. 'Ye...ees.'

'Lallie...' she repeated and sat up on her knees.

'Ma...aaay?'

'Why did Harley thank you like that when he left?'

'Because he's The Good Polite Child,' her sister said, automatically referencing a story they'd read as children. She missed this short hand communication they had, and the closer she got to leaving, the closer she came to understanding what she was leaving behind.

'No. Come on what was it? It was like he was thanking you for a particular thing, not "thank you for having me."'

Lallie shrugged dismissively and shoved a box towards May with her foot. 'I didn't notice anything,' she said blandly, writing on the box in marker pen, CHRISTMAS FAIR. May knew she wasn't going to get any more so she just said, 'What's in that one?'

'Clothes.'

'Lallie, I've had an offer for my flat and I've accepted it.'

Lallie didn't reply. Her movements became more emphatic in the silence that opened between them.

'When I get back I'm going to talk to the Bartons, see if

they'll sell.'

Lallie sat back against the wall and finally looked at May. 'With Harley?'

'We haven't discussed it. But that's not important really. I'd be doing it anyway and I want you to know.'

'God,' Lallie said in a small voice. 'I don't know what's worse, you wanting to live so far away just because, or because you've met someone.'

'Lallie, I'm so sorry.' May felt it welling up from deep inside her. 'I really am, I feel as though I'm abandoning you and letting you down, but I can't live here. I just can't. I love you, but I don't love here.'

'I know.'

May waited for Lallie to say more; to remind her that she was all she had and that they had promised to be there for each other always, but she didn't.

'I want you to be happy, May. I really do.'

Harley met May at the airport and they stood holding each other for so long that the arrivals hall had begun to thin out before they walked to the car holding hands. Harley chatted about Matthew and the animals, about Carlos and Maryanne and all the time, May was aware of the soft exchange of looks, a tenderness and of time stretching loose and languid ahead of them.

'So Maryanne's got a place at SCAD.'

'What's that?'

'Savannah College of Art and Design.'

'Oh my, my… Georgia.'

'Uh huh.' Harley let go of her hand to shift gear as he eased out onto the highway, then took hold of it again. 'Great for her, not so great for Carlos.'

'How's he taking it?'

'Oh, he's a good guy, he's psyched for her, of course he is and he wants to hire a truck and take her down when it's time to go, but... well, you know.'

Yes, she thought. It'll be hard for Carlos to see her go. As they drove through town May's pulse started to thump.

'I've missed it all so much.'

Harley squeezed her hand and smiled as he checked the rear-view mirror.

'It missed you,' he said.

She sat up a little straighter in her seat, looking out at the iced river, its banks covered in snow, at the black patches of water where the ice had melted. A whole year, she thought. This time last year I was with Lallie and didn't know if he was going to be alright.

At last, Harley turned his truck into the gate and crept slowly along the densely packed snowy drive, pulling up at the porch.

He looked almost shy as he walked along beside her and she glanced at him wondering why he suddenly looked so nervous and smiley.

She stopped at the top of the steps and turned to look out over the snowy garden. The light was leaching away from the sky and there was a chilly, rosie-orange throb of colour in a fat swell over the snow-covered hay fields, the edges were streaked with purple and teal and the farthest edges of the field seemed to shine bright and polished with the last burst of winter sunshine.

'I want to show you something.' Harley grabbed her hand and began to walk into the house, leaving her suitcase standing by the door. He was in an eager hurry suddenly; his mood changed now as though he'd remembered something. He took the stairs two at a time and May, tired from her long trip struggled to keep up with him.

'What?' she laughed, a little breathless.

Harley stopped abruptly at the door to their bedroom. It was closed, which made her wonder. She usually kept doors open in the same way she kept windows uncurtained; she liked the feeling of freedom it gave her.

'Close your eyes.' She did and they fluttered open, so she squeezed them tight and heard Harley laugh.

'You look like you're waiting on Santa, hope it's worth it.' She felt him nudge her gently forward and heard the door open.

'Okay...' he said.

She opened her eyes and for a moment it looked as though the room was bathed in sunshine through a stained-glass window. The bedside lamps were on and pouring pools of soft, gleaming light onto their bed, which was covered in patches and strips of glowing, jewelled colours. May sank to her knees at the foot of the bed, fingering the edge of the quilt, stroking a garnet velvet square.

'Oh, Harley... Harley.' She turned to him, tears in her eyes, tried to speak and gave up.

'Lallie sent me and Sam to get it, then she wrapped it for me to bring back, she wanted to surprise you. She's never going to like it, sweetheart, but she gets it and that's good enough for me.'

He nudged himself up off the doorjamb and walked over to where May was still kneeling, hand extended. She took it, stood up and they lay down together, wrapping the quilt around themselves.

'Welcome home, baby.'

May woke hours later in the still darkness, as wide awake as though it were midday, still on London time. Harley lay breathing steadily next to her, one arm flung across her, Thunder's dark shape nesting in the space between his feet. She slipped quietly out and wrapping her quilt around her, crept over to the window seat. The cat stretched languorously, springing silently down and padding across the floor to rub against her legs as she stood gazing out at the snowy landscape.

The moon hung luminous and clean edged in the blue-black sky, reflecting off the undulating folds of soft banked drifts that rolled over the garden down towards the snow-covered pasture fence. Phoenix would be tucked up in her stall with Drum, blanketed against the cold, the chickens roosting and fluffed out in the barn and Matthew would be sleeping with The Warhorse on guard against foolhardy critters.

The world was gleaming, reflecting, softly glowing. May sat for a long time, quietly watching. Finally a little stiff and beginning to feel sleepy again she made her way back to bed. She stopped as she glanced out of the eastern window. Through the skeletal trees, cloaked in softest snow, she could see the very beginning of a rose-gold sunrise.